Coming Home to Glendale Hall

Coming Home to Glendale Hall

Victoria Walters

hera

First published in Great Britain in 2019 by Hera

This edition published in the United Kingdom in 2019 by

Hera Books
28b Cricketfield Road
London, E5 8NS
United Kingdom

A CIP catalogue record for this book is available from the British Library.

Print ISBN 978 1 78863 607 0
Ebook ISBN 978 1 91297 310 1

Printed and bound in Great Britain by Clays Ltd, Elcograf S.p.A.

For Uncle David, in loving memory

Chapter One

'Izzy, we're not in London any more,' I murmured under my breath so I wouldn't wake my sleeping daughter beside me as I drove our ancient car along country lanes.

There was darkness all around us. I had forgotten just how dark it got out here. After ten years living in a city, it was strange not to see any streetlights or passing cars, the only light coming from the main beam of my headlights and the stars in the sky, visible to me for the first time in forever. These roads had once been as familiar to me as breathing, but I found myself frowning with concentration, making my way cautiously, searching for the house I had vowed never to return to.

I could see my breath in the air. The heating in the car didn't work all that well and I hadn't paid too much attention to it before, but it was the depths of winter in Scotland and I cursed myself for not getting it fixed. Glancing at the satnav, I saw that we were almost there. My younger self would have mocked me for having to use it for directions, but I would have already got hopelessly lost without it. Glendale Hall really is in the middle of nowhere. My city brain couldn't fathom how long it had been since I'd seen another house. In London, we lived in a tiny flat, squished in between other buildings like sardines in a tin, but here, beyond my windscreen, there was nothing but trees.

You have reached your destination

Driving through the open, imposing iron gates, the satnav informed me that we had arrived, as if the goosebumps which had run down both my arms weren't enough of a clue. I slowed the car right down as we drove through. Even in the darkness the sight of the house was impressive, with its cream stone, and ivy climbing up over the large oak front door.

Parking on the gravel drive, I sat for a moment in the dark, still car sucking in a few deep breaths. I needed all my courage to get out, to be honest. It had been ten years since I had last walked through that front door. My childhood home. I had thought it was lost to me forever but here I was, back again, and wishing I could turn the car around and run.

Like I did when I was sixteen.

'Izzy, we're here,' I said, instead, touching my daughter on the arm to rouse her. It had been a long journey and we were both exhausted. I craved sleep but I wasn't sure if I'd be able to do so back in my childhood bed. 'Come on, love.'

Isabelle stretched and yawned. 'Is this it?' she asked, sleepily, looking out of the window at the house. 'Mum, it's massive.'

'It is. Wait till you see it in daylight. Right, let's grab our bags and go in. Hopefully we can just go straight to bed.' I'd tried to time our arrival perfectly: too late for us to have to really talk to anyone tonight. I wanted to get my bearings a bit before I faced my family.

We climbed out and heaved our two large suitcases from the boot, shuffling up to the front door like the two strays we were. I touched Izzy on the back as I knocked, trying to reassure both of us I think. She was excited that she was finally going to see the house after begging me for years to let her see it, and because I'd taken her out of school early for the Christmas break to do it, but I could tell she was nervous. Like me.

'Beth!' The door swung open and in front of us stood a small, smartly dressed older woman, a wide smile on her face.

I relaxed just a little. 'Sally,' I said, smiling back. 'Here we are.'

'Here you are. And Izzy. Come on in you two, you must be shattered,' she said with her strong Scottish lilt.

I had lost most of mine during my decade in London. In the light of the hall, I reached for her and we shared a long hug. I had missed her. It had been ages since she had been down to London to see us. Phone calls just weren't the same.

'Everyone is in bed,' Sally said when we drew back, raising an eyebrow, obviously working out what my plan had been.

Relaxing even more, I glanced around the vast hall. 'It looks different,' I said, the décor lighter and simpler than I remembered it. The large, imposing grandfather clock, one of our family's heirlooms was still there though, ticking loudly, the only sound in the silent house. A shiver ran down my back at the memories pouring in.

'I'll take you to your rooms, let you get a good night's sleep.' Sally took one of the cases and led us up the wide, ornate staircase.

I thought about how I used to slide down the banister as a child. And how much I was told off for doing it. And then I thought about the last time I had walked down it – hurrying as softly as I could, trying not to wake anyone, about to do a midnight flit. Sally had been with me then, too, helping me out of the back door, even though she had begged me to stay.

Everywhere was quiet at the Hall. The household all in bed except for Sally waiting up for us. She had been the housekeeper at Glendale Hall since I was a baby, and long before. She was probably nearing retirement, I thought, not that anyone would dare to mention such a thing to her. Sally was as permanent a fixture as the staircase.

'I thought you'd like rooms next to one another,' Sally said, opening up one of the guest bedroom doors for Izzy.

'This room is almost as big as our flat,' Izzy said in wonder when Sally switched on the light. There were eight bedrooms in the house, all spacious with high-ceilings. Izzy had never known anything quite like it.

'I'll come and say good night in a bit,' I told Izzy, leaving her to get settled as I went next door, pausing in the doorway as Sally wheeled my case in. I had never planned to be back in this room. I slowly walked in behind her. My childhood bedroom now looked like any other guest room, all neutral and clean and tidy. The only sign it had once been mine was the small teddy bear sitting on the chair by the window. 'Ted's still here,' I said in surprise.

'He's been waiting for you,' Sally replied. 'It's good to have you back here, Beth. We weren't sure that you would come.'

'Nor was I. This is so strange. I didn't think I'd ever sleep here again.'

'The house has never been the same since you left.' She looked away, and I felt a lump rise up in my throat. 'Sleep well,' she said, shortly, leaving hastily.

I looked around and shivered again. The last time I had stood in the room, I had been throwing as many of my things as I could into a bag, tears streaming down my face. Ducking out before memories from my past could overwhelm me, I went to check on Izzy. She was already in her pyjamas, brushing her teeth in the en-suite bathroom. On her bed waiting for her was a book, and her own teddy which she'd had since she was a baby.

I shook my head at how organised she always was. She'd been packed for two days, whereas I had packed half an hour before we left.

'Everything okay?' I asked, perching on her bed.

She finished brushing her teeth and switched off the bathroom light. 'The bed is massive,' she said, eyeing it almost fearfully.

'Hey, I'm right next door if you can't sleep, okay? But I'm sure you will.' Pulling back the duvet for her, I patted the bed and she climbed in. Tucking her in, I smiled down at my pride and joy. We both had thick, wavy hair that never behaved itself even if we tried to straighten it. Hers was a deep auburn, flowing down her back, whereas my dark brown hair grazed my shoulders. Izzy was well on her way to being as tall and willowy figured as me, but she had pale skin that turned lobster red in just a hint of sunshine. My eyes were dark brown, but Izzy's were blue, which she had got from her father. 'You going to read for a bit?'

'Just a couple of pages,' she replied, picking up her book. I rarely saw her without one in her hands.

'Good plan.' I leaned over to give her a kiss. 'Sweet dreams.'

She nodded. 'You too. And it'll be okay, Mum, we're here together.'

I smiled. 'Everything is okay when we're together,' I agreed. 'Come and get me when you're up,' I added before leaving. Izzy always woke before me and I didn't want her facing downstairs alone. Or maybe I didn't want to have to do that myself. A bit of both, I decided, shutting the door and heading back to my own room.

Once there, I sank down onto the king-sized bed, exhausted from the journey and everything I was feeling. I had come home because of a mixture of guilt and duty, and I was planning to leave again as soon as I could. I ran my hand over the crisp duvet and looked up at the painting of white horses hanging over the fireplace – which my dad had moved from his study up there for me because my six-year-old self had loved it so much – and I was glad I had the first night back at the Hall to myself. It was surreal to be here as if no time had passed, when so much had.

I had no idea what kind of welcome I would receive in the morning, but there was no turning back now.

Chapter Two

'Wake up, Mum.'

I groaned as Izzy pulled back the duvet. Rolling over, I saw her standing next to my bed, hands on her hips. 'It's too early,' I mumbled, about to turn back towards the wall.

'It's eight o'clock and I'm hungry, so come on, let's go downstairs.'

Groaning again, I took in Izzy more clearly. She was already dressed. She might have been off school, but she was still up and ready at a ridiculous time. Honestly, sometimes I wondered if she really was my daughter.

'Please, Mum.'

I sighed. 'Okay, okay,' I said, rubbing my eyes and trying to pull myself out of my sleep haze. 'I'm coming.'

'You're the one who didn't want me to go down by myself,' she reminded me as I slung a leg out of the bed. I had forgotten how comfortable the beds were at the Hall. And how warm the house got, thanks to the new heating system Mum had installed in the bedrooms when I was a child, and the log fires always burning downstairs. The Scottish winter was beaten back with a very large stick.

I got out of bed and stretched and yawned. 'Did you sleep okay?'

'Yeah, once I got used to being in a different bed. You look like you didn't though.'

'Thanks, love,' I replied dryly. It had taken me a long time to drop off: thoughts of the past keeping my mind too busy for sleep. 'I need a vast amount of coffee. Right, let's face the music then.'

'Hadn't you better get dressed?'

I knew that there would be comments if I went down in my PJs, so I shuffled off into the bathroom. After a quick shower, I pulled on jeans and a long black jumper. Leaving my hair loose, I glanced in the mirror and decided that I would have to do like that. I was never going to be as polished, as my mother and grandmother, and I'd given up fretting about the fact a long time ago.

'Right, I need sustenance and I need it now,' I said to Izzy, following her out of the room. We headed downstairs side by side. The house was super quiet. Our flat in London was never really quiet: we could always hear our neighbours and the traffic outside. It had taken me a long time to get used to living in the city and I now had to readjust to countryside life again.

'Which way?' Izzy whispered when we reached the hallway.

'Um…' It took me a moment to remember the layout of the house, especially as in the daylight I could see it looked very different to how I remembered it. It had been built by my great-grandfather, Leslie Campbell, in the 1900s, and had been rich in wood and our clan tartan, but was now neutral and light since Mum had a decorating spree after I left. 'Well, I can smell bacon so let's go this way!' Led by my nose, we turned right and walked down a long, twisting corridor until we found the bright kitchen and breakfast room. There was a large floor-to-ceiling window looking out to the garden and a long pine table providing a perfect view for breakfast and, behind it, the cream and pine kitchen where Sally was bustling about. She was the only person in there and I felt another pinch of relief.

'Morning,' I said to her back.

Sally turned from the Aga with a wide smile. 'Hello, you two. Sit down, it's almost ready.'

'Blimey,' I mumbled as Izzy beamed in delight. The table was already laid with coffee, tea, orange juice, a basket of muffins and pastries, two racks of toast, a vast array of jams and marmalades and a big bowl of fruit. I sat down facing the garden and looked out at the grounds. The garden had always been my favourite part of the Hall. The sun was starting to climb higher in the sky, and I could see a white coating of frost on the dewy grass and the tips of large oak trees in the distance blowing lightly in the breeze.

'Here we are,' Sally said coming over with two plates piled high with eggs, bacon, sausages and tomatoes. 'You two need a good breakfast after your journey,' she said.

I smiled. Sally had always been a feeder, which was perfect for us as we liked to eat. A lot. I put it down to struggling to scrape enough money together for food when Izzy was tiny. 'Your father has already left for the office. Your mum will be down soon; she was just checking on your grandmother,' Sally told us. She went back to the kitchen and brought out another plate. 'Thought you might like these too,' she added, putting down a stack of pancakes drizzled with lemon and sugar.

'This beats cornflakes,' Izzy said, her eyes wide.

I grinned. 'I might not be able to wear my new skinny jeans after this, but I really don't care.' I poured myself a large mug of coffee and passed Izzy the juice and we tucked in.

Sally came over to sit with us with a mug of tea and a plate of toast.

'How is Gran doing?' I asked her, my mouth full of pretty much the best breakfast I had eaten in ten years. Maybe there were some things I had missed at the Hall after all. My grand-

9

mother was the reason we were here. She had been ill for a while, and it was now terminal. The doctors thought this could well be her last Christmas so my dad had called me to beg me to come home to say goodbye and to support my mother. Despite the fraught relationship I had with my family, I hadn't been able to refuse such a request.

'She's already asking for you,' a voice replied from behind me. I turned, mid-mouthful, to see my mum striding in. Caroline Williams was always perfectly put together. Mum was petite and slim with a sleek chestnut-coloured bob and a cloud of Chanel N° 5 perpetually following her. 'It's lovely to have you both here,' she said smoothly, coming over to kiss me on the cheek and hug Izzy. Mum and Dad usually came down to London twice a year to see us, but it was the first time I'd come up to Scotland since I had left ten years before. It was so strange to be with Mum at the breakfast table and watch her pour herself a coffee. I knew that she wouldn't be eating anything. She barely did and especially not breakfast.

'You arrived very late last night, Sally said,' Mum said, after sipping her coffee. Disapproval dripped from her cultured voice. She barely had a Scottish accent. Gran had sent her to elocution classes when she was a little girl. They tried to do the same to me, but I was so disruptive the teacher told them I wasn't welcome any more.

'Lots of traffic,' I lied, grabbing a piece of toast. 'I'll go and see Gran after this. Dad has already gone to work then?'

'You know what he's like,' she replied with a sigh.

My dad was pretty absent from life at the house usually. He worked in banking over in Inverness, and worked God knows how many hours. I barely remembered spending any quality time with him growing up. He was quiet and calm and not prone to getting involved in much, so when he phoned and told me I was needed at home, I knew it was serious. I had still hesitated though. I hadn't wanted to come back, especially because Gran was the main reason I had left in the first place. But then Sally had called, too, and told me she thought I would regret it if I didn't come home. Plus I knew Izzy was desperate to finally see where I had grown up, mainly because it sounded like a house out of one of her favourite books. I had always said it was too far to visit, what with school and work to sort out, but she had kept asking, so in the end I had come back for her as well as my grandmother.

'How is Gran?' I asked then, already nervous to see her. Growing up I had always been intimidated by her. And for ten years, I had never been able to forgive her because she was the reason I'd felt I had to run away.

'The doctors are doing all they can to keep her comfortable,' my mother replied. She looked at Izzy. 'You have grown again.'

'I'm almost as tall as Mum,' Izzy replied with pride.

'You both get your height from David,' Mum said with an envious sigh about what we'd inherited from my dad. 'You better go up and see your grandmother, Beth. She gets very anxious at the moment. Isabelle can stay with us and we can find out all about what you've been doing.'

Why did anything my mother suggest sound so ominous? I swallowed the rest of my coffee and grabbed a muffin to take up with me.

'Breakfast was delicious,' I told Sally. 'You'll be okay down here?' I checked with Izzy, wishing she could come with me. I wasn't at all ready to face my grandmother, but I knew I should see her alone first. I needed to prepare Izzy for how sick she might look. They had met only twice, both times when my grandmother had deigned to join my parents in London to see us, but the last visit had been a long time ago. She hated to leave Scotland was the excuse my mum always gave, but I was certain it was because she had never got over me going against her wishes as I had.

'Of course she will,' my mum answered for her.

Izzy piled more food on her plate, making me smile as I left. I knew she would be fine really. My family all loved her.

It was me who was the black sheep.

Chapter Three

Gran's bedroom was at the front of the house. It was her father who had built Glendale, and it was she who owned it now. Leslie Campbell had made his money making whiskey. As he approached retirement, and with only a daughter and old-fashioned views about passing on family businesses, he had sold it all off to a big brand, and had made even more money in the process. We still owned shares in the company, and those, along with the money from the sale, had kept the family in comfortable wealth ever since. Gran's husband and my dad had both worked though they didn't really need to, but my grandmother and mother never had. It was yet another difference between us. And one of the reasons I was so stunned when I received my first wages from the café I worked in when I got to London, and saw how little I had to live on.

Gran liked the fact that she had a view of the driveway to keep an eye on the comings and goings of the house. I asked her once if she minded living with my mum and dad and Gran said this house needed people to fill it. I wondered if it had felt different after I left but, in my heart, I knew it had.

I hesitated outside the door. I had fallen pregnant with Izzy when I was sixteen, and Gran was the one who found my pregnancy test. While we hadn't ever been what you would call a close family, I had hoped that she might support me but she had been furious and disappointed, and our relationship had never recovered. 'Don't be a chicken,' I whispered to myself and, taking a deep breath, I pushed open the door softly.

Margaret Mackenzie was in bed with her eyes closed. I tiptoed in and walked towards the bed, leaning over to look at her. I was taken aback by how different she looked from the last time I had seen her. She was pale and thin, her usually dyed hair now allowed to be its natural white, cut a lot shorter than she had ever worn it.

'Gran?' I whispered and her eyes opened to reveal the same brown eyes that Mum and I shared with her. She smiled faintly, and I went to perch on the edge of her bed. 'How are you feeling?' Perhaps a stupid question, to be honest. She bore hardly any resemblance to the formidable woman that I had spoken to there in that very room just before I had run away from the house.

'Beth, it's really you,' she said, reaching out with a cold, bony hand to touch mine briefly. She had never been particularly affectionate and, even now, the touch barely registered. 'You're back.'

'Dad told me you wanted to see me.'

'Thank you for coming,' she said with a small cough. She struggled to prop herself up a bit to look at me. 'All grown up now. And Isabelle...'

'She's here too. You can see her when you feel up to it.' I sat down in the chair beside the bed.

'How is she doing at school?' Gran asked, ignoring my comment.

'Brilliantly, as usual. She reads more than I've ever seen anyone read.' I tried not to let my anxiety about that show to Gran. I loved that Izzy was so enthusiastic about books but sometimes it worried me how she seemed to prefer to live in a fictional world. I wasn't about to let Gran know any of that though. In front of her, I needed to be as strong as I could be.

She sighed, then her eyes fixed on me. 'Ten years is a long time. I never dreamed you'd stay away from here for so long.'

'Well, my life is in London now. And it's a long way...' I mumbled, not meeting her eyes. The truth was I had been too nervous to come home. I had tried to forget the Hall, even though that had proved impossible.

'I've been thinking a lot about the past, stuck here in bed,' Gran said, her voice throaty and faint as if she hardly used it now.

'I suppose you would do.'

'It's been hard on your parents, well on all of us, with you and Isabelle living so far away from here.'

'It's been hard for us too,' I replied, wishing I could keep out the trace of bitterness in my voice, but that was impossible. Izzy and I had had to survive on our own, and she must have known that it was because of her, surely? I sighed though, seeing her sad expression. I couldn't help but feel a rise of pity inside for her. 'We're here now though,' I added, soothingly.

She nodded. 'Yes.' She closed her eyes briefly. I looked around her bedroom. It was exactly the same. Mum had obviously been banned from decorating it along with the rest of the house. I thought back to that final conversation between us. Gran had told me so many reasons in that very room why I shouldn't have my baby. I was so young. I wasn't married. I had my whole future ahead of me. What about my dream of being a landscape gardener? Of going to college and university? What would people say? And then the argument that had reached my heart. How could I do it to Drew? How could I destroy his future right alongside mine?

'It's good to have you back,' Gran said then, opening her eyes again and drawing me back from the past to the present. 'What does Isabelle think of Glendale Hall?'

'I'm going to show her around later. She can't believe how big it is.' I smiled. Thank goodness Izzy was with me. I felt like I could handle anything with her by my side. As I'd had her so young, we were often mistaken for sisters, and she felt like my best friend, as well as daughter. We were as close as I had hoped we would be when I walked away from my family with her growing inside me. Although I wished she didn't worry about things as much as she did. I had known as soon as I decided I had to keep her that I would be nothing like Mum or Gran, that I would raise my baby with affection and honesty, and I would try my hardest to give her everything she needed from me. It hadn't been easy at all, but I had done my very best. Gran coughed again and her eyes closed for a moment.

'You look tired. I should let you rest.'

'But it's been so long.'

I nodded and stood up. It was hard to reconcile the woman in front of me with the one who pushed me to go. I needed time to adjust. 'We're here for Christmas so don't worry. There's plenty of time. I'll come back later.'

'There is so much to say.' She closed her eyes again. 'Thank you for coming, Beth.'

I watched her drift off into sleep. It didn't look good at all. I wasn't sure quite how I felt about that as I left softly, closing the door behind me. It felt wrong to be angry with someone who was so sick. But I was, I realised. It was there, bubbling up under the skin as if it had been lying dormant all the time in London. It all felt raw again.

There wasn't a moment when I regretted having Izzy but those first few months were bloody tough. Being a single mother far away from my family and my home had been a test of all my determination and survival instincts.

'There you are,' Izzy said, rounding the corner and spotting me. She looked relieved.

'What's wrong?' I asked, instantly on alert.

She smiled. 'Nothing. I just came to find you.'

'Come on, I want to show you the garden.' I slung an arm around her.

–

Growing up, the grounds had always been my favourite place. We grabbed hats and scarves from our rooms. The sun had finally risen but it was that kind of watery wintery sunshine that failed to produce much warmth. There was no breeze, though, so it didn't feel too biting when we walked out of the French doors onto the still-dewy grass.

The house sat in around eight acres of grounds. There was a formal garden to the side of the house that burst with colour in summer, a wide green lawn that led down to a stream and the woodland area, as well as a vegetable patch and long greenhouse. In the midst of the trees was a small, pretty cottage where our full-time gardener, John, lived. As a kid, I had spent a lot of time in the garden.

'I used to love coming out here,' I said, wrapping an arm through my daughter's as we strolled away from the house together. 'I even had my own patch.'

'Where?'

'Let's find it.'

We walked under a large archway, which in spring was draped in wisteria but was now just a skeleton, to the side of the greenhouse where a square patch was marked out. John had let me plant what I wanted there, and I had found the prettiest and most colourful flowers that I could for it. I was surprised to be able to see it from a few feet away.

'There it is, it's still here,' I said, pleased, bending my knees to look more closely at it. The flowers weren't in bloom in December and a thin layer of frost covered the plants there. It was clearly still tended to carefully though as every inch of the grounds always had been. 'God, I miss having a garden.' The worst part of moving to London was having to live in a flat. We had a tiny balcony at our place where I could fit two pots of flowers, and that was it. Out there, being with nature again I found myself smiling. The cold morning didn't dampen the spring in my step as I stood back up. 'I had dreams of being a gardener, you know.'

Izzy looked at me. 'Really?'

She, of course, had never known me as anything but an admin assistant at her school. When I was pregnant, I had worked in a coffee shop and then managed to scrape by when Izzy was tiny, looking after a family who let her come with me, and then when she started school, I took the office job there so I did the same hours as her. It had worked well, although we never had much money. 'I loved being outdoors and learning about plants. I loved growing things. All summer, I was in the garden. As an only child, there wasn't always much to do in the house, but in the garden, I always had something to do. I hadn't realised how much I had missed it.'

'It's pretty,' Izzy said. 'Did you say there's a stream?'

'Up here, we call it a burn. Come on, I'll show you.' I knew she was just humouring me but I led her towards it. Isabelle was an indoors girl. Happiest with her books, she had always been capable of occupying herself. I had tried to get her interested by taking her to gardens and parks in the city but I had never really succeeded. I was determined not to stop trying though.

18

We walked further from the house and I felt lighter than I had since we arrived. I looked down and was pleased to see Izzy had a smile on her face too. I was happy I could finally show her the grounds that I had loved so much. Perhaps coming home wouldn't be a complete disaster after all.

Chapter Four

'I heard a rumour you were back,' a voice called out to us as we approached the water's edge.

I turned to see John sloping down the lawn towards us. He was nearing fifty, broad-shouldered and freckled, his skin always tanned from being outdoors and his fair hair now had streaks of grey in it. 'Unfortunately, the rumour is true.'

He grinned. 'Well, at least Christmas won't be boring now.' He gave me a quick hug then turned to Izzy. 'And this must be the famous Isabelle. Your grandparents have got me searching all the grounds for the best Christmas tree I can find just for you.'

'Really?' She looked at me, her eyes all lit up.

'Can you top the one we had when I was twelve though?' I asked him. The tree had touched the ceiling in the hallway, taking up half of the massive room.

'I'm going to do my best. It's good to see you out here again. How's your garden at home?'

I frowned. 'We only have a tiny balcony so right now I just have a pot of pansies, and some heather out there.'

John shook his head. 'That's too bad. I always wanted to see what garden you'd have when you had your own place. Right, I better head off, I need to find that perfect tree, don't I?' He winked at us and carried on his way.

I looked at the house behind us, rising up tall and proud in the wintery sunshine, the cream stone as bright as ever, and I sighed. Turning back to the stream, I followed Izzy towards it, the sun dancing on top of the water. It was hard not having a garden of my own. Being out in the garden was making my fingers itch with wanting to touch the earth again. I had had a place at college in Inverness to study horticulture when I was sixteen, which my parents were happy to let me do as they assumed that like my mother and grandmother, I'd get married before I started a career anyway. But then I did something that none of us had planned for – I fell pregnant. I wouldn't have changed having Izzy for anything, but I couldn't deny my heart had been broken when I realised I would never get to go to college.

'I can't feel my nose,' Izzy complained as we walked along the stream. It was getting colder, and we were not used to it.

'I think we need one of Sally's famous hot chocolates. Let's head back,' I replied, changing direction. 'What do you think of Glendale Hall then, Iz?'

She looked at the house as we started to walk back to it. 'It's amazing, Mum. I can't believe you used to live here.'

'I know, right?'

'I can't wait to see it decorated for Christmas. Could we help, do you think?'

I thought back to Christmases when I was younger – my mother would arrange for people to come in and decorate for us; I never had the chance to do anything. In London, Izzy and I always spent a day decorating our flat together playing cheesy Christmas songs as loudly as we could, and eating far too many chocolates. 'I'll ask Sally to make sure you can help with something, don't worry.' Sally was bound to be doing a lot of festive baking that Izzy could help with if my mum was still against children being part of Christmas.

As we got closer to the house, I looked up and saw a figure at the windows, watching us. My mum was upstairs, looking at us walking across the garden. I couldn't fathom the expression on her face. When she saw me looking, she quickly turned away. I wondered how we had drifted so far apart. I couldn't even pin it on me leaving. We'd always been so different, I supposed, and I'd always resented how she'd tried to mould me into someone who would be just like her and Gran. Which was why I hadn't turned to her when I fell pregnant, and why we struggled to communicate with each other now. My grandmother had certainly made things even harder between us. Gran had expected a lot from her daughter, and Mum in turn, had expected a lot from me. That was one of the reasons I left to raise Izzy, I wanted to have a different relationship with her. I wanted to raise her to be the person she wanted to be. I just wanted her to be happy.

'Sally, we are in need of emergency hot chocolate!' I called as we walked in through the back door to the kitchen.

Sally was kneading dough. She actually baked bread. 'Good job there's some ready to go then.' She went over to the cooker to turn the pot on. We took off our boots on the doorstep and left them outside, knowing my mum would have a fit if we trailed mud into the house. We shed our outside coats and hung up them on the hooks by the door before heading over to the table where Sally joined us, bringing over a steaming mug of hot chocolate for all three of us.

'How was your walk?'

'It was lovely to see the grounds again.' I sat holding my hands around the mug to try to get some feeling back in them. Izzy was blowing on her drink, her nose as red as I was certain mine was. It was going to take some getting used to how cold it was. 'I've missed them.'

'Can I go and get my book, Mum?' Izzy asked, obviously sensing it was adult chat time and wanting to avoid it. I couldn't say I blamed her.

'Take your drink up with you if you want to read in your room.'

She beamed and hurried off, clutching the mug to her chest. I shook my head. 'She hasn't inherited my love of the outdoors at all. I keep trying to get her nose out of a book but it never works for long.'

'It's a shame you don't have a garden in London.'

'There's no way I could afford to move somewhere with one. I hadn't realised how much I've missed it.' I looked out of the French doors, already wanting to be back out there again. 'Hopefully John will let me help out while I'm here.' I turned back to Sally. 'How is everything here? Really?' I hadn't missed the fact that I hadn't seen my dad yet and my gran seemed to not be doing well at all. The house seemed so quiet, so downcast, to how I remembered it. I tried not to worry that somehow it was my fault, but it was perhaps inevitable that my absence had left its mark on the house, and on my family.

Sally sighed. 'Mrs MacKenzie has been ill for a long time. The cancer is everywhere now. Your mother has found it very hard; we have a daily nurse coming in but she's taken on most of her care by herself. You know your father, he's always at work so hasn't been around to help much. I don't think your mother is coping that well.'

'She's drinking a lot?' Each time we'd met up with them, I'd noticed Mum ordering more and more drinks.

Sally gave a small nod. 'She seemed to perk up, though, when we knew you were coming. It means a lot to her, to everyone, that you've come home for Christmas.'

'You think it will be Gran's last one then?' There was no need for Sally to answer that. We both knew it would be. I couldn't reconcile the thought in my mind – it had seemed as if my grandmother would always be there, holding court over everyone, ruling the house and the family – and I wasn't sure what would happen to any of it once she was gone. 'And how are you, Sally?'

Sally and I always been close, so when Gran found out I was pregnant and left me in tears, I ran straight to her. She had been there for the whole of my life, not just running the house but doing my hair in the morning before school, helping me with my homework when I got stuck, and when I was older listening to me tell her how amazing a boy called Drew was. Whenever I'd had an argument with Mum or Gran, I'd run to Sally for advice, and she had always been the peacemaker between us, encouraging me to apologise when I stubbornly didn't want to.

Sally had asked me what I wanted, which was something Gran hadn't even thought to do. I told her I was desperate to keep my baby, and she supported my choice. Perhaps because of her own situation. Sally's husband had died when I was a teenager. They hadn't had a family and I knew she had always regretted that, although she was close to her niece, Emily.

Emily had spent school holidays running around the Hall with me, although she was four years older, but she and her parents had moved to London when she was fourteen and we had lost touch. Sally had phoned Emily, who was at university, and she had let me stay in her tiny student flat in the city until I scraped enough money from working in the coffee shop to afford a deposit to rent my own tiny flat. Izzy and I hung out with her in London a lot and when Sally came down to see her family, we had all spent time together. I knew that Sally missed them, but she had never wanted to leave Glendale, the place where she and her husband had grown up and been so happy. She did concede to moving into the Hall, though, after he passed away, and I didn't think she'd ever leave.

'I'm fine, you know me. There has been a lot to do here; it keeps me busy. And I'll be going to my Emily's to celebrate Hogmanay as I always do.'

'I've missed this,' I said then, to lift the conversation a little. I gestured between us. We had often sat at this very table drinking hot chocolate together.

Sally smiled. 'Me too. The house was so quiet after you'd gone. I wished I could have come down to London more often, but you know me, much happier in the country.'

'And working,' I said with a wry smile. Sally didn't like resting all that much. Idle hands and all that, she used to say. I knew, though, that keeping busy helped her to not miss her old life as much. Perhaps we were more alike than I had realised.

Sally looked at me more seriously. 'Everything is okay in London, isn't it? On the phone last month, you didn't sound yourself.'

I looked down at my drink. 'I think I was just so tired. There's a lot to do at work and I had to stay late a few nights, which made it tricky being there for Izzy. Plus, I had to pay out for a school trip and it all got a bit tight moneywise but, honestly, I'm fine.'

'Well, you're good at putting a brave face on things for Izzy, I know that.'

I looked up. 'What has Emily been saying?' I knew that they talked about us. They always had. Emily was as kind as her aunt, and I was always careful not to lean on either of them too much.

'Only that she thinks you have a lot to deal with all by yourself. Well, let's face it, you always have. It's okay to accept a bit of help sometimes.'

'I'm fine,' I repeated. I didn't like complaining to Emily or to Sally: they had been such a help when I arrived in London alone and scared, and I didn't want them to have to worry about me any more. I wanted to be able to handle it all but, sometimes, it wasn't easy. That was true.

'Well, you're here now and you can relax a bit. I know it's not the best reason to have to come home, of course, but now that you're both here, let us take care of you. Okay?'

I smiled. 'You're still as bossy as ever.'

'You never want to hear it but I'm going to say it again: you should be proud of the life you've built for you and Izzy. Izzy is a wonderful girl. And you're a great mother to her.' She got up, picking up our empty mugs. 'Right, I can't sit here all day chatting to you,' she said breezily, walking away as if she hadn't given me a compliment. I looked away, pretending that my eyes hadn't welled up at her words.

I had phoned Sally a lot when I first got to London, confessing that I was worried I had made a huge mistake, but she encouraged me, told me that I could do whatever I wanted and made me even more determined to get it right. I had called my parents as soon as I got to London to let them know I was safe. I kept quiet about the help that Sally gave me. Even though she was pretty much indispensable at the Hall, I didn't think my parents would have understood why I had turned to her and why she hadn't told them I was going to leave.

It wasn't until a few weeks after Izzy was born that I let my parents come and see us. They had tried to persuade me to come home with them, but I had wanted to cling to my new found independence as hard as I could. Once I knew that I could do it on my own, I decided that's what I should keep on doing. London let me be myself and live the way I wanted to. Maybe I had clung to my independence too much, and too hard, not coming back to Glendale for ten years, but the longer I stayed away, the easier it had been to just stay where I was

'Thanks, Sally,' I said when I was able to speak again. I wanted to ask her my next question but it scared me more than any of the others. 'Do you ever hear anything of Drew?' I said, watching her back as she loaded the dishwasher.

She stood up and looked at me. 'Only that he's still in Boston, working in a hospital there. A doctor, like he always planned to be.'

I nodded, my parents had told me that and I had felt relieved that he had fulfilled his dream. And I was happy for him. Even though it was the reason that I had let him go without telling him I was pregnant.

'Have you thought about contacting him again?' Sally asked then.

'No.' Alone on Izzy's first birthday, I had watched her fall asleep in our cramped bedsit and broken down in tears. I loved her with all my heart, but I was lonely, and I thought of Drew miles away from us in America and I wondered if I had made a huge mistake in not telling him about her. I had written him a letter, slipping a photo of her inside, and sent it to his university over there. I hadn't heard a word from him since. 'He knows where we are and has decided not to get in touch,' I replied. 'Izzy has asked about him, but I told her that he'd left before I realised I was pregnant and there was no way to get in touch with him. I don't want her to know that he decided he didn't want to know her.' It had been hard when I hadn't heard back from him but I had planned to raise Izzy alone and so I got on with doing just that. It still stung though. Drew had once

27

meant everything to me, and when I caught glimpses of him in our daughter, I still wished things had turned out differently.

Drew was someone I usually tried not to think about, but being back in Glendale again, it was proving to be impossible not to. He was two years older than me, someone that I had always known at school, but it wasn't until I was sixteen when we were both cast in a school play that we really spent any time together. We just clicked. I fell head over heels in love with him. We were inseparable.

But soon after we became a couple, Drew told me that he'd accepted a place on an exchange programme – he would receive a free ride to study at Harvard University in exchange for a US student coming over to study in Scotland. Drew had always wanted to become a doctor and the scholarship was a dream come true for any eighteen-year-old. He hadn't known that he was about to fall in love for the first time. His parents had died in a tragic car accident just after he had accepted his place over there, and I knew that they had been so proud of him when he got it there was no way he could turn it down. His brother Rory was a few years older and had taken over running their family farm and was determined that Drew should still go too.

Drew felt he would be letting his whole family down by not going. I couldn't have let him do that for me. Which was why I had decided not to tell him I was pregnant, and that would always be the hardest choice I've ever had to make in my life.

'Well, he's crazy not to want to know her,' Sally interrupted my thoughts. 'And neither of you need him in your life if he doesn't want to be part of it. You both deserve so much more than that.'

I knew she was right. Although I did still wonder why he had never replied. Perhaps he just couldn't forgive me for not telling him I was pregnant. Or maybe he was just too settled and happy in America, so he'd decided it was best for us to stay apart. I would never know, I supposed. 'It's all for the best,' I replied with a shrug.

Sally glanced at me but didn't say anything.

Sometimes people had to let you believe what you needed to.

Chapter Five

Dad finally made an appearance that evening. Izzy and I walked into the drawing room to find him in his work suit, tie off, drinking a glass of the family whiskey. My mother was wearing a camel twinset sat on the opposite sofa, drinking her usual gin and tonic. It didn't seem as though they had been speaking when we entered. It had never been my favourite room. It was long and narrow and usually only used when we had guests over. There was a grand piano in one corner, bought by my great-grandfather, which was now never played, and on top were family photographs all in gold frames. Mum had updated the décor but left the original fireplace, which crackled at one end merrily, and the blue and green family tartan upholstered armchairs in the corner. Candles flickered on the mahogany coffee table and the sweet scent of their perfume filled the room.

'There's my girl,' Dad said, getting up and holding out his arms to Izzy. He gave her a big hug and then turned me. 'And Beth, thank you for coming.'

'Good to see you, Dad. I thought you were a figment of our imagination for a minute,' I said, giving him a kiss on the cheek. I went over to the drinks table and poured myself a glass of wine and got a juice for Izzy. We sat on the sofa together.

'What do you think of Glendale Hall then, Izzy?' Dad asked her as he sipped his drink.

'It's so huge but I love how the log fires make it cosy. And the food is really good here. We went in the garden today, and tomorrow Mum is going to take me on a tour of the house.'

'I'm glad you like it here,' my mum said to her. She glanced at me and I caught the unsaid meaning behind it. *Why does Isabelle like it when you so obviously didn't?*

'And Mum said we can walk to the village.'

'Why do you want to go there?' Mum turned to me, eyebrow raised.

'We can't stay in the house for the next three weeks,' I replied, knowing we'd go stir crazy if we didn't leave the Hall at all before Christmas. Plus, I spent so much time in Glendale growing up and I wanted to see the place again. I was surprised that Mum seemed confused as to why I'd want to show it to Izzy.

Sally poked her head around the door. 'Dinner is ready.'

I hated that Sally served us still, but I knew better than to say anything about it. We trooped into the formal dining room. A room I'd always hated, preferring to eat in the cosy kitchen instead. The long shiny oak table was set up at one end for the four of us, and Sally brought in steaming plates of stew and mash topped with homegrown vegetables. It smelled amazing. I had forgotten how hearty her meals always were. I glanced at my mother, certain she wouldn't be wanting much of it. She never did. She was knocking back her gin though.

'Thanks, Sally, it smells amazing.'

Sally smiled at me as she left, and I managed one back. I wished she would stay.

'Has the village changed much?' I asked my dad as we tucked in.

'I hardly go there,' he replied with a shrug. 'There's nothing of interest there now.'

'It's not what it once was,' Mum said. 'The whole place has gone downhill. Something really needs to be done about it. It's meant to snow overnight, so you won't want to go anywhere in that.'

'Snow?' Izzy looked at me in wonder. We rarely saw anything more than flurries in the city. She had no idea how deep it could get out here. 'We have to go out if there's snow!'

My mother's face flashed in annoyance. She didn't realise she would make Izzy more likely to want to go out with her weather forecast, not less. 'Beth—'

'Mum,' I cut in firmly, suspecting why she wasn't keen for us to go into Glendale. 'I know that I've been away for a long time, and I'm sure there was a lot of gossip about it, but we're back for Christmas and we'll go stir crazy if we stay inside the whole time. I'd like to see the place again and to take Izzy there. I know that we might see people we know, but you were the ones who begged me to come home. If they're going to talk, they'll do it with or without seeing me. Won't they?'

'It's not that,' she said with a sigh. 'Honestly, the village isn't what it used to be. But you'll see for yourself, I suppose.' She drained her glass dry.

I wondered if Mum was serious or whether she was trying to put me off going because it was likely I'd bump into people we knew. Sally had told me that after I'd gone, there had been a lot of gossip in the village about why I'd left so suddenly. My parents had kept quiet about me being pregnant at sixteen, which I supported as I didn't want anyone telling Drew or his brother, only mentioning that I had a daughter once I was older. I think my mother pulled away from being involved in the community because of that. But we had had a lot of friends in Glendale and I felt guilty that Mum appeared to have cut herself off from the village because of me. I decided it was best to change the subject. 'How's everything going at work, Dad? Izzy was asking about what you do,' I said, turning to him.

My dad launched into a boring conversation about his banking company to which Izzy listened politely. Mum drained another gin and tonic and picked at her food, and I ate my food as fast as I could, hoping we could escape the table soon.

'Who's for pudding?' Sally asked when she came in to take our plates. Izzy clapped, and my heart sank.

—

After I said good night to Izzy, I followed my mum into Gran's bedroom. I looked closely at her as she drew the curtains and tucked Gran up under the covers. Mum's face was far more lined that it had been last time I saw her, the circles under her eyes poking through the expensive make-up she always wore. Sally was right – Mum looked exhausted. We watched as Gran closed her eyes.

'Should you not have some more help?' I asked Mum gently.

'Why? Am I not doing everything I should?' she snapped back.

'That's not what I meant! You look tired, that's all. It must be hard, and you and Sally can't be with her twenty-four seven.'

She relaxed a little. 'No, we can't. We have a nurse coming in every day now, and the doctor pops in when he can. There's not much anyone can do for her. We just try to keep her comfortable.' She led us out of the room. 'It has been hard though.'

'Of course it has. Why don't you go and have a bath and have an early night?'

'She needs a hot water bottle.'

'I can do that.'

33

Mum looked at me for a moment as if she was going to say something but then she gave a swift nod. 'Okay.' She headed for her room.

I went downstairs and made two hot water bottles, thinking Izzy might want one too. I took one into her then I took the other to Gran, slipping it under the covers for her. She was sound asleep. I looked over at the chair by the window which my mum sat in when she was with her. She'd left a half-finished glass of gin and tonic there, so I picked it up to take down to the kitchen. I saw a letter then on the chair. I recognised my writing on the envelope. Instantly, I knew what it was.

Why was she reading this? I couldn't believe that she had kept it for all these years.

Sitting in the chair, I leaned towards the lamp and opened up the letter to read it. I thought back to the scared, confused but determined sixteen-year-old who had written it, leaving it for her family to find. I barely recognised her as myself.

> Mum, Dad, Gran,
>
> You'll read this when you discover I've gone. It might be a cliché to do a midnight flit but I knew there would be more arguments if I didn't leave in secret. I can't take any more arguments. I know what you all think of me being pregnant. I know I've let you all down. I'm sorry but I love this baby already. It's a piece of me and Drew, and I can't let that go.
>
> I know you'll never let me keep it so that's why I have to leave. Start fresh somewhere new, just me and my baby. I'm sorry that I wasn't the daughter you wanted me to be. But I have to do this.

When I'm settled, I'll let you know where
I am.
    Beth

I looked at the window. Flurries were starting to fall outside.
Mum had been right about the snow then. Izzy would be
excited when she woke. I put the letter back in the envelope.
Why had Mum been reading it? Was my coming back here
making her think about the past, just like it was doing to me?
I tried to put myself in her shoes when she had read it back
then. I knew I would be heartbroken if Izzy left me: we were so
close. I had never felt close to my family in the same way. They
were always reserved, always more interested in what people
thought about us, in us doing the 'right' thing, not so much
about showing love and affection. But I knew that they must
have been upset when they had read my letter.

My gran had told me my parents felt the same way she did
about the baby, and I had been heartbroken. I had hoped my
mother might support my pregnancy and I had never felt so
alone than in the moment I realised she wouldn't. Gran told me
she had booked me in to see the doctor the next day to have
an abortion. 'You'd be going against all of our wishes if you do
this. I've spoken to your parents. And they are as disappointed
as I am. You're too young for this. Drew is going to America.
You can't destroy his future along with yours. You can't be a
single mother. What will people think? What will they *say*?'

Tears streaming down my face, I had asked her if my mum
had also agreed that I shouldn't have the baby. I had still been
holding a small flicker of hope that she would step up and stand
by me for once, that she'd want her grandchild even if it had
seemed like she had never wanted me.

My gran had looked at me and shaken her head. 'Your
mother thinks as I do. You can't have this baby, Beth. But,

don't worry, we will sort it out quickly. I'll take you to the doctor myself in the morning.'

I tried to tell her that I wasn't sure, but she swept out of the room. I remember thinking that surely I had a say in the matter. Wasn't it *my* body? *My* choice?

I sat on my bed in tears, not knowing what to do. I touched my stomach. I started to imagine what it would be like if the baby kept growing inside me. Would it look like me or Drew? I thought of Drew and how much I loved him. I was carrying a part of him too, wasn't I? How could I not love it too?

Perhaps if I had thought more rationally, I would have weighed up that love against how hard it would be becoming such a young, single mother, but I couldn't seem to get my head to ignore my heart. In that moment, all I could think about was the love I already felt for that baby. Love that I thought my family didn't feel for me.

My grandmother had never paused to ask me what I thought, to check how I felt, she had just decided what was best for me, like she and my mum always had. And that made me angry. And reminded me once again about how much I longed to be free of my family's influence. To do what I wanted to do.

I knew that if I was going to keep the baby, I couldn't stay. I had already imagined leaving Glendale and making my own way in the world away from them, so I could just do it sooner than I had planned. Now, I had a reason to do it.

My sixteen-year-old stubbornness kicked in. I felt as if I could take on the world by myself, and so I decided to do just that.

I looked back at my sleeping grandmother who was nearing her last days on earth. I wondered if she had ever regretted what she said before I ran away. I was sure I'd never know. My family don't do apologies or forgiveness. There was still a wall between us all. I had wondered if coming home would help to break it down, finally, but maybe it would always stay that way.

Chapter Six

We woke up to a blanket of white outside. Snow covered the garden and every surface, layers deep, powdered and thick like I hadn't seen since I left Glendale.

Izzy bounded into my room, up before me as usual, eager for us to walk in it. It was lovely to see her so excited to go outside so I suggested we left the tour of the house I had promised her until later, and that we go to the village first. It looked like a Christmas card outside. I couldn't wait for us to leave our footprints in it.

We ate breakfast alone. Sally told us that Dad had gone to the office and Mum was upstairs with Gran. I promised to take Izzy up to see her as soon as we got back home. We ate quickly and then pulled on our coats, hats, scarves and boots. It had been a long time since I had walked through the snow. We opened the door and almost cried at the bitter wind that greeted us.

'Are you sure about this?' I asked Izzy, wondering if my mother had been right about staying in today.

'Mum, it's snow, we have to!'

I laughed and clutched her gloved hand with mine as we stepped gingerly off the front step. John had cleared a path to the front gate already, but beyond, although the road had been gritted the pavements were still completely covered, so we walked single file along the road.

Glendale village was a twenty-minute walk from the house, down a small winding lane with countryside surrounding it. There wasn't another house for miles. I had done the walk so many times in my life before I could have probably done it blindfolded, but it felt unfamiliar because Izzy was beside me. The sky was blue, and the sun was out, shining down on the white ground beneath our feet. There was something about snow that made the world feel peaceful. It was silent, the only sound the crunching of the snow underfoot as we walked carefully away from the Hall. Izzy was beaming, enjoying the feel of walking through deep snow for the first time in her life. I snapped some photos of her on my phone and took a selfie of the two of us with silver birch trees behind us, covered in snow.

'Is that it?' Izzy asked, squinting as some buildings came into view, forcing their way into the landscape in front of us.

'That's it.' We soon passed the sign indicating that we were in Glendale village and found ourselves in the small narrow high street. It was strange to walk down it again. We were the only two people in sight. I thought back to summer days as a teenager, running to the village almost every day to meet up with my boyfriend Drew and our friends. We would buy ice creams and walk to the small green in front of the church to eat them. The church still dominated the scene, its steeple was dusted with snow.

I looked around in surprise. 'Where is everyone?' I wondered aloud to Izzy, who shrugged. I didn't think the snow would be a deterrent to hardy Glendale residents, as it would have been in London, but there was an eerie emptiness to the village.

We strolled down the road. There were just two shops open – a convenience store and a florist – as well as the doctor's surgery and the library. The rest of the shops had been boarded up. 'There used to be so much more here,' I told Izzy. It had been thriving when I was younger. I had often dragged my mum into the cafe for a sweet treat when she had brought me with her on errands. We always saw someone we knew and I used to roll my eyes at how long she would talk to people in there, bored as soon as I'd finished my shortbread. I wondered how long it had been since she had walked down the road like we were doing. Would she still stop to talk to people here, or had my leaving changed all that for her? I felt guiltier with each step.

I tried hard to find some resemblance to the past village I had known. It felt like that had been a different place. 'At least the pub is still here,' I muttered, seeing it still standing at the end of the road, its thatched roof covered in white. I smiled as I remembered hanging out there as a teenager, sitting out in the beer garden, even though it was too cold, to hide the alcoholic drinks bought for us by older kids. Snuggled up to Drew, I never wanted to go home after nights like that.

'And they still have a library,' Izzy said then, breaking through my memories, pointing ahead eagerly. 'Can we go, please? I definitely need more books,' she begged, her eyes having lit up at the very idea of books.

'Izzy, we talked about you not disappearing into a book every moment of this trip, didn't we?' I said. I loved that she got so excited about books, but I also wanted her to want to spend time with people. In London, she found it hard to connect with kids her age. She had always enjoyed books, and we had read together a lot, but once she started school, she spent more and more time reading. I tried to encourage her to be more sociable by inviting kids in her class round or taking her to birthday parties but she just didn't seem to enjoy it, and I hated forcing her into it. I knew that as an only child without family around, she had spent more time alone or just with me than many of her peers would have done, but I worried that there was more to it. Izzy always tried to protect me, I knew that, telling me that everything was okay and avoiding asking me for money unless she really had to, trying to help out around the house when she saw that I was tired; it was tough us being alone and there being a smaller age gap between us than most mothers and daughters, but I didn't want her to miss out on anything.

Izzy pouted. 'Can we just have a look though? Don't you want to see it again? It's part of the village tour, isn't it?'

I couldn't say no to the hopeful look in her eyes. 'Okay, fine, just for a few minutes and then we're getting hot drinks, I can't feel my face,' I said, letting her lead the way to the small building at the end of the high street. It certainly hadn't been somewhere I had spent much time in growing up. My mother had always bought books brand new for me, and never having been the studious type, I had done the bare minimum in studying outside of school, working as fast as I could until I could get outside again. Izzy, however, had always been very much at home in a library. On my limited income, it had been a godsend with such a bookish daughter. We walked inside and the warmth that greeted us was very welcome.

Izzy marched us straight to the children's department and let out a gasp. 'Oh my god, look!' She pointed to a display of Harry Potter books draped with the house scarves and dotted with figures from the films, and wands and mugs, and basically every piece of merchandise you could think of. 'This is amazing.'

The Harry Potter series had always been her favourite. She loved the magic, obviously, but had especially loved the fact there was not only a red-haired main character but a whole, large family all with red hair in it too.

'Do you like it?' We turned to see a petite blonde walking over to us.

'I love it!' Izzy cried. 'Although you don't have a Ginny figure and she's the best.'

'You're right. I'll have to get one,' the woman replied, smiling at Izzy. She turned to me and stared, her mouth slowly falling open into an 'oh' shape.

I touched my face, wondering if I had breakfast left on it or something.

'Oh my god. You look so much like… Beth?' She said in a thick Scottish accent.

'Yes?'

'It's me – Heather!'

Then it was my turn to stare. She broke out into a huge grin as I smiled. 'Oh my god, it is you!' I recognised her too, then. My childhood best friend.

Heather grabbed me and gave me a tight hug that took my breath away. 'Bloody hell! It really is you. I heard rumours you were back in town.' The couple in the corner turned around to shush us. 'Oops,' she said in a lower voice. 'I should really know better. Then this must be…?' she asked, looking down at Izzy.

'I'm Izzy,' she replied, standing a little straighter.

'What a lovely name!'

'I can't believe we've run into you,' I said, shaking my head in disbelief.

'I know! It's been, what, ten years? Please say I can tempt you to a cup of tea?'

I hesitated, glancing at Izzy who promptly sat down, cross-legged on the floor, pulling a book down on to her lap. 'It would be nice to catch up. You'll be okay here, Iz?'

'Of course,' she replied, pointing to the book.

Following Heather to the desk at the front, I sat in the seat she gestured to and watched as she put the kettle on. 'I can't believe you're here,' I told her.

'Me? I'm always here! But you, I haven't seen you in Glendale in forever. You still live in London, don't you? I tried to find you on Facebook a few years ago actually, but I couldn't find you,' Heather replied.

I remembered her rapid-fire conversation from when we were teenagers. It was nice to see she hadn't changed.

'I still live there,' I confirmed. 'My grandmother isn't well, so Izzy and I have come back for Christmas. And I'm not on Facebook at all,' I told her, smiling as she handed me a tea and sat down in the desk chair opposite me. I had avoided social media, too worried that I'd resort to stalking Drew online. It was better to be in the dark about his life, for both Izzy and me. It made his absence from ours somewhat easier.

'You're probably wondering why the hell I'm still in Glendale, huh? Well, I did get out for a bit. I went to uni and all that, but my parents needed me, so I came back and got a job here.'

'How are your parents?' I asked, taking a sip of the tea.

Heather sighed. 'My mum passed away a few years ago, so it's just me and Dad now.'

'Oh, I'm so sorry!' I remembered all the times I spent at Heather's house in the village when I was growing up. I loved her cosy, warm house and her loving parents: it always felt like a respite from life at Glendale Hall. 'I wish I had known.'

'It was a shame that you went so far away,' Heather agreed. 'But I did understand. Sally came to see me like you asked her to.'

'I couldn't just leave without telling you.' I had begged Sally to go and see Heather to tell her why I'd had to run from Glendale.

'I'm glad you did. I wished I could have helped you in some way though.'

'It all happened so fast. I realised I was pregnant, and then Gran found my test. I didn't have a chance to talk to you, to anyone really. Sally was a huge help. I went to stay with her niece to start with.' I glanced over at Izzy and smiled.

Heather looked at her too. 'She looks just like you expect for the red hair. That's all Drew,' she said, whispering his name. 'Does she know about him?'

'Yes. She knows that he never knew I was pregnant, which is why she's never met him.' I didn't want to confess that I had reached out to Drew and had been rejected.

'I'm sorry you had to do it all on your own. You didn't ever meet someone then, in London?'

I shook my head. 'I suppose it wasn't easy being a single mother; I always put Izzy first.'

'And you were so in love with Drew,' Heather replied, looking at me with understanding.

I felt my cheeks warm up more than I could blame on the tea. 'I suppose I have compared people to him. It's hard not to. First love and all that…' I tried to laugh. 'But what about you? Anyone special in your life?'

'Unfortunately, you don't tend to meet Prince Charming working in here. What do you do in London then?'

'I do admin at Izzy's school.'

'The girl who hated school now works in one!' Heather hooted with delight. 'I never told anyone that she was Drew's,' she continued in a low voice. 'Your parents kept quiet the real reason you had gone, but obviously there was a lot of gossip about it. One of the theories was that you'd gone to a young offender's place.' She shook her head. 'In the end, most people assumed you'd run off with another boy. And then your mum told someone that you'd had a baby in London, which seemed to confirm all of that. It was all a bit of a scandal though. Beth Williams leaving Glendale Hall and her family… the village was shocked.'

I sighed. I could just imagine how much people had talked about it all back then. It explained why my parents appeared to have retreated from village life. They would have been mortified being gossiped about. 'And what about Drew? Have you seen or heard anything about him? Did he hear all the gossip?' I asked her, anxiously.

'Rory told me that Drew had been devastated when you didn't turn up to see him at the airport. He took a lot of convincing to get on the plane to America. Rory didn't tell him about the rumour you'd gone off with someone else, I don't think.'

'It was the hardest thing I've ever done, not going to that airport.'

'I bet. I've briefly seen him on and off over the years when he's been home if him and Rory have come into the pub, just to say hi really, not much more. He seems like he's doing well. I don't know if you want to hear that or not though,' she added.

I was about to reply but Izzy came over then. I shook my head, that conversation had to be over for now. 'Now, why do you have four books with you?'

'They look really good.'

'You won't have time to read them, we will be spending time with the family and you brought a pile from home.'

'Mum, you can never have too many books!'

Heather chuckled. 'A girl after my own heart. How did you produce such a bookish daughter? I was friends with your mum when she was young, and I never saw her reading.'

'You like Harry Potter though, don't you, Mum?'

I grinned. 'Well, of course, I do.'

'Take them all home with you; it's lovely to see someone using the library,' Heather said. 'I'm not sure how much longer we'll be here, so you might as well.'

'Why not?' I asked.

'The council keep threatening close it down because they are losing Government funding for it, apparently, as people just aren't using it enough. The whole of the high street seems to be shutting down. The council put all the rents up and it forced most of the shops to shut. There's a rumour that they want to sell off the whole street to some developers, but I don't know if that's true.'

'That's awful,' Izzy said, her face twisting up in outrage at the very idea of closing the library.

'What will they do with the buildings if they do sell them?' I asked Heather.

'Put up flats, apparently, sell it as a commuter estate for people working in Inverness. I don't know, maybe it would be better, the high street is like a ghost town.' She shrugged. 'But if they do close the library, I'll have to get a job in Inverness as there will be nothing around here for me.'

'That's such a shame,' I said, thinking that explained why it had all felt so different to the village I remembered. I wondered whether my parents knew how bleak Glendale had become; they had always been so active in the community when I was growing up. It used to annoy me that they would constantly tell me we had to keep up our good family name in the community, so it was strange to see them not at all interested in the village now. 'I hope it can be saved.'

'We'd need a lot of money though. Anyway, we should talk about brighter things. What are your plans for Christmas then?'

'Tomorrow we're cutting down a tree and I'm going to help decorate it,' Izzy said, excitedly.

'Your mum is going to allow that?' Heather looked at me in surprise.

I grinned. 'She doesn't know about it yet.'

'I'm glad that some things stay the same,' she replied, smiling back.

'Excuse me, Heather?' An older lady came over. 'Can you help me find a book, dear?'

'Of course, Mrs Smith,' Heather said, jumping up. 'Wait here,' she added to us.

The lady started to follow her but then stopped, staring at me. 'You look so familiar, dear.'

'I used to live here. I'm Beth Williams.'

The lady turned that over in her mind for a moment. 'Beth! Oh, my goodness, I used to teach you piano! Do you remember? Well, it was only for a couple of months until you announced you hated it and refused to play so your mother stopped the lessons.'

I shook my head, smiling. 'I do remember. I'm so sorry, Mrs Smith, I hated being stuck in having to practise it. I just wanted to be out in the garden. Was I a horrible brat to you?'

She chuckled. 'I've had worse, don't you worry. Lovely to see you back in Glendale. I know your family have missed you while you've been living it up in the big city.' She waved merrily as she went off with Heather.

I wondered if she was right; they had never actually said that to me.

When Heather came back, she signed Izzy up to the library and handed over the books she had picked. 'Let me have your number, Beth, so we can arrange a night out. Lord knows, I'm in need of one.'

'I'm relieved to see Glendale Arms is still open at least,' I said, putting my number into her phone.

'Yes. If the pub ever shuts, you'll know that Glendale really is dead.'

Heather chuckled but I could tell how sad she was about what was happening to our village. It was weird how much I had put it all out of my mind in London, but being back in Glendale, I felt my old affection for it rising up again and I understood how she felt. It had almost changed beyond recognition. I was glad, at least, that some of the old faces were still around.

'It's been really good to see you.'

'You too. We are definitely going for a drink while you're here.'

'Deal!'

Heather glanced at the clock and squealed. 'We've been talking for ages, oops! I better get some work done.' She looked at me and shook her head. 'You always were a bad influence.'

'I will forever plead my innocence,' I replied with a grin.

Chapter Seven

'You two must be frozen!' Mum greeted us when Izzy and I walked in through the front door when we came back from the village. The snow was falling in earnest again and I was glad to be back inside. 'What have you got there, Izzy?'

'I got some books at the library,' she said, showing the bag to her grandmother.

'The village seems quite rundown now,' I said as we shed our outside layers.

'I told you it wasn't worth visiting. We can go into Inverness once the snow clears a bit.'

'But aren't you worried about Glendale?'

Mum sighed. 'People have to accept that some things need improving; we can't just keep things the same as they've always been if it's not working. Everyone around here is so afraid of change. The council wants to regenerate the whole area, and everyone is being very difficult about it. Good riddance to the place, I say.'

I was confused why my mother seemed so keen for the village to be redeveloped. I had thought she always loved the history of the place, the fact that the village and countryside were unchanged, that the community was so strong. It seemed that hiding herself away at the Hall meant she didn't care as she used to. I felt like I needed to do something to change that, as it must have been because of me that she had stayed away for so long, but I had no idea what.

'Are you okay to come up to see your great-grandmother now?' Mum asked, putting an arm around Izzy. Izzy glanced at me to see what I thought about it. 'She keeps asking after you.'

'Now as you know, your great-grandmother has cancer, and is very frail,' I said to Izzy. I had gone to see her alone first but now it was time for Izzy to say hello, and I wanted her to be prepared for what would greet her. 'She may not be up to talking much but she's been really looking forward to seeing you, so do you want to just go in for a few minutes?' Izzy nodded but looked a little worried.

'She'll be needing her nap soon anyway,' Mum agreed as we headed upstairs together.

Even though it had been a while since they had seen each other, Gran had always sent lavish gifts for Izzy's birthdays. I had wondered to myself whether they were gifts to try to ease her guilt, but I doubted she would even admit that to herself, let alone anyone else.

We entered her room softly, but I was relieved to see that Gran was sitting up in bed, propped up with pillows, waiting for us. She was wearing a silk nightdress, her hair neatly tucked behind her ears. The room smelled of her lavender perfume, the old-fashioned scent she had always worn.

'There she is,' Gran said, smiling at Izzy. 'You've grown a lot since I last saw you.'

Izzy briefly glanced at me and we shared a look; she was forever being told she had grown a lot, like every kid was. She was going to be as tall as her father, I was sure of it.

'Come and sit by me.'

Izzy went over and perched on the bed. Mum walked to the window and gazed out, fiddling with the gold chain around her neck. I went to sit in the chair by the bed. 'You must have so much time to read stuck in bed all day,' Izzy said. I bit my lip to stop myself from laughing. I loved how innocently she framed the question. Of course Izzy would envy anyone able to read all day.

'I find it hard to concentrate on books,' Gran replied. 'You love to read still then? Are you doing well in school? Do you like school?'

Izzy bit her lip. 'It's okay. I like the learning part of it and the books,' she replied, trailing off a little at the end. I frowned, wishing it didn't worry me that studying was her favourite part of school. I loved how seriously she took her schoolwork, of course, but I thought about Heather and all the fun we'd had in our classes and wished she had that too.

'And what do you think of your first trip to Scotland?'

'I love it so far,' Izzy said, suddenly much more animated. 'This house is so cool. I haven't even seen half of it I don't think. I love all the fires, and I can't believe it actually snowed today! It's like being in a book.'

I smiled as that was the biggest compliment that Izzy could give somewhere.

'Well, I'm glad to hear you're enjoying Glendale so much.' Gran said. She looked over at me then. 'She's a credit to you, Beth, dear.'

I almost fell out of the chair. Even Mum turned around from the window. I had never had any praise from my family about my mothering skills. 'I'm very proud of her,' I said, once I had found my voice.

'Caroline, it's lunchtime, isn't it? Bring some food up for us all; Isabelle, go with her,' Gran said then. Her tone was familiar from growing up with her – such as to brook no disagreements.

My mum glanced at me then nodded, gesturing for Izzy to follow her.

Once we were alone, Gran turned her gaze back on to me. 'Come here, Beth.'

Dutifully, I got up and sat where Izzy had sat. Gran's face was sallow and hollow, but her eyes were still fierce. Her bony hand reached out to touch my arm. I wondered what went through your mind when you knew that your time on earth was nearing its end. Did you think back over your life? Or did you think of all the things you'd be missing out on in the future? Or did you try not to think about any of it? Sometimes I wondered how differently things would have gone if ten years before Gran had told me she would support me. Would I have stayed at Glendale Hall? Would I have still gone to college and become a gardener? Would Izzy and I have been as close as we were? I tried to shake my mind clear. Questions like that could drive you crazy. I made my choice back then and we were where we were.

'You and Isabelle have a strong bond,' Gran said. It was a statement not a question, but I nodded anyway. 'Stronger than I have with Caroline and stronger than she has with you. I have been thinking a lot about the past. That day when I told you that you shouldn't have your baby.' She closed her eyes for a moment as if the recognition caused her a moment of physical pain. I wanted to tear my arm out of her grip as that night flashed back, but I stayed still. She met my gaze again. 'I didn't listen to you, to what you wanted. When I woke up to find the house in chaos and you gone, I knew that it was my fault.'

How could I respond to that? It *was* her fault. What did she want me to say? She waited for a response. I opened my mouth, closed it again, then tried a second time.

'I wouldn't have gone if you hadn't booked a doctor's appointment. I felt I had no choice.'

She nodded. 'I know. I didn't know what kind of mother you'd be, Beth, if I had known… if I could have foreseen Isabelle then…'

'Why are you saying this now? You've never before shown any regret for what happened.'

'I felt it, but I didn't show it. I thought showing regret made me… weak. Now, lying here, I can't stop thinking about the past. I want you to know you did the right thing. Ten years ago. Walking away like that. You're so much stronger than me, Beth. All I cared about was trying to protect the family name. I didn't know that being strong, being brave, being determined, they are the things to be proud of, not how we look to others.'

I stared at her. I was stunned to say the least. She was accepting that she was wrong. More than that, she seemed to admire me for what I had done. I never thought for a moment she felt like that. I thought they all still thought I'd done the wrong thing in choosing to keep Izzy. That they disapproved of me, of us, of our life in London. But it seemed as though Gran, at least, didn't feel that way. 'I wish you had told me that sooner. I wish you could have asked me what I wanted back then, that you had given me a choice, a chance. Maybe then we would all be closer. I was sixteen. I was scared and alone. So alone.' I whispered the final words, choking up on them, as I thought back to that painful night.

Gran started to say something else, but the door opened and in came my mother carrying a tray, Izzy on her heels carrying a jug of juice, so she stopped. My mother looked at us as she entered, and I wondered if she had heard some of what I said. Her mouth was fixed in a straight line. Not giving anything away as usual.

I jumped up and backed away from the bed, hurryingly wiping my eyes so Izzy wouldn't see that I was upset. I tried never to let her see me cry.

Turning away from them, I gazed out at the wintery wonderland outside and felt a little of the weight I had always carried around lift ever so slightly.

Chapter Eight

Izzy and I followed John out across the lawn towards the wood-land area of the garden. It had stopped snowing, but it still lay thinly over the ground. John was going to cut down the Christmas tree and Izzy was eager to watch. Two men from a nearby farm had come to help and we stood there with Sally under the chosen one – it was huge, as John had promised Izzy, and would make a stunning addition to the entrance hall: the only place big enough for it, which was really saying something. As we waited for them to get it ready, shivering a little in the bitter wind, my phone vibrated in my pocket. Pulling it out, I smiled at a message from Heather.

> **How about that drink in the village tonight? H x**

I replied that I would meet her in the Glendale Arms at seven. It would be nice to have a distraction. My heart was still heavy from my conversation with Gran.

My mother had been even frostier with me than usual and I wasn't sure why. Through the years, my parents had become adept at never mentioning the fact they hadn't wanted me to have Izzy. When they had first come to see us, they had begged me to come back with them as if it had never happened, and I hadn't understood why they had been so upset when I refused to. It had never really been mentioned between us again. But I was beginning to think that we did need to talk about the past. To have an honest conversation like the one I'd had with Gran, and maybe lay things to rest once and for all. I just wasn't sure where to start.

'Okay, here we go,' John said, pulling me back to what was happening right in front of me. I put my phone away as the chainsaw started. We watched as he hacked at the bottom of the tree, the two men ready to help bring it down safely. I remembered watching John do this when I was Izzy's age and it was nice to have her see some of the traditions I had loved myself. I realised that after I had left, I had thought more about the bad parts of the house and my family, probably to protect myself and convince my heart that I'd done the right thing in walking away, but there had been a lot of magic in growing up here.

I thought about Heather then and the village, and I turned to Sally. 'I heard the library might close and some developers are trying to buy up the high street. What's going on?'

Sally shifted on her feet. 'Yeah, it's been hard. Most of the shops have closed through the years; the village has been going downhill for a while. Apparently developers are offering the council a fair bit of cash to sell to them.'

'And no one is doing anything to stop it?'

'There would need to be a lot of money found to do that. I don't think there is anyone willing to take the council on.'

'And Mum and Dad haven't got involved at all?'

Sally looked away. 'You should ask them about that. I don't think they're as tied to the community as they were once. Which is a real shame.'

'I'm really surprised,' I said, thinking back to how much being part of Glendale had meant to them.

'Beth, it's not my place but—' Sally's words were cut off by the sound of the chainsaw getting louder and we turned to watch John finish cutting down the tree. I wondered what was making Sally look so awkward and I supposed I'd have to talk to my parents about it, which wasn't something I really wanted to do but I just didn't understand why they weren't worried about the village. Something told me there was more to this than people were telling me.

I looked at my daughter's face, watching in wonder, as the tree finally toppled over. We started clapping as it hit the ground with a loud thud. 'This beats our fake tree at the flat,' she said to me.

'It does,' I agreed. I was determined we'd get to continue our Christmas traditions up there though. As we walked back to the house, the men carrying the tree between them, I nudged Sally with my arm. 'Izzy and I want to decorate the tree this year. We always make a day out of it at home.'

'I think your mother has booked the decoration company, so you'd better speak to her about it,' Sally replied with a look that said, 'good luck'. Christmas wasn't about making your decorations look like they could have come direct from Harrods' windows, it was about having fun putting them up, getting into the festive spirit together. I left Izzy with Sally to watch the men stand the tree up and I headed to find my mother to plead my case. I might have been an adult, and a mother myself, but I still felt a flutter of nerves as I found her at the kitchen table having a coffee.

–

'Room for one more?' I asked, pouring a mug for myself and sitting down opposite her before she could reply. 'We just watched the tree being cut down.'

'Oh, I'll go and have a look,' she replied and started to move.

'Wait. I wanted to ask you something,' I said, quickly, and she paused. 'Izzy is really excited for Christmas. One of the things she loves the most is decorating the tree each year. We usually make a big thing of it, put on music, bake some cookies and decorate it together. She would love to help decorate the tree here. I know that you usually bring in people to do it, but please, just this year, while we're here, can we do it?'

'I've already booked them for tomorrow,' Mum said.

'Mum, it's Christmas, it's all about the kids. Izzy is so excited to do it. We don't have anyone here but us. Why does the tree need to look like some kind of showcase?'

She sighed. 'It's what I've always done.'

'Don't I know it? I always wanted to help do the tree when I was growing up. Can't you see that doing things the way you always have isn't working?' I felt my voice starting to rise as my frustration grew. This was how I had felt as a teenager – that she never really listened to me. I took a breath and tried another tack. 'Why not let us do it and if you really hate it then they can redo it? How about that?' I suggested, trying to keep my voice as calm as I could. 'Please, for Izzy?'

She sighed. 'Fine, if it's that important to you.'

'Why don't you do it with us?'

She looked surprised. 'Really?'

'It's Christmas, Mum. Let's decorate together,' I replied firmly. I knew that Izzy would love it and it would be nice to show my mum that Christmas was a time for fun and family. Glendale Hall really seemed like it could do with a big dose of both.

Chapter Nine

It was freezing as I drove to the village to meet Heather, far too cold to walk. I wore my thick coat and scarf over my skinny jeans and black shirt but still shivered during the drive over. Parking outside the pub, the lights and noise emitting from it were very welcoming as was the heat from the crackling log fire that stood near the door when I walked in.

'Beth!' Heather called my name from a table in the corner, waving madly at me. I smiled and walked over to her. She had shed her outside layers and was wearing a long-sleeved wool dress, her hair curled over her shoulders. 'You made it,' she said as she jumped up to hug me. 'I wasn't sure with all the snow.'

'I must admit after being in London for so long I'd forgotten how to handle it,' I replied, pulling off my coat and scarf.

'I got us wine, I hope that's okay?' she asked, sitting down.

I joined her and picked up my glass. 'Definitely okay but I did drive here.'

'Oh, I'm sure we can find lifts home. Don't worry. Here's to catching up after ten years.'

'Cheers.' We clinked glasses and I took a long gulp. 'I needed that.'

'Being back home is hard, huh?' she asked, her face screwed up in sympathy. 'I know when I first moved back it was a big adjustment.'

'And you get on with your family.' I let out a small laugh, but I knew it sounded hollow. I sighed, fingering my glass on the table. 'I thought I'd put everything behind me, you know, but being back here… there are so many unsaid things in my family, so many unresolved issues. We've ignored them for ten years, but I don't think we can keep doing that. My gran is really sick so if we don't face them now, we might never be able to. I guess I'm still angry with them and they're still disappointed with me. How do you move past that?'

Heather thought for a moment. 'I think you have to talk it all through. They might not be disappointed. Sometimes it's hard for people to show how they really feel. I'm sure they're proud of the life you've made in London. And look at Izzy, she seems like a wonderful kid. And that's down to you. I think at some point you all have to forgive each other for what happened. That's the only way to move on, isn't it?'

I wondered if I could ever forgive my family for pushing me away. As soon as the words left Heather's lips, though, I knew she was right. Things were still difficult between us because I couldn't forgive them for not supporting me, and I assumed they couldn't forgive me for running away and having Izzy against their wishes. 'I'm not sure we do forgiveness,' I replied. It seemed like a handholding, therapist sharing kind of concept, one totally against our reserved, stiff-upper lip way of doing things. Although Gran had brought up the subject herself, hadn't she? She had seemed to want to finally talk about, and face, the past. Perhaps forgiveness *was* on her mind. Regret was certainly. 'Coming back here has dragged up all kinds of ghosts.'

Heather smiled. 'Including me.'

'You're a good ghost though. I'm sorry we didn't keep in touch.'

'We both had our lives to get on with, right? And it doesn't matter. Friendship just doesn't stop because you don't see each other every day. We've been through so much, you can't shake that kind of bond, right?'

I thought of all the times we spent together growing up, and I nodded. 'We did have some good times. Remember when we came here for your sixteenth birthday? We ended up dancing on the tables in the beer garden, even though it was freezing.'

'I was so sick that night,' she replied with a shudder. 'I've never touched vodka since. Fact. And what about when Drew stole Rory's car and hit a tree and we had to ring him and admit what we had done?'

'He was so angry,' I said, thinking back. 'And he gave us that three-hour lecture about car safety. To be fair, I've never had an accident since.'

The door to the pub opened then, letting in a gust of bitter air, and I glanced over at it as a tall man with auburn hair strode in, his cheeks red from the cold.

'Oh, God,' Heather muttered, seeing him. 'Are you stalking me again, Rory?' she said, louder, as he passed by our table.

He stopped and grinned. 'I think we already established it's you who has the unrequited love problem, Heather,' he replied, his Scottish accent thick. I looked up at him, and my heart bounced in my chest. He noticed me. 'Who's this? Hey...' he said, catching the familiarity of my face. His eyes widened. 'Beth? Beth Williams?'

'Hi, Rory,' I managed to say, my breath caught in my throat as I greeted Drew's older brother.

He started. 'Blimey, I didn't think I'd be seeing you here tonight. Actually...' He turned to the door, looking awkward. 'Maybe I better—'

Before he could finish his sentence, the door swung open again, and this time the three of us turned to watch as someone else walked in, looked around and waved when he spotted Rory, then headed straight for us.

It felt as if the floor slipped from under me. I grabbed the edge of my chair to steady myself. He looked just the same. Taller, thinner maybe, and with a slight tan but his red hair was still in the same floppy cut, there was still a faint line of stubble on his chin and that smile was exactly the same.

'Oh my god,' I said, under my breath, not able to take my eyes off of him.

'Over here,' Rory said, waving him over.

'No worries, I paid for the taxi,' Drew said with an eye-roll in his brother's direction then he noticed Heather who was staring open☒mouthed at me. She quickly turned to him.

'Oh, my goodness! Drew? I haven't seen you here for ages,' she said, her voice a little squeaky. She brushed her foot against my leg under the table. I couldn't believe my eyes.

'I thought you were in America,' I found myself blurting out, causing all their eyes to turn to me. I was surprised that I could speak – my throat felt as if it was closing up. It was all coming back. The kisses. The way he held my hand. His fingers in my hair. The stolen moments at his farm. The day I realised I couldn't tell him I was pregnant. The letter I wrote, tears streaming down my face, telling him about our baby.

Drew's eyes met mine then. There was a long pause as he stared at me, as shocked as his brother had been to see me in there. I wasn't sure which one of us was more shocked actually.

Rory jumped in to save us all. 'Back for Christmas, aren't you? And in need of a beer I bet, shall we?' Rory asked, gesturing to the bar.

'Beth? Is that you?' Drew said, finally, not seeming to have noticed his brother speaking. I managed to nod.

'Beth is back for Christmas, too,' Heather said, quickly. 'Her grandmother isn't well, so here she is, back in Glendale after all this time!'

'It's been ten years, hasn't it? Rory asked, his voice a little hard. 'Look, how about we get some drinks, eh, Drew? We have a lot of catching up to do, don't we?' he said, patting Drew's arm.

That seemed to shake Drew out of staring at me. He looked at Rory and nodded. 'Yeah, I think I need a drink,' he said. I noticed he had a slight American edge to his accent now. Rory hurried off to the bar, glad to escape it looked like. I saw Heather reach for her wine and take a long gulp.

Drew turned to go, and then paused to look back at me. 'It's been a long time,' he said.

'It has,' I agreed.

'You look… well,' he said then turned and practically ran after Rory to the bar.

I exhaled and slumped in my chair. 'Oh my god,' I said.

Heather refilled my wine and pushed the glass towards me. 'You need that. Are you okay? You look white as a sheet.'

'I can't believe he's here,' I said, taking it gratefully and draining half of the glass down my throat in one gulp.

'I haven't seen him in ages. Rory's often in here but I never thought. I can't believe you two are back here at the same time! What are the odds?'

I shook my head. It felt like the universe was playing a really cruel trick on me.

Heather leaned forward then. 'So, he doesn't know anything about Izzy? Right?'

'Actually...' I leaned closer and in a low voice confessed to writing to Drew when Izzy was one. 'I never heard back from him.'

Her eyes flashed. 'The utter bastard! And to see you here and not even ask about her!' she glanced behind her, and we saw Rory and Drew sitting at a table in the back, beers in front of them. 'I just can't believe that.'

'I feel like such a fool. I was so in love with him, Heather. And I've never felt that way about anyone since. I know that it must have been a shock to find out about her but to not say anything. I have tried to let it go, to move on, but seeing him here now, it brings it all back.' I really hoped I wasn't going to start crying in the middle of the pub.

'We should go,' Heather said, firmly. 'You shouldn't have to be in the same room as that man.' She got up and pulled on her coat, so I did the same, feeling dazed. I looked over at Drew's back, wondering what he was thinking about seeing me here. Was he not curious about Izzy at all? Did he really hate me that much that he didn't care at all about his daughter?

I knew that I should be angry and upset, but mostly I was confused. The boy I had loved all those years before would never have treated me like that.

I let Heather lead me out of the pub. I saw Rory notice and as we walked through the door, I glanced back and caught Drew turning around to watch us go. Our eyes met for a moment, and I thought he might be about to call out something, but then the door closed behind me, and he was gone.

Chapter Ten

'Mum, are you alive?'

I opened one of my eyes and groaned. Izzy was leaning over me, frowning at my lifeless form under the duvet.

'You made a noise, so you're alive,' she said, climbing up to perch on the bed. She patted my arm. 'It's ten o'clock and everyone is asking where you are.'

I bet they were. I opened the other eye and groaned again. 'Come here,' I said, pulling Izzy down to hug her. She squealed.

'What's that?' she asked as something slid off the bed. She pulled away to pick it up. 'A photo album?'

Heather had wanted me to go back to her house, but I wanted to be alone, so I'd gone back to the Hall and ended up staying up into the early hours drinking too much of my dad's whisky. I hadn't been up that late drinking for years, and my head was not thanking me for it today. When I'd finally got to bed, I'd been too wired to sleep, running everything that happened over and over in my mind. I'd pulled out my old photo album from the bottom of the wardrobe and ended up falling asleep with it on my lap.

I watched as Izzy opened the album. 'From when I was a teenager,' I said, my voice croaky. Izzy began flicking through the photos. I couldn't help but watch her, thinking of Drew. She really did look like him.

'Who are they?' she asked, pointing to a photo of me in my school uniform, arms draped around three other people at school. 'Wait is that…?' She trailed off, recognising her father.

I nodded. 'That's me, Heather, your father and his friend.' I was never happier than when I was hanging out with them. They were my refuge. I had taken a couple of photos with me to London, so already Izzy had seen what her father looked like, but there were so many more in the photo album and she now looked with interest at them all. Drew's smile from the previous night was playing on my mind. Their smiles were so similar.

'What was he like?' she asked then as we looked at one of me and Drew at a school dance. He looked smart in a suit borrowed from Rory, and I was wearing an expensive blue dress my mum had bought for me.

I tried to stop my heart from aching as I thought back to who he was then, but it was impossible. 'He was funny and kind, very loyal; he always looked out for me back then. He was just easy and fun to be with. He was my best friend.' I wondered how the two people in that photo could have become such strangers. My teenage self would have been devastated if she had known how estranged we would become.

'Did he come to this house a lot?'

'Not too often. My family didn't really like my friends. They wanted me to socialise with the children of their friends, and I hated them all.' I smiled at her. 'You know me, I wanted to do everything my parents told me not to.' Including having you, I added silently to myself. 'Right then, I better have a shower, and I need a lot of coffee and maybe some bacon.'

She looked at me. 'You're hungover, aren't you? Granny said you probably were; that's why you were still in bed.'

I sighed. I wished my mum wouldn't say bad things about me to Izzy. 'I just had a couple of drinks, but it was a late night so that's why I slept in. Anyway, we have a lot to do today. It's tree decorating time!'

Izzy grinned. 'I can't wait!'

I smiled at her excitement, pleased I'd persuaded Mum to let us do this. We would have a good day, I thought, despite the cloud from last night still hanging over me. I would make sure of it. 'Want to stay here until I'm ready?'

Izzy nodded and tucked herself up under the duvet with the photos. I wished she could have known her father back then. He had obviously changed beyond recognition now. It was for the best she didn't know him, I decided, as I headed to the bathroom; but even as I told myself that, the hurt from him not even asking about her last night refused to budge from my chest. It had settled there, making it hard to take a deep breath. I had been confused last night and now I was angry. For Izzy and for the girl who had loved him so much back then. We both deserved better. That I knew for sure.

All I could hope was that I wouldn't run into him again while we were in Glendale.

–

Slade blasted out of my iPhone as the smell of cookies in the oven filled the kitchen. Sally was supervising Izzy and me as we baked cookies ready for our afternoon of festive decorating.

We had made our signature chocolate chip cookies, but we needed Sally's help to work out the Aga. She decided to make some shortbread, so we had the full Christmas biscuit assortment.

Mum had come down after seeing to Gran, her face barely hiding her disapproval at the mess she found the kitchen, and us, in. Baking always got very messy when Izzy and I were around. Flour was smeared across my face and Izzy had a piece of dough stuck to her elbow, but that was the fun of baking, wasn't it? And eating a bit of the raw cookie dough too. To which my mum practically self-combusted when she saw us.

'Right, while they bake let's go and get all the decorations,' I said, going to the sink with Izzy so we could wash up.

'John has brought the boxes down from the loft and put them in the hall,' Mum said.

'Excellent. We can choose what we want to put on the tree then, Iz.'

'At least colour coordinate,' Mum muttered. 'I'm going to get a drink.'

'No need, Sally has made mulled wine,' I replied, ignoring her colour comment. I wasn't going to let her suck the fun out of this for us. 'And hot chocolate for you,' I added to Izzy who beamed at me. She brought a mug over to Sally to pour her drink in, and I grabbed two glasses for me and mum. At least she had no disapproving comment to make about mulled wine – she never turned down alcohol. Sally said that she'd bring us the cookies when they were ready.

'Let's go!' Izzy cried, leading the way out of the kitchen. Chuckling I followed, with Mum behind me walking more reluctantly.

I loved to see Christmas through Izzy's eyes. I didn't use to be excited about it even when she was little. Being on my own, all I could think about was making sure I had enough money for her presents, though I couldn't stop myself from wondering what was happening at Glendale Hall. We always spent the day at Emily's parents' house, but it was hard not to think of my own family. My parents usually came down Christmas week to see us for lunch, but it wasn't the same, which is why I started to come up with so many traditions for me and Izzy. I wanted to make sure neither of us felt the hole of my missing family, that we always had a special holiday.

The tree took up most of the entrance hall, rising up to almost touch the ceiling. Boxes of decorations waited on the floor and Izzy got stuck straight in, sitting on the floor, crossing her legs and rifling through them. The scent of pine needles filled the room sending me right back to my childhood with a nostalgic bang.

'Lights first,' I reminded Izzy, showing her which box housed them. At home, Izzy liked multi-coloured lights, but I knew that we only had white lights at Glendale: my mother thought coloured ones were gaudy. The lights had been expertly wound by the professional decorators the previous year making it easy for us to drape them around the tree. John returned with a stepladder to put them on the top half of the tree.

Once the lights were all up, Sally came in with the cookies, which were delicious and even my mum had one. Izzy gathered up the decorations she wanted to use, and we stood around the tree to hang them. John and Sally joined in and my mum directed us to make sure we spaced them evenly. Izzy chose all the sparkly ones, so the tree was soon glittering with gold.

'Remember this one?' I held one up to show my mum. We had made them at my school when I was about Izzy's age. It was an angel covered in glitter. I remembered being so proud of it. I was crushed when I realised that it hadn't been used on the tree because 'it didn't match anything'. 'I made it at school,' I added when she looked blank.

'Oh, you made so many things; they were always sending you home with something that I had to try to find a place for.'

'Let's put it on the tree!' Izzy took it from me, excited to be holding something I had made, while I faced my mum, feeling the hurt I had felt all over again. And a buzz from the mulled wine.

'I'm sorry I was such an inconvenience,' I snapped. I felt Sally's and John's eyes on us. 'Kids make things, you know, and are excited to bring them home. All I wanted was to hang my angel on my Christmas tree.' I turned to see Izzy hanging it right in the centre. God, I loved her. 'Only took twenty years,' I added, under my breath.

'I'm sorry I was such a disappointing mother,' Mum hissed from behind me. When I turned to reply, she was stalking out of the room.

'Mum, what do you think?'

I took a breath and walked over to Izzy. 'It looks beautiful.'

'Does Granny not like it?' she asked, noticing she had gone.

'She's gone to check on your great-gran. You're doing a brilliant job.' I felt a lump rise up in my throat and I tried to force on a smile for my daughter's sake, because that's what you did for your kids at this time of year. So, why was it so hard for Caroline Williams to do the same?

'Why have we never come here before?' Izzy asked me then.

'London is a long way away,' I replied, passing her an ornament to hang.

Izzy looked at me, eyebrow raised. 'Mum, I'm not a kid.'

I bit back a smile. 'I wasn't always that happy here, so when I left I didn't really want to come back. And your grandparents always came down to see us, didn't they?'

'Didn't you miss it?'

I started to say no but I realised that wasn't strictly true. 'I missed walking in the gardens, waking up on Christmas morning to snow outside and the smell of the turkey cooking downstairs; I missed summers lying on the grass under a tree dreaming of everything I wanted; I missed how safe and peaceful it was here. London was a big shock to the system. But I had you to focus on; I didn't think about this place because I had so much else to think about.' The house had shaped so much of who I was. I realised I had tried to block it from my heart, but being back, I did remember how much I had loved growing up here. My family were a different matter entirely but the house was special.

'Why did you go to London, Mum? Why didn't you stay here to have me?'

It was a good question with a potential thousand responses. 'I thought we'd be happier there,' I answered, halfway to the truth. 'And we have been, right?'

Izzy seemed to be avoiding my eyes. 'This house is a lot bigger than our flat. It must have been weird to go from this... to that.'

I smiled back. 'It was weird, but it was worth it. I'm glad I got to show you this house though. You like it, don't you?'

'I love it here,' she said, quietly.

I was about to ask why she was suddenly asking so many questions about the past, but then John brought in another box of tree decorations and Izzy hurried over to look. I watched her, pleased that she seemed to be enjoying Glendale Hall so much. But it gave me a small stab of guilt too. I used to be so sure I was doing the right thing in keeping Izzy from the house, and at arm's length from my family, but things suddenly didn't feel so clear cut.

Chapter Eleven

While Izzy was helping Sally prepare the dinner, I went up to see Gran again. My mum was in there sitting in the chair by the bed reading while my gran slept. 'How is she?' I asked, looking at Gran with her eyes closed, seemingly peaceful in her bed.

'She's been sleeping most of the day. The doctor is coming in the morning, so we'll see what he says,' she replied shortly. 'I hope he can make her more comfortable.' Gran started to stir then. 'Mother, how are you doing?'

'Just tired,' she said, her voice croaky as she struggled to sit up. I started to move but Mum jumped up and hurried over to help prop Gran up on her pillows. She smiled. 'You're both here. Sit on the bed. Please.' We both sat by her. 'Family is so important, you know that, don't you?' She touched my hand. 'Beth has come home finally. I know that things haven't been easy between us but that has to change now. Life… it's too short.'

I glanced at Mum who avoided my eyes. 'I wish things were different,' I admitted to them both, voicing what I'd been feeling the past few days since I had come home. Putting up the tree should have been enjoyable, but it ended in Mum walking out. I was grateful she had left the tree exactly as Izzy and I had decorated it, but it was a shame she hadn't been able to enjoy doing it with us.

'They can be. We just need to be honest,' Gran said then. 'I have something to tell you both.' She started coughing.

'You need to rest, we can talk tomorrow,' Mum told her. 'We'll still be here.'

'I have so many regrets,' Gran continued, ignoring her. 'But most of all that it's my fault you two aren't close. Beth, I see you and Izzy, and I wish it had been like that for you two,' she said, her voice croaky. She reached for some water. 'I thought I was doing the right thing. That it was for the best. But I know that it cost you two your relationship.'

'What do you mean, Gran? What did you do?' I asked, not sure what she was trying to say.

Gran closed her eyes, looking exhausted. 'I'm just so tired.'

'It's okay, Mum, you go to sleep,' my mother told her gently. 'Don't push her, Beth.'

'But what is she talking about?'

'She's getting confused. She needs rest.'

'But she said it was her fault we're not close.'

'There's nothing wrong with our relationship,' Mum snapped, standing up.

I shook my head. 'You know that's not true.'

'She needs to sleep,' Mum said, firmly, starting to walk out. I sighed and got off the bed to follow her.

'Why can't we talk about it?' I asked, frustrated. 'There are too many things left unsaid in this family.'

'I don't want to row, Beth. I've had a long day with your grandmother, I want to lie down. We can't change the past. You left us. We can't ever get those years back.'

'So, it's all my fault? Even though you all forced me to go?'

She spun around in anger to face me. 'Forced you to go? How can you say that! Don't you realise that you broke my heart when you left? Having you here with Isabelle, it's what

73

I've always wanted but it's painful for me. I missed out on so many Christmases with you. I missed out on it all.' With a sob, she pushed past me to her room.

'But…' Confused, I let the word hang in the air as I watched her door close. How can she talk about her heart being broken? If she had wanted me to stay, why didn't she support me?

My hands rose up and then fell to my sides. As usual it was all my fault. The past had been rewritten by my family to solely blame me. I didn't know why I was so surprised. I turned around and headed downstairs to the kitchen, desperate for the warmth, and love, of Sally and Izzy, because I sure wasn't going to find it anywhere, or with anyone, else.

–

The following day, my phone buzzed with a call from Heather as I stepped out into the garden. The sun was out, and the breeze was gentle, so it wasn't too bracing in my coat and boots. I was planning to find John and beg him to let me do something in the garden. I was feeling restless. Izzy had gone with Sally and my mum to do some shopping in Inverness, but I hadn't wanted to join them. Mum and I weren't really speaking, and I knew the atmosphere would be frosty. It was better Izzy went alone and actually had a nice day. As I trekked across the grass to find John, I picked up Heather's call. 'Hiya.'

'Oh, hi, Beth. I just wanted to check in with you. How are you feeling about… everything?' She said the last word in a whisper as if she was worried someone would hear her.

'I'm okay,' I replied. 'It just hurt seeing him again, but I accepted long ago that he wasn't going to be part of our lives. I just have to make sure I can avoid him for the rest of our stay,' I replied, knowing I was avoiding speaking his name aloud because it did still feel so raw, no matter how hard I just had to convince myself, and Heather, that it didn't.

She clucked sympathetically. 'Hopefully he'll just stay out on their farm. It sucks, Beth. Christmas should be fun but we're both being put through the ringer.'

'Why? What's up with you?'

'I've had the worst day! I was called in to the office by my manager, and it's definite. The council are going to close the library in the new year. They have almost signed the deal with the developers. I knew it was on the cards, but I really hoped it wouldn't happen.'

'I'm really sorry, Heather. I can't believe they're going to let the library go. And they're really going to turn the high street into flats? I just don't get it.'

'It's so sad. For everyone. But everyone just goes into Inverness for what they need now. There's no reason to come into the village, I suppose. I really don't want to have to look for another job. I love it here. Ugh. But I think the council have given up on the village, and no one is doing anything to fight them. It seems such a shame that no one can breathe life into the Glendale again.'

'Surely everyone who lives here wants to save it?'

'Everyone I speak to does but no one seems to have any ideas as to what we can do. Everyone has just accepted that it's inevitable I think. I better go, my break is almost over. I just wanted to check in on you.'

'Thank you. And I'm really sorry about the library. We could meet up at the weekend, maybe?'

'That would be lovely. I'm so glad you're here, Beth.'

Heather hung up, and I put my phone in my pocket, feeling deflated. I decided I had to talk to my dad about what was happening in the village. Mum seemed not to care but my dad had always weighed in on things happening in Glendale. Surely, he didn't want it taken over by these developers?

'John!' I called, spotting him pushing a wheelbarrow across the lawn. I caught up with him. 'I'm going crazy inside. Let me do something please?!'

'Today, I'm clearing snow. You want to help do that?' He was grinning, a challenge in his eyes.

'Perfect.' I ignored his raised eyebrows and followed him to the shed, where he passed me a shovel. Then we went around to the front of the house where the snow still covered the driveway. The snow had turned icy now, no longer powdery and pretty, but sludgy and dark. It was hard work moving it into piles. Even though it was chilly, I soon shed my coat as I heated up with the manual labour. John whistled as he worked, no need for talking, for which I was grateful. I put all my anger and frustration and confusion into the shovel.

'Here,' he said, finally. He was leaning against his shovel and passed me a thermos. I stopped, standing up with a groan as stiffness had started to set in. I took a sip of the coffee and sucked in some deep breaths. I hadn't done worked outside for so long, I had forgotten what hard work it could be.

'Want to talk about it?'

I looked at him. 'Where to start? I knew it wasn't going to be easy coming back, but everything seems to be going wrong. My parents are barely speaking to me, Gran keeps talking about regrets and mistakes, the village is about to be bulldozed and Drew is back for Christmas.'

'Sounds to me like you need to think about what you can do about all of that. It's no good listing all your problems if you don't also think about what the solutions might be.' He picked up his shovel again. 'You're older now, Beth. You're all grown up. It's time to start acting like it.' He started whistling again and carried on moving the snow as if he hadn't just hit me with a verbal attack. I watched him for a moment, mouth open, ready to argue back but, how could I? I wasn't the sixteen-year-old girl who left here ten years ago. I was grown up. I was a mother. I'd made a life for me and my child. If I had a problem with how things were at Glendale Hall then I had to try and fix them. Why did it always sound so obvious when someone else told you what you needed to do?

I sighed and picked up my shovel, hoping there would be answers somewhere within the snow. I knew in my heart the answer to all of it was to start talking. I needed to talk to my parents and to Gran. And there was a part of me that felt frustrated about my brief interaction with Drew at the pub. I had a lot of anger that I really wanted to let out. I wanted to tell him exactly what I thought of him ignoring Izzy for all her life, but that would mean opening up all of my old wounds. Did I really want to face that?

I felt like crawling under the pile of snow I had made and letting it cover me, but Izzy would be home later, and I had to step up for her. She was enjoying building a relationship with her family; I owed it to her to try to heal some of what was broken between us, didn't I?

And I knew, deep down, even though I had tried to deny it for years, that she wished she knew Drew. He was right here in Glendale. Should I let him walk out of her life without trying to get him to see her?

Chapter Twelve

We had a family tea that night. My parents were already drinking at the table when Izzy and I joined them. I eyed their full drinks. I was starting to notice just how much they drank. Apart from my night out with Heather, which I was still hurting from, I didn't drink halfway as much as my parents seemed to now. I sometimes had a glass of white wine when Izzy went to bed but that was it. My mum had a massive G & T on the go, and my father a large whisky. Wine was poured out on the table as well. I had never thought of them as big drinkers in the past. It added up to another thing that no one seemed to be acknowledging in that house.

They were sat in silence when we walked in, and both turned to us, the relief obvious on their faces that they were no longer alone. Had they run out of things to say to one another? Was that just what happened when you'd been married for almost thirty years?

'It's the weekend tomorrow so why don't we all do something together? Sally said there's a Christmas fair we could go to,' I suggested, brightly.

'Your father is going to the driving range. Again,' Mum replied, taking a gulp of her drink.

'Surely, you can miss it this once, as we're here,' I pressed him, determined to draw a family outing out of them. They exchanged a long look. What was going on? 'Dad?'

He sighed. 'Yes, okay fine. We can go in the morning and I can go to my club in the afternoon, if that's what you want.'

'What will they have at this fair?' Izzy asked me as Sally brought in the food.

'Lots of stalls selling Christmas decorations and presents, and I heard a rumour that Santa might make an appearance.'

She rolled her eyes. 'Mum, you know Santa isn't real.'

I sighed. I still tried to make her believe but everyone at school had long given up on the idea. As we tucked into the cottage pie, I took the opportunity to talk to my dad. 'So, Dad, do you remember my old friend Heather? She works at the library in the village now, and she's really upset as they're going to close it down.'

'Why would anyone want to close a library?' Izzy looked up from her plate, glaring at her grandfather.

'They're not used all that much now,' Dad replied. 'Especially our one. People just buy books online. Plus, most of the shops are shut so there's not much reason to go into Glendale anymore at all. The village is dead. It's better for everyone if it's redeveloped.'

'But what about the people who do use it? Who can't get to Glenmarshes or Inverness? Especially in winter. Or who can't afford to? And the owners of the shops in the high street, they will be out of a job.'

'They're being paid very well,' he replied, unmoved. 'They can set up again elsewhere if they want to. The best thing for the village is if the council sell off the high street.'

'But what about community?' I turned from him to my mum. 'You two were always all about the community when I was younger. Won't it change the way of life here? How long before they offer us money to turn this house into a block of flats?'

Mum looked outraged. 'Well, of course that won't happen, I mean we—'

'Caroline,' my father said in a warning voice. Then he turned to me, patience gone. 'Beth, this really isn't anything to do with you. You've been gone for ten years and once Christmas is over, you'll be back in London. I'm going to my study.' He picked up his whisky and swept out of the room.

'Mum, what the hell is going on around here?'

She pressed a hand to her temple. 'I have a splitting headache now. I'm going to bed. I can't take any more arguments, please, Beth. Good night, darling,' she added to Izzy, picking up her own drink and leaving the room as well.

'Does that mean we get their share of the chocolate cake I made earlier?' Izzy said into the silence.

Despite everything, I chuckled, and she grinned, happy she had cheered me up. I leaned over to kiss her head, grateful we had each other.

–

As nine a.m. approached, I went searching for my parents. I wasn't hopeful that after last night's disastrous dinner they were still planning to come with me and Izzy to the Christmas fair, but I wanted to give them a chance to do so – for her. When I reached the drawing room door, I heard tense voices within. I paused, unsure whether or not to go in, then curiosity got the better of me and I leaned closer to the door.

'I'm not stupid. I know you're not going to be playing golf,' my mum snapped.

Dad sighed loudly. 'You know I play golf every other Saturday. I can't just change my plans on a whim.'

'You mean you don't want to.'

80

'After yesterday, not so much no. This is a stressful time for you…'

'Oh, it's always my fault! I'm tired, David. Tired of it all. And Beth is not stupid, she can see…' Mum's voice grew quieter, so I missed the last few words.

'She'll forget about it all as soon as she's gone,' Dad said after a moment. 'You know she will.'

'I'm sick of all the lies in this house!'

I turned away, frustrated. So, they *were* lying to me. And maybe to one another, too. I supposed some things never changed. As I walked away as fast as I could, I saw Sally standing there. 'Are they always like that?' I asked her as she followed me to the hall.

'Lately, more and more,' she admitted.

I stopped before we reached Izzy. 'Drew's back,' I told her. It was the first moment we'd had alone since I'd seen him. 'I ran into him at the pub.'

'What did he say?' Sally asked, her eyebrows raised.

'Hardly anything. He didn't even mention Izzy,' I replied, in a low voice, in case she overheard.

'I don't understand it. I honestly thought Drew was one of the good ones.'

'Me too. I better go. Izzy deserves a fun day out.'

'And so do you,' she told me, firmly. She waved me on. I smiled at her and carried on into the hallway where Izzy was waiting for me. I was so happy we were both going out for the day. I hoped I could forget about everything and just have fun with her, but I wasn't sure it would be that easy.

As I watched Izzy looking at the Christmas tree, a happy smile on her face, I suddenly felt ashamed. My parents were lying. But was I any better than they were? I hadn't told Izzy that Drew was in Glendale. I was trying to protect her, I knew that, but it was still another secret under this roof.

'So, just you and me then, love,' I said to Izzy, forcing on an upbeat smile for her. We headed outside together. The snow had all melted, but the air was still bitingly cold and whipped around us as we hurried into the car.

–

The Christmas fair was in the neighbouring town of Glenmarshes in their church hall. Izzy turned up the radio so we could sing along as we drove there down winding lanes, the sky thick with grey clouds above us, looking out at the sloping hills marking our way. It was certainly a scenic route compared to the city driving we had done together in the past. I liked seeing the smile on her face as she took it all in.

My phone rung then and I answered it on speakerphone, hoping it was one of my parents calling to apologise, but it was Heather.

'What are you doing today? I'm at home feeling really sorry for myself,' she said when I answered.

'We're on our way to the Glenmarshes Christmas fair; why don't you meet us there for lunch?' Heather said she'd love to come so we arranged to meet there at twelve. I felt really bad that her job was about to go. I knew that Dad was right in a way – I wasn't going to be here for much longer – but I couldn't help the feeling deep in the pit of my stomach that what was happening to Glendale village just wasn't right. I also just couldn't understand why my parents weren't as outraged as I was. I was still sure there was something I was missing. And after hearing them argue, I was even more convinced of the fact.

But what was it?

When we reached the church, there were plenty of people heading inside. We followed the signs and parked on the field behind, which was already filling up with cars. Climbing out, we headed into the large hall to the side of the church, which was lined with stalls selling all kinds of arts and crafts. There was also a food area with the smell of chestnuts and mulled wine inciting you in and draped around it all were twinkling lights.

I was determined to get my Christmas spirit back. For Izzy, and for myself. 'I think we should spend some money that we don't have,' I told her as we walked towards the stalls, holding up my hand. She laughed and high-fived me. Izzy's eyes lit up everywhere we went, and I found some of my earlier stress starting to melt away as we examined all that was on offer. Izzy fell in love with a Christmas bear on one stall, so I bought it for her, and she clutched it to her chest for the rest of the day. I got myself a delicious-smelling candle to light later, and we bought a bagful of chocolate and fudge from another stall after we took too many samples than was probably polite.

I knew I needed to get the family something for Christmas, even if right now I didn't really want to, and when we spotted a homemade smellies stall, I picked up some bubble bath and hand cream for Gran, Mum and Sally. Then we found gloves for Dad and John before it was time to meet Heather. We walked towards the food area and spotted her there, waving madly at us. She gave us both a big hug and we got hot drinks and sandwiches and found a free table to sit down at. Izzy showed her what we had found so far.

'That all looks brilliant. I hope I can get something for my dad: I'm so behind on my shopping this year,' Heather said. She sniffed my candle. 'Oh wow, I need one of these! This was such a good idea, thanks for inviting me. I really wasn't looking forward to a day wallowing.'

'Have you heard anything more?'

'My manager said that they will be giving us our notice soon and we should see if there is anything available at another library, but the nearest one is in Inverness now.' She poked at her sandwich miserably. 'It looks like it's all over.'

I shook my head, it all seemed like such a waste to me. 'And you don't think anyone could come up with something? To make the council have a rethink?'

'They seem to think Glendale high street is finished.'

'But there used to be such a wonderful community in Glendale! There must be something that would bring everyone together and show the council that we need the high street? That the village is worth saving?'

'Like what though?' Heather asked.

'Something Christmassy. Everyone likes that,' Izzy suggested.

I looked at her and beamed. 'That's a great idea, Iz. If we could show them that the village wants to fight to save itself then they'd have to change their plans, surely?'

Heather seemed to perk up a bit. 'I guess they would. But how do we get everyone together? What could we do?'

I sighed, willing a great idea to come to me. 'If only my parents weren't so disinterested, I'm sure they could rally people. They know everyone.'

'I'm not sure if I should tell you this...' she trailed off, anxiously.

'What is it?'

'I was googling the development company who is trying to buy up the shops and...' Heather looked awkward suddenly. She glanced at Izzy who was playing with her teddy. Heather leaned closer to me. 'Your father's name was on the list of directors.'

Chapter Thirteen

I stared at Heather as her words sank in. 'Are you serious?' Suddenly, it all clicked into place. Why my parents didn't seem to care about the village being sold off – they stood to benefit from it for God's sake! I dropped my sandwich. 'This is why they've been so weird with me. I knew they were keeping something from me. They really didn't want me to care about what was happening. It's because it's all down to them!'

'I'm sorry, Beth,' Heather said quickly. 'I didn't mean to upset you.'

'No, I'm glad you told me,' I said. 'This explains so much. I'll talk to my dad and find out why he's doing this. They've always loved Glendale – why now are they trying to ruin it?'

Heather shrugged. 'I guess it's all down to money. The village hasn't been doing well for a long time.'

'Then we should be trying to fix it, not destroy it. Ugh.' I couldn't finish my lunch. I pushed my tray away and stood up. 'Will you guys be okay while I pop to the loo?' They both nodded so I weaved my way to the toilets, my head spinning. Well, now I knew what my parents were lying about. Why couldn't my family ever be honest with one another? I tried to ignore the little voice in my head telling me I had grown up to be just like them.

After I went to the loo, I came out and almost collided with a man. I stepped back as he let out a little gasp. I looked up and my heart did a little skip. 'Drew,' I said.

Drew looked as shocked to see me there as he had in the pub. 'Beth! What are you doing here?'

'Christmas shopping,' I said lamely. My eyes moved to where Heather and Izzy were but they had their backs to us, thankfully, and couldn't see us. I wanted to flee but I stood my ground. I wasn't going to let him off by running away as I had the other night.

'Oh, right. Yeah, me too,' he replied, running a hand through his hair, which I knew from the past he did when he was nervous. 'Well, it was, uh, good to see you again,' he said quickly, turning to go.

'You're *really* not going to ask about her?' I blurted out. I couldn't stop the anger, and hurt this time. I had to know why he wouldn't even acknowledge our daughter, sat just behind us.

'Ask about who?' he asked, stopping with a sigh. 'Look, Beth, we don't know anything about each other's lives any more and just because we're both back in Glendale doesn't change that fact.'

'And whose fault is it that we don't know about each other's lives?!' I cried, causing a few people to look at us curiously.

Drew's face hardened. 'Certainly not mine.' He stalked off then, his long legs striding briskly as he walked through the shoppers. I looked after him, stunned, but I wasn't going to let him get away with that.

Tearing after him, I caught up and grabbed his arm, forcing him to stop and look at me. 'How can you say that to me? After you ignored my letter?'

'What are you talking about?' he cried, shaking my hand off. 'What letter? I haven't heard from you in ten years!'

I opened my mouth to continue my rant but then his words registered. I stared at him. He was looking serious and a little hurt too. 'But...'

Drew sighed. 'I get it, okay? We were young, and you obviously didn't feel the same way about me as I felt about you. It hurt when you didn't come to the airport to say goodbye. Really hurt. But I had to accept it, and I went off and I lived my life. Like you have lived yours. Shouldn't we just leave it at that?' He looked away then, but not before I saw the pain in his eyes.

'Drew,' I said, more softly. I touched his arm. 'I'm so sorry that I didn't come to the airport. But I wrote to you. A letter. It was a year later... To explain. To tell you why.'

His eyes met mine and he frowned. 'What letter?'

'I sent it to you at university. I tried to explain everything. I thought that when you didn't reply... I thought you didn't want anything more to do with me. With us.'

He shook his head, confused. 'Us? What do you mean?'

'I...' I opened my mouth and then shut it. 'You mean you really didn't read my letter?'

'I didn't get any letter, Beth. I promise.'

My hand dropped from his arm. We looked at one another as people walked around us, Christmas music playing in the background, but all I could see were Drew's blue eyes staring back at me. If he didn't get that letter then he knew nothing about Izzy. Izzy! My hand went to my mouth. I couldn't let her see him. Not when he seemed to know nothing about her. I had to try to explain. To them both. But how?

Everything around us came back into focus then. I couldn't do this here. 'Drew, I need to tell you what was in that letter. But not here, not now. Can I come and see you at the farm? Please?'

He hesitated. 'Do you really think…?'

'It's important,' I interrupted him. 'I wouldn't ask if it wasn't.'

After a moment, he nodded. 'Okay.'

'I have to go,' I said, and I turned before he could say anything else, fading into the crowd to get back to Heather and Izzy, my pulse racing along with my thoughts. I didn't look back at him this time. I couldn't bear to.

'Are you okay?' Heather asked me when I went back to them, and I wondered what my face looked like. I tried to adjust my face into a less shell-shocked expression so Izzy wouldn't know that something was up.

'Drew's here.' I managed to mouth to Heather when Izzy wasn't looking.

Her mouth hung open. 'Text me later,' she mouthed back with a nod at Izzy.

'I'm tired,' Izzy announced then, and I almost cheered.

'Why don't you two head off? I'm going to go back to the candle stand,' Heather said, quickly, jumping up. I hastily gathered up our things and we moved to the edge of the food area. Heather gave me a hug. 'Everything will be okay,' she said into my ear.

I wished I could believe her. She hugged Izzy and we headed out to the car park. I had two bags of gifts and Izzy had her teddy, so it had been a successful fair for Christmas presents at least. As we headed to the car, I kept an eye out for Drew but I couldn't see him anywhere.

I hadn't thought coming home for Christmas would be quite *this* stressful.

Not only did I have to face Drew and our past, but also Heather had told me that my parents were part of the reason the village was falling apart. And then there was the actual reason we were up here – to say goodbye to my grandmother. I suddenly felt forty not twenty-six.

We climbed into the car and Izzy requested Christmas songs as we drove home. I was pleased to turn up the music and let her focus on that so I could think in peace.

As we drove along country roads, I couldn't stop thinking about Drew. Was it fate that we were both in Glendale at the same time in ten years? I hated that, for all that time, it appeared that he had thought badly of me. That he thought I hadn't turned up to say goodbye at the airport, and cut off all contact, because I didn't love him, when the truth was exactly the opposite.

And I had spent that time both angry and hurt that Drew hadn't wanted anything to do with our daughter, or me. What a mess. How was I even going to begin to explain it all to him?

It was hard not to wonder then if I had done the right thing all those years ago. I glanced over at Izzy. She had fallen asleep cuddling her Christmas bear. I smiled. I was happy that she had had a lovely festive day at least. There was never a day when I regretted having her, but I certainly had had many moments of being unsure whether I had done the right thing in leaving Glendale and raising her by myself.

Seeing Drew again brought back all those sleepless nights in London, longing to reach out to him. When I finally did and he had ignored me, I banished any fantasy of him and Izzy ever knowing one another.

But if he really hadn't received my letter then there was a chance now that they could finally meet. I had no idea what Drew was going to say when I told him about her. I knew Izzy would be shocked but happy to know he was in Glendale, too – she had always wanted to meet her father. Would he feel the same though?

I made a choice when I was sixteen. One that I still wasn't sure had been the right or wrong one to make but all I could do now was finally face up to it.

Part of me wanted to just turn around and run back to London and not have to face Drew and our past, but I knew that wasn't an option this time around. I was an adult now and I had my daughter to think about. I knew that for her sake I had to tell Drew the truth finally.

I had to try to make it right, somehow.

Chapter Fourteen

When we arrived back at the Hall, my mum met us at the door, looking anxious. 'I'm glad you're home, your grandmother wants to talk to us both. She's getting quite distressed.'

'Okay,' I said, already exhausted from all the revelations of the day and not particularly excited to have to deal with any more. 'Iz, why don't you go into the living room and pick out something for us to watch? I'll come down in a bit and join you.' Izzy hurried off and I slipped off my coat, following Mum slowly up the stairs. I just wanted to curl up with Izzy, but my mother looked so worried, I had no choice but to go up with her.

'She's here,' Mum said as we walked into the bedroom. Gran was sitting up in bed, sagging in relief when she saw us.

'I can't put it off any longer,' Gran said, her voice sounding even weaker. I couldn't help but wonder if she had much time left with us. 'I have to tell you what I did. It's all I've been thinking about.'

'Calm down, Mum,' my mother tried to soothe her, sitting down in the chair by the bed and reaching for her hand. 'It's okay.'

I went and sat down on the other side of her, having no idea what she was so distressed about.

'It's not okay though. I have to tell you about what happened ten years ago. And the lies I told.'

I looked at Mum and then back at Gran. 'What do you mean? What lies?'

'You have to know that I didn't mean for it to tear the family apart. If you only knew the distress it has caused me over the years. I have often wished I could have taken it back. I know now how wrong I was. Thinking that it was for the best, keeping it from you both but I'm running out of time. I have to get this off my chest. I can't bear to keep it to myself any longer. I should have told you both long ago…' she trailed off, upset.

I had no idea where this was going. Gran, the great Margaret MacKenzie, didn't do apologies or forgiveness, she didn't explain anything to anyone – what she said went – and there she was looking stricken, about to confess something. I leaned forward in my chair, feeling uncomfortable and nervous but also burning with curiosity it must be said. 'It's okay,' I reassured her. 'You can tell us.'

'I'm the real reason Beth left ten years ago. I lied to you both. And I'm so sorry.'

'What do you mean you were the real reason she left?' Mum asked, frowning. She looked stumped.

I glanced at her. Surely, she knew what Gran said to me before I ran away? To *make* me run away?

Didn't she?

'I told Beth that we all felt the same about her being pregnant – that she shouldn't have the baby,' Gran said to my mum. 'I said that I, you and David were all disappointed in her. I told her I had booked a doctor's appointment for her the following day, that she needed to get rid of the baby. That's why she ran away,' Gran said, her voice gaining strength as she finally unburdened herself after all these years.

'What do you mean?' Mum asked. 'You told her we didn't want her to have the baby? But we didn't even know she was pregnant.'

A shiver ran down my spine as I turned to look at my mum in shock. 'You didn't know? But…'

'I lied,' Gran admitted. Her voice was croaky but determined as she finally explained her role in the past to us. 'I was shocked: I was thinking about the family name. I knew it would be a huge scandal. I also didn't want her to throw her life away.' She turned to me. 'That's what I thought you'd be doing if you had that baby, Beth. So, I tried to convince you not to have it. I told you that your parents thought the same as I did: that you'd ruin all our lives if you had the baby. And when Beth left, I didn't tell you what I had done, Caroline, I let you think she had just decided to leave us. That she wasn't able to tell any of us she was pregnant.' She dropped her head to her chest. 'I am so, so, sorry. I was wrong. I know that now. But at the time, I thought I was doing the right thing.'

'The right thing for who?' I cried. I jumped up, unable to stay sitting there a moment longer. I turned away from the bed and walked to the window. I couldn't believe she had lied like that. Made me think I had no choice. Forcing me to run away and raise my baby all by myself because I thought my family wouldn't support me. 'How could you do that?' I whispered, turning back to look at her, tears welling up in my eyes.

'I thought you didn't want to tell me you were pregnant,' Mum said then, walking over to me. 'That you hated me that much, you wanted to get as far away as possible so I couldn't be involved. I was heartbroken when you left, Beth. If I had known what she said…' She looked at her own mother then. 'You took my daughter and my granddaughter away from me.'

A tear rolled down my cheek. 'I thought I was all alone,' I said.

'I was wrong,' Gran said, feebly, closing her eyes for a moment. 'Have you ever done something that you thought was for the best only to realise years later that it wasn't?' She opened her eyes again and met my gaze.

I felt sick. She had made me think the right thing for me to do was to leave my home and my family, and that I had to run away to raise my daughter alone. She'd made me feel like I shouldn't tell Drew, that I should let him go off to fulfil his dreams never knowing that he had a daughter. I thought I had made the only choice that I could. 'Drew doesn't know he has a daughter because of you,' I managed to say. 'I am a single mother because of you.'

'You tore this family apart,' my mum added, and then she walked out of the room. I didn't blame her.

Gran started to move as if she wanted to try to get out of bed, but I shook my head. 'You need to let us process this,' I told her, firmly. Then I followed my mother out, leaving my grandmother alone in her room with the knowledge that she had at last told the truth.

Ten years too late.

Mum and I went downstairs to the drawing room where she went straight to the drinks cabinet and poured herself a brandy and passed me one without asking. I sat down shakily on the sofa and clutched it. Mum drained hers in one gulp, poured another and sat down in the armchair.

In the silence, I could hear the grandfather clock ticking out in the hall.

I sipped my brandy and winced at the strength of it. 'I really thought that I had to go,' I said, finally breaking the quiet.

'I thought that you didn't want me near your child,' Mum replied. She sighed. 'I should have realised by your letter you thought that we all knew you were pregnant. By what you said. I wouldn't have been pleased if you had told me you were pregnant, of course. You were sixteen and I wanted so much for you. But I would have supported your decision, Beth, I promise you. I know that I don't say it enough… maybe ever, but you are a wonderful mother, and Isabelle is a credit to you.'

A sob escaped my throat. It was all I had wanted without realising it. My mother's approval. Maybe it was what all of us wanted really. 'I don't know what to do,' I said then. 'I thought I was doing the right thing in not telling Drew about Izzy, but a year after she was born, I just couldn't do it any longer. I wrote to him in America. I told him that we'd had a baby. I sent him a photo of her. And I never heard anything from him.'

'He didn't respond?' Mum asked, shocked.

'He's back in Glendale, Mum. I've seen him, talked to him. He told me that he never got my letter. And I think I believe him. I have to go and tell him about Izzy, don't I? But how do I even find the words?' It was possibly the first time in my adult life that I was asking my mum for advice, I realised.

Mum thought for a moment. 'You tried to make the right choice at the time… for all of you. You were sixteen and you thought you were alone in the world. I'm so sorry you had to deal with that, Beth. That you had to cope with making that decision. You were just a child yourself. Things are very different now. So yes, I think that you do need to tell him.'

'Will he understand?'

'You can make him understand.'

I smiled faintly. 'I hope that he wants to meet her. Izzy would love it, I know that. It's all so complicated though.'

'I know. But I think it will work out. Follow that heart of yours, Beth. Unlike my heart, yours seems to guide you right.'

I was unused to praise from my mother: somehow her saying it made it feel true. I hoped she was right. I looked at her then, the wall between us felt as if it was slowly, finally, starting to crumble. I had to ask the question that had been burning inside me since I had come home. 'Mum, what's going on with you and Dad? You're not happy, I can see that.'

She sighed. 'You know what your father is like, working all hours. It's been hard here alone looking after my mother. We don't seem to be able to talk like we used to.' She looked down at her glass then, seemingly hesitant. 'And, there's something else. But, I feel so ashamed even saying the words aloud.'

I leaned forward. 'You can tell me,' I reassured her. I wanted us to be able to be honest with one another now. About everything. It was about time after all.

'A few weeks ago, I went to his study to try to talk to him. And I heard him on the phone. To… *her*.' She almost spat out the word and quickly drank more of her brandy afterwards.

'He's having an affair?' I wasn't surprised exactly. My dad had always been absent from life at Glendale Hall when I was growing up; it wasn't a massive stretch of the imagination to think there had been other women but, on the other hand, appearances were everything to my family so I wondered why he would be willing to jeopardize that.

'I saw them together. He was telling me that he was playing golf so often, but after that phone call, I knew he was lying. So, I went to the golf club and there they were – having lunch together. Cathy, that's her name. I've even met her. She came to a dinner party here once. She owns the development company who want to buy up the village. Your father is on the board of directors.'

'Are you serious? Why haven't you kicked his sorry arse out of here?' I asked her, outraged that not only had he been cheating but the whole village was suffering because my dad couldn't keep it in his pants.

Mum looked at me and then, to my shock, burst out laughing. 'None of this is funny but... sorry arse,' she choked out between giggles. And despite all we had learned in the past half an hour there seemed nothing for it but to laugh right along with her. Then she came over to the sofa and for the first time in ten years, reached out and gave me a hug. 'I'm glad you're here, Beth,' she said before pulling back quickly. She had never been much for affection. We could work on that though.

I nodded. 'Me too. We're going to fix everything. Together. Deal?' I looked at her fiercely. I really wanted us to rebuild our relationship. It seemed she needed me as much as I needed her. We had to sort out everything that had been going wrong in this family for all this time. And we needed to do it together.

I could have been wrong, but I was sure I saw a flash of pride in my mother's eyes. 'Deal,' she agreed.

Chapter Fifteen

I got up early the next day, having not slept much the night before, my mind whirring with everything that was happening. It felt as if there was so much to try to sort out, but I knew that I needed to see Drew as my first priority, before I chickened out, but also before he and Izzy bumped into one another. I had forgotten what a small world Glendale was: the Christmas fair had been a close call. I hated not telling Izzy the truth but I couldn't yet. I knew she'd be devastated if I told her that her father was in Scotland too but he didn't want to meet her – I had to protect her, and be sure that he wanted to meet her first.

Sally was making coffee when I walked into the kitchen. It was still dark outside and I could barely make out the garden through the French doors.

'Have I ever seen you at this time before?' Sally asked when she saw me.

'Ha ha ha, I have no sense of humour before coffee,' I replied, grabbing a cup. She poured me a strong black coffee, and one for herself. 'I was too nervous to sleep. I'm going to go and see Drew today,' I explained after I had taken a huge gulp.

'All those years you thought he wasn't interested in knowing Izzy…'

'I don't understand how he never got my letter,' I said, sitting down at the table with her. She brought over a rack of toast, but I couldn't face eating. 'But his surprise seemed genuine. I had convinced myself that he just couldn't forgive me for not telling him about Izzy and was too happy with his new life in America. Now I know he didn't get the letter – how do I tell him he's missed out on the first ten years of her life?'

'Just be honest. Explain why you made the choice that you did and that you tried to tell him the truth.'

I nodded. 'I hope that he will want to meet Izzy, but if he doesn't, well, we have each other, don't we?'

Sally smiled. 'Exactly. It'll all be okay, Beth, I know it. You're here now, where you should be.'

'Even though everything seems to be turning into a bigger mess by the day?' I took another gulp of the coffee. It was waking me up slowly.

'Sometimes things have to get messy so you can discover the best way to put them right.'

'I just hope that I'll be able to.'

–

Drew's family farm was a short drive from Glendale Hall down twisting country lanes. I found that I could remember the way as if it was burned into my memory. I used to beg John to drive me out there most weekends, and almost every day over the one summer we spent together, bribing him with promises to do the garden jobs he didn't want to.

The sun began to slowly rise as I drove out there, my stomach fluttering with nerves. It had been so long since I had set foot on the farm. Rory, who was four years older than Drew, still ran the farm after taking it over when their parents died. He'd worked there since leaving school having always loved farm work, and knowing that Drew wanted to do something else.

I turned into the gravel driveway and drove up to the farm-house. It was a pretty stone house situated within acres of land. I had loved coming to the farm, pulling Drew away from his books to drive the tractor through the fields with me. Or sharing a picnic together on the grass, the sun beating down on us. Helping Rory with some of the chores. And rolling around in the hay together, kissing until our lips got sore. I remember watching the sunset lying on the bonnet of Rory's battered old car, the radio playing from inside, holding hands and talking about the future – certain as only teenagers could be that we would be spending it together.

Parking my car, I stared at the house, wondering for a moment what had happened to those two kids who had been so happy and carefree – and in love.

But, of course, I knew exactly what had happened to them.

I couldn't help but think back to *that* night. Drew and I had spent the summer together. Practically every day we'd been together. I was so in love with him and so ready to take the next step. Drew, wanting to be a doctor, had taken precautions seriously, and after discussing it, I had gone on the pill to be ready. I had paid less attention to taking it, though, and those few missed tablets had changed everything.

Shaking off my memories before I became lost in them, I climbed out of the car. The sky above was turning blue and the sun peeked out from behind the farmhouse as I walked up to the door and knocked.

'Beth,' Rory said, his eyes widening, as he opened up the door.

'Oh, hi. Is, uh, Drew in?' I asked, wondering if Drew had given him a heads-up that I might be coming to see him. They had always been close, so I suspected they had discussed it.

'He's in the kitchen. Go on through. I need to head out and feed the chickens,' he replied, slipping past me. He paused and looked back. 'Look, it's none of my… you guys are all grown up.' He groaned in frustration. 'I'm just trying to say that you broke his heart back then, so promise me that you won't do it again, okay?'

'If it's any consolation, I broke my own heart as well,' I replied.

He looked at me for a long moment, nodded and then walked off again, hands thrust in his pockets. I watched him go, knowing that Rory wouldn't have said that if he didn't mean it. Drew really had loved me as much as I had loved him then. I wished I could go back and change it all but that was impossible. All I could do was try to make things right now.

Cautiously, I let myself into the house and walked towards the kitchen. The smell of frying bacon hit me instantly. Drew stood by the cooker, poking at the pan, his shirt sleeves rolled up, wearing dark jeans, his hair still wet from the shower. I watched him for a moment before I realised he hadn't noticed I was there. 'That smells good.'

Drew started at my voice, turning from the cooker as I hovered in the doorway. 'You came,' he said, simply.

I nodded. 'I had to. Is it okay if I come in?'

'Oh, of course!' He gestured to the round pine table. 'Sit down? Tea? Coffee? Juice? I was just making breakfast. I mean, would you like some?'

'Just coffee, thank you,' I replied, relieved that he seemed nervous too. I took off my coat and sat down, pouring out another coffee as Drew came over with a plate of scrambled eggs and bacon and a large mug of tea. I raised an eyebrow. 'You didn't use to be able to cook,' I couldn't help notice.

'No, I had to learn at university,' he replied. 'I burnt a lot back then,' he added with a grin remembering. 'But, actually, I really enjoy it now.' Drew took a sip of tea, his gaze fixed on me. Finally, he sighed. 'It's so strange seeing you here, in this kitchen, again. I often thought when I came home that I might run into you, but you never seemed to come back to Glendale.'

'This is the first time I've been home in ten years,' I confirmed. I wondered whether he had hoped to see me all those other times, but I didn't dare ask.

'Such a long time.' Drew put down his knife and fork, his appetite seemingly gone like my own. He leaned forward, putting his elbows on the table. 'I heard of you through the years... I mean, there was a lot of talk about why you left. Rory said he'd heard there was another boy.' Drew looked at me with a raised eyebrow.

I shook my head, my throat feeling very parched. 'That wasn't the reason why I left,' I replied, carefully. 'I heard about you over the years too. That you still live in Boston?' I asked, trying to take the heat off of me for a moment so I could decide how I was even going to begin to tell him everything.

'I loved it as soon as I started university there. After medical school, I was offered a residency in a local hospital so I moved into the city once I graduated.'

I nodded. 'You really did it. Became a doctor. Like you always wanted.'

He smiled a little. 'Yeah, I did. What about you though? I know that you live in London. And everyone said you had a daughter a while back,' he said, steering the conversation back to me. 'Why did you come here, Beth?'

I took a deep breath. 'It's about the letter I sent you—'

'The one I didn't get,' he interjected, still studying me closely. His gaze made me even more nervous. He had always been able to read me too easily, to tell what I was thinking and feeling. And I had been the same with him, but I had no idea if we still had that connection. So much time, so much life, had passed.

I nodded. 'The one you didn't get.'

'So, what did it say?' he asked, impatiently.

As I watched his forehead crease with frustration, I was struck by how similar Izzy looked when she made such a face at me. And the thought of her gave me the strength to finally make my confession.

Chapter Sixteen

Clearing my throat, I looked down at the coffee cup I held tightly in my hands and began. 'Well, as I said at the fair, I wrote to you about a year after you'd left for America. There was a reason that I didn't come to the airport to say goodbye, a reason why I felt I had to cut off all contact with you, why I left Glendale, and ran away to London. I thought I was doing the right thing at the time.' I sucked in a deep breath. I knew I was speaking too fast, but I just had to get the words out.

'I made the hardest decision of my life. But one night, I just broke down, and I… missed you, and I wanted to tell you everything, and so I wrote to you. And when I didn't hear back, I thought… Well, I thought that you didn't want anything to do with us.'

There was a beat of silence. 'Us?' He promoted me.

I forced myself to lift my eyes then. I started to reach across the table to touch him but then I stopped, too scared to, and pulled my hand back. 'You really didn't get my letter?'

Drew shook his head slowly. 'I promise you I didn't. I never understood why you didn't at least tell me that you didn't want us to stay together. I waited at the airport for you until I was the last passenger to board the plane. Rory was the one who pushed me onto it. I almost ran to find you. But I had to accept that you didn't love me.' His voice broke a little on the word 'love'.

'Oh, Drew,' I said, fighting back the tears. 'It was never about that. If anything, it was because I loved you *too* much. I didn't want to stop you from making all your dreams come true.' The tears rolled down my cheek then, and I tried to hold it together to get the words out. 'I knew how much being a doctor meant to you and to your family, to Rory. How… how could I stop you from doing that?'

Drew got up and came around to my side of the table. He kneeled down beside me and reached for my hands. 'Beth, just tell me, please.'

My heart broke at how gently he spoke to me. He was being kind, as he always had been. But how would he react when I told him? I turned and gripped his hands with mine. 'The reason I ran away when I was sixteen was because I was pregnant. Drew, we had a baby.'

There was a long silence as we looked at one another. Slowly, Drew let go of my hands and backed up on his knees to put space between us. My skin felt the loss of the warmth of his instantly.

'What are you talking about?' he whispered. His face had gone pale.

'I'm so sorry, Drew. I don't know how to explain. My gran, she found out that I was pregnant, and she was furious. She wanted me to have an abortion. She kept telling me how I would destroy both our futures,' I told him, my voice breaking at the end. 'I didn't know what to do. I loved you, and the minute I knew I was carrying our baby, I loved her too. I couldn't give her up, but I didn't want to stop you going to America. That's why I left. I ran because I didn't feel like I had any other choice.' A sob rose up in my throat at the end.

Drew stood up, shaking his head. He walked over to the window and leaned against the sink for a moment, looking out to the farm. Then he turned, slowly, back to me. 'You're saying that your daughter – she's mine?' he said, finally.

I nodded. 'Isabelle – Izzy. I wrote to you on her first birthday. I missed you so much. And I wanted you to know the truth. I was scared I'd made a huge mistake. And I felt so… so guilty. I didn't know what else to do, so I wrote to you. Hoping. Begging. For you to try to forgive me. But when I didn't hear back… I thought you couldn't. That you didn't want to know… her.'

He stared at me in stunned silence. 'How could you think that of me?' he asked then.

I didn't know how to answer that. At the time, I had thought it was only what I deserved.

'And you didn't ever try again? To contact me? To tell me about her?' he asked then, his voice becoming harder.

I looked down again, unable to bear to see the anger in his eyes. 'I thought you were happy without me, without us. I didn't want to intrude in your life.'

'Intrude! Beth, we had a daughter, and you thought it would be intruding to tell me about her!' He shook his head in disbelief.

I couldn't stop the tears rolling down my cheek. 'You don't understand. I was all alone, raising her all alone; I felt so hurt, so rejected when you didn't respond… And I love her. So, so much! I couldn't bear to have her disappointed, to have her rejected. I didn't want to raise either of our hopes. It seemed better for us if I just accepted that you didn't want to have any contact.' I looked down. 'I have always tried to protect my daughter. To do the best I could. And I thought I was letting you live the life you wanted to.'

There was a long silence. Finally, Drew let out a puff of air to break it. 'Do you have a photo of her?'

I pulled out my phone and showed him the screensaver picture of me and Izzy walking to the village in the snow earlier in the week.

Drew took the phone off me and leaned back against the counter as he stared down at it. 'She looks like you,' he said after a long silence.

'She has your hair and eyes though – and your smile.'

'She's beautiful.'

I sniffed and wiped at my eyes. I needed to get a hold of myself. 'She's such a great kid, Drew. Really special. I know I'm biased in saying that… but she is.' I smiled despite what was happening, thinking about her.

'How could you not tell me?' Drew asked, looking up with tears in his eyes. 'You should have known I would have been there for you.'

'That's why I didn't tell you when I found out about her. I didn't want you to give up your future because of me.'

'That wasn't up to you! I should have had a say in the matter.' He turned away as if he couldn't bear to look at me.

'I know that now. All these years, I have gone over and over it in my mind. But I was sixteen and terrified, I felt so scared and alone. My family turned their backs on me, or so I thought at the time, and I felt as if there was no other choice. I thought about your parents and how proud they were of you when you got that scholarship and…' I couldn't go on. I covered my face with my hands, words failing me. How could I expect him to understand? I had kept our daughter from him. How could I ever try to make that okay? I remembered fantasising after I sent him that letter that he would knock at the door and sweep us both into his arms. The reality of him finding out about Izzy was far removed from that, but it was only what I deserved. He should have been angry with me. I was angry with myself too. I had thought I was protecting him, letting him have the future he had dreamed of, but I knew now that I hadn't really considered how much he would be missing out on by keeping our baby from him.

Drew came back to the table and put my phone down. He sat down in the chair opposite me. 'This is such a mess.' I nodded, trying to swallow down the lump in my throat. 'Is she here? Our daughter?' I nodded again. 'God, I can't believe I'm saying that word. That I'm a father. All this time…'

'I don't know if you can ever forgive me. I'm not sure I deserve you to. But Izzy, she has always asked about you. She would love to meet you. I have to ask you for her sake. If you'll think about it… please. If only just once.' I begged him then. I had to hope that the two of them could have some kind of relationship.

Drew looked down at my phone again, touching the screen to light up the photo of her. I knew he could see himself in her: there was no denying the resemblance, it seemed to only grow stronger as she got older. 'I don't even know where to begin, what to say, how to navigate this. It all needs to sink in. I mean, I know that you were just sixteen, and your family were never easy… But, Beth, you should have told me. If not then, before now. Ten years! I've missed out on ten years.'

'I thought when you didn't reply to my letter it was what I deserved after not telling you the truth at the time. I thought you had a new life over there, and that you thought it was best that we had nothing more to do with one another. Perhaps I thought I should be punished. That I deserved to be… alone.' I admitted the darkest thoughts I had had during that time. I had lost the love of my life and I had no one else to blame but myself.

He was quiet again for a moment, letting my words sink in. He sighed heavily, and I wished I knew what he was thinking. 'So, you raised our daughter all by yourself? In London?'

I nodded. I wanted to reach out to him, for him to hold me again and tell me that it was all okay, but I knew he couldn't. Because it wasn't.

'I want to meet her,' he said then. 'I have to meet her.' He looked at me. 'When can I see her?'

'Tomorrow. Give me a chance to tell her that you're here. To make sure she's okay with it all.'

Drew nodded. 'Tomorrow,' he repeated. 'Isabelle?' He asked then. 'Why Isabelle?'

I wondered if he would remember. 'That song we listened to all summer. The one we danced to outside here, to the radio in your car. Do you…?'

His lips curved into a small smile. 'Of course, I do. That night…' He trailed off, not needing to say it. It had been our first time, that song playing as we made love, not knowing we were also making a baby. That night was so special in so many ways. When I had held our daughter in my arms for the first time, I knew it was the perfect name for her. And as our eyes met across his kitchen table, I knew that Drew thought so too.

A little hope sprang up in my heart then that one day he might understand the choice I made, if not be able forgive me. But until then, I was just happy that my little girl would get to meet her dad, and that Drew would finally get to know how special our daughter was.

Chapter Seventeen

After I came back to the Hall from Drew's farm, I made sure that Izzy and I had the afternoon to ourselves. I took her into the dining room and suggested we made some Christmas decorations together to hang up in our bedrooms. 'I've got paper for us to make snowflakes and some popcorn and cranberries to string. And, look, John brought in some pine cones from the garden, so we can use them too.'

'We can cover them in glitter,' Izzy said, pulling out the box of paints and crafting bits she'd brought from home. I was always trying to encourage her crafting efforts, as it was something we could do together and it took her out of her book world for a while. I had noticed, though, that she hadn't slunk off to read by herself during the day so often as we seemed to have something going on every day, and I was pleased that she was enjoying other things while we were in Scotland. 'And Granny said we could take the fairy lights we didn't use on the tree upstairs if we want.'

'Our rooms are going to look so festive after this,' I told her with a smile. I started to cut up the paper into snowflakes as Izzy covered the pine cones in glitter. I was relieved I'd put a sheet over the table as the glitter had a habit of going everywhere, and I knew my mum and Sally would kill us if we got any on the wood. 'So, how are you enjoying our holiday up here so far?' I asked her, wondering how to bring the conversation around to

Drew. I had left the farm with a plan to meet him at a cafe in town with Izzy and I wanted to prepare her as best as I could. I knew that she worried a lot about things, despite trying to hide it from me, and I wanted her to see this as a good thing and not be anxious about it. I would likely be anxious enough for both of us anyway.

'It's nice and relaxing, and I love how festive everything is here. And it's nice to be with family too.'

'That's great. I'm so happy you like it here.'

'I wish we could stay longer,' she added, biting her lip as she twisted the pine cone round to make sure it was fully covered in glitter.

That surprised me a little. 'Are you not missing London then?'

She shook her head. 'I even like having a garden,' she added, grinning at me.

'I am shocked!' I joked. 'Izzy likes something outside! We need to make a banner or something.'

'Mum,' she groaned, rolling her eyes. 'I hope it snows again.'

'I think it probably will.' I hesitated then, knowing that I needed to broach the subject of Drew – the afternoon was slipping away. I watched her for a moment, so proud of her and full of love. I knew that once I told her, our life of just the two of us would never be quite the same again. But I also knew that I would be giving her something she had always wanted. And I just wanted my daughter to be happy. 'Listen, love, I wanted to tell you something. And it might come as a bit of a shock. It was for me too,' I warned her, as gently as I could.

Izzy looked at me. 'What is it?' She already looked wary.

'It's something good, don't worry,' I added, quickly. 'It turns out that we're not the only people who have come home to Glendale for Christmas. I bumped into someone, and they are really excited to meet you. But I told them that I wanted to check with you first.' I reached over and put my hand on hers. Her eyes watched mine, cautious as they always were with change or anything new. She was more like her dad in that way than me. I gave her fingers a reassuring squeeze. 'Iz, your father is here in Glendale, and he would love to see you if you'd like that.'

'He is? Isn't he in America?' Izzy put the glitter down. 'I thought he didn't know about me?'

'He's come to stay with his brother for the holidays. But I've told him all about you, Iz. It was a huge shock for him, but he would really like to meet you. And I know that you've always wanted to meet him, so this is a good thing. Isn't it?' I asked her.

She nodded slowly. 'I can't believe he's really here. I mean, I would like to see him but...' she trailed off, biting her lip.

'But what?' I asked her.

'But what if he doesn't like me?'

'Oh, love.' I pulled her into my arms. This was what I had wanted to protect her from. That feeling I had felt when it had sunk in that Drew wasn't ever going to reply to my letter. I never wanted her to feel like that. But now that Drew knew about her, he had been swift in his desire to see her. Surely in time he would love her just as fiercely as I did? 'You are a really special little girl. How many times have I told you? You have nothing to worry about, okay?' I knew whatever happened, I would make sure my little girl wasn't hurt somehow. Out of all the mistakes I had made, she would never be one, and she deserved only happiness.

She nodded and leaned back to look at me. 'What's he like, Mum?'

'Well, he's a lot like you. You have the same hair and smile,' I said, tugging on a strand of her auburn hair. 'And he loves books almost as much as you. He's clever and kind, too, just like you are.'

Izzy smiled. 'It's weird, isn't it, that all three of us are here at the same time?'

'Like it was meant to be,' I replied. Goosebumps pricked my arms. It did feel a little bit like fate had had a hand in all of it. 'So, how about we meet him for breakfast tomorrow in town?'

'You'll be there too, won't you?' she asked, picking her pine cone back up.

'Of course I will.'

'Okay, then,' she said with a nod, making her decision after weighing it all up, just like she always did. My heart swelled with love for her. I watched her go back to painting and my chest sagged a little in relief. She seemed to have taken it all in her usual practical way. So much like Drew in that respect. I knew she'd be nervous, but I also knew that she had longed to meet her father. She had tried to hide that from me, to protect me, but that longing had been there all her life.

And now I finally could give her something that I had been scared that I never would be able to.

I was opening our cosy little world of two to someone else and it was bloody terrifying, but I hoped that if the boy I had loved was still there inside the man Drew was now, then it would all work out okay.

–

After I said good night to Izzy that evening, I went down to the kitchen where my mum and Sally were sitting with a glass of wine each in front of them. 'I need this,' I said, pouring out a large glass as I joined them.

'How did it go today?' Mum asked.

'Honestly, I don't know what Drew thinks of me or my decision but I'm holding on to the fact that he wants to meet Izzy, and that's the most important thing. She's excited to see him, too, but nervous, I can tell. She's worried about whether he's going to like her.'

'I'm sure Drew is worrying about the exact same thing.' Mum gave me a smile. 'You've done all you can. You've told him everything, and you're letting them build a relationship. It won't be easy but once he's come to terms with it all, I think he'll understand what you went through back then. It took me a long time to accept your decision to go to London and have Izzy; I didn't know all the facts about you leaving either and it was hard, but never for a moment did I question whether having Isabelle was the right choice. You know that she was. And Drew will too.'

'He will love her, won't he?' I asked, taking a sip of the wine. I was so nervous for Izzy. I wanted their meeting to go well for both of them but especially her. She deserved all the love in the world.

'How could he not?' Sally said. 'She's such a wonderful girl. It's a shock for him but, by all accounts, Drew has his head screwed on right; he's doing a great job of being a doctor over there: his brother is always saying how proud he is of him.'

I raised an eyebrow. 'I thought you said you didn't know much about him.'

'Well, I didn't want to make you feel bad,' she admitted.

'It does change things knowing that he didn't turn his back on us, you know? All this time, I thought he rejected us when he didn't respond to my letter but now I know that he never read it.'

'I always thought it was unlike him,' Sally replied. 'But people change, so you never know what they will do.'

'That's true,' Mum said, darkly.

'Is Dad still at work?' I asked, guessing that's who was in her mind. His absence from the Hall was becoming more conspicuous by the day.

'I don't know where he is,' she replied with a sigh.

I frowned. I really didn't like how my parents seemed to be living separate lives. They had kept up a good pretence of being as they always were when they had come to London, but now I was with them every day, it was noticeable how little time they spent together. 'Shouldn't you talk to him, Mum—?'

'Don't you worry about us,' she interrupted. 'We have enough to deal with in this house right now. Your grandmother has slept most of today. I think she's getting weaker. And you have Izzy to worry about, too. You need to focus on what's important.'

I nodded but it worried me that she didn't see her marriage as a priority. Perhaps it had just kept on slipping down the list. There was a lot going on at the Hall. But that's why it was so strange that Dad was never around.

Surely everyone needed him here more than ever?

Guilt settled over me once again when I saw how much things seemed to have changed both at home and in Glendale over the past ten years. It felt like something needed to happen to make things better, but I had no idea what.

I needed to sort out my own mess before I could tackle anything else. Still, it was there in my mind that I wanted to do something that would help everyone. It felt important before I walked away from them all again.

First though, I had to make it through tomorrow.

Chapter Eighteen

I drove Izzy to the neighbouring town of Glenmarshes the next day. Sleet was floating down from a grey sky as we parked outside the cafe where we had arranged to meet Drew. Izzy had changed her outfit three times, bless her, and had settled on a black wool dress with boots. I had gone with my usual jeans, boots and long jumper and we both had our hair loose over our shoulders. I wasn't sure who was more nervous out of the two of us. Izzy was quiet on the drive, so I turned up the Christmas music and tried to take her mind off things by singing along loudly and off key, which at last raised a giggle from her and she joined in for the final one.

Pulling into a space outside the cafe, I switched off the engine and turned to her. 'Listen, Iz, everything will be okay. I promise. I love you loads, you know that, right?'

She nodded. 'I know, Mum. Let's go.'

'Okay,' I said, proud of the determined expression she had on her face. She was far braver than I had been at her age. Sometimes I hoped she wasn't trying to grow up too fast, taking too much on her young shoulders, but I knew some of that was her personality and I wouldn't have changed her for the world. I squeezed her hand and we got out and went into the cafe.

It was a cosy vintage place with white tables and floral tableclouths, the smell of freshly baked cakes filling the air. The bell rang cheerily as we walked through the door and straight away I spotted Drew at a table in the corner. He sprang out of his seat when he saw us, and I could see that he was just as nervous as we were.

'Hi,' I said, when we walked up to his table. 'Drew, this is Izzy. Izzy, this is Drew.' I watched as Drew stared at his daughter for the first time: he did a double take – there was no mistaking the fact he was her father.

Izzy actually held out her hand to him. 'Hi,' she said. I bit back a laugh, but Drew very solemnly shook it. 'You have red hair like me,' she said, looking up at it. I knew she had often wished for my colour hair, so she would be pleased to see where hers came from.

Drew ran a hand over his hair. 'We can blame my grandfather for it,' he replied, smiling at her.

We sat down and the waitress came over, so I ordered a strong coffee for myself and Izzy asked for a hot chocolate. Drew was already on his second coffee he said and I could see his knee bouncing against the table as he declined another one. The cafe was busy, and they were playing Christmas songs, so the short silence after the waitress left the table wasn't too painful, but I knew that it needed to be filled.

'So, Drew, tell us all about Boston. We've never been to America, have we, Iz?' I said, taking a sip of my coffee and giving him an encouraging smile. She shook her head and fixed her gaze on Drew.

He cleared his throat. 'Well, it's very different from Glendale, that's for sure,' he replied. 'When I first got there, I got really homesick. I still miss Scotland a lot, but I like the fact that summers get really hot there and I can go running every morning in the park by my apartment. I love baseball and try to go to as many games as I can, although my hours at the hospital make that tricky sometimes. It's always busy and bustling there, which took some getting used to.'

'Mum said you have a farm here?' Izzy asked him then.

'That's right. My older brother, Rory, runs it. I miss winter mornings getting up in the darkness to feed the animals. And just the peace of all the open space here. You're never alone in Boston.'

'I've never been to a farm,' Izzy said.

'Well, you'll have to come over and help us feed the animals. If you'd like to?'

Her eyes lit up. 'Can I, Mum?'

I smiled. 'Of course.' I was pleased they were both talking about spending more time with one another.

'What about you guys, Izzy? What's life like in London?'

She licked some whipped cream off the top of her drink. 'Well, it's a bit like Boston I think. Really busy, and there's always lots of noise and people everywhere. We live in a flat in south London, and I can't believe how much space there is up here. I really like Scotland.'

'And what about school? Your mum said you're a big reader. Do you know what you'd like to do when you're older?'

Izzy shook her head. 'I just like reading and learning new things. We go to museums quite a lot, which are my favourite places in London. Mum prefers the parks though.'

'When you let me walk in one,' I replied. 'Although you like the garden at the Hall, don't you?'

'It's pretty, especially when it's snowing,' Izzy conceded. 'We've never had a garden before.'

Drew looked at me in surprise. 'You don't have a garden in London?'

'I can't afford a place that has one,' I told him ruefully. 'So, it's been great to get back into the one here, I must admit.'

'You didn't become a gardener then?'

'I work at Izzy's school, actually. Just office admin. It pays the bills,' I replied, taking a sip of my coffee. 'And it means I get weekends and holidays off to be with her. Which is why we were able come up here for Christmas.'

'That makes sense,' Drew said. 'Although it's a shame that you didn't get to be a gardener like you wanted.'

I nodded and wondered why his words made me feel emotional all of a sudden. They started talking about the Science Museum, and as Izzy chatted, Drew watched her with a smile on his face. My heart swelled to see them finally together.

–

'Drew needs to come back to the house with us,' Izzy announced as we stepped out of the cafe an hour later. The sleet was coming down faster then, blurring our view. It was freezing and I was looking forward to the cosy warmth of the Hall.

I looked down at her. 'Izzy, Drew might have things to do—'

'It's okay,' Drew interrupted me, placing his hand on my arm for a moment. The contact silenced me instantly. 'I don't mind.'

'I need to give him something, it's important,' Izzy insisted. I knew when she was like this, it was hard to persuade her from her course of action.

'I'll follow you back,' Drew said with a smile.

'Are you sure?' I checked as Izzy skipped towards the car.

'It's fine. Izzy wants to give me a copy of the book I promised to read,' he replied.

'I hope you know what you've let yourself in for,' I said with a smile. 'See you back at the house then?' I watched him duck his head to avoid the sleet and hurry over to his jeep. I went to our car and climbed in, turning on the heating straightaway.

'He's nice, isn't he, Mum?' Izzy asked as we started to drive home. She was smiling, and I was so relieved that their first meeting had gone so well.

'He is, my love.' I glanced in my rear-view mirror to see him driving behind us. He smiled as our eyes met. My cheeks turned a little pink and I wasn't sure that I could blame it on the hot air blowing out from the vents.

Chapter Nineteen

When we walked into the Hall, shaking off the snow from our coats, Izzy pulled off her boots and raced off straight away to get the book. Drew watched her go in wonder. 'I can't believe that's our daughter,' he said. 'She's so grown up already,' he added, glancing at me, a slight frown on his face.

Guilt settled in my chest again. 'Thank you for today. I know... I can't imagine what a shock all of this still is.' I led him through to the living room where I had spent a lot of my time growing up. It was smaller and cosier than the formal drawing room with comfy chairs and a huge TV and a fire crackling merrily in the corner. The rest of the house was quiet. Mum and Sally were both out running errands they said, so there was a nurse upstairs with Gran. Dad was at work as usual.

'It's still hard to get my head around it all,' Drew admitted as he followed me in. He looked around as if trying to remember everything about the place. It had been a long time since he had set foot in the house. He went to the armchair and settled in it, so I sat down on the sofa opposite him. 'I've missed out on so much.'

'I'm so sorry, Drew,' I said, hating that I couldn't give him back those ten years. 'I know that doesn't even begin to cover it though.' I thought about my gran upstairs and her own apology to me. There had been so many mistakes made.

Drew sighed. 'It's hard seeing her and knowing that she grew up without me there to see it all. I mean, she seems like a great kid. And I can see myself in her. And you. So much of you, too.'

'Really?'

'Of course. Although you never got excited about books.'

'That's true. I was always trying to stop you studying. Wasn't I?'

'We got thrown out of the library on more than one occasion because of you talking.' He smiled then and it was so good to see.

'And that one time…' I trailed off, my cheeks turning even pinker as Drew nodded, remembering along with me. We had been caught by one of the teachers kissing rather too amorously against a bookshelf. We had got into a lot of trouble over that.

'Here it is,' Izzy announced, coming back in. She went over to Drew to show him. 'Now, do you know anything about Harry Potter?' she asked, her face dead serious. I tried to bite back my laugh.

'Well, I have seen a couple of the films, but I've never read the books. I'm willing to be educated,' he said. 'If you think I should read them then I will.'

Izzy beamed at him. 'You will love it. It's my favourite.'

'And, why is that?'

I stood up, knowing it would be a long conversation. 'I'll go and get us some drinks,' I told them, heading out to the kitchen and letting them discuss all things Harry Potter together.

Waiting for the kettle to boil, I looked out into the garden. The sleet had left a white layer that looked like dust scattered across the grass. As you grew older, you stopped seeing snow as some magical thing but that was what it felt like in that moment to me. It was hard to believe that Izzy and Drew were in the next room. I had fantasised about the two of them meeting on and off for years, but I had decided it would always be just a fantasy. Yet there they were. Somehow the world had worked its magic and finally the three of us had been brought together.

Carrying in a tray with three mugs of hot chocolate, I paused outside the door as I tried to balance the tray and push it open without spilling them everywhere. I was about to call out for some help when I heard Izzy speaking.

'I like them the best because they have red hair and they don't seem to mind having it at all.'

'You know, when I was at school,' Drew said, 'I was teased a lot for having red hair. It wasn't cool for a boy to be a redhead.'

'That's what happens to me!' Izzy cried. 'They all call me carrot head or laugh because my skin goes red a lot. "Lobster Izzy" some of the boys called me the other day. I wish I was in Harry Potter so I could cast a spell on them and turn all their hair red, and then they couldn't laugh at mine.'

I sagged against the door. I had worried that there was more to Izzy's apathy towards spending time with the kids at her school than she let on. She had always told me everything was okay at school but I now knew she had been hiding the truth from me. Anger rose up like a flare in my chest that kids were picking on my lovely girl. There was no way I was going to put up with that.

'I wish I had had a wand back then, too,' Drew said. 'But, you know what, the reason they all talk about your hair is because it's so beautiful. They are jealous that they don't have lovely coloured hair of their own. That's why I think this family you like in the book all have red hair. They sound like a special bunch and so they needed to have special hair.'

Izzy was quiet for a moment. 'You might be right about their hair. They are a special family. Do you really think that's why our hair is red?'

'I really do.'

I couldn't hold the tray any longer, so I bustled in noisily to give them warning. When I walked in, Izzy was kneeling on the floor beside Drew, the book on his lap as she pointed things out to him. I wanted to gather them in my arms and tell them that they were both special, but instead I beamed, put the tray down and started babbling. 'Right, here we go. I made your favourite, Iz. I hope you like still hot chocolate, Drew, otherwise we might not let you come back. Right, Iz?'

She giggled and came over to take one of the mugs.

'Of course I do,' Drew said, smiling as I passed him his mug. 'And I really think I'm going to be a fan of this book once I start reading it. It sounds pretty awesome.' He took a sip of his drink. 'And this is awesome too!'

'I honestly never thought I'd hear you say "awesome" so much,' I replied with a laugh.

'I couldn't help pick up a few Americanisms, I'm afraid.'

'Mum's always telling me off for speaking like a Londoner,' Izzy told him.

'If we stay here much longer, I'll definitely revert back to my Scottish accent,' I said, sipping my drink.

'I always pick it back up again when I come home,' Drew agreed.

'Teach me some of the American things you say,' Izzy said, and they started talking about the different words they had for things. I leaned back and smiled as they debated sneakers versus trainers, rubbers versus erasers, and the time when Drew called something 'bonnie' and no one had a clue what he was talking about.

'I did a presentation at school once about Hogmanay, none of my class had ever heard of New Year being called that,' Izzy chipped in.

'They are missing out then,' Drew replied with a smile.

I wanted to freeze the moment and replay it over and over again.

–

When the sun began to set, Drew got up and said he should be getting back to the farm as he'd promised to help Rory with some things. My mum and Sally arrived back at the Hall then, and Izzy gave Drew a hug and rushed off to the kitchen to tell them about her day.

I showed Drew out. 'I can't thank you enough… she's so happy,' I said, as I opened the front door, letting in a blast of cold air.

'I am too, to meet her, I mean. To know her. I just wish that I had known about her sooner,' he replied.

'Drew, I know that nothing can make up for the years you've missed…' I began, feeling the lump in my throat return with a vengeance. 'But I hope that you two can spend lots of time together while we're up here.'

Drew nodded. 'I would like that. I do need to think about everything, Beth. Everything has changed now. I know you never intentionally kept us apart, I know that things were hard, that you made the choice you thought you had to but… it's still difficult to come to terms with.'

'I understand,' I said, softly. 'I wish I could go back and change things; I wish I could make up for the time you lost; I wish I had tried again after that letter…' I broke off, finding it hard to carry on.

'I wish you had as well,' he said, his own voice sounding emotional. He looked away from me. 'I'd love to show her my farm, if I can? Will you bring her? Rory would love to meet her, too.'

'Of course I will,' I promised, hating that he was hurting so much. That I had caused it.

'See you, Beth,' he said, and the words shook me — it was how he always said goodbye to me.

'See you, Drew.' I closed the door and sagged against it. I wiped away a tear that had formed in the corner of my eye.

Chapter Twenty

Izzy and I walked into Glendale village with my mum the following morning, which had dawned bright and dry. I had wanted to draw Mum out of the Hall and show her the village, to see if I could get her onto my wavelength about how much of a shame it was to see it so changed. We had arranged to meet Heather for lunch as I thought we could try to get Mum interested in helping us to do something that might help the high street and the library.

There was a sharp breeze in the air and we were all wrapped up in coats and scarves. 'Do you remember the cafe that used to be here?' I asked as we walked to the library to pick up Heather for her break. 'It was run by that couple who used to make the best sandwiches and cakes. I was always begging you to take me there on the way home from school.'

'I wish there was still a cake shop,' Izzy said, longingly. I knew just how she felt.

Mum looked around the high street as we walked down it, passing the two shops still open. 'And there was that knick-knack shop where I got the fairy that sits on top of the Christmas tree,' she said, thinking back. 'And what else was there? The bakery and the butchers.'

'And a bank,' I said, screwing up my eyes as I thought back. 'Blimey, it's changed so much.'

Mum paused as we passed one of the open shops. There were no customers inside. 'It was always busy here, wasn't it? I walked into the village a lot when you were younger to get us both out the house, and we knew everyone here.'

'People are now forced to shop elsewhere. If we could bring back good shops then surely people would come back? I bet the rents just got too high.'

'I very much doubt the council would lower the rents though.' She sighed as we started to walk towards the pub again.

'Do you understand now why I've been so upset?' I asked her. 'It's so different to how I remember it.' We paused outside as Izzy went into the library to get Heather.

'To be honest, after you went to London, we came here less and less,' Mum replied. 'I suppose I didn't want to face people, knowing you'd left us,' she said, quietly, so Izzy wouldn't hear. 'I knew everyone was talking about it. And I never got back into the habit of coming into the village, so I hadn't noticed how much it had gone downhill. When your father started talking about redeveloping it, I thought that sounded like the best idea for everyone.'

'Dad is only thinking of profit though. I'm sure the new flats would make us money but the place we live would lose its identity. I think people need this village, whether they realise it or not. Surely we should be fighting to keep it?'

Mum smiled then. 'It's nice to hear you being so passionate about Glendale.'

'Hi, guys,' Heather said, coming out with Izzy, her coat pulled tightly around her. 'I'm starving.'

'Let's go to the pub then,' I said, smiling at her. We set off for the Glendale Arms, the only place left in the village where you could get lunch. Pushing open the door, the warmth from their log fire greeted us and we found a corner table close to it. The pub was almost empty save for us, another reminder that things weren't as they used to be in Glendale. 'Why is the village so empty now?'

'A vicious circle,' Heather replied. 'People started going into Glenmarshes or even to Inverness for shopping so what with that, and the high rents, the shops shut so there was nothing here, and then more people had to go elsewhere.'

'It's such a shame, there was always such a community here when we were younger. And those people must still be around?'

'If only we could show the council that the community is still alive,' Heather said. 'But how?'

'You need to bring everyone together,' Izzy piped up as she looked at the menu. 'So they can see the village is still a cool place to be.'

I looked at her. 'You're right but what can we do? Are the council set on this plan or can we persuade them to invest in the village again?'

'You know,' Mum said, 'one of my friends' son works for the council. I wonder if I could get us a meeting with him, to find out what they're thinking and see if there's any hope of changing their minds about selling.'

'What would Dad say though?' I asked, biting my lip. I certainly didn't agree with what he was doing but I also didn't want to see him ruined.

'We don't need to tell him anything just yet. Yes, his company would make more money if this goes ahead, so we would make more from our shares, but I'm sure they can find somewhere else to invest in. And I'll be honest, I won't lose any sleep over upsetting the board over there,' Mum said, darkly. She hadn't mentioned Cathy, the woman who worked there who Dad was having an affair with, much but it must have been on her mind a lot. I couldn't imagine how she felt. It must have been tearing her apart. I didn't understand why she didn't seem to want to do anything about it. I resolved to make her realise it wasn't something she should just accept.

'Do you think you can get us in to see the council though?'

'Oh, don't you worry about that.'

I was pleased to see that determined look back in her eyes, the one I remembered from when I was a child and she had wanted me to do something that I really didn't want to do.

'And in the meantime, let's come up with a way to bring the village together,' Heather suggested, pulling out a notebook and pen.

I went up to the bar to order us some food and drink and glanced back to see their heads bent close together as they tried to brainstorm ideas for how we could save the High Street, and bring the Glendale community back together again. It was lovely to see them all energised and wanting to help. I was sure that if we took the lead then others would follow, and help make Glendale somewhere people wanted to be again. I thought about what Izzy had said about bringing people together and doing something festive, and an idea popped into my head. I hurried back over to them after ordering, hoping they would all like it.

–

We all stood in the garden in a line – Mum, me and Izzy, and John who we had pulled away from the greenhouse to join us. Heather had had to go back to work but she'd been bouncing with enthusiasm as she left us, planning to work all afternoon on my suggestion at lunch. The three of us had come straight home to see if John thought it was something we could do.

'What do you think? Can you picture it?' I asked John anxiously.

'It could be really stunning. A lot of work but we could pull it off. Even with the short deadline. We'd need to ask people to pitch in and help. And you could design it all. But would people come?'

I bit back the urge to reply, 'if we build it, they will come', so I nodded instead. 'People care about Glendale, they'll come. Plus, the chance to see Glendale Hall after all these years and get a glimpse of the black sheep daughter, who could resist?' I said with a grin.

'What about David?' John asked with a shuffle of his feet.

'He's not going to like it,' I admitted. I turned to my mum for her verdict.

'It's not his house at the end of the day, though, is it?' she replied.

I hadn't thought of it like that, but she was right. Gran owned Glendale Hall, not my father, and I didn't think she was about to refuse us anything as she wanted to make amends for the past. I looked out at the garden and tried to picture my idea fully formed. I had remembered taking Izzy to Kew Gardens last Christmas, where we had walked their trail of lights together. I thought that we could create our own festive trail at the Hall and invite everyone who lived Glendale to come along. And even get them all to help build it. It seemed like a perfect idea to pull everyone together and bring some much-needed festive cheer to the village. 'We could invite the council to come on opening night and really show them that we're willing to fight for our village,' I said then, hoping that we'd be able to change their minds and make them see that there was a community to save.

'We have a lot of lights already,' John said. 'But we'd need to buy more. We'll probably need to hire an outside generator, too.'

'Okay. Heather is going to try to drum up support in the village. She was always good at art: we'll need leaflets, posters and social media buzz.'

'What about me?' Izzy asked, keen for a job to do.

'Find the leftover decorations you didn't use and see if there's anything suitable for the trail,' I told her. 'I think we'll need to go to the garden centre and buy more things though. I'm going to do some sketching of what we want it to look like.'

'We need an inflatable Santa!'

'Start making a list,' I replied to Izzy. 'Come on, Mum. Let's go and get Gran on board.'

'An inflatable Santa?' she hissed as we walked back towards the house. 'Won't that lower the tone?'

'The kids will love it though,' I said, biting back a laugh. Some things really did never change.

We went upstairs to my gran's room. She was propped up in bed holding a book, which she dropped onto her lap when we went in. She was looking more frail by the day, but she smiled when she saw me.

'Hello, Beth,' she breathed.

'We are on a mission and we need your help,' Mum said, going to sit in the chair by the bed. She nodded at me. 'Beth, why don't you tell her what's been going on?'

I told her about the council's plans for Glendale: the fact that Heather was about to lose her job and the village was about to not only lose the library but its complete identity if the plan to turn the high street into flats went ahead. 'We've decided we want to go and see the council to find out if there's any way we can stop their plans. We also think if we can show them that there is a thriving community in Glendale, they might take us more seriously. So, we've decided to make a Christmas trail in the garden here.'

'I missed all the events we used to have here. The garden parties every summer… the whole village would come. A trail, a trail would be wonderful.' She looked at me. 'I think this is a great idea. We were once right in the centre of things in Glendale. Ever since the Hall was built really but we've let that slide. Let the village fall around us. You're right, Beth, we have to fight for it. My father would have been mortified to see us turn our backs like we have. And my grandfather… he built this house and this family to be a prominent part of the community here.'

'You're right – we've neglected the village,' Mum said. 'I have turned a blind eye to things for years because I was too worried about what people thought of us. Walking down the high street today was depressing. Glendale used to be thriving, and I think it could be again.'

'I think you need to try to do all you can,' Gran agreed. 'I want to help. Let me pay for everything you need.'

'That's very generous, mother,' my mum said in surprise.

'What's the point of hanging on to all my money now,' she said with a weak attempt at a smile.

'Thank you, Gran,' I said.

She looked at me. 'I know how much Isabelle loves it here. We're doing this for her and for her generation. I wish I had known about all of this sooner, before I became stuck in this godforsaken bed.'

'I just accepted what David said,' Mum said with her head down. 'I don't know why I didn't try to get involved more. I have had my head stuck in the sand for far too long. About a lot of things.'

Gran sighed. 'I can never change what I did in the past, but I hope you'll let me help you both do this. Maybe I can make some amends for everything that happened. I am truly sorry.'

'I know you are,' I conceded. I didn't doubt her sincerity, but I wished it hadn't come so late. My mum and I had lost a lot of time being angry with each other, and my daughter had missed out on having a family around her. And Drew had missed out on everything. I knew that my gran wanted me to say that I forgave her, but I wasn't ready for that yet. 'I'm glad we know the truth now. And I am happy we are going to work on saving Glendale together.' That was the best I could do for her right now. She nodded as if she understood that.

'I'm proud of you both,' Gran said. It was something that she never would have thought to say before, I knew that. She was trying now. We all were, I supposed. I did feel a lot of sympathy for her. She was bedridden and would be watching us build this trail from her room. I couldn't begin to imagine what it was like for her.

'Right, I better get this meeting with the council set up,' Mum said, getting up.

I followed her out, thinking about how much had changed in such a short time in our family. There had been so many years of misunderstandings between us, but now we knew the truth, we had a chance to fix all of that.

I was still angry with Gran, though. I thought of Drew then, and how he must feel the same about me: could either of us forgive the mistakes that had been made? We were caught up, still, in the pain of the past. I wasn't sure if we could let it go. But I also knew that we would only end up hurting ourselves if we didn't. Forgiveness was as much about you as it was the person you forgave.

We all needed to focus on the future. I just wished that I knew if that was something we'd be able to do.

Chapter Twenty-One

I sat beside Izzy's bed that night. I watched her climb under the covers, pulling a book onto her lap for her usual bedtime reading. I hadn't seen her with a book all day, she was as excited as all of us about creating this trail, and it made me happy to see her enjoying being with the family. Though I couldn't help but think about what I overheard between her and Drew.

'Iz, you know that you and Drew were talking about what you love about Harry Potter? Well, I heard you talking about your red hair…'

Izzy bit her lip and looked down at her book.

I put my hand on hers. 'Have people been giving you a hard time at school?' She nodded, and I felt my heart break a little bit. 'Oh, love, why wouldn't you tell me about that?'

She sighed. 'I didn't want you to worry. You worry about so much, Mum.'

'Izzy, listen to me, I always want to know everything that's going on with you. I don't want you to keep anything from me. I want you to be happy, that's all I care about. And when you tell me something, we can sort it out together so neither of us have to worry about it. Okay?'

'Okay.'

'You promise me, Iz? You'll tell me if something like that happens again?'

Izzy nodded. 'I promise.'

'And when we go back home, we're going to sort it out. I'm going to make sure no one upsets you again.'

'I wish we didn't have to go back to London. I really like it here,' she said, lying down under the covers. 'I'm tired. I don't think I need to read.'

'Okay,' I said, her words having stung me. I got up and leaned down to kiss her. 'You have sweet dreams. And tomorrow we're going to see your dad on his farm, so that will be fun, won't it?'

'I hope I get to feed some animals.'

'I think you will.' I turned off her light. 'I love you, Izzy.'

'Love you too, Mum.'

I slipped out and went into my bedroom, sinking down onto my bed in the darkness, Izzy's words ringing in my ears. Had I really been so caught up with day-to-day survival that I'd missed just how much Izzy didn't like school? I knew she didn't have lots of friends, but I hadn't realised that she was being picked on, enough to make her wish she wouldn't have to go back in the new year. I sighed. Why couldn't I protect her from everything?

I hated that she felt she had to keep it from me, worried that I had enough on my plate to deal with. I didn't want her to feel that way again. I wanted her to tell me everything. There were just sixteen years between us. Sometimes that felt like a lot but sometimes it felt like it was nothing. It often seemed like we were sisters, not mother and daughter, but Izzy needed to feel like she could just be a child and not try to deal with things on her own.

Coming to Glendale Hall was helping that, I could see it already. I felt like I could take a breath here and she was free to enjoy herself. I was determined to make this our best Christmas yet. Izzy deserved it. I hoped the house would continue to work its magic on all of us. I turned to look at the window and saw large white flakes floating down, as if it was promising to do just that.

—

We drove through the Fraser Farm gates and I felt the same jolt as I had the last time. Izzy let out a gasp from the back, and I looked across at Heather who gave me a reassuring smile. The two of us had spent a lot of time there as teenagers so it was surreal to be back there together. I had invited Heather to come to lunch with me after dropping Izzy off to be with Drew so I wouldn't spend the time worrying about how it was going. Plus, Mum had secured us a meeting with the council, and we needed to plan for that.

'Look, Mum,' Izzy said, pointing out of the window. We passed a pen of sheep, huddled together at the entrance to a barn, keeping out of the cold wind, and opposite them two horses draped in blankets were eating from a trough of hay. We twisted down the gravel track towards the farmhouse.

'Don't suppose you see anything like this in London, Iz,' Heather said.

'No way,' she replied. 'Just pigeons.' We laughed, and some of the nerves in the car evaporated a little.

As we pulled up, the door opened, and Drew and Rory came out. Standing together you could see how alike they were with their tall, broad frames and auburn hair. Rory was slightly shorter, although he was older, and had a beard. Drew lifted his hand in a wave. They both wore jeans, wellies and thick jumpers ready for farm work.

'Hi, guys,' Drew said as we climbed out of the car. 'Ready to see the farm, Iz?'

'Definitely,' she said, hurrying over to him. They looked at one another, a little bit unsure what to do, but Drew held out his arms and she gave him a hug. I had to look away to compose myself.

'This is your Uncle Rory,' Drew said to her.

'Hey, kid. Welcome to the farm. You ready to feed some animals?' Rory asked her. She nodded and he held out his hand for a high five, which she gave him. Rory looked at us then. 'You stalking me again, Heath?'

'You wish. I'm taking this one for lunch,' she said, nodding to me. She smiled at Rory, though, and I wondered if she'd spent more time with him over the years than I knew.

'You should stay here,' he replied. 'We've got a feast prepared, and we could always do with more hands. Don't you think, Drew?'

Drew's eyes met mine. 'Uh, sure. You should stay,' he said.

I smiled, wishing that I wasn't worried about the memories that might come back being with Drew on the farm again.

'Please, Mum,' Izzy begged then, so I had to agree.

'I'm so not wearing the right shoes for farm work,' Heather said, pointing down to her heeled boots. 'But I'll watch.'

Rory rolled his eyes. 'Why am I not surprised? Come on, Izzy, let's show her what real work looks like.' Rory, Drew and Izzy began to walk around the back of the house.

Heather slipped her arm through mine. 'You okay with staying?'

'It's just crazy to be back here,' I replied as we set off after them.

'I know what you mean. Remember that summer you were with Drew, we were here practically every day? It seems like a lifetime ago but also like it was yesterday. They seem to be getting on great,' she added in a low voice as we watched Drew open a gate to let Izzy through to the field.

'They are a lot alike. I'm so happy that they are getting on so well, but it hurts too. I try not to think about what might have been but…' I leaned on the fence, Heather beside me, as we watched Drew and Rory show Izzy the cows and the sheep. The smile on her face was amazing to see. 'I made the wrong choice back then, didn't I?'

Heather thought for a moment. 'Maybe there wasn't a right or wrong choice, you know? You made the one you thought you had to. You can't change it, hun. They're together now, aren't they?'

I nodded but I wondered if I'd ever be able to let go of the guilt I felt. I had tried so hard to do the right thing, but perhaps what Heather said was true and it wasn't possible in that situation to do the right thing, only what your heart told you to do at the time. I was only sixteen, too. I had a second chance now, and this time I was determined to get it right.

Chapter Twenty-Two

We all trooped into the farmhouse at lunchtime, hungry after a couple of hours spent outside. Izzy had loved watching them move the sheep to another field. She had helped collect the eggs from the hens and had squealed when a couple decided to chase her. Drew had ended up picking her up and running away with her. They had such an easy way with one another already. Rory had got the tractor out then and given Izzy a ride around the back of the farmhouse on it.

I left them to go to the bathroom. When I came out, I passed a row of photos stuck to the wall. I looked at Drew's graduation photo. Him in a cap and gown, gripping his diploma, a grin on his face. He looked so happy in the picture. He had become a doctor. His dream had come true. Like I had wanted it to. Maybe it wasn't black and white, like Heather said, maybe there really hadn't been a right choice for me back then. I really wasn't sure any more.

'Hey,' a soft voice said. I turned to see Rory watching me. 'I went over to see him graduate. I had almost burst with pride.'

'I bet,' I replied with a smile. 'Your parents would have been so proud.'

Rory nodded. 'Drew told me that was part of the reason you didn't tell him about Izzy. I get it, Beth. Maybe more than he does right now. I worked so hard after they died to make sure he still went to university. He wanted to stay, you know, and help me run the farm but I told him there was no way he was doing that. I miss him like hell, but I know I was right to make him go.'

I looked at Rory. I had always liked him, but we'd never shared a heart to heart or anything. He had just been my boyfriend's brother who liked to tease me and joke about us being so in love it made him feel sick. His words touched me then, though, more than he probably knew.

'Seeing this photo, and how happy he was to graduate, it does help. I didn't want him to give up anything for me. I hope one day he will understand that. I know he'll never forgive me – I don't think I'll forgive myself – but maybe he'll understand.'

'I think he already does. You were in an impossible situation.' Rory nodded towards the kitchen. 'Come on, let's go in and eat. Izzy's a great kid, Beth. You did good.' He turned and sloped off again.

I took one last look at the photo and then I followed him.

Drew had laid the table with an array of food, and everyone was sitting down. There was freshly baked bread, chunks of cheese, chutney, sausage rolls, tomatoes, hard boiled eggs fresh from the hens and slices of ham and beef. Drew poured out glasses of homemade lemonade for everyone.

'An indoor picnic,' he said, giving me a small smile as I joined them.

'This looks amazing,' I said. I sat down next to Izzy whose cheeks were pink from the fresh air. 'I'm going to be a stone heavier after this Christmas at this rate.'

'I never knew you two were so domesticated,' Heather said as Rory sat down next to her. 'I should come here more often.'

'Only if you wear wellies,' Rory replied, sternly. 'In fact, I might buy you a pair for Christmas.'

'I'll only wear them if they're sparkly.'

'Bloody hell,' he muttered under his breath as he handed her the basket of bread.

Izzy let out a cry then, peeking under the table. 'Oh, it's a cat,' she said, when she realised what had brushed against her.

'That's Tabby, our mouse hunter,' Rory told her.

'Tabby? Honestly, what a name,' Heather said, shaking her head.

'Tabby is a rubbish hunter,' Drew said to Izzy. 'I don't think he's ever caught anything. Prefers just to eat and sleep.'

'I wish we had a pet,' Izzy said, popping a tomato into her mouth. 'Our flat doesn't allow animals though.'

'Same for me in Boston,' Drew said. 'We'll just pretend that Tabby is ours for now.'

Izzy 'accidentally' dropped a bit of her ham on the floor. 'That's a good idea. Maybe we could get Granny to have a pet at the Hall?'

I smiled at her. 'I'm not sure you'll have much of a shot with that, but you can try. I think she'd be too worried about cat hairs around the house, to be honest.'

After lunch, Rory took Heather and Izzy out to see the goats and I helped Drew wash up the lunch things. The radio was on softly in the background and the wintery sun streamed in through the window by the sink. I looked out at the three of them walking towards the back field and I couldn't help smiling.

'She seems to like it here,' Drew said, catching my smile as he passed me a plate to dry.

'She loves it. I knew she would. I loved coming here. Your house was always warm and cosy and full of life, so different from mine.'

'How has it been coming home?'

'Better than I thought. My mum and I seem to be finally getting past some of our issues, after we found out that a lot of what we thought about the past was wrong. I think she's been quite lonely lately. My gran being ill has been hard on her, and my dad hasn't helped much. She's happy to have us there I think.'

'I'm sure she is. What about your gran – how is she doing?'

I told him about her illness. 'They don't think she'll last much beyond Christmas. It really feels like it's almost time to say goodbye. It's hard. I spent so many years resenting her...' I told him then what she had said to me before I left. 'She really made me feel as if I was all alone and had no choice but to leave. And now I know my parents didn't even know that I was pregnant.'

Drew was quiet for a moment. 'I wish you had told me, Beth. I had a right to know. I could have helped. We could have decided what to do together. You know that, right?'

I nodded. 'I know that now. Back then, it wasn't so clear. I was scared, so scared, and I didn't want you to give up on your dreams for me.'

'I know.'

'If I made the wrong choice, I did it out of love. For you, for Izzy, for all of us. I got it wrong, I can see that now. But if you had not gone to America, I would have never forgiven myself and maybe you would have resented me in time. I don't know.'

'I don't know either.' He sighed. 'What I do know is I am happy that I get to be with Izzy now. She is special, isn't she?'

'She is.' I nudged him then. 'We made her. Can you believe it?'

'I really can't.' He smiled, and it felt as if we had turned a corner and maybe things would be okay. 'I just wish I didn't live so far away. It's going to be so hard going back to Boston now.'

'I know. But there are so many ways to stay in touch. You will always be in each other's lives now.'

'You promise?'

I met his gaze. 'I promise.' He handed me a dish and our fingertips brushed. I didn't know if he felt it, but heat flooded through me at the simple touch. His hand moved away, and I felt the loss instantly. I wished he would touch me again. My skin seemed to crave it. I looked away from him in case my face betrayed me.

It was crazy that his touch could still do that to me after all the time we had been apart.

Chapter Twenty-Three

Mum, Heather and I piled into mum's Range Rover and we drove to Glenmarshes for our appointment with a Development Officer on the local council. Mum's friend had got us the meeting with her son, a Mr Murray, to discuss their plans for Glendale village. As we'd agreed, we didn't say anything to my father about the meeting or our ideas for Glendale.

The three of us marched purposefully from the car park into the low-rise office building. Mum was in her Chanel suit complete with pearls and court shoes, Heather had on a black wool dress with boots and I had put on my smartest jeans with a camel cashmere jumper Mum bought me for Christmas the previous year, which I had never had anywhere to wear it to before now. We were directed, once inside, up to the first floor where the receptionist showed us into Mr Murray's office. It was a tiny room with an even smaller window looking out over the car park. The man himself was small in a grey suit that looked as if it had seen better days, and he was much younger than we were expecting. I saw Mum hide a smile. I knew that she thought we could take him. I was feeling much more hopeful myself.

'Mr Murray, I am Caroline Williams, and this is my daughter, Beth, and this is Heather Douglas, who works at Glendale library,' my mother said in her poshest voice.

We all shook hands and I could see Mr Murray was a little nervous. Even though my family had drawn back from village life, the Hall was known throughout Glendale – as was our family's money – so for one of the first times in my life, I was glad that such things had an influence on people, and hoped they would on Mr Murray. He sat down behind his desk and we perched in the three plastic chairs opposite him.

'Mr Murray—' my mother began.

'Oh, please, call me Edward,' he interrupted.

My mother's eyes narrowed. 'I asked for this meeting because I have been stunned to hear the news that not only is the Glendale library being closed down, but you are selling off the high street to developers who are going to turn it into flats.'

'We are in talks to do so yes and we will be having a public consultation in the new year, where residents can raise objections if they have any.'

'I have reason to believe that will be too late by then,' Mum replied. We knew that Dad's company were meeting the council to finalise plans before then so I was sure this public consultation would just be lip service.

'What we'd like to know is what we can do to change your mind about selling to them,' I said then. 'Surely you would rather keep the high street for the local community to use? I understand this company is offering you a lot of money, but isn't it in the best interests of Glendale to find a better alternative?'

Mr Murray thought for a moment. 'What alterative is there? All but two of the shops are empty.'

'Because of your high rents!' Heather burst out then looked embarrassed and sat back quickly.

'People just don't use the village any more,' he continued. 'The two businesses left are keen to sell, so there really isn't any other option. The library isn't used enough for us to justify funding it any more when we have other priorities in the local area that we need to pay for.'

'What if we could show you that there is still a community in Glendale? One that you should be fostering, not destroying?' I asked.

'Well, how would you do that?'

I told him about our plan to build a trail and bring the village together. 'It'll be a great opportunity for everyone to be involved, a community project, and one that will show you people do want to save Glendale.'

'I'm sure that would be lovely, but it wouldn't help with the problem of the empty premises on the high street.'

'What if we could fill all the empty premises? What then?' Heather asked him.

'If you could find businesses that are able to pay the full rent then we would consider that seriously.'

'So,' I said, quickly. 'You're saying that if we could fill the high street with local businesses able to pay the rent you currently charge then you wouldn't sell to these developers?' I asked him.

'Well, now, I would have to speak to—'

'Mr Murray, you were born and raised in Glendale as all of us were. Surely you want to keep it for the local community? Surely the council want that above anything else? I mean, the local press would have a field day if they knew you would rather sell it off and ignore a perfectly good alternative plan…' Mum said, pointedly.

'Of course,' Mr Murray roused himself then. 'If you can come up with an alternative plan then we would obviously rather that than selling off the premises. I don't think we need to contact any journalists until we have sorted things out between ourselves, do you?'

My mother smiled. 'Of course not. We will see you at the trail, Mr Murray, and then you'll see how keen everyone is to save our village.' Mum stood up and held out her hand to him. 'And in the meantime, we have your word that nothing will be agreed regarding the redevelopment of the high street?'

'We have a meeting on the fifth of January with New Horizons to discuss their bid so, yes, nothing will be agreed until then.'

'Thank you for your time,' Mum said, shaking his hand firmly.

We marched out the way we had come, each of us feeling like we had secured a reprieve for the village but knowing we still had a monumental task ahead. Not only finding people willing to run a business on the high street again, but creating a trail that would knock the council's socks off and make everyone believe in Glendale again.

'But we have hope,' Heather said when we were back in the car. 'And that is something we didn't have this morning.'

'We are going to need to talk to your father,' Mum said, looking across at me. 'He won't be happy his deal isn't going to be signed before Christmas now. And then we need to talk to all the businesses that have closed up and see what can be done to get them to reopen.'

'We could have a village meeting,' Heather suggested. 'I can rally everyone, I'm sure I can.'

'If we can show the council that everyone in the village really wants this, maybe they would budge on the rents. Maybe do a deal with us?' I wondered.

'Maybe,' Mum said. 'Let's do all we can to make it as hard as possible for them to sell off the high street.'

'I don't think they'll budge on the library, though,' Heather said, sadly. 'It really isn't being used enough.'

'We'll try,' I told her. 'That's all we can do.' I really hoped we could do something to make a difference. I couldn't leave without knowing I had done all I could to change their minds. I had started this trip counting the days until I could go back to London, but suddenly there didn't feel like there was going to be enough time to do everything that needed to be done before I would be leaving Glendale.

Chapter Twenty-Four

I curled up on the sofa with Izzy as the rain hammered against the window. We were in the living room, a tartan blanket over our knees. We had just put on *The Muppet Christmas Carol*: a film we watched every festive season. As the menu flashed up, I looked across at my daughter. 'Tomorrow we need to buy some things for the trail.'

'Can Drew come with us?'

'I can ask him.' She nodded so I pulled out my phone to text him. 'We definitely need a lot more lights.'

'And an inflatable Santa.'

'Well, don't tell Granny we're getting one.'

She giggled, and I started the film, sending off the message to Drew to see if he wanted to join us on our mission. I leaned back to watch the Muppets and it was nice to have a quiet moment with Izzy, just the two of us. This Christmas felt like a period of massive change for us, and everyone around us, and I was grateful to take a moment doing something we had always done. I tried to shut off my mind from thinking about everything else that was going on.

Later though, that proved to be impossible. The film over, we put on *Home Alone* – another classic Williams festive film – but Izzy fell asleep halfway through, so I put the blanket over her and left her to go and see what was happening with my parents. Night had wrapped itself around Glendale Hall by then, and I padded softly on the carpet towards my dad's study, where I heard raised voices coming from inside.

'Why won't you put your family first for once?' Mum flung at him.

I stood in the open doorway. My father was sat at his desk, my mother standing nearby, looking furious. 'Everyone okay in here?' I asked, at a loss for what else to say. I flashed back to listening to an argument between them when I was about Izzy's age; it had scared me in a way I hadn't understood at the time. I think I feared that it meant they were going to split up. Now though, I wondered if that would be the best decision for them both.

'Your mother has just informed me that you're all doing your best to ruin this deal with the council for me,' Dad replied in a dry tone.

'I hardly think this deal not happening will ruin you,' Mum flung back.

'We have shares in this company, Caroline… it's in our interest for the deal to go through.'

'But we'll be fine if it doesn't,' she replied. 'This is about your fancy woman being angry if it doesn't go through, especially if she finds out your family were the ones who scuppered it.' She crossed her arms over her chest. 'You used to care about Glendale.'

'The village will be better if we take it over. It's a ghost town. This will bring life back into it.'

'But there won't be anything for the community,' I reasoned with him. 'Just flats. How will that help anyone but your profit? This isn't your company, Dad, you're just on the board; can't you see that what's best for Glendale is for us to help it, not destroy it?'

'I'm going to have to tell—'

'You will not,' Mum roared furiously. 'You are not to tell anyone anything. We have until after Christmas to make our case to the council and then they will decide. I won't have you upping your offer or making any deals behind our backs. Otherwise, you can pack your bags right now and get out.'

Dad and I stared at her. Not once had I ever heard her speak to him like that. I kind of wanted to give her a cheer, to be honest, but I sensed that wasn't the best move. 'I have to tell Cathy,' he added more quietly. He was slumped in his chair now, sensing defeat perhaps.

'How dare you even say her name to me.' Mum spun around then and marched out of the room, her head held high.

'Dad, how could you do this? Can't you see how much you are hurting her?'

He looked at me and shook his head. 'It's complicated, Beth.'

'It doesn't seem all that complicated to me. You're having an affair. You clearly don't care about Mum's feelings any more. Why are you still here? Why don't you just leave?'

'Do you know what people would say if I left her?'

'Jesus, you did not just say that. That's pathetic. No one cares what we do any more, Dad. You've not only cut yourself off from Glendale but you're trying to tear it all down, so what exactly are you worried about? That you won't be welcome at your golf club any more? That no one will ask you to dinner parties? That's enough, is it, to put Mum through all of this? Do you even care about this family any more? Or do you only care about your other woman? You know what, she's welcome to you.' I left him then, hoping some home truths might shake some sense into him. In my mind, there were two options – move out to be with Cathy or break things off and try to repair his marriage to my mother.

I found Mum crying into her G & T in the other room. 'Mum, you should not be crying right now. All of this is on him. And you really shouldn't be drinking again.' I took the glass out of her hand. 'Everything is going to be okay, you know that, right? If he leaves, you will be fine.'

She looked up. 'You think so? Really?'

'Of course I do.'

'It's been a miserable few years. I am stuck in this house with nothing to do. And now my mother…' She let out another sob.

'Listen, there's no need to stay stuck in the house. There is so much you could do. And we're starting with this project. We're going to save this village, and then we'll work on what you can do next. You're not alone any more, Mum.' I had spent so many years feeling resentful of my family, especially of my mother, believing that she hadn't supported me when I needed her the most. Now I knew that hadn't been the case at all, so I sure as hell was going to support her now when she needed me the most.

'You're right.' She wiped her eyes. 'I have a project now. Your father isn't going to win this one, Beth. And if he wants to be with *that* woman, then so be it.'

I never thought I'd hear my mother speak about Dad like that. I loved them both, they were my parents after all, but I couldn't not be on my mother's side on this one. My father wasn't being fair. He was seeing another woman, for a start, and clearly didn't care who he hurt in the process – not my mother, or the whole of Glendale.

Chapter Twenty-Five

Drew had jumped at the chance to come out with us and picked me and Izzy up in his jeep to take us to the garden centre. I told him on the way all about our plan for the trail.

'I think that's a great idea,' Drew said. 'I haven't liked seeing how much Glendale has changed whenever I've come home. I think we probably have noticed it more than your family or Rory as we don't live here. It's a shame. Growing up I loved going into the village. I would be happy to help out all I can.'

'Really? That would be great, wouldn't it, Iz?'

She nodded. 'I can't wait to buy lots of cool things today.'

'We might need reining in, we tend to go big at Christmas – although our small flat doesn't let us go too crazy – but now we have acres at our disposal,' I said to Drew.

'Mum, if you can't go big at Christmas then when can you?'

'I've taught you well,' I replied with a grin.

'I'm nervous now,' Drew told us. We just laughed.

The garden centre was huge and packed, most of the inside had been set aside for Christmas things, which rendered Izzy and I a little bit speechless when we saw it. 'Wow,' I said, taking it all in. Izzy immediately ran forward into the thick of it.

'You guys really are big on Christmas, aren't you?' Drew asked with a laugh.

'You used to be, too. Remember when you made me go to that panto in Inverness? It was hilarious.'

'Unintentionally,' he agreed. 'I suppose Christmases here were always magical, weren't they? Boston goes pretty overboard with lights and trees, but it never feels quite the same without family, which is why I like to come home if I can.'

'I know what you mean,' I said, picking up a box of snowflake lights which I thought would look pretty on the trail. 'In London, we've tried really hard to develop our own festive traditions, but I always think about Glendale Hall. I'm glad Izzy finally gets to have a Christmas up here.'

'I think she'll love it,' he agreed.

'Mum, look!'

We hurried over to Izzy who was pointing excitedly with both fingers at something. 'Oh my god,' I said when I saw what she was looking at. There was a six-foot, inflatable, lit-up Santa on the floor. 'We have to have it!'

'And this,' Drew said, pointing to the matching snowman. 'You could have them at the start of the trail, one on each side.'

'Yes!' Izzy cried. 'And we could have a banner hanging across the trees so people know it's the start of the trail.'

I laughed. 'You two are on a roll. Iz, text Heather and ask her to make a banner.' I passed her my phone. I knew Heather would make a really beautiful one, and it would be the perfect entrance to the trail.

'I'll get a trolley for these,' Drew said, picking up two boxes and putting them at my feet.

'Mum is going to kill us for buying these; we better pick up some more tasteful bits too,' I said to Izzy. She hurried off again, eager to find more things. When Drew came back with the trolley, we put the inflatable Santa and snowman boxes in along with the snowflakes lights and set off after her. 'John had already started hanging the lights we had back at the house.

I feel like we need something else other than just more fairy lights though.'

'What about these?' Izzy showed me a set of reindeers in different sizes made out of lights. 'They are so pretty.'

'They would be lovely,' I agreed. 'Let's get a set for sure.' Gran had given me her credit card before we left, which I was grateful for as I was sure these were going to add up to a fairly hefty amount. 'And these are cute,' I said, picking up some star lights.

'How about these?' Drew came over carrying a box of icicle lights. 'You could hang these in a bush or round a tree?'

'Perfect,' I said with a smile. We loaded the trolley and agreed that we should get out of there before we bought the whole place. Drew picked up a set of lights for the farm, saying that they needed to decorate the outside of the house. It seemed our festive spirit was contagious.

'I really do want to come and help, if you can stand to spend more time with me?' Drew said as we loaded the car up with our purchases.

'Honestly, that would be great, we need all the help we can get.'

'And those mince pies would help, too,' Izzy suggested sagely, nodding at the packet he had bought inside.

Drew chuckled. 'You're a real chip off the old block.'

'What does chip off the old block mean?' Izzy asked as we piled back into the overflowing jeep.

'It means you're going to turn into me one day,' I replied, giving her a shocked face.

She groaned. 'But I hate coffee.'

'I hated it when I was your age, so watch out.'

'As long as I don't start liking wine, I'll be okay.'

Drew and I burst out laughing. 'I'm going to remind you of that sentence when you're a teenager, you know that, right?'

'Fine because I'll still feel the same way then,' she said, stubbornly.

'I think we need to bet some money on this,' I said, still chuckling.

'I think we definitely need it in writing,' Drew agreed. We headed off back home. It was a second before I realised what I had thought to myself – that Glendale Hall was home. It had been a long time since I had felt that way, but as we drove back there, it really did feel like it.

–

We all stood in the garden, wrapped up against the chill, after unloading our purchases, so we could plot out the trail. John had found three men from the village to come to help and with Drew as well, they made quick work of getting everything out of the car.

I had drawn a diagram of how I pictured the trail, and we were debating how we could create it for real. 'We're going to need lots of help with this. Can we really pull it off by Christmas Eve?' I asked them.

'We can do it,' Mum said, firmly.

'How about this?' I walked over to two fir trees which stood tall and proud with a walkaway between them. 'If we start here, then people will walk through all the Christmas trees and end up at the stream. We could guide them around it and out towards the rose garden, which would make a good finish to the trail as it's close to the driveway,' I suggested. Everyone looked at me. 'What?' I asked, wondering why they had all gone silent.

John strode forward. 'Beth, that is perfect. We can hang all the fairy lights in this section, then by the stream put up the standing lights and in the rose garden we can have the grotto.'

In my absence, they had decided we needed a finale for the trail, so we were going to create a grotto using a tent Heather's dad had loaned to us and turn it into a winter wonderland, complete with fake snow, and a sleigh inside which one of John's friends was hiring from his brother in Edinburgh. Everyone seemed excited, and the idea just kept getting bigger and bolder so no one could blame Izzy and me for getting carried away by Christmas: it seemed like the whole village was along for this ride.

'Great, let's get started then,' I said, passing out lights and pointing to where they should be hung. John had already hired a generator and they were sorting out the cabling under my mother's directions. Together Drew and Izzy carried the inflatable Santa over to the start of the trail.

I saw a car pull into the driveway and I waved when I saw Heather hurrying over to us. 'Wow, you guys are already in full swing,' she said. 'What do you think?' She thrust a leaflet at me. *Glendale Hall Christmas Trail* proclaimed the leaflet promising twinkling lights and a winter wonderland. She had designed it beautifully.

'It's perfect!'

'I wanted to come and see where this banner is going to hang so I get the size just right,' she said, as we set off to the garden together. 'And then I'll drop off the leaflets around Glendale. I'll obviously have them in the library, the pub, and the shops that are left,' she said with a sigh. 'I'll leave some here for you guys as well. I've also posted on the Glendale Facebook page so make sure you ask everyone to share that, okay?'

'You've thought of everything,' I said. 'Here's where the trail will start.' We watched Drew and Izzy put the snowman on the other side of the Santa creating a pathway for the trail. 'So, we can hang the banner here between these two trees,' I said, pointing upwards.

Heather looked up. 'Right, I need to head to an art shop then, I need a much bigger paintbrush.'

'You really bought an inflatable Santa?' My mum appeared then, putting her hands on her hips.

'You have to have something tacky at Christmas,' I replied. 'It's a festive law.'

She rolled her eyes. 'Sometimes I do wonder where you came from,' she said before going up to Drew and telling him to move it so it looked straighter.

We all got stuck in to the work and time seemed to fly by. Sally called out from the back door that there was tea inside, so we all gratefully trooped into the kitchen. As it was Sally, there was not only hot tea for everyone but an array of cakes and biscuits too.

'I'm going to make chilli for later,' she told us. 'You're all welcome to stay for it. I think you'll be needing it by the looks of it.'

'Sally, you're a star,' I told her. I took a sip of the hot, sugary tea. 'Thanks so much for helping out, guys,' I said to the room. 'This is what I missed about Glendale – everyone pitching in together. This really will remind everyone what our village is all about.' Everyone cheered and raised their mugs of tea in agreement.

After we had had our tea break, we all went back out into the chilly afternoon and made good progress on the trail before the sun started to set. Heather left to go shopping to make her banner, and my mum returned inside to see to Gran. I placed the reindeer lights along the trail and watched as Izzy gripped a ladder so Drew could string lights on a tree.

'How's it looking?' Drew called down to her.

'There's a bare patch there,' she called back, pointing to where he needed to add more lights. It was lovely to see them working as a team on the trail. For us all to be working on it.

I loved seeing Izzy outside and having fun; the problems of London seemed like they were irrelevant out here. For me, too. My worries about money and being a single mother, and trying to juggle it all, were all very far away. London seemed like a different universe to Glendale.

'Beth, are these straight?' Drew called out to me then, so I went over to check. I wrapped an arm around Izzy as we looked up. 'Perfect,' I said, giving her a squeeze. She grinned at me. Drew gave us a thumbs up and started to climb down the ladder.

I knew then that we'd made the right decision to come back. It felt like Christmas would really be a special one for us all.

Chapter Twenty-Six

We worked on the trail until we had completely lost the light, and then Sally called us all inside. 'You folks deserve this, I think,' she said as we walked into the cosy, bright lit kitchen. The smell of the chilli hit my nostrils instantly, and my stomach rumbled on cue. Everyone grabbed a plate and queued up for Sally to spoon chilli and rice onto their plates and then we crowded around the table. Mum was pouring wine and handing out beers, her hair for once wavy and free around her face, and she looked happier than I had seen her since we arrived.

'Working outside suits you,' I told her as I took a glass of wine from her. She, of course, had a large glass on the go for herself already but I couldn't begrudge her that.

'You too,' she replied with a smile. I knew she was right. Being outside in the garden had given me a glow that I hadn't had in a long time. I hadn't quite realised just how much I'd missed gardening, and I was already wondering what I could do about that when I was back in London. I sat down next to Izzy as we tucked in. I don't think we have tasted a better meal than we did that night.

'Sal, I need the recipe for this, it's so good,' I said, knowing that I'd never get it to taste quite like she made it.

'I'll have to give you my recipe for mac and cheese,' Drew said. 'It's taken me years, but I have perfected it now.'

'Have you ever uttered a more American sentence?' I teased him.

'What's mac and cheese?' Izzy asked. Drew described it for her. 'Pasta and cheese, why have we not had this before?' she demanded of me.

'We have but we used a packet mix, and it was awful.'

'Right, that's it, I'm going to make it for you,' Drew declared.

'Yay,' Izzy said, going back to her food. I smiled across at him, pleased that he wanted to cook us a meal. Izzy. Cook for Izzy, I corrected myself, feeling my cheeks grow warm.

My phone buzzed with a message from Heather – a picture of the banner in progress. I showed the table, to murmurs of approval, and replied to her to say it was looking good. 'I think this trail might give the one at Kew a run for its money,' I said to Izzy.

'What is it like?' Drew asked. 'I've never been.'

'I'll show you our pictures of it,' I said. We had had a lovely evening, Izzy and I, walking the trail on a crisp December evening, mesmerised by the lights, and I hoped if we could capture some of that magic, everyone in Glendale would have a lovely time and remember just how special our community was.

After we finished the chilli, followed by chocolate cake, we helped Sally clear everything up, and then everyone started to disperse. Drew showed no signs of wanting to leave, so after Mum went up to check on Gran, I took him into the living room with Izzy and pulled out my laptop so I could show him what the Kew trail had looked like. We sat side by side on the sofa, and Izzy curled up in the armchair and put on *Home Alone* again after falling asleep last time. Sally had draped the mantelpiece in holly and berries from the garden lending a wild festiveness to the room, and we were perfectly cosy with the fire lit underneath it.

'It looks stunning,' Drew said, looking at the photos on my laptop. 'But they don't have an inflatable Santa, and we do.' He smiled across at me. 'Do you think the council will think again?'

'I really hope so. I hate the idea of just giving up and letting the village go.'

'Even though you don't live here any more?' he asked, gently, seeming interested in why I cared so much.

I closed the laptop and leaned back against the sofa. 'It never left me though. I fought for so long, and so hard, to make a new home for myself, so much so that I thought I'd left it behind. But coming back, and seeing it so changed, it has upset me. More than I ever thought it would. I want to help get it back to how it was. Back to the Glendale I remember.'

'I understand. I may live far away from Glendale, but I don't think it's ever stopped feeling like home, you know?'

'I know what you mean,' I agreed. I looked over at Izzy who chuckled at the film. I suddenly wished I hadn't kept this place from her for so long. If only I had known what Gran revealed earlier then we maybe we could have spent every Christmas at the Hall. But at least we were here now. She yawned then. 'Iz, you should go up to bed: it's been a long day, and it's getting late.'

'Just a bit longer, please? The film is nearly finished,' she pleaded, giving me puppy-dog eyes.

I sighed. 'Okay but straight to sleep then, no reading.'

Izzy nodded. 'Okay, Mum. Could I have a cup of tea, though?'

'Actually, that's a good idea, I fancy one too. Drew?' I asked, getting up.

'I should be going soon,' Drew said, looking at his watch.

'Have a cup and then head out,' I suggested.

He came with me to the dimly lit kitchen as I put the kettle on and got out three mugs. I leaned against the counter to wait for it to boil and watched as Drew looked at a photo propped up by the sink. It was a school photo of Izzy when she was eight. I remembered sending it to my parents, never knowing they had put it out on display. I saw a shadow pass over his face, and I felt the lump in my throat return. I hurriedly made the teas, trying to pull myself together, though I couldn't stop thinking about how much time together the two of them had lost.

'Are you all right?' Drew said, from behind me.

Reluctantly, I turned around, sure that he could see my eyes glistening. 'Watching the two of you together today… it's my fault that you both missed out on that for all these years. I am so sorry.'

Drew was thoughtful for a moment but then he reached out and squeezed my hand once. 'I can't pretend that I haven't thought about all the milestones that I missed out on, but I do understand why you didn't tell me back then. I wouldn't have got on that plane if I had known.'

I nodded. 'I know.' I had always known that, which was why I had let him go without telling him.

'I'm glad that I know now. I can be there for the rest of it. I want to be here from now on, Beth.'

'I'm so glad,' I said. 'Izzy already loves you being here.' It would be tricky living in different countries, but I was pleased that Drew wanted to keep building a relationship with Izzy. It would mean the world to her. It meant the world to me, too.

'I love being here,' he replied, and he smiled, and it felt as if the past ten years had melted away.

We went back into the living room, and drank our tea, the film playing to itself as we chatted. I curled my legs up beside me on the sofa as I watched Drew and Izzy on the opposite one, talking about their favourite Christmas movies. It was everything I had always wished for.

And I let myself pretend for a moment that we were just like any other family.

Chapter Twenty-Seven

'It's Christmas week!' 'Izzy cried as she came into my room the following morning. She jumped on the bed, and I laughed as I sat up. The morning was only just beginning to lighten up and I could see frost covering the garden outside. It was clear and bright though – perfect for working on the trail. But before that, we had a town meeting to go to. Izzy was, however, more excited about how close we were to the Big Day, and I couldn't say I blamed her.

'This is your last chance, you know,' I told her, as I slid my feet into my slippers.

'Last chance for what?' she asked. She had finally learned that we were on holiday and was still in her PJs and dressing gown, although she was way more bright and chirpy than I could ever be at that hour.

'To make sure you're on the good list,' I said, pulling on my own dressing gown.

She gave me A Look. 'Mum, we've been through this. I know it's you that gets me the presents. And even if he was real then you know I'd be on the good list. You, on the other hand…'

'Hey!' I picked up a pillow and tossed it at her. She ducked and giggled. It was a shame she no longer believed in Father Christmas, another sign that she was fast growing up.

When we went to the kitchen, Mum was at the table drinking coffee, and Sally greeted us with a big smile as she made scrambled eggs. Izzy bounced over to her, telling Sally that I was grumpy and needed coffee and asked if she could please have some juice. I joined Mum at the table. She looked as if she hadn't slept.

'Are you okay?' I asked when I sat down.

'Not really. I was up half the night. Your grandmother is not doing well. And your father didn't bother coming home at all,' she said in a low voice so the others couldn't hear us in the kitchen. 'I just hope this meeting goes well today.' We had booked the village hall and invited everyone we knew in Glendale, trying to spread the word as far as we could, not only to publicise the council's plans, but to draw support for our trail and see if there were any businesses interested in coming back to the high street. We didn't have much time left.

'I'll go up and see Gran before we go into Glendale,' I told her. I felt bad that all the strain of my grandmother's illness was on her shoulders. I knew I needed to step up despite all the pain of the past clouding us. But my dad I was less sure about. 'Where do you think he is?' I asked quickly as Izzy was heading our way.

'With *her* I assume,' she replied, draining her coffee dry. She stood up. 'I need a long shower.'

I sighed, thinking my dad had a lot to answer for around here. Izzy and I tucked into our scrambled eggs and toast, and I hoped that the day would turn around for my mum.

'Can Drew come back for dinner after the meeting?' Izzy asked then.

'If he wants to,' I said with a smile. She was keen to spend every moment she could with him.

'Is there enough food, Sally?' she asked.

'Of course,' Sally replied, crossly, as if it was an insult to suggest that there wouldn't be.

'Can I text him, Mum?'

'Go on,' I said, pushing my phone across the table to her. 'I'll go up and see Gran.'

'We really should get him something for Christmas, shouldn't we?' Izzy said to my retreating back.

'Okay, you have a think about what you want to give him,' I replied, smiling at how excited she was. It was all I'd ever wanted for her.

–

I walked up to Gran's room. The curtains were drawn back to let in the morning light, and she was propped up on her pillows, her eyes opening as I went in. I saw immediately why my mum was worried. Gran's skin looked almost grey. She weakly nodded at me as I perched at the side of her bed. Her breathing was laboured now. It seemed to take much more effort than it should for her to look at me. 'How are you doing?'

'I'm okay. You have your big meeting today Caroline said? I hope you can help the village, Beth.'

'Me too,' I replied, frowning because she was clearly not okay.

'And you've been seeing a lot of Drew?'

'Drew and Izzy are really becoming close,' I replied, smiling at his name. I couldn't help it.

She smiled, too. 'I'm glad. What matters now is the future. I wish I could be around to see it. Promise me that you'll always focus on your family. You and Izzy, and your mother. You need to look out for each other. I have done a poor job at that,' she said, coughing a little. 'I loved you, though, all of you, very much, even if I didn't show it like I should have done.' I winced at her already talking about herself in the past tense. 'I hope one day you will realise that.'

I reached out and touched her hand again. It felt too cold for my liking. 'Every one of us has made mistakes. You're not alone in that. I wish I could have spent more time here with you all, but what is done is done. All we can do now is try to make it right. Do our best from now on.'

'Maybe it was a good thing that you left us, because you've turned into a special woman and raised a daughter to be proud of. Maybe we would have stopped that from happening. We have been a mess these years. We have lost our way. But now you're here to help this family. You may think you're saving Glendale, Beth, but you're saving us.'

'I don't know about that. Dad didn't come home last night.'

Gran closed her eyes briefly then opened them. It seemed to take her a moment to gather enough strength to speak. 'It might be better for everyone if he does leave,' Gran said then. 'Sometimes you have to let go to be happy. You know that, Beth. Your mother and David haven't been happy for a very long time. Perhaps now you're here they are finally realising that. That's okay, you know. Some things come to an end as others are beginning. That's the way of life. Look at you, and me, here now. My life might be coming to an end, but yours is just beginning.' She closed her eyes again – and I felt a burst of panic – but then I saw her chest rising and falling. She had just fallen asleep.

Carefully, I let go of her hand and climbed off the bed, trying not to disturb her. Perhaps she was right that this Christmas was a crossroads, not only for the village, but the family, for all of us. It certainly felt that way.

Chapter Twenty-Eight

Glendale Village Hall was behind the church, and I remembered having some parties there as a kid – discos where the boys stood on one side, skidding on the floor on their knees, and the girls on the other in their pretty dresses, wondering if anyone was going to ask them to dance. It still smelled the same. Like floor varnish and bleach. I joined Heather and my mum at the front facing the room lined with chairs that were starting to fill up. They had conjured up most of the village between them, I was pleased to see.

Drew arrived then and came over to me. 'Well, this is a great turnout. And thank you for the dinner invitation.'

Izzy bounded over. 'Drew, I saved a seat for you by me!' she said, tugging on his hand.

'Good luck,' he said quickly to me, letting her pull him away.

Mum called everyone to order then. 'Thank you all for coming,' she said, her voice clear and loud after she had introduced the three of us to the room. On the roof, I could hear a light pattering of rain. I looked out at the faces in front of us, most I recognised in some way, and I felt proud that we had managed to get everyone together in one room. Now we just needed to get them all behind us. 'When Beth came back to Glendale, she was shocked at how much the village had changed,' Mum said. I looked at her in surprise: I hadn't known she was going to talk about me. 'She immediately wanted to know what was going on, and what we could do to help. To be honest, I brushed her off at first. I thought that the idea of this village was defunct now. That we didn't have a community any more. That the best thing would be for the high street to be turned into flats. But she has shown me that I was wrong. Heather, you felt the same, didn't you?' she asked, turning to Heather.

'I work in the library, and when the council told me it was going to be shut down, I was heartbroken. I know so many people who live alone and might not speak to anyone else all day, but they know they can come to the library, or the shops, or the pub and see people and get what they need. When I was younger, this place was always busy. Our community was strong. I know that times are changing and many of us go into Glenmarshes, or to Inverness, to do our shopping and we don't think we need each other as much any more, but that seems like a real shame to me. I want Glendale to be a place I'm proud to live in again, don't you?' There were a few nods and murmurs of agreement around the room. 'We've spoken to the council who have given us until the fifth of January to come up with ways we can save our village, and that's why we called this meeting – to see how we can work together to do just that.'

I stepped forward then and told them about our Christmas trail idea. 'We are hopeful we can show the council there is still a community here but, to be honest, with them I think it's mostly about the money. They need to fill the empty shops. And we don't know if there's anyone who would want to help to do that?'

A man at the back stood up. 'I used to run the bakery, but the council doubled the rent and then I just couldn't afford it. Are they going to cut them?'

'They haven't budged on rents at the moment,' Mum said. 'If we put the rents to one side, do we think anyone would want to go back to the high street, and would people actually shop here again if they did?'

A lively debate followed.

'I wouldn't bother coming to the village: there would never be everything I need here like there is in Inverness,' a woman said at one point.

Mrs Smith, my old piano teacher, got up then to disagree. 'The only reason I stopped shopping locally was because the shops disappeared. If they came back, it would be much easier for me. I don't drive and the bus is ridiculous, one an hour and so slow… I'd much rather walk into Glendale for what I need.'

'I've always liked the idea of opening a farm shop,' Rory said at one point. 'Ever since the supermarket cut our contract, we have been struggling to sell our produce and keep everything afloat. But as you said, Tom, I couldn't afford high rents, I'd make no profit.'

I glanced at Drew who looked worried about what Rory had said. Clearly the farm had been struggling. Like me, Drew had been too far away to do anything about it.

'If we can make the Christmas trail a success and go to the council with businesses willing to open up, then maybe they would make a deal on rents,' I said. 'We just need to convince them that they need to go with us and not sell to this development company.'

'Hang on,' a lady said then. I vaguely recognised her. She stood up and faced us. 'Isn't your husband behind this development company? What does he think of you trying to block this deal?'

My mum cleared her throat. 'The development company are doing this for business reasons. They see that they can make a profit by turning the high street shops into flats. They aren't thinking about the impact that would have on our village. But we know the impact it would have. We are the ones living here. So, we need to show the council another way. We need to try to make this the best place to live that we can. For all of us.' Mum ended her speech passionately. I looked around at nodding heads. I was impressed with how she had steered the conversation away from Dad. Mum should really have gone into politics.

The woman who had asked the question sat back down. 'I just didn't want there to be a conflict of interest for you. I think this is a good idea, if we can actually pull it off.'

'I think we can,' Mum told her firmly. 'Right, come and see us if you want to go on the list as being interested in opening a business on the high street, and please take one of Heather's leaflets for the festive trail at the Hall. If anyone has any other thoughts, please do let us know. We can only save Glendale if we do it together.' There was an enthusiastic round of applause and then everyone hit the tea table.

'I think that went well,' Mum said to me and Heather. 'And I'm wondering whether to put my own name on the list. Don't you think we could have a Glendale Hall shop, Beth? We could sell plants and flowers grown in the garden, and make other products, too.'

I stared at my mother. 'Really? That sounds great but it would be a lot of work.'

'Well, I have plenty of time for it,' she replied, before walking off to talk to the minister. I watched her go, amazed. She was definitely getting back to the determined woman I had grown up with. It would be perfect for her to have a project like that. I worried it was going to be lonely for her once Izzy and I left; Gran wouldn't be around for much longer it seemed like, and who knew if my dad would return. And I wouldn't be there to help her either.

'Your mum is amazing,' Heather said. 'I'm coming to the Hall after this so I can show you the banner and help with anything you need for the trail. I can't thank you enough for this, Beth.'

I smiled. 'Don't thank me yet, we don't know if this going to work.'

'That doesn't matter. You have brought everyone together, and that's a huge achievement in itself.' She squeezed my arm and went off to talk to a group standing by the biscuits.

I allowed myself to feel good about what she had said. I looked around the room and it was lovely to see everyone animated about fighting back. My eyes found Drew standing with Izzy. I went over to them. 'What did you think?'

'You did a great job: everyone will rally around, I'm sure of it,' Drew said. He nodded to where Rory was talking to Heather. 'I was thinking of making that mac and cheese I promised you, Iz. Shall I ask Rory and Heather, too? Something tells me they'd be keen for a dinner party.'

I followed his gaze. 'I think you might be right,' I replied. I turned back to him and we smiled at one another. I never thought I'd be trying to matchmake Heather and Rory with Drew a couple of weeks before, but there we were, and it felt right somehow.

Chapter Twenty-Nine

When we got back to the Hall, Izzy, Drew and I went outside to see how the trail was getting on.

'The sleigh has arrived,' John called when he saw us stepping out into the garden. 'Come and see!' Izzy tore after him and, laughing, Drew and I followed her through the trail – which was really coming together now – to the tent that was becoming the grotto. The sleigh was huge and ornate, painted red and gold, and would soon be filled with presents. It took up most of the grotto, but it did look amazing.

'Wow,' Izzy spoke our thoughts aloud.

'It works, doesn't it?' John said. 'And when my friend found out why we were doing this, he said we can use it for free. The convenience store in the village is letting us have some chocolates to give away as presents, too.'

'Everyone has been so generous,' I replied. 'I knew the community was still here, it just needed teasing out. Surely the council won't be able to deny that when they see all of this?'

'Let's hope not. Right, I better cover everything, the weather isn't looking good,' John said, marching out at his usual rapid pace. I could tell he was thoroughly enjoying himself on this project.

'Can I sit in it?' Izzy asked. Drew lifted her into the sleigh, and she perched on the wooden bench. 'It's a shame we can't have reindeer as well. You should get some on your farm.'

Drew chuckled. 'I'll pass your suggestion on to Rory.' He winked at me, and I laughed at the idea of Rory looking after reindeer.

'I can't wait to see it all lit up,' Izzy said as we made our way back to the house. 'Do you think it'll be better than the one at Kew, Mum? I think it will.'

'It'll be smaller scale but no less magical,' I told her. 'It's been fun making it all, hasn't it?' She nodded. 'I've missed working outdoors,' I admitted. I looked around at the trees in the twilight, leaning in the breeze, guiding our way back to the Hall. It was hard to think I'd have to say goodbye to it all again soon.

'If it's something you want to do,' Drew said, looking across at me, 'then you should find a way to do it.'

I was surprised at his words but perhaps he was right. I had taken my job for its usefulness with Izzy, not because I had any passion for it, but it was tough when everything came down to you. 'Maybe one day,' I replied. Maybe when Izzy was older and didn't need me to be at home as much. But I couldn't see how I could find something that would pay what I currently made straightaway; I'd be starting at the bottom especially with no qualifications, and that wouldn't work with all the bills I had to pay.

I saw Drew frown a little at my response, but we went into the kitchen, then, where Mum was chatting to Sally as she prepared the meal, so he didn't say any more. Being a doctor was such a vocation, it was probably hard for him to put himself in my shoes and think about doing a job he didn't really want to just for the money, but I knew I was far from alone in doing just that.

'Let's eat in here,' my mum suggested. She seemed to be thriving organising the trail and the village and seemed to be relaxing a little more. She helped Sally bring over the food to the kitchen table, and we all sat down together to eat the lasagne, salad and crunchy bread. 'So, Drew, how is everything in Boston? Do you ever get homesick for Glendale?' Mum asked as she sipped her wine.

'I do,' Drew admitted. 'But, to be honest, I'm usually working such long hours there isn't a lot of time to dwell on it. When I come back here, though, it hits me. Especially this year because the farm isn't doing as well as we would like. I wish I could be here to help out more, you know? Rory is excited about maybe opening up a farm shop though.'

Mum nodded. 'I think it's a really good idea. I'm just hoping we can do something to make it financially viable. That's why so many businesses left the village – the high rents. It's so short-sighted of the council. Surely they would rather have thriving shops paying a fair rent than an empty high street because they're charging too much?'

'But now they've had the offer from New Horizons, they don't have a great incentive to change,' I said.

'They will after they see the trail and how much people want to keep the village,' Drew replied. 'At the end of the day, they won't want to do something they can see is that unpopular, surely?'

'We shall have to wait and see,' Mum said. 'At least the trail is coming on beautifully.'

'I had a quick look,' Sally said. 'I'm amazed at how fast you have pulled it all together.'

'We've had so much help,' I agreed, pleased that so many people had pitched in.

'It's been a lot of fun,' Drew said, smiling. 'It's true that there is more of a community here. I barely know any of my neighbours at home.'

'Same for us,' I agreed. I was always too busy to reach out to anyone in our building. We all had such busy lives it was easy just to pass by one another without saying anything. 'That's why I think it's so important for us to fight for Glendale.'

'Here's to Glendale,' Izzy said, raising her glass of squash. We all lifted our glasses and toasted the village along with her. I really hoped that all our hard work would pay off. It would be so sad to leave for London and know that the village wouldn't be there waiting for us.

After dinner, Izzy begged Drew to stay and watch a film with her, so they went to set it up, and I helped Sally clear up while Mum went to take Gran some food, not that she was able to eat much.

'It's lovely to see how close Drew and Izzy are becoming,' Sally commented as I carried over the plates to her at the dishwasher.

'I know,' I agreed. 'I honestly never thought they'd be together this Christmas.'

'Glendale brings people together,' Sally said. She gave me a shrewd look. 'You look worried.'

'I was just thinking about what is going to happen after Christmas. I can't imagine us going back down to London and Drew flying off to America. It's like we're in this bubble up here. I just don't want it to end.'

'I'm sure both of you will be able to make it work: there are so many ways to keep in touch nowadays. Right?'

I sighed as I wiped down the counter. 'I know. It'll be hard for Izzy, though, to say goodbye.'

'And for you,' she said, raising an eyebrow at me. 'I can see how happy you are that he's back in your life.'

'Is it that obvious?'

Sally smiled. 'Perhaps only to me. You seem so much lighter already. Happier. As if a weight's been lifted off your shoulders. And you light up when you're around him. This place is good for you, and so is he.'

'Is it crazy to feel that way?' I asked, admitting maybe for the first time to myself, and certainly to anyone else, that he did still light me up.

'Not to me. My husband was my childhood sweetheart. I never loved anyone but him.'

'I'm sorry you lost him, Sally. I know how much you still miss him.'

She nodded. 'That's why if you do have feelings for Drew now then don't let him go back to America without knowing. Life is too short. People can be taken from you in an instant. Grab any chance of happiness while you can.'

I knew she was right, but our situation was so complicated. 'How could he feel the same after what I did?' I said, biting my lip. I really didn't think he could be that forgiving of the past. But I couldn't stop my heart from wishing it.

'You'll never know unless you ask.' Sally patted my shoulder as she passed me. 'You deserve to be happy, Beth. You just need to decide what will make you happy and then go out and grab it.'

It sounded so simple coming from her lips. I thought back to Drew telling me I should go after a job that would fill me with passion. And now Sally was saying I should follow my heart. I wanted to follow their advice, I knew that I should, but life wasn't always that straightforward, was it?

I went to find Izzy and Drew and saw them curled up on the sofa together watching *Elf*. I stood in the doorway, leaning against the frame, watching them. My lips curved into a smile. My two favourite people in the world. Sally was right about one thing, though – I felt as if everything had changed since we'd come to Glendale, and I really didn't want things to go back to the way they were before.

Chapter Thirty

The next morning, I came in from the garden where we were working hard to finish up the trail, to grab an extra jumper, and walked straight into my dad in the hallway. The Christmas tree lit up the room against the grey clouds outside. Light was rapidly fading, and we were all out there working as hard and as fast as we could to get the trail ready for the grand Christmas Eve opening. Dad was carrying a case and his coat, and he jumped when he saw me. Evidently, he had been hoping to come in and go out again without any of us seeing him.

'Dad, what are you doing?' I asked. Just as Glendale was coming together, my family was fracturing. My father looked tired and unshaven.

Sighing, he put his bag on the floor. 'I'm checking into a hotel for Christmas.'

'Seriously? But Izzy and I have come home to spend Christmas with you all.'

'I'll still come over for Christmas Day lunch but it's best that I don't stay. Your mother and I need some time apart. And I really can't stay here with all of that going on outside.' He waved his hand in the direction of the garden. 'I can't be seen to support your trail, Beth. I am on the board of the company trying to develop the high street shops. How would it look if I was here helping you stop them?'

'It's all about how things look for you, Dad, yet you're happy to bulldoze the place you've lived for thirty years. How does that look? Like you care more about money than people, that you don't believe in community or your own family? I don't understand.'

'I love her, Beth. Cathy – I love her.'

I sighed; I couldn't believe he was doing this to my mum. 'Why are you not staying with her then?'

He wouldn't meet my eyes. 'She will be with her husband over Christmas.'

'Wow, Dad. You're not only breaking up your own marriage but hers too. Is it really worth it?'

'I won't stand here and explain myself to my daughter.' He picked up his bag again. 'We were fine until you came back and poked your nose into everything. Your mother knew about Cathy and it didn't bother her before.'

'You can't really believe that,' I snapped at him, furious that he was blaming me for all of this. 'Of course, it bothered her! She's devastated. How can you not see that? She's looking after her sick mother, and all you care about is what your other woman thinks. You're so selfish.'

He snorted. 'Coming from the girl who has hidden herself away for ten years. Where were you when Margaret got sick? In London. You only came back because I begged you to.'

I hated that he was right. I had left my mum to deal with way too much on her own. 'I'm here now, and I am going to keep poking my nose into things. Because you're wrong. About everything. We're going to save Glendale, and I'm going to make sure Mum knows she is worth so much more than being stuck in an unhappy, loveless marriage.' I spun around and ran up the stairs, my hands shaking slightly. I was so angry with my dad. He was right though. Mum had had to deal with so much alone. I couldn't change not having been there before, but now I was back, I was going to help as much as I could.

After I put on an extra jumper, I popped my head into Gran's room. 'Do you need anything?'

'I heard raised voices,' she said, looking away from the book she had been reading.

'Dad came back to pick up some things: he's going to stay in a hotel. I'm dreading telling Mum,' I told her.

'This has been a long time coming, Beth.'

'He basically told me it's all my fault.'

'If giving people the encouragement they need to make changes is wrong then you're doing an excellent job. I have never advocated a marriage splitting up, you know that, but times are different now, and your father has shown himself to be incapable of being the man I thought he was once. You will be there for your mother, won't you? After I'm gone I mean. She will need you, and Izzy. She has never been alone, you know.'

'I know. I'll help her, don't worry.'

'This is helping you too, isn't it? I can see the old spark in your eyes is back. Glendale is good for you. Don't fight it. I think you're exactly where you need to be.'

I watched as she went back to her book. I wondered if she was right that a spark had returned in me. I left her to it and made my way back out into the garden. Seeing Izzy come to life here had warmed my heart. We were surrounded by family, which I had missed even if I hadn't allowed myself to admit it. There was also the relief of everything being out in the open. No more secrets. The pain of the past seemed further away than it ever had. And there was Drew. He was back in our lives. And that was making both me and Izzy happy.

I hadn't even realised that my spark had been missing but years of raising Izzy alone, dealing with everything myself, had dampened it. It wasn't just Izzy who had come to life at Glendale Hall I knew then. I had too.

I looked at Heather shouting to John and another man to move the banner up a bit to make it straight, and I headed over to them. She had drawn the huge banner with festive flourishes and the words were bright red and green; it brought a big smile to my face.

Glendale Hall Christmas Trail

'What do you think?' she asked me.

'I love it.' I wrapped an arm around her shoulder and squeezed her. 'You're a genius.'

'I better not tell you that I had to start over when I realised I had written 'trial' and not 'trail' then.' She looked at me and we both started giggling.

I spotted my mum then and hurried over to her. 'I just saw Dad,' I said, falling into step with her as she headed towards the winter wonderland, her arms full of holly and ivy for it. 'He's going to stay at a hotel.'

She sighed. 'Typical of him to not even talk to me about it. I don't think that man has ever had an honest conversation his whole life.' She glared at me. 'There's no need to look so worried. Right now, I'm focused on getting this trail ready and making sure we all have a lovely Christmas. I will deal with your father after that.'

'This isn't my fault, is it? That you two are fighting. I mean, all of this…'

'You've given me a kick up the backside when I needed it the most, that's all,' she replied. 'Now, come on, we need to decorate the fireplace,' she said, ducking through the entrance to the grotto.

'Yes, sir,' I muttered but I smiled as I followed her inside; it finally felt as if Mum and I were putting the past behind us and growing closer. We'd always be different, but we had a common purpose right now and I thought we were making a pretty good team.

Chapter Thirty-One

The day before Christmas Eve dawned bright and sunny, if freezing cold.

We were all in the garden at the trail: Mum, Sally, Izzy and me, John, Heather and her dad. The banner was swinging slightly in the breeze, and the inflatable snowman and Santa were smiling and ready to greet guests. All the lights were in the perfect place. Excitement flooded through my veins. It looked magical even before it was all lit up, and I was sure that everyone would be impressed.

John was standing by the generator. 'Right, I think it's time to test everything and make sure all the lights are working.'

'Five!' I cried, and the others joined in loudly, Izzy's voice above the rest. John rolled his eyes but waited for us to count down anyway. 'Four! Three! Two! One!'

John pulled the levers down, and the generator started up. We turned around, but nothing happened. The trail stayed dark.

'Uh-oh,' I said.

'What's happened?' Izzy asked, her face falling in dismay.

'I have no idea,' John said, frowning. 'Right, we need to check everything.' He rushed over to the cables to check them, and we all fanned out looking for anything amiss. My heart sank. We were due to open tomorrow and our trail was dark – had we failed before we'd even started?

'Oops!' Heather was waving frantically so I hurried over to her. 'Look,' she said, pointing down to her feet. Her spikey boot was standing on a cable. She pointed, and I could see she had pulled it out of a socket: the cables were all on a loop, so it had stopped any electricity getting to the lights.

'Seriously, you need to get a pair of wellie boots,' I said, remembering what Rory had said to her at the farm. 'John, we've found the problem!' I called him over, shaking my head.

The others all joined us. John looked at Heather. 'Don't you dare turn up tomorrow wearing those,' he said, grumbling under his breath as he went to sort the issue.

'Honestly, my boots are being discriminated against,' Heather said, her cheeks pink.

'No countdown this time,' John said then, reaching for the levers once again. I crossed my fingers as he pulled them down.

We watched as all the lights around us came on. I breathed a sigh of relief as Izzy cheered beside me.

'All's well that ends well,' Heather said, cheerfully.

I laughed, unable to believe our trail had almost been called off because of her boots. We slowly walked down the trail. We couldn't see the full effect in the daylight, but the lights twinkled through holly and berries, reindeer sparkled in front of the oak trees, and the glow of the Santa's grotto could be seen from far away, beckoning you into its warmth. It was full of festive magic already, and I knew it would be stunning at night.

'It's perfect,' Mum said, smiling at me.

We went into the grotto. Inside was dark enough for us to see the lights draped over the sleigh, and across the ceiling of the tent, and the piles of presents, which glittered in red and gold ready to be claimed by the children. I knew that everyone would be excited to see it, which made me think it had all been worthwhile even if the council didn't come around to our thinking, but I desperately hoped that they would.

'All that's missing is Christmas music,' Izzy said then.

I turned to her. 'You're right! We need music. I have just the thing. Come and help me, Iz.' We left the others and went back to the house, Izzy following me up to my room.

I went to the wardrobe and shifted under everything until I found an old box, relieved that it was still there.

'What's that?' Izzy asked from her perch on the edge of my bed.

'A boom box. We can put it in the tent and play one of our Christmas CDs for everyone.' I took it out of the box. 'I used to listen to music on this as I did my make-up before I went out to meet your dad. You know, you were named after our favourite song.'

'Can I hear it?'

I had played it for her before, but I always indulged her. I found it on my iPhone, and we listened to the singer crooning about his lost love 'Isabelle'. I closed my eyes and pictured me and Drew dancing to it together. We had never dreamed in that moment that we would have a little girl together. I wondered what our younger selves would say if they could have looked into the future.

'You look sad, Mum,' Izzy said when the song had finished.

'Just thinking back to hearing that song for the first time, that's all.' I smiled at her. And then I played the song all over again.

–

The fairy lights we had bought with Drew at the garden centre greeted us as I parked outside the farmhouse. We were the only car: Heather hadn't arrived yet.

The earlier sunshine had faded away, and a cloudy afternoon had taken its place. Izzy jumped out of the car and raced to the door to ring the bell. I followed more slowly, feeling a little nervous. I had changed my outfit twice. I had settled on black jeans, my cashmere jumper, a pretty scarf and boots, and I had attempted to straighten my hair. Izzy had put on her green dress, and I had styled her hair into two plaits.

'Hi, guys.' Drew opened the door with a wide smile, and I felt slightly more at ease. He hugged Izzy and gave me a kiss on the cheek as we walked through into the house. He was wearing a dark shirt and jeans, and I tried not to drink in the smell of his musky aftershave. It was the one he had always worn and the familiarity of it was disconcerting.

'Rory has gone to pick up Heather as her dad needed their car tonight,' Drew explained. 'They won't be long.'

'Something smells good,' I said, as he led us through to the living room.

'I've made my signature dish as promised,' he said. 'Let me get us some drinks. Take a seat, make yourselves at home.'

It was a simple sentence, but it still made my pulse speed up a little. I sat down on the sofa, and Izzy went over to look at his Christmas tree standing at the edge of the room. 'Let's put his present under here,' she said. I took it out of her bag and passed it to her. 'There are two here for us,' she hissed at me. I was immediately curious as to what he could have got for me.

Drew returned with wine for the two of us and a Coke for Izzy, who stepped away from the tree quickly, and he turned on the radio softly. 'Merry Christmas,' he said, raising his glass. We returned the toast and took a sip of our drinks. 'I'm glad we're all here together,' he added.

'As we're not seeing you on Christmas Day, maybe we should open our presents now,' Izzy suggested, trying to look solemn as she said it.

Drew chuckled. 'As we're waiting for the others, I think that's a good idea actually.'

'Go on then,' I said, smiling. I knew that Christmas to Izzy was really all about the presents: it was for us all when we were kids. And this was the first year she'd get one from her dad, so I couldn't blame her for being eager to see it.

'Open ours first!' Izzy rushed over to the tree to grab it. She went to sit beside him on the sofa, and we watched as he unwrapped the silver paper and pulled out a photo album. 'It was Mum's idea,' she said.

'Well, I wanted you to have something that might fill in some of Izzy's childhood for you. I know it'll never be the same... it's not a consolation...' I stopped babbling and tried to smile. 'We just wanted you to see everything.' We'd had our favourite photos on my phone printed out for him, and Izzy had put them all in an album.

'That's really thoughtful,' he said, looking across at me. He smiled a little and then opened it up. 'Tell me what the photos are of then,' he said to Izzy. I sat back and sipped my wine as Izzy and Drew took a journey through her childhood. I had documented as much as I could, perhaps thinking that one day he might get to see it, but also because of how much all of it meant to me. I could see it affected him. He paused over each photo, asking questions, listening and smiling at his daughter now as he compared her to the pictures. His voice broke a couple of times, and I saw a tear escape his eye when he saw her first school photo. It was painful to see how much he regretted missing those years, and I felt guilty, but he smiled as well, and

I knew he was touched by our gift. It was a real mixture of emotions for all of us I think.

'That really was the perfect gift,' Drew said. 'Right, time for you two.' He got up and grabbed one from the tree. 'This is for you, Iz.'

Izzy ripped into hers quickly. She pulled out a Harry Potter notebook.

'I thought as you loved reading so much that maybe you should start writing your own stories,' Drew said. 'And I thought what better than a notebook to write them down in?'

'I love it!' she squealed. 'Thank you, Dad,' she cried, giving him a big hug.

I started. It was the first time she had called him that. Drew's eyes met mine, and he beamed. I could see how much it meant to him for her to call him Dad, and my heart swelled with warmth.

'Look, Mum,' she said, coming over to show me.

'That's such a great idea. I bet you could write a great story,' I told her, giving her a squeeze. 'I can't wait to read it.'

'Time for your gift now,' Drew said, passing a small box to me. His eyes met mine as our fingers brushed, and I felt a shiver run down my spine.

I opened up the present, wishing my heart wasn't beating quite so hard. I was worried that they'd be able to hear it. When I opened the box, I let out a small gasp. I pulled out the delicate chain which had a crescent moon and small star hanging from it. Drew had bought it for me for my sixteenth birthday, but I had left it in his car before he had gone to America. 'You kept it all these years?' I asked him, slipping it through my fingers.

'I thought you might one day come back for it,' he replied. 'Here let me put it on.' He jumped up and lifted it around my neck. I tried to keep my breathing steady as he held up my hair to do it up. 'I got this for your mum when she was sixteen,' he explained to Izzy. 'It was to remind her that wherever in the world we were, we were still both under the same moon and stars.'

'I missed it,' I managed to whisper.

'Can I see?' Izzy came over to look at it. 'It's so pretty.'

'Just like your mum,' he replied, and then looked a little startled by his words. I kept my eyes on Izzy, not daring myself to let my eyes meet his. I touched the pendant. I had always seen it as a good luck charm, and I hoped that it still would be.

We heard the front door open then, and Drew jumped up to greet Heather and Rory, Izzy hurrying out after them.

I stayed where I was for a moment, still touching the necklace, my heart beating hard beneath it.

Chapter Thirty-Two

'Right, I think our food will be ready now so let's go into the kitchen,' Drew called out then.

I got up and followed them into the kitchen. Heather gave me a hug. She looked lovely in a velvet dress, and Rory looked the smartest I had ever seen him as he poured out wine for all of the grown-ups. Drew was lighting candles on the table, and Izzy was putting out cutlery. I sat down at the table and took a long sip of wine. Butterflies were still dancing in my stomach at Drew's words earlier, and the necklace he had given back to me felt like it was burning a hole straight through to my heart.

'Right, direct from America, my signature dish,' Drew said, when everyone was sat at the table, carrying over a steaming bowl. He lifted the lid with a flourish and we all leaned forwards to breathe in its delicious smell.

'I feel two stone heavier already,' I commented as he handed me a plateful of macaroni and cheese, bubbling, with crispy pancetta on top.

'Calories don't count at Christmas,' Izzy quipped.

I laughed. 'I think they are very wise words,' I said, tucking in. 'Wow, Drew, this is so good.'

'I told you it's world famous,' he said, with a grin.

'You're a modest cook, aren't you?' Rory joked to his brother.

'Sometimes you have to be honest about your qualities. What do you think, Iz?'

She just smiled as she tried to swallow a massive mouthful.

'I think she's a fan,' I replied. He looked at me across the table, and we shared a smile.

'So, are we all ready for tomorrow?' Heather asked as she tucked in.

'I think so,' I replied. 'Mum phoned the council to invite them along to the opening, so hopefully, someone will be there, and they'll see the village is worth saving.'

'I really hope so,' she replied. I knew how much it meant to her to keep the library from closing, and I hoped that we could do it.

We somehow polished off the mac and cheese, and then sat back, all feeling stuffed. What was it about Christmas that gave you the green light to eat twice as much as you usually would? Whatever it was, I was fully on board with it.

After we cleared up, we all went back into the living room. It was pitch black outside, but the room was warm and cosy. Drew closed the curtains and lit a candle on the mantelpiece. The smell of frankincense filled the room.

'Have you already opened presents?' Rory asked, looking at the tree.

'Well, we're not seeing one another tomorrow,' Drew explained with a shrug.

'In that case then...' Rory grabbed a package and handed it to a surprised Heather. 'You better have yours too.'

'For me?' she asked, staring at it.

'For you,' he confirmed. 'Go on then,' he said, turning to us with a wink. We watched as she ripped open the wrapping and pulled out a pair of sparkly silver Wellington boots. 'You said they had to be sparkly for you to wear them,' Rory said as Heather burst out laughing.

'Oh my God! I love them,' she said, jumping up and giving Rory a kiss on the cheek. To say he was now the surprised one was an understatement.

'Well, I expect to see them on you next time you come to the farm,' Rory said, sitting down, his cheeks a little pink.

'That sounds like an invitation,' Heather replied. Drew and I exchanged a smile; it was impossible not to notice their flirting. I wondered if they were even aware of it.

Drew turned to Izzy and me then. 'What do you both usually do on Christmas Day in London?'

'We usually go to Emily, Sally's niece who lives in London too, for lunch. Then we go back to our flat and watch a film or play a game together. It'll be strange to be at the Hall again. But nice, too.'

'I can't wait for Sally's food,' Izzy said. 'Do you think they will all play a game with us?'

'What's your favourite?' Drew asked her.

'Monopoly, but it's not fair because Mum is so good at it. She always wins.'

Drew raised an eyebrow at me. 'That sounds like a challenge.'

'Only if you can accept inevitable defeat,' I replied with a smile.

Heather and Rory's attention was called away from her boots, and Izzy set up the game on the coffee table; Drew bringing over more drinks, and a tub of Quality Street.

'I want to be the dog,' Izzy said. 'Mum, do you want the hat?'

'It's my good luck charm,' I said, grabbing it for myself.

'Go easy on us,' Drew said to me, smiling across the table.

'I'm sorry, guys,' I replied. 'But I'm not called The Champion for nothing.'

'No one calls you that,' Izzy piped up.

'Well, they should,' I replied.

'What is it about board games that makes everyone so competitive?' Rory asked. 'I remember Drew sulking for a week once when I beat him at Guess Who?'

'I did not sulk,' Drew retorted.

'You just either have it or you don't,' I replied. And he threw a cushion at me. 'Hey!' I spluttered. 'Seriously? How old are you?'

'Come on,' Izzy complained. 'Let's start.'

We quietened down to get the game going, and they were soon moaning that I was getting all the best properties. I just laughed. I loved this game. 'I can't afford any of these in real life so that's why the universe lets me have them in the game,' I told them.

'Is there a Scottish version? We should play that one up here,' Izzy said.

'I'll find out,' Drew promised. 'But I might not let your mum play it with us.'

'That's just sour grapes,' I said. I rolled the dice and landed on the property I had been eyeing to groans from the group.

'Don't let her have any sweets for that,' Rory said, snatching the tin from me.

'I warned you all,' Izzy said, in a sing-song voice, when the game was over and I'd won by a landslide.

'There might be money in this – we could hustle unsuspecting strangers,' Drew suggested.

'Hustle? Bro, you really need to leave Boston,' Rory told him. 'Right, we need more drinks!'

'Can I have a quick word?' Drew said quietly to me as Rory went to the kitchen and Heather and Izzy went to look at the other board games they had. I followed Drew out, curiously, and we walked into the hall. He grabbed a bag hidden behind the door. 'I bought Izzy a few more things: can we put them in your car, and you can surprise her Christmas morning?'

I smiled, touched by his thoughtfulness. She would love that. 'Of course.' We went outside into the cold night. The sky above us was clear and shining with stars. There was a stillness to the air, and I wondered whether more snow was on the horizon.

Drew carried the bag over to my car and heaved it into the boot.

'You didn't need to do that,' I said, as he shut it again.

'I wanted to. There's something else in there for you, too, something I actually paid for this time.'

'Nothing could top this,' I admitted, my hand reaching up to touch the necklace. I never wanted to take it off again. 'I still can't believe that you kept it for all these years.'

Drew smiled. 'It belongs to you, and I knew I'd see you again.'

'You did?'

'I knew one day you'd come back here. Glendale is your home. I can't imagine you in London, you know.'

'I can't really imagine you in Boston either.'

'Actually, I wanted to talk to you about something. Get your thoughts on it…'

'Oh?'

'Not now. We better be getting back.' Drew nodded towards the house. He looked up. 'The stars are out tonight.'

'It feels like it might snow.'

'Izzy would love a white Christmas, wouldn't she?' He looked at me, and we shared a smile. 'I certainly didn't expect to be spending time with my daughter when I came back.'

'Coming home really has been full of surprises,' I agreed. Not least the reigniting of all my old feelings for Drew. Alone, under the stars, I looked across at him and I wished I knew how he felt about me.

'It certainly has,' he agreed. He ran a hand through his hair. 'Maybe I should tell you now. I…' He began, looking a little nervous. It was impossible to stop hope from flooding through my veins. Maybe he felt this was a moment, too. He was about to continue when we heard gravel crunching; light suddenly flooded the driveway. Confused, Drew turned, and I followed his gaze to watch a car drive up to the farmhouse. 'Who could this be?' He wondered aloud.

The car stopped by us, clearly a taxi, and out of the backseat emerged a pretty, blonde woman. I looked at Drew whose mouth had dropped open.

She climbed out, and then the taxi driver got out and went around to the boot to grab a suitcase.

'Hi, baby,' she said when she was standing in front of us, beaming at Drew, her American accent out of place in the Scottish countryside. I felt like a bucket of iced water had been drenched all over me as she threw her arms around him. Drew's eyes met mine. I looked away: their embrace was too painful to watch. 'Well… are you surprised?'

Drew pulled back. 'Really surprised. What are you doing here, April?'

'I've come for Christmas. Like you wanted!'

'But you said—'

'I know, I changed my mind. I missed you so much.' She finally noticed me. 'Oh, who's this then?' she asked, her voice staying upbeat, but I didn't miss her eyes narrowing a little.

'This is, uh, Beth,' Drew replied. He wouldn't look at me.

She wrapped herself around Drew and smiled at me, flashing dazzling white teeth in the glow from the taxi headlights. 'Hi there. I'm April – Drew's girlfriend.'

Chapter Thirty-Three

'Mum! We're going to play Cluedo next…' Izzy's words faded away as she stood in the doorway, calling to me, before noticing that Drew and I were not alone.

Izzy broke me from my spell, staring at April open-mouthed after her revelation. I turned quickly and hurried over to Izzy.

'Actually, Iz, we need to be going. Drew's, uh, friend from Boston is here and they need to catch up,' I hissed at her, dragging her into the farmhouse with me as she looked over my shoulder curiously at the newcomer. I saw April turn to ask Drew who the little girl was, and I had a flash of pity for how he was going to explain to his American girlfriend that he'd just discovered he had a daughter, but then I remembered he hadn't mentioned April to us, at all, and my sympathies faded somewhat.

'What's going on?' Heather poked her head out of the living room.

'Drew has a visitor,' I said, trying to keep calm, as Rory was behind her and I didn't want to show how upset I was. 'His girlfriend has come over from Boston.'

Heather's eyes widened. 'Girlfriend?' She spun round to face Rory, her hands on her hips. 'Did you know he had a girlfriend?'

Rory looked a little surprised at how furious she was. 'Yeah, they've been together a while. They live together over there.'

'They live together?' I repeated, dumbfounded. Why hadn't Drew said anything? 'Izzy, grab your things, we need to go,' I implored her. Then I heard the front door close.

'You're not going?' Drew said from behind me.

I just couldn't face him, terrified about what my face would betray. 'I think we better, it's getting late and there will be loads to do tomorrow before the trail opens.' I sighed with relief as Izzy reappeared with our things. I pulled my coat on quickly and reluctantly turned around. Over Drew's shoulder, April stalked upstairs with her suitcase, clearly annoyed that her surprise hadn't gone as planned. I was relieved she was going out of sight.

'Wait, I wanted to introduce—' Drew began.

'Can we do that when we see you tomorrow?' I begged him, not sure I could bear to watch Izzy meet April just yet. I needed to get my head round this. 'That is, if you're still coming…?'

'Of course I am,' he replied. 'Okay. Izzy…' He went over to her to say goodbye.

Heather hurried over to hug me. 'Call me in the morning,' she whispered as she gave me a tight squeeze. I nodded and waved to Rory over her shoulder. He still looked a little shell‑shocked.

Drew led us out, opening the door for us. Izzy went out to the car, but as I passed Drew, he touched my arm and I was forced to stop. 'Beth, I feel like I need to explain—'

'There's no need,' I cut him off firmly, hoping that my voice didn't sound as shaky as it felt. 'Good night,' I said before I hurried out after Izzy, willing myself not to turn around.

'Who was that woman, Mum?' Izzy asked when we were in the car, ready to leave.

My knuckles were white as I gripped the steering wheel. 'Drew's girlfriend – apparently,' I replied, switching on the engine. Drew was still in the doorway, watching us. The evening had promised so much and now that was all over. I took a deep breath and forced myself to remain cheerful for my daughter. 'Right, let's go home.'

Izzy waved to her dad as I drove out of the farm. I couldn't stop myself from glancing in my rear-view mirror as I drove down the gravel driveway, but Drew was already walking back inside.

'Are you okay, Mum?'

I turned on the radio to save me from having to answer, and she was soon singing along to the Christmas songs, leaving me to try to hold it together until we went to bed, when I had no doubt the tears would come. I had deluded myself that Drew might not only be able to forgive me for the past but might see his future with us too. It was all just a fantasy though. He had a life already in Boston and someone to share it with. I would just have to let my fantasy go and ignore the fact that I had started to fall in love with him all over again.

I woke up the next day without any time to dwell on last night's events.

'Happy Christmas Eve!' Izzy cried when she flung my bedroom door open early in the morning. 'Come on, Mum, get up! It's the trail day!'

I smiled as I heaved myself out of bed. 'Go get breakfast started, I need a shower to wake up,' I told her, watching her skip off. I couldn't suck any of the excitement out of the day for her; I had to push Drew to the back of my mind as much as possible. I stood under a steaming hot shower and closed my eyes, letting it pour over me, wishing I could erase the image of Drew hugging his girlfriend in front of me out of my head.

I just hoped by the time of the trail opening I'd be able to do that.

I was confused that Drew hadn't mentioned her, a little hurt as well, but then again, I had kept a huge secret from him so perhaps I didn't have any right to feel that way. I was disappointed too, I couldn't deny it. It suggested that any moments I had thought Drew and I had shared had all been in my head. I was also a little worried for Izzy. I had no idea how this April would react to Drew having a daughter, and I really hoped it wouldn't stop Drew and Izzy's blossoming relationship in its tracks.

There wasn't much time to keep thinking about it, thankfully. After a quick breakfast, we all headed outside into the garden. John, and all of the village helpers including Heather, arrived early to help us get the trail ready for its grand opening and check once again that everything was working perfectly. We knew the trail looked as good as we could make it, but everyone was nervous. We wanted people to turn up, to love it, and for it to do some good for the village, and we had no idea if we could pull that off.

I found my mum and Sally by the grotto, restringing a set of lights around the door that had moved in the breeze, Izzy barking orders at them. My phone vibrated in my pocket and when I saw Drew's name on the screen, my pulse began to speed up instantly. I quickly handed my phone to Izzy. 'It's your dad,' I said. She grabbed it eagerly, walking off to speak to him. I let out a sigh.

'How was last night?' Mum asked, noticing the look on my face.

'We all had a lovely time.'

'But?' Sally prompted with a raised eyebrow.

'But then Drew's girlfriend turned up,' I replied.

'Girlfriend?!' My mum and Sally said in unison, exchanging a look with one another.

I nodded. 'Yep. They live together in Boston, apparently, and he hadn't thought to tell us about her. She surprised him last night. God knows what she said when he told her about Izzy.'

'Beth…' Mum began, but then Izzy came back over, and she stopped speaking.

'Dad wants to talk to you now,' Izzy said, thrusting the phone at me. I looked at my mum who gave me a reassuring nod. I knew I couldn't get through it with them all watching, so I took the phone and ducked inside the grotto with it.

'Hello?' I said, finally, leaning against the sleigh, which looked shiny after John had polished it the previous night.

'Hi, I just want to say sorry again for your visit being cut short yesterday,' Drew said in a low voice.

'It was a surprise, I must admit,' I replied, hoping that my voice didn't break.

'I know. I honestly didn't think April would turn up like that. She had definitely decided not to come with me. Before I left Boston, things had been… difficult between us.'

'It's none of my business,' I said, quickly, at the same time wishing he would tell me everything. I was dying to know what she had said when he had told her who Izzy was.

'You must have wondered why I hadn't mentioned her to you or to Izzy. I honestly thought that when I went back she wouldn't be there. I really didn't think— Oh, she's coming downstairs,' he said, breaking off abruptly.

'You better go,' I said, clutching the phone to my ear, wishing he would stay on there for the whole day.

'I had a great time last night,' he said in a low voice. 'I wanted you to know that.'

'Me too,' I managed to whisper back.

'I'm looking forward to tonight – seeing the trail and you guys.'

'Us too.'

'Would it be okay if April comes too? She's dying to meet Izzy. She loves kids, so she was thrilled when I told her.'

I swallowed the lump in my throat. 'Sure. I have to go now. Bye!' I hung up before he could stop me. I closed my eyes for a moment. April was 'thrilled' about Izzy and would be at the trail opening. How was I supposed to act happy about that? Drew said that they had been close to splitting up but, suddenly, April had flown over, clearly to make sure that didn't happen. But what did Drew really think about that? I wished I knew how he felt about her.

All I hoped was that April didn't take Drew back to Boston with her any earlier than he had planned to go. I didn't want Izzy to have to say goodbye to him any sooner. I tried not to let myself think about how I would feel saying goodbye.

I walked back out of the grotto, knowing there was still plenty to do; I wasn't going to let them spoil the day.

'Okay?' Mum asked when she saw me.

'Yep,' I said, smiling at her. I was determined to be.

We ate an early dinner of stew and mash and then we all piled into our coats and headed outside. Darkness had fallen and the clear, crisp sky was dotted with a thousand stars. We all held torches to walk to the trail, which wouldn't be lit up until everyone had arrived.

We decided in the end to make the trail free as Gran had bought most of what we needed, and the rest had been donated or lent to us by people in the village – it seemed the best way to draw as many people as possible to Glendale Hall and prove to the council our community spirit was well and truly alive.

Heather was the first to arrive with her dad, and they walked over to where we stood under the banner she had designed. 'The driveway is already filling up,' she said as she hugged me. 'The whole of Glendale will be here tonight, I'm certain of it.'

'Fingers crossed! Your banner looks so good.'

'I had forgotten how much I love to draw. It's been a long time.'

'Same for me with gardening. This trail has been so much fun to work on.' I was really proud of all we had achieved in such a short space of time. I looked at the trail ready and waiting for people to view them, and a shiver of excitement ran through me. More people joined us, and a large crowd started to build up. Pretty much the whole village was there. And then Mum nudged me and nodded in the direction of two men walking across the grass – it was Mr Murray from the council with another colleague. At least they had done as promised and had turned up. I just hoped they saw enough to change their minds about their plans for the village.

Once the crowd was large enough, Mum, Heather, Izzy, Sally, and I moved to the front, assembling ourselves together in a line. John went to the light switches, ready for his cue.

'Thank you all for coming,' Mum said, loudly drawing everyone's attention to us. 'This project has been a real labour of love for all of us. We wanted everyone to have a lovely evening when we created the trail but, as you know, what we wanted to do was to bring our village together again. This has been a real team effort – so much has been donated and so many people lent their time and expertise too. I'm so proud of how quickly we put this together and I really hope you will all love the finished product. Beth?' She turned to me.

I hadn't planned to say anything. I cleared my throat. 'We know how much you all love living in Glendale. Coming back here, I've been reminded of just how special this place is. I really hope we can work together to make it a village to be proud of again.' I glanced at the two men from the council and hoped that they felt the same. 'I think it's time we opened the first ever Glendale Christmas Trail, don't you?' There was a scattering of applause. 'Okay then, let's the start the countdown!'

Voices rang out in the silence loud and strong.

'Five!'

'Four!'

'Three!'

'Two!'

'One!'

I found myself crossing my fingers as I turned around. The trail behind us burst into light. I breathed a big sigh of relief as a cheer went up from everyone. We stepped aside and watched as people entered the trail. I couldn't help but hope as I saw their faces lit by the fairy lights that this might become an annual tradition.

'I'm going to get your grandmother,' Mum said then, heading back to the house. Gran had begged to be allowed to see the lights for herself, so we had got her a wheelchair and Mum was planning to push her down through the trail. I was happy we had found a way to let her see it, particularly as she had funded so much of it.

'This looks incredible,' a warm voice said from behind us.

'Dad!' Izzy cried as we turned to see Drew, Rory and April walk over to us.

'Hi, guys,' Drew said with a warm smile. I couldn't help but look at Drew's hand entwined with April's. My stomach lurched. I looked up slowly and found his gaze on me. I didn't want to look at April at all, but the curiosity was too strong. She was as pretty as I had thought she was in the dim light outside his farmhouse – blonde, blue-eyed and tanned, with a dazzling, sparkling white smile. I felt dizzy all of a sudden. And then April had to drop her hand as Izzy launched at Drew and they shared a big hug. I hated that I was glad about that.

'See how good it looks!' Izzy said when she pulled back.

'It does look great,' Drew replied. 'Iz, this is April – she's my girlfriend from Boston,' he said in his easy way.

'Hi there, lovely, aren't you gorgeous?' April said, bending down a little to greet Izzy.

'Hi,' Izzy replied, stepping back towards me, a little unsure of this new woman in our lives. I put my hand on her shoulders to give her a squeeze.

'Is Heather already here?' Rory asked, straining to see behind me.

'Yeah, she and her dad are walking the trail. You could catch them up though,' I replied.

'You wanna show us the trail? I can't wait to see it!' April said then to Izzy. She actually held out her hand and Izzy, with a brief glance up at me, stepped forward to take it. I tried not to let myself feel jealous, but it was hard not to when they all waved merrily and walked off towards the twinkling lights together.

Drew looked back at me for a moment, but I wasn't sure what the expression on his face meant. I forced on a smile, and they faded away.

'Beth, you look as if you have the whole world on your shoulders,' Sally said, finding me then.

'It just feels like so much is changing, so quickly. I certainly didn't think Izzy would be spending Christmas Eve with her father when I came home.'

'Things don't always turn out how we plan but they also have a way of working themselves out,' Sally replied. 'Glendale needed you back. Look at what you're doing for the village and for your family.'

'I wish it was as easy to sort myself out,' I said with a wry smile.

'I used to tell you that you were too impulsive, that you just followed your heart and didn't think enough about where it would lead you,' Sally said. 'But it sounds like you need to remember that girl. Sometimes we think *too* much when we're older.'

'I can't believe you're telling me to be more impulsive,' I replied with a shake of my head. Sally was Mrs Sensible and had always been that way. I had always been the rebel of the family. But she was right: as you grew up, you tended to weigh things much more carefully. And usually that was a good thing, but perhaps, sometimes, you did just need to go with the flow.

'Are you joining us, Beth?' Gran called, as Mum wheeled her to the trail. I followed them, looking at Gran, whose eyes were wide, and then at my mum who was smiling. There was something about Christmas that brought out the child within us all.

It felt as if the three of us were getting a second chance. Just for one night, all our problems, Gran's illness, our past, all the regrets, the lies and our worries about the future, could all be put aside as we disappeared into our winter wonderland if we let them.

Chapter Thirty-Four

Drew came to find me later. I was in the kitchen warming up with a cup of coffee. 'There you are. I wanted to catch you before we head home,' he said, appearing behind me and making me jump. I had been lost in thought, staring out at the garden, sipping my drink. 'We all loved the trail. You have a real talent for making things beautiful,' he said, his voice soft as he stood close by me. 'You're wearing it,' he said, smiling, as he reached out to touch the necklace he had given me. I had taken my scarf off inside and the star and moon pendant sparkled in the kitchen light.

'I promised you when you gave it to me that I always would. And then I left it in your car. I've missed it all these years.' I looked away from him, not wanting to add that I had also missed him. The necklace reminded me of the two of us as teenagers, giddy with our young love, feeling like we had the whole world at our feet. I missed them. I had wanted to take it off when I saw April, but I knew that was just a knee-jerk, childish reaction. I kept it on to remind me of what we once had. It was clear now we would never get that back but maybe one day I'd find that kind of love again. It reminded me that I was capable of loving someone like that at least.

'I hoped I would get it back to you one day. What's wrong? You look sad, which is crazy, as tonight is going so well,' he asked his eyes focused on me. He was always able to read me, which was kind of annoying, but I also liked that he hadn't lost that ability.

I lifted my face and met his gaze again. 'Just thinking about the future, I suppose. Our time here seems to be going by so quickly, but also so much is changing it's hard to keep up with it all. I feel a little bit lost I think.'

'I know what you mean. Before April came back, I was going to tell you guys that I have been offered another job. At the hospital in Inverness. It would mean I could finish my residency here in Scotland.'

'Wow.' I tried to ignore the fact my heart had sped up a little at the idea of Drew being so much closer than he currently was. 'How do you feel about that?'

'I don't know. It was the reason that things were... tense... between April and me before I left. She was angry that I was even considering it. She believed our life was in Boston and pretty much said if I took the job then we were over. But I was thinking about Rory. If I was here, I could help with the farm, and I have missed Scotland, you know?' I nodded; I felt the same. 'But now April doesn't seem so against the idea. That's why she came to surprise me, to tell me that, and see Scotland for herself.' Drew let out a heavy sigh, and then he turned to stare out into the garden as if it might hold the answer he was looking for. I wish it did for both of us. 'And now I know about Izzy, well, that's even more of an incentive. We have a lot to talk about, I guess.'

'Have you two been together long?' I asked, unsure what answer I was hoping for.

'We met at university. She was the sister of my roommate Dan so the first day I moved in, she was there, but it was a while before we became a couple, and we've been together, on and off, since then. Things were so weird before I left, it's hard to get my head around her being here, and her saying that we could move here and build a new life, have a future here... together.'

I didn't like the idea of Drew building a future with April, but I couldn't deny that Drew moving to Scotland would make Izzy incredibly happy, so I would have to deal with that, accept it and be happy about it, for her. I swallowed hard. 'Izzy would love it if you moved back here,' I said. 'You know that.'

'April already loves her, you know. They're getting on like a house on fire. April can't wait to have her own family,' he replied, not realising how painful his words were for me. I looked away. 'But how do you really know if you're meant to be with someone forever?'

I shook my head. 'If you ever work that out, please let me know.'

'I knew once,' he half whispered.

I couldn't look at him. I touched the necklace around my neck. 'Me too.'

'Do you think?' He coughed. 'Do you think we would have lasted forever?'

'There was a time when I was so sure of that.' I dragged my eyes to his. He was standing so close to me, it felt if either one of us took just one step then our lips would meet. I wished he would, but I knew he wouldn't. And that I couldn't. 'Sally just told me that I needed to follow my heart. I think that's good advice.'

'If only I knew what my heart wanted,' he replied with a rueful smile. I wished it did too if only to put me out of my agony.

'There you are!'

We both jumped this time, and Drew quickly stepped back from me as we turned to see April walking in. It felt as if we had been caught doing something we shouldn't have been.

'I think it's time to head off, Drew, we'll have to be up early to get the turkey cooking,' April said, smiling, but I saw her eyes flick between us uncertainly.

'Of course,' Drew said. He turned to me. 'I'll call Izzy tomorrow to wish her a merry Christmas, and we can arrange a time for me to see her?' I nodded, not trusting myself to speak. 'And congratulations again.'

I watched them walk out together, Drew's arm resting on the small of April's back as they left.

And I exhaled slowly, and shakily.

–

When I stepped outside again, my mum waved me over: I joined her and Mr Murray and was introduced to a Mr Tom Walker who was in the council's finance office.

'I've just been telling these gentlemen about all the people who are keen to open up businesses on the high street again. As they've seen tonight, the community here really wants to have a chance to rebuild the village together. I am, though, very worried about the high rents that are being charged.' She gave them an arched look.

'The problem is, I'm afraid, the need for distribution of resources,' Mr Walker replied. 'Although the rents may seem high, they are necessary to keep the buildings, which are very old, maintained, as well as the high street itself – the hanging baskets in the summer, the trees at Christmas, the road sweeping, the potholes etc. We have one pot that everything comes out of. Some of the rent money goes towards social care too, which as I'm sure you're aware is costing more and more.

For instance, if we decided not to sell to New Horizons and then also cut the rents, we would have to cut resources to other, perhaps, you could argue, more significant areas. I sympathise, I really do. I don't want the high street to become flats, but we are running out of other options.'

'Can we still have until the fifth of January to come up with a solution?' Mum asked, clearly determined not to give up. 'After all, as is clear tonight, you must agree selling off the high street is not what people in this village want.'

Mr Murray nodded. 'We are impressed with the community spirit here tonight, Mrs Williams, but it does, I'm afraid, all come down to how we can balance those books. You still have until January; I really hope you can find an answer.' We all shook hands, and then they left, leaving me and my mum standing on the grass, feeling a little deflated.

'I thought they might budge on the rents,' I admitted once we were alone. 'Was that really naïve of me?'

'No, just hopeful.' She smiled. 'Don't worry, we have time to come up with something. We aren't giving up yet, okay?'

'Okay,' I said but I was at a loss as to what we could do next.

John came over to us then. 'A kid got too excited in the grotto and has tripped the lights so I'm going to find a new fuse. It might be a good idea to start winding things up before we lose any more lights,' he said with a shake of his head. 'Bloody kids,' he muttered as he sloped off.

I laughed. 'John is happiest just alone with his plants, isn't he?'

'You've got that right. I can't say I blame him.' Mum smiled. 'Let's clear the trail then, shall we?'

'Whatever happens, we can be proud that we did this, can't we?'

We both looked at the lights ahead. 'Definitely.'

Chapter Thirty-Five

Later, when everyone had gone home and we had turned off the trail lights, I went up to say good night to Izzy who was reading in bed and paused outside my gran's room on the way. Her lights were still on, so I peeped in and saw her eyes were open as she lay in bed. 'How do you think it went?' I asked her, softly.

She smiled as I stepped inside. 'It reminded me what I loved about Glendale. You know, I have lived my whole life in this house,' she said. 'I had dreams of going to the city once. But then I fell in love with your grandfather. He worked for my father when we still ran the family business. Like me, he was born and bred in Glendale, and once we were married and I had Caroline, there was never a question of us leaving.

'And Caroline, she never really had dreams of moving away. When she married your father, they decided they would live here. Your grandfather had only just died and your mother didn't want to leave me alone, but perhaps she too found it hard to be parted from this house. It becomes part of you. I think when you left, it shook us all because we couldn't imagine living anywhere else. And perhaps we all fell a little out of love with this house and the village. But you've shown us that there is still so much to love here, and we should be trying to keep it for the next generation.' My gran spoke slowly and softly but her speech was full of emotion, and her voice broke at the end of it.

I would never be sorry for leaving. I'd had to do it. I was sure of that. It was important for me. It had allowed me to grow and become the woman I was, raise Izzy the way I wanted to and create a bond between us that could never be broken. But I also understood why they had never left. 'It is special. I think coming back after so long has made me see it with completely new eyes. I maybe didn't appreciate it when I was younger or maybe it didn't appreciate me. I am so glad we are trying to preserve Glendale. I'd like Izzy to enjoy it as she grows up.'

'And you always loved our grounds, didn't you? It must have been hard not to pursue your passion for gardening, to let that all go. I hadn't thought about it before but seeing the trail tonight, I realised how it must have broken your heart to not do what you wanted.'

I nodded. 'Being back here has reminded me how much I did love it. Working on this trail has been really special.' I tried not to think about how I would feel in January going back to my desk job, every day the same, no window even in my office to see out of. A world away from Glendale. But we all had to do things we didn't want to, surely. That was what life was about. 'I did what I had to do, though.'

Gran nodded. 'Perhaps now you can let yourself dream again.' She closed her eyes. 'Before you run out of time.' She was asleep suddenly as if she had been pulled to it by a hidden magnetic force. I shut the door softly and left her alone, wondering if I could.

Chapter Thirty-Six

When I opened my eyes on Christmas Day, my room was in darkness and there was a stillness in the air that I knew could only mean one thing. I rolled over and sighed when I saw the time on my phone was five a.m. Sitting up, I pulled back the curtains and peered out of the window at the thick white carpet covering the garden. 'A white Christmas,' I whispered. Despite waking up so early, I couldn't help but smile at the snow outside, knowing that Izzy, sleeping next door, would be beside herself with excitement.

Climbing out of bed, I pulled on my fluffy dressing gown, and slippers, and put my hair up into a messy bun. Padding softly out of my room, I went into Izzy's room and smiled down at her curled up, sleeping under the blanket. 'Iz, wake up,' I said, softly, giving Izzy's sleeping form a nudge.

'What is it?' Izzy mumbled, rolling over sleepily.

'It's Christmas,' I told her.

'It's Christmas!' Izzy's eyes flew open and she sat bolt upright.

I laughed. 'I have something to show you. Come on!' I held out her dressing gown as she climbed out of bed. I passed her slippers and she shuffled into them. 'Merry Christmas, love,' I said, giving her a kiss.

'Merry Christmas!' she repeated, a smile spreading across her face. I took her hand and we walked softly downstairs. Glendale

Hall was still and silent. We passed the huge Christmas tree, packed with presents underneath ready to be opened soon, and went into the kitchen where I took Izzy over to the patio doors. She let out a little gasp as we stood side by side and looked out at the winter wonderland in front of us.

'What about the trail?' she asked with sudden panic.

'It's okay. John made sure everything was covered, and if it's still snowing tomorrow, we'll have to get up early and clear a path. But I think it will make it feel even more magical.' I knew that John would be grumpy about the snow despite what I told Izzy, but I smiled at it. I had missed it living down in London. It reminded me of my childhood, and I was thrilled Izzy was getting to experience it. 'Makes it feel really Christmassy, doesn't it?'

'Can we go for a walk in it later?'

'Definitely. How about some hot chocolate then?'

'Can I open my presents from Santa?'

'Oh, so now you believe in him?'

She poked out her tongue, and I laughed. 'Go and get your stocking from the mantelpiece, and I'll make our drinks.' I watched her rush off and shook my head with a chuckle. When she was growing up I had tried hard to make sure Izzy had the best Christmases that I could but it wasn't always easy on my own. Now we were ready for our first Christmas with our family and I was a little nervous about how the day would go but I was determined to make it special for my little girl as I always had.

'There are so many!' Izzy said, coming back in and struggling a little to hold all the presents in her arms. She put them on the table.

I took over two hot chocolates and we sat down at the table together. It was a silver lining to being up at the crack of dawn

– a moment with just the two of us. Like we always had at this time of year.

'It's a shame Dad can't come over,' Izzy said as she opened up her first gift.

'We'll see him tomorrow. And he will ring you later.' Now that April was here I was relieved that it had already been agreed we'd spend the day apart.

'What are you two doing up?' Sally said when she walked in a while later.

'We saw that it had snowed and had to come and see it,' I replied. 'Merry Christmas, Sally.'

'You too.' She came over and gave us both a kiss. 'I'm going to put the turkey in and then I think we all need a bacon sandwich and a glass of Buck's Fizz. Just the Buck for you though, Iz.' I liked that as it was Christmas she sat with us like one of the family. Which is what she was to me. She would be off to London soon to see Emily but it was right she was here for our first Christmas back at Glendale Hall.

'What is she talking about?' Izzy hissed at me as she opened her new diary from Santa.

'I never really know,' I whispered back. 'Looks like you were on the good list after all,' I said, gesturing at all the gifts on the table.

'And, once again, you weren't,' she replied, reaching for the chocolate snowman. She held it up hopefully, but I shook my head.

'At least have your bacon sandwich first. We have to pace ourselves today, Iz. Sally will make enough to feed an army; I can promise you that.'

'I'll need a helper though,' Sally said as she pulled out food from the fridge. 'What do you think, Izzy?'

'Can I be the taster too?'

I laughed. 'I have taught you well.'

Izzy jumped up to help Sally get the turkey into the Aga. I wrapped my hands around my mug and gazed out at the garden. Outside, large snowflakes fell down gently as if they were feathers.

The year before, as Izzy and I had got ready in our flat for Christmas dinner at Emily's house, I had told myself that I didn't miss being at Glendale Hall with my family, but I'd known I was lying. This would be my first Christmas here for ten years. It was crazy to realise that. Maybe I had stayed away too long. Looking at Izzy's happy face, I knew that at least I had done the right thing in coming home this year.

–

'Beth, your grandmother wants to come downstairs for Christmas dinner,' Mum said, finding me as I came out of my room showered and dressed. I was wearing my traditional Christmas jumper for the day. It was black and fluffy with the face of a reindeer on it, the nose of which flashed red.

Mum stared. 'What is that?'

'The best jumper ever,' I replied. 'Wait until you see Izzy's. We always wear them on Christmas Day.'

She rolled her eyes. Despite our relationship improving no end since I had come home, Mum still hadn't got to grips with our festive spirit and love of all things tacky at this time of year. I wished I had bought her a jumper to wear just to see her face. 'Anyway, will you help me?'

We went into my gran's room. I could understand why she wanted to be downstairs. I couldn't imagine being bedridden for as long as she had been. I didn't like how she looked. It didn't seem as if she had long with us. Sally was waiting there and between the three of us we lifted Gran out of her bed and carried her downstairs into the living room, helping her into the armchair with a stool to put her feet on. Mum draped a heavy blanket over her even though there was a roaring fire in the room. Gran smiled at being there despite the obvious pain she was in. It was still strange to see the woman who had been so formidable and such a force of character through my childhood looking so frail and weak now. I still didn't know if I was ready to forgive the lies she had told but only someone with a heart of stone wouldn't feel pity for her.

'Can we open presents now?' Izzy asked, appearing behind us. Her jumper had a penguin on it and was pale blue and sparkly.

'Your father used to make you wait until after lunch: do you remember how upset that made you?' Mum said to me with a smile. 'Well, he isn't here yet, so yes, I think we should. Izzy, why don't you bring them in from under the tree? I think we'll be nice and cosy in here for opening them.'

I grinned as Izzy skipped off happily. I quite liked this new-found rebellious nature of my mum's. I loved my dad, of course, but he was so in the wrong in my opinion, not only seeing another woman behind my mum's back, but also in putting money before the community, and helping to destroy Glendale. I hoped his time away might be making him change his mind about everything.

I sat down on the sofa and Mum passed me and Sally a glass of mulled wine. Soft Christmas music played in the background, and Mum had lit candles: it was sending me back to Christmases gone by with the scent of frankincense and myrrh.

Izzy's face lit up as her dad phoned to wish her a merry Christmas. She skipped out to the tree after speaking to him to collect all the presents.

'What a difference a Christmas makes,' I said aloud, thinking about all the changes that had happened to us while we had been here.

'How are you feeling about Drew?' Mum asked me, gently.

'I'm happy he's in Izzy's life now.'

'And his girlfriend?' she prompted, curling up her lip in distaste.

I shrugged, trying not to betray the disappointment in my heart. 'What is there to say? We were over a long time ago, Mum.'

'You were kids back then, and now you have one together. That changes everything.'

Izzy came back in, struggling with a pile of gifts so I couldn't respond. I watched her make piles for each of us and smiled at how much fun she was having. I was disappointed about Drew and April, there was no denying it, but I had spent ten years without him. All that mattered was Izzy and how happy him being in her life was making her. My heart would be okay as long as hers was. I had to believe that.

Chapter Thirty-Seven

Once we had a pile of gifts, and a pile of ripped up wrapping paper, Sally had to leave to check on the turkey, and then my dad walked in.

'What did you get for Christmas then, Iz?' he asked, sitting down on the sofa in his suit, flashing us all a smile as if nothing was out of the ordinary. My family really were experts at pretending nothing was wrong. Izzy showed him the beaded bracelet I had got her, with a book charm hanging from it. We had seen them at a market in London, and I had gone back to buy her one on my lunch break.

'I'm going to go and help Sally,' my mum said, fleeing for the kitchen.

'David, what are you doing?' Gran said, opening her eyes from the nap she'd been having. I looked at Izzy who was cross-legged on the floor studying the set of nail polishes Sally had given her. I hoped an argument wasn't about to erupt. 'You should go and talk to Caroline.'

'Stay out of this, Margaret,' Dad muttered. He sighed and rubbed his temples.

'I think if you only had a short time left, you wouldn't stay out of anything either,' she replied. 'That's my daughter you are treating appallingly. There is only one choice – you leave, for good, or you stay, and you work at your marriage. Do you even care how she is feeling about you being here today?'

With a resigned sigh, my dad got up from the sofa. 'Fine, I'll go and talk to her. But I have every right to be here, this is my house and my family.'

'I think,' Gran said to his retreating back, 'you'll find this is my house, and it appears to be your family only when it suits you.'

Dad didn't reply but I saw his cheeks grow pink as he went to find my mum.

I had been on the receiving end of my gran's cutting remarks before, but it was hard to feel any pity for him.

'I like that colour,' I said to Izzy, hoping she hadn't paid too much attention to their heated words. I wanted her to enjoy her first Christmas at Glendale Hall. 'Shall I help you paint your nails later?' I looked at Gran – she had closed her eyes again. 'Iz, go and see if Sally needs any help with lunch, I'll be there in a sec.' When Izzy had gone, I went over to Gran's armchair. 'Can we all call a truce for one day? For Izzy?'

'We can,' Gran said, opening her eyes. 'But I had to tell him what I thought. I am ashamed to call him my son-in-law. I know that my opinions haven't always matched yours, but I think they do now.' I sighed and nodded. 'You will help them, Beth, I know you will. I just don't want to go with any regrets. If I don't say how I feel now, I may never get the opportunity. Do you understand?'

'I do. I know it won't be easy but I'd like us to all enjoy this day together.'

She patted my hand. 'We will. This family means more to you than you care to admit I think. Maybe you had to leave us to realise this is where you belong.'

'I like being back here, Gran, but London is my home now.'

'Hmm. Your home isn't a place, it's the people you share it with. Izzy is your home. And so are we.' She closed her eyes again, signalling the conversation was over.

–

Lunch was spectacular. I don't know what my parents said to one another, but everyone was on their best behaviour as we made our way through the turkey, pigs in blankets, roast and mash potatoes, honey-drenched carrots, cauliflower cheese and parsnips. Izzy made us all wear the hats from our crackers, and I kept smiling every time I looked across at my elegant mum with one on her head. Gran managed to have a small meal but as soon as we were finished, my dad carried her back to bed so she could sleep. We had Christmas pudding with brandy butter and then all piled into the kitchen to clear everything up. It was late afternoon by the time it was all done, and Izzy begged to have a walk in the snow before we lost the light. Sally went off to phone her family, and Mum went to check on my gran, so Izzy, my dad and I stepped out into the garden wrapped up in our warmest clothes.

'I need this, I'm so full after all that food,' I said, my boots sinking into the soft powdery snow. We couldn't see any grass peeking through, it was white for as far as the eye could see. We padded our way across the lawn; it was slow work as our boots sunk deep into the snow.

'I'm going to make a snowman,' Izzy said, dropping to her knees to make a ball. My dad and I continued to walk on slowly. It was the first time we'd really been alone since we'd arrived in Glendale.

'Let me show you the trail,' I suggested. We walked towards the fir trees, Heather's *Glendale Christmas Trail* banner moving in the gentle breeze. 'This really isn't about me and Mum doing something just to piss you off,' I said to him. 'I didn't even know you were involved at the beginning. But when I walked into the village and saw how deserted it was, it made me really sad. I remember walking there one Boxing Day with you and Mum to have tea and cake. It had snowed just like today, and the cafe was full of people, really cosy and warm. Don't you miss that? You've lived here all your life, just like us, do really want to see it turned into flats?' I said all this gently so he didn't get defensive. I was actually curious as to why he thought this development idea would be good for Glendale.

'I loved going into the village too, but after you left, it became hard especially for your mother. We felt as if everyone was talking about us. Caroline explained that Margaret told you we all knew you were pregnant and didn't want you to have the baby. I'm sorry, Beth, that you felt so alone you had to run away. We blamed ourselves, and you, and I wish we could all have spoken about it more and found out the truth sooner, but Glendale became a place for us to hide from. We drifted away from the community, so when I joined the board at New Horizons, I suppose I just didn't feel any kind of emotional attachment to the village any more. When the idea was suggested, I could see the financial benefits for the company, and that's all I was really thinking about.' He looked at the covered lights as we strolled through the trees. 'You've all put a lot of work into this, haven't you?'

'So many people are upset at the thought of the village being destroyed,' I said. 'We've had so much help. I wish you could have been here last night: the whole village came out to see it. It really felt magical. The council came too, and I think they feel as we do: that the village should be saved, but they need money, and that's why your offer is so appealing to them.'

Dad looked across at me and sighed. 'My company have put a lot of work into our plans. I still support what we want to do. I haven't told anyone at New Horizons about what you're trying to do because you're family, but that's all I can do.'

'Does Cathy know?' I hated to even say her name.

'No, and she will be furious with me when she finds out. Do you think the council will change their minds?'

I lifted my shoulders. 'Honestly, I don't know. I hope so. We just felt we had to try. Dad, this Cathy, is she really special enough to throw away everything you have with Mum?' We passed by the stream then, the sunshine creating a sparkling coating on top of it.

'Your mother and I haven't been happy for a long time, Beth. We have been living separate lives really. I know that it's a shock to find out about Cathy, but she is special to me. I have so much respect for your mum, I do love her, but our marriage is not as strong as it once was.'

I sighed. It was nice in one way to have an honest conversation with my dad, but it was hard to hear what he was saying. 'Are you really at a hotel then? Not staying with her?'

'She wanted to be with her family over Christmas. Their children live far away and are staying for the holiday but after that...' He glanced at me. 'We have discussed moving in together.'

'Oh, Dad.'

'I'm glad of one thing, though – that you and Izzy are here. Even if you are stirring up all kinds of trouble with this trail. It is nice to see you all engaged in something together, I have to admit. And your mum, she seems to have some of her old spirit back.'

I smiled. 'I think we all do. We all needed this project. You're right, it has brought us closer together.' We walked into the grotto. 'What do you think?'

Dad shook his head. 'It is wonderful. You've all done a great job. I am proud of you and your mum for taking a stand, you know. I wish it wasn't against me, of course, but it's nice to see.'

I smiled. 'I just wish we knew what was going to happen.'

He looked at me. 'No one knows that, Beth. But I do know that whatever happens, you'll take it all in your stride. You always have.'

That was as close to praise as I'd ever had from my dad. I followed him out and we walked back to find Izzy and see how her snowman was coming on.

'He looks like he's eaten too much turkey,' Dad said when we saw the rather round snowman.

'I know the feeling,' I said. I put my arm around Izzy, and she snuggled into my side as we watched Dad pick up two stones and use them for the snowman's eyes.

'I've lost all feeling in my fingers,' Izzy complained.

'We better get you inside then. Mum wants to show you her favourite festive film.'

Dad smiled a little. '*It's A Wonderful Life*,' he said. 'We still watch it every year.'

'I'm glad you kept up the tradition,' I said. I remembered the three of us watching it when I was younger. I wondered then what might happen next year. It was hard to imagine that my parents might not be together then, but I knew that they both deserved to be happy and perhaps that would be easier if they did let each other go. And at least I would be there for them if that did happen. I wasn't going to slink back to London and sever all ties with my family again. I wanted to keep building on our growing bond and make sure Izzy always had her family around her.

And I needed them, too. It had been hard dealing with everything by myself for ten years; I had been lonelier than I admitted to myself. I liked being back at the Hall surrounded by them. And seeing how much Izzy had blossomed here. Glendale seemed to be good for both of us.

When we went back inside, we all crashed in the living room in front of the film. Izzy and my mum on one sofa, my dad in the armchair and me on the other sofa. The night started to draw in and we passed around chocolates, the fire roaring in the corner, and I smiled as I looked around at my family, glad that I had come back to Glendale Hall for Christmas. My family was flawed, yes, maybe a little bit broken and battered from the past too, but we had healed a lot of our wounds since I had returned home, and we would keep on healing and being there for each other.

I had found my family again. And that felt like the best present of the day.

Chapter Thirty-Eight

'What if I fall over?' Izzy hissed to me as we walked towards the ice rink behind April and Drew, who were holding hands in front of us. It had been April's idea, apparently. A trip to the local outdoor ice rink as a chance for us all to get to know one another. I had tried to get Izzy to come skating with me in London, but she had always turned her nose up at the idea. My daughter was never one to be outside, or doing sport if she could help it – but Drew had promised her a trip to a bookshop afterwards, so she had reluctantly agreed.

'I won't let you fall,' I promised. I hadn't skated in years but had loved it growing up. At this very rink. I had come every week with Heather in winter when we were teenagers and had done so more than once with Drew. I wondered if he remembered as we got our skates and sat down to put them on.

'This place is so cute,' April said as she laced her boots, looking out at the large rink, which had a Christmas tree in the centre, and was blasting out festive songs. 'We didn't get to go to the rink in Boston before Drew came over here, so this will be fun. Have you skated before, Iz?'

I tried not to wince at April calling my daughter by the name I always used. I knew she was trying to make friends with her, and I knew that would make Drew happy, but there was no denying that we made a strange foursome.

'You're going to show me up as usual, aren't you?' Drew said as Izzy told April this would be her first time. He grinned at me, showing he did remember our dates there. He spent the whole time gripping the sides as I tried to pull him around, before giving up and skating off, full of teenage confidence. It had been nice to find something that I did better than him.

It was soon apparent that Drew hadn't become much better at skating through the years. April also clung to the side almost as much as he did, both of them wobbling as they tried to steady one another. Izzy held my hand as we went on to the ice and I pulled her into the middle straight away, not wanting her to get comfortable holding on to the rail. We skated around side by side until she wanted to try on her own. After an unsteady couple of circles around the rink she found her footing, so to speak, and I was pleased to see that even though like Drew she preferred the indoor world of books, she could skate pretty well.

Izzy went over to the others to try to help them, and I was able to skate around the rink alone a few times. It was fun to do something I hadn't done for so long, to enjoy the breeze whipping around my hair as I glided over the ice, which much like riding a bike had come back to me almost immediately. Finally, I was out of breath and I came to a halt by the three of them, my cheeks warm and the smile wide on my face.

'You're better than I remembered,' Drew said smiling back at me.

'It's just about balance really, isn't? Not really skill?' April said, with a toss of her blonde hair. I raised an eyebrow at the snide comment. 'I felt like Bambi out there,' she added quickly as though she hadn't said what she had. She looked at Drew, wrapping an arm through his. 'Let's get out of here, baby.'

'Come on then, we all need refuelling I think,' Drew agreed.

'Did you like it, Iz?' I asked as I helped her off the rink.

'It was better than I thought. Better than PE at school anyway.'

'Maybe now you'll come with me in London,' I said hopefully to her.

'I was a cheerleader at my school,' April said, catching up to us. 'I'll have to show you some photos.'

I tried not to roll my eyes. Of course she had to have been a cheerleader.

It was a short drive to the bookshop cafe Drew had found online for Izzy, and we all piled inside, eager to warm up. We found a cosy corner table and then Drew went off to order with Izzy, leaving me and April alone for the first time.

Chapter Thirty-Nine

'So, how are you finding Scotland?' I asked her, searching for something to say as we sat down, taking off our coats.

'Oh, I love it,' she replied, brightly. 'Like something out of a film, although it's even colder than Boston, which is saying something.' She looked over at the counter. 'Drew is so sweet with Izzy, isn't he?'

'It must have been a shock for you to come here and find out about her,' I said, trying to put myself in her shoes.

'It was but I love her, she's adorable.' April smiled. 'I love kids: I have a big family, and I can't wait to have one of my own,' she added, looking down at the table, her cheeks turning a little pink.

I tried not to let her see how much the idea of her starting a family with Drew upset me. 'Have you… have you talked about that?' I couldn't stop myself from asking her even though I really didn't want to know the answer. I wasn't sure why I was trying to torture myself like that, but perhaps it would help my heart get over him to keep reminding it that he was with her and not me.

'We have, even more since I surprised him here. He wasn't sure I was keen on the idea of moving here, but he knows now that I'd move anywhere to be with him.'

'Wow. You must really love him.'

'Oh, I do,' she replied, fiercely. 'He's perfect and I know we'll be together forever. But you mustn't worry about Iz, I just love her, and I think we'll all be super close.'

Her words cut deep into my skin.

'I can't imagine what it was like raising Izzy all by yourself,' she continued, oblivious to my misery. 'It's such a shame Drew missed out on so much; I know he's devastated about that, but you had your reasons, didn't you?' She rested her chin on her hand to give me a sympathetic look.

'I did,' I managed to reply. 'And I tried to put it right but—'

'Oh, yeah, the mysterious letter. Kind of convenient, wasn't it – that your letter never showed up?'

My mouth fell open at her words.

'Here they are!' April straightened up, throwing on a bright smile as if she hadn't just implied I'd made the whole letter up. Drew and Izzy arrived with a tray of drinks and food, and I was forced to pretend everything was okay, but inside I was seething. I also wondered if she had suggested just that to Drew, making sure that there was no way he would forgive me for the past.

'I got you your favourite,' Izzy said, sitting down beside me and pointing to the coffee and brownie on the tray for me.

'Thank you, love,' I replied, hoping I'd be able to swallow it down okay.

'After this, I told Izzy she can choose a few books,' Drew said, sliding a skinny latte over to April. She wasn't having a cake.

'If you buy any more this Christmas, we won't be able to fit them in the car,' I said to her.

'I can keep some here for when we next come up,' Izzy replied, taking a bite of her gingerbread man. She seemed certain we would be back. I thought about that as I took a sip of my drink. I didn't know what would happen when we had to leave. She was going to be upset, I knew, and I was beginning to realise that I would be too.

April asked Izzy then about her favourite books. She did really seem to be trying to get to know Izzy, but I couldn't help but think that it was all for Drew's benefit. He was watching them with a smile on his face, clearly happy to see them getting on so well. I felt like such a bad mother feeling jealous that Izzy seemed to like her. I knew it would be a good thing for her, because if Drew and April did stay together, Izzy would still be able to have a closer relationship with her dad if April encouraged it. But it was still hard for me to watch.

After we'd finished our drinks and cake, we walked into the bookshop. It was a small, twisty shop with lots of nooks and crannies. Izzy was in her element and pulled April over to the children's section. I wandered over to the new releases to see if there was something I could pick up for myself and Drew followed me.

'They seem to be getting on well,' he commented, looking at the books in front of us.

'Hmmm,' I replied. My eyes moved over the romances, sure I couldn't bear to read one, so I grabbed a dark looking thriller instead. 'And what did April think of Inverness?' I asked, remembering that they said they went to look at the city where Drew had received a job offer.

'She liked it. It's been a real turnaround. I think she's keen on the move idea now, which I never thought she would be.'

'Perhaps she thought she'd lose you if she didn't come around to the idea,' I said, looking at him to gauge his reaction.

Drew looked up to meet my gaze. 'I think that was part of it. I really feel like it might be time to come back to Scotland but it's a big decision, for both of us. I think if she did come here with me she would want us to get married.'

'Oh,' I replied, my heart sinking. 'And is that what you want, too?'

'Honestly, I'm not sure but—'

'Mum!' Izzy came around the corner then. 'What do you think of these?'

'Show me over here,' I said, pulling her with me to the corner to get away from Drew. I just couldn't bear to look at him any more, my face I was sure betraying every emotion I was feeling. Izzy had found five books, and I just wanted to get out of the bookshop and back to Glendale Hall, so I had no will to argue and let her give them all to Drew to buy. I rushed up to the till with my serial killer book so I could have a moment to compose myself.

Waiting in line, I tried to get a grip. This was crazy. Drew was obviously serious about April despite what he said about them almost breaking up and not mentioning her to us before she turned up – more serious than I would have imagined. April had come to claim her man, to tell him she would move to Scotland if they got married, and Drew was seriously considering doing just that. I imagined Izzy in a pink bridesmaid dress as they got married in Glendale parish church and I felt a little bit sick. The same church I had fantasised about the two of us getting married in when I was younger. I clearly needed to let that fantasy go. And yet sometimes when Drew looked at me it still felt as if I wasn't the only one feeling like things weren't as clear-cut as they appeared to be. Perhaps that was just my wishful thinking though.

But April was certainly not missing any chance to take a dig at me, and I knew she wouldn't pass up any opportunity to make sure Drew had no warm feelings towards me. Could I blame her? She was clearly desperate for them to have a future together. If Drew loved her, and was happy with her, I had to accept that. He deserved to be happy. I just wished I knew if April would make him happy.

'Oh, I couldn't bear to read a book like that,' April said, suddenly behind me in the queue, peering over my shoulder to look at what I was buying. 'I like a cute love story,' she said, waving the book she was buying.

I wanted to say something sarcastic back, but all I could think was that I wished I could have her cute love story for my own. Thankfully, I was saved from having to reply when I was called up to the counter.

Chapter Forty

I walked into the kitchen the following morning, eager for a coffee. The sky outside was still black. Somehow, I had transformed into someone who got up early, earlier than Izzy. Too much on my mind, I supposed. I paused in the doorway as I heard low voices from within. I saw that my mum was at the table with John, two mugs in front of them. She sniffed, and he put an arm around her.

I stepped back, feeling like I was interrupting something important.

'Beth?' Mum said, noticing me, hastily wiping her eyes. John dropped his arm from her and leaned back in his chair.

'Are you okay?' I asked, still hovering in the doorway.

'I'm fine. Come in and have a coffee.'

'I need to get to the village to pick up some bits,' John said, getting up.

'Don't go on my account,' I said, walking in to the kitchen. I was confused about finding them together like that; I didn't think they ever really chatted alone or maybe I had just never seen them do it before.

'See you,' John said, ignoring my comment. He walked out quickly, further reinforcing the feeling.

I brought a steaming mug of coffee over to the table and clearly saw that Mum had been crying. 'What's wrong? And don't tell me nothing,' I said to her gently.

She wiped her eyes. 'I went to the hotel to see your father yesterday. I thought we needed to talk, and it's proving impossible with him there and me here. But when I walked in, I saw him in the restaurant having lunch with… *her*.'

'Oh, Mum.' I moved to the chair next to her and rubbed her arm. 'I'm sorry. Did they see you?'

She nodded. 'I just walked straight out. He called out, but I couldn't bear to answer him. They looked so happy together. And it made me realise that this is it, you know? That he really is actually going to leave me.' Then she leaned against me, and for the first time in my life, my mum cried on my shoulder. 'I feel weak for being upset because he's cheated on me, and I should be furious, and I am but I'm also sad too.'

'Of course you are, and that's okay,' I said. 'He's been your husband for thirty years, of course you're going to be upset. That's not being weak. But if you want to cut up his suits, I fully support that.'

She smiled a little through her tears.

'Are you going to leave him?' I asked her when her tears had grown quieter.

'I think he's already left me,' she replied, and my heart broke for her. She sat up and used a tissue and sipped her coffee. 'I'm glad you're here, Beth.' She squeezed my hand.

'What were you and John talking about?' I asked then.

'Just about David. John has worked for us for twenty years; he knows everything about us, Sally too, and often they have been the only people I could talk to.'

'I'm sorry, Mum. I should have been here.'

'I should have been there for you, too. But I'm hoping that now we will be?'

I nodded. 'Definitely. What will you do about Dad?'

'I'll talk to him when I'm ready. I know that I will be okay. I have things I want to do now: I have you and Izzy, I have friends, I have the village to save.' She smiled a little. 'I have been drowning a little bit in self-pity but I'm not going to do that any longer. And I'm not going to drown all my sorrows in glasses of gin any more either. When I think about your grandmother upstairs, it puts things in perspective, you know? We only get one, short life and we need to make the most of it.' She gave me a look. 'I told your grandmother that I forgave her last night. For not telling me you were pregnant, for making you feel as if you had to run away. I know she was wrong. She tore us apart, but in a twisted way, she thought she was doing the right thing, and I know how hard it was for her to finally admit the truth. I couldn't bear to see her so ill and so worried that she had destroyed our relationship. She's my mother. I told her that I forgave her, and I think it brought her some peace.'

I swallowed. 'I'm sure it did.'

'If there is anything you want to say to her, don't leave it too late. That's all I'm saying. Bitterness, anger, regret… don't be like her: let go of it, Beth. In the end, they only hurt us and not the person they are directed against.' She got up then. 'I better go and see to her. Thank you for listening.' She bent down and kissed me.

After my mum had left, I sipped my coffee in the silence. I didn't know if I forgave my gran. You could say that everything had worked out in the end but, at the time, it could so easily have gone the other way. And even so, my heart had been broken and I thought I was all alone when I wasn't. It was hard to even contemplate letting her off for that. But then I thought of her in bed, in pain, slipping away and I couldn't help but feel pity. And compassion.

Was my mother right?

Would letting go not only help her but me too?

—

'How are you?' I asked Gran when I went up to see her that evening.

'Oh, just fine,' she replied, with a wave of her hand. 'Are you ready to open the trail again?'

I nodded. 'Everyone seems to love it but I'm not sure it's actually done much to help Glendale. The council aren't budging on their rents or changing their minds about the library.' What with that, Mum and Dad at breaking point, and April, things at Glendale seemed a lot bleaker all of a sudden. I sat down by her bed and tried not to look sad; after all, she had things much worse than I did.

'But you've got everyone to think about the village and to try to fight to save it. That's something.'

'Maybe.' I hated feeling dull, it wasn't my nature – I preferred to just get on with things – but I had to admit, there wasn't a whole lot to smile about.

'And you enjoyed making the trail, didn't you?'

'I loved it.'

'You really should be focusing on that, Beth. What are you going to do in the new year when you go back to London? I worry you're just going to go back to your old life, but you won't be happy.' She looked quite fierce then – some of the old Gran coming up to the surface again. 'Please, promise me, that you won't do that.'

'I don't want to but it's not easy changing your life, Gran.'

'Of course it's not,' she snapped. 'But that doesn't mean you just don't do it. Right? When have you ever shied away from doing something hard?' She gave me a sharp look. 'It isn't like you to sit around feeling sorry for yourself. You need to decide what you want and go after it.'

I smiled at how animated she had become. 'I will try.' I thought of Drew then but pushed that thought away.

'Hmmm. Well, make sure you do. Now, off you go and open up that trail and have a nice night. Turn that frown upside down as my mother used to say.'

I rolled my eyes, but it was nice to see Gran with some of her spirit back. I said good night and then went back downstairs, knowing that she was right and feeling sorry for myself wasn't something I wanted to do for much longer. I just wasn't sure how to turn things around yet.

Outside in the garden, Mum, Sally and John were with Izzy at a table filled with teas, coffees and cakes, welcoming everyone who wanted to see the trail. We had planned to open it each night until Hogmanay and then take it down. There were already a bunch of people coming into the garden, and one I recognised. I smiled as she walked over.

'There you are,' Heather said. She peered at me. 'Are you okay, Beth?'

'Just overthinking about things, I guess.'

She frowned. 'Well, that's never good, is it?' she lowered her voice. 'Is it about Drew?'

'Partly,' I admitted. 'And the village, and my gran, and my parents and what will happen when Izzy and I go back home. The whole lot, to be honest.' I turned to look at the banner floating in the breeze, the bright lights of the trail beyond it. 'Do you ever think about the things you missed out on?'

Heather nodded. 'It's funny you say that; my dad gave me a brochure for Inverness College the other day. They have a lot of classes for adults there. I'd been going on to him about how much I'd enjoyed making the banner and the leaflets for the trail and how I'd missed designing things, drawing, all of it – I used to love it so much but when I came home after uni, and had to get a job, I just put all of that to one side. Now I'm wondering whether I should go back to it.'

'That's a great idea!' I cried. 'You definitely should do that. You are really talented. I'm sure you could find a part-time job while you did it. You should go after your dream, it's never too late.'

Heather smiled. 'And what about you and the dreams you gave up?' she asked me, pointedly. 'It's not too late for you either, you know.'

'I have really enjoyed working in the garden since I've been back,' I agreed. 'But I'm not sure if there's anything I could do about that in London. I do sometimes think about what it would have been like if I had done my degree… but it wasn't meant to be.'

'Just don't discount it now. Maybe we can both go back to school.'

I laughed. 'God, remember our school days? I really hated it there. If it wasn't for you, and Drew, and all our friends, I probably would have never even turned up.'

'And speaking of Drew – what about him and April?'

'I think he's going to marry her.'

'Oh my god, no, really? Can't you tell him how you feel?'

'I can't. It's too selfish. After everything I did… how can I do that? He loves her, not me, and I have to accept that.' I looked across the lawn then as Drew and April arrived with Rory.

'It's Hogmanay soon, anything could happen,' Heather said.

'Perhaps a midnight kiss with a certain someone?' I asked, teasing her.

She rolled her eyes. 'I have no idea who you're talking about.'

'Yeah, right.'

'Anyway, shhh, they're coming over.'

'Hi, guys,' Drew said when the three of them walked up to us. 'You two look deep in conversation, are we interrupting?'

'We were just talking about the Hogmanay party at the Glendale Arms,' Heather lied smoothly. I looked at her: she hadn't mentioned that. 'You're coming too, right?' She put her arm through mine and squeezed it. I was glad she was there. 'It's a costume party and I've had the best idea what we can go as.'

'Why am I suddenly feeling nervous?' I replied, shaking my head.

Chapter Forty-One

I had planned to make an early dinner, before we opened up the trail again, for Sally as she was going down to London to spend New Year with her family. It was a strange swap for us – usually Izzy and I would see her at the party Emily had at her small house each year – but we would be at the Hall instead. Izzy, of course, begged me to include Drew, which meant April too, so I also invited Rory and Heather. The more people between me and April, the better.

When everyone arrived, I was in the kitchen, Sally, Mum and John at the table, Christmas music playing softly in the background. Izzy had rushed to answer the door when the bell sounded, and she returned with our guests.

'Mum is making stew,' Izzy said when she came in. 'I have no idea what it will be like.'

'Charming,' I said, over my shoulder. 'It will be delicious.' I had used one of Sally's recipes, so I was hopeful. 'Are you keeping an eye on the potatoes?' I asked her pointedly, so she quickly ran back to the Aga to check. I left the stew cooking to say hello to everyone and poured out wine for all.

'How's it all going?' Drew asked my mum as he sat down. She had a notebook out on the table and she and Sally and John had been brainstorming ideas for the village.

Mum sighed as she closed the notebook. 'We're running out of ideas as to how we can compete with the development company. We have people who want to run businesses on the high street again, but the council won't budge on the rent costs. Even if the council does want to be seen to be upholding the community, they say they'd have to move resources from other services if they helped the shops. What if we've done all this for nothing?' She gestured outside where you could just see the lights of the trail trying to twinkle through the rain.

'It definitely wasn't for nothing,' Drew told her firmly. 'You have brought the village back together, and even if we fail, I think everyone is passionate about trying to save Glendale, and we will think of another way to do that, I'm sure. Don't be downhearted by all that you've achieved, because you've done more in the last couple of weeks than most people could do in a year.'

'You'll be changing careers and becoming a motivational speaker soon,' I teased him. I was worried, though, like my mum – it did feel as if we'd hit a huge roadblock with no way to navigate our way around it.

'Drew is right,' April said, eagerly. 'Giving up is the last thing you should do.'

'Any ideas as to what we can do instead?' Mum asked with an arch to her voice.

I hid my smile. 'Right, it should all be ready in a minute.' I left the table and went over to drain and mash the potatoes. I heard them all still talking about the village and hoped someone might come up with an idea we could use. I didn't want to give up on saving the village, but it was starting to feel impossible. I thought back to what Gran had said about me not getting down in the dumps but doing what I wanted. It was easier said than done, however.

Izzy came to join me then. 'It smells good,' she said as I pulled the large pot of stew out of the Aga.

'See? Oh, ye of little faith,' I replied, nudging her with my elbow.

'I just remember the lasagne incident, that's all,' she said, referring to the burnt mess of pasta I made us one Saturday night. In my defence, our oven seemed to cook things twice as fast as any recipe instructed. We'd had to order a pizza that night instead and Izzy hadn't been able to stop laughing. I hadn't tried to make it ever again.

I was relieved that everything seemed to look tasty tonight, not wanting any of them at the table to witness a culinary fail. 'Take the green beans over, would you? And remember I swore you to secrecy about that lasagne.'

Izzy grinned. 'I'll take it to my grave, Mum.'

We served up plates for everyone and joined them back at the table, where we all tucked in. I noticed Mum was eating much more, which pleased me, but April picked at it, evidently not enjoying it. Everyone else seemed to, though, so I just ignored her. I was beginning to wonder what Drew saw in her, apart from her looks. They seemed very different, but maybe I was just reading what I wanted into that.

'I was thinking we should do something big for Hogmanay on the trail,' John said. 'It'll be the last night – let's go out with a bang. How about we put on a fireworks display?'

'Everyone will be at the party at the Glendale Arms though,' Heather said, taking a sip of wine.

'They could all come back here for the countdown maybe,' I suggested, liking the idea. I got up to put the dessert in the oven – Izzy and I had made a big apple pie – and saw that Drew had followed me.

'Just getting April some water,' he said, going to the sink. 'Your family had a big firework display the Hogmanay we were together, do you remember? You and your mum had had an argument about what you were wearing, so you refused to come down and we watched the fireworks from your bedroom window, didn't we?'

I remembered it well. It had been our only one together and at midnight, I had wished that every new year would be seen in with Drew by my side. I avoided his gaze, knowing I couldn't let myself get sentimental about it. 'Mum wanted me to wear this hideous dress she had bought me, and I just wanted to wear jeans. She still hates that I refuse to dress up.'

'But you seem to be getting on much better now?' He filled up the glass and leaned against the counter as I put the pie in the oven.

'We are. I think that now we know the truth about why I left, it's been better. And I'm older now, so not so stubborn,' I replied with a smile. I stood up and looked at my mum at the table chatting with John. 'She's had a lot to deal with recently, and I hope that having me here has helped a bit.'

'Of course it has. She'll be sorry to see you go.'

'Like Rory will with you,' I said, looking across at him. He nodded and was about to say something else when April called out his name.

'Your food is getting cold!' she called, straining to see what we were doing.

We both went back to the table, and April narrowed her eyes at me. I just smiled at her.

'I was just saying to Iz,' April said, brightly, turning pointedly away from me towards Drew. 'My sister used to have red hair, but she dyes it blonde like mine.'

My head turned sharply in her direction. Was she saying my daughter needed to dye her hair?

'Izzy's hair is beautiful,' Drew replied, coldly, to my relief. He nudged Izzy who was next to him. 'It has magical powers, right, Iz?'

'Right,' Izzy agreed, smiling up at him.

'Oh, yes, it's gorgeous,' April said, quickly, her cheeks turning a little pink. 'I was just saying she could if she wanted to when she's older.'

'Actually, Iz,' Heather said, breaking into the conversation. 'Your hair has given me inspiration for my Hogmanay costume,' she said to her. I threw her a grateful smile. Across the table, April's eyes were on her plate. She looked like she might cry but it was hard to sympathise with her. 'I need to pick your brains about it.'

'Okay,' Izzy agreed, seemingly oblivious to the tension around her.

'When do I get to know what I'm wearing?' I asked Heather.

'On the night. Me and Iz have got it covered.' She winked at Izzy who giggled.

The back door opened then and we turned in surprise to see my dad in the doorway. 'Oh,' he said when he saw everyone at the table. 'I came to collect some things,' he said, and ducked his head, walking past us briskly and out of the kitchen.

Mum stood up. 'Excuse me,' she said, following him out. I really didn't want her to have to deal with that on her own, so I followed her, apologising to everyone as I left the kitchen. I found my parents in the hallway, facing one another angrily.

'You can't just turn up when you feel like it,' my mum said to him.

'This is still my house!'

'Well, actually, no: it belongs to my mother, but that's beside the point. You've moved out, David. You can't just come and go when you feel like it.'

'I just came to get some things, not to start World War Three,' he replied, wearily. He noticed me then. 'Beth, we don't need a referee.'

'I just came to see if you're all right,' I said to my mum.

'I'm fine,' she said with a nod at me. 'David, you're either part of this family or you're not. You've chosen to leave, so we need to do this properly. You need to call before you come here again.'

My dad stared at us, a little dumbfounded. 'Caroline—'

'I think we need to call this what it is – a separation. So, we should do it properly. Go and get what you need now but, in future, we can arrange if you need anything from the house. And I know you suggested we celebrate Hogmanay together but we're having a fireworks display on the trail and I'm sure you will think that it wouldn't be right for you to be seen at that by your... company,' Mum said, faltering a little on the word, no doubt thinking of Dad's mistress. She spun on her heels and walked back into the kitchen. I kind of wanted to applaud her but obviously I didn't.

'Is this your influence?' Dad said, turning to me.

'Dad, the only influence at work here is yours.'

I left him alone in the hall, hoping he'd finally realise that he was throwing away everything of value in his life.

Chapter Forty-Two

After we'd finished dinner, I sent everyone into the living room with their coffees and started to put everything in the dishwasher. I didn't notice Drew had stayed behind until he brought over a stack of plates. I smiled at him.

'Are you okay? After your dad, I mean?' he asked, handing them to me.

'Just worried about my mum really. She's devastated but putting a brave face on it all. I think he's moved out for good. I don't see how they can come back from this.'

'I'm sorry. It's hard, isn't it, watching people struggle but sometimes you have to let them find their own way out. I know you; you want to help fix it, but it's not something you can do.'

'I know that you're right. I just hate seeing them hurting, especially my mum. She doesn't deserve how he's treating her, but I think she's finally realising that.' I shook my head 'Who'd have thought I'd be fighting my mum's corner? This Christmas really has changed everything.'

'It's nice to see you two getting on so much better. Maybe you're really all grown up now.' He smiled.

'That's right. I'm mature and sensible now. Wonders never cease, right?'

'You haven't changed that much,' Drew replied with a grin.

'Oh, really?'

'Your hair is still the same for one thing.' He reached out and tucked a flyaway strand back over my shoulder. My breath hitched in my throat. 'But you're a posh southerner now.'

'You can talk with your American accent,' I replied, busying myself by rinsing a saucepan, wishing he wasn't standing so close – it made it hard to concentrate.

'I think being back here is calming it down a bit. The longer I'm in Scotland, the more Scottish I become again.'

'Actually, I think my Scottish accent is returning a bit too. People in London won't be able to understand me when I go back.'

'How do you feel about going back? I settle back into Glendale life so much whenever I visit that it feels strange to leave again. And this has been one of my longest trips for a while, I can't believe that I'll soon be on a plane back to Boston.'

With April, I thought to myself with a sinking feeling in my stomach. I tried to shake off my sadness. 'It's the same for me. I really didn't want to come back. If my gran hadn't been so ill… But Izzy and I have really settled in to life here. I will miss Glendale when I get back to the city. And I really didn't think I'd ever say that.'

'I know you've lived in London for ten years, but I always thought of you here. Working in the garden, running through the house, walking to the village, that's how I always thought of you in Boston. Not living in a flat and working in an office.'

'You thought of me in Boston?' I turned to him in surprise.

Drew smiled. 'Of course I did. Beth Williams, you've been hard to shake off, you know.'

'But you did shake me off?' I asked, my voice barely above a whisper.

'Mum, John needs sugar!' Izzy said, bustling in loudly.

I tore myself away from Drew's searching gaze. 'Okay, love,' I said, hurrying to the cupboard to get it.

'What are you talking about?' Izzy asked. I wondered what the expressions on our faces looked like to her.

'What a pain you are,' I replied, handing her the sugar bowl. 'We're coming in now anyway,' I said, following her out before Drew could say anything.

I could feel his eyes burning a hole in my back. My breathing was too fast. I told myself not to put too much stock in our conversation: Drew must have moved on from me a long time ago.

I just wished that I could have said the same.

–

'Did you love my dad?' Izzy asked as I went in to say good night to her. Outside, the trail lights had been turned off and the garden was dark and still. The rain had started back up again, creating a pounding soundtrack in the silence of her room. I sat on the edge of her bed as she looked at me seriously.

'Of course I did. Why do you ask?'

'I just wondered why you aren't still together, I suppose,' she said, trying to shrug casually but it was clear she had given this a lot of thought. Perhaps with April appearing on the scene it had made her wonder.

'Well, Drew won a scholarship to go to university in America so he could be a doctor. When I found out I was carrying you, I didn't want Drew to walk away from his dreams, so I decided that I would go to London and look after you by myself. Why do you ask? Are you worried about him going back to Boston?'

Izzy nodded. 'A little bit. We will keep in touch, won't we?'

'You will always have him in your life now, I promise.' I knew Izzy would be over the moon if Drew chose to take the job in Scotland, but I had no idea if that would happen so didn't want to get her hopes up by telling her about the offer.

Izzy smiled. 'That's good.'

'We both love you, and even though we're not together now, we will always love you. You know that, right?'

She nodded and lay down on her pillow. I turned off her lamp, plunging the room into darkness. 'I love you, Mum,' she said sleepily.

I smiled even though she couldn't see me. 'Sweet dreams, love.' I tucked the duvet around her and left her to fall asleep, hoping that I had eased any concerns she had. I supposed it was confusing to her why her parents weren't together, but I was happy she loved having her father in her life. I had no doubt their bond would continue to get stronger even if Drew did remain in Boston. I tried not to think about how much more we could see him if he did come back to the UK.

Or how much I desperately wanted him to.

Chapter Forty-Three

'Who are you supposed to be?' Mum screwed up her eyes as I walked down the stairs and found her and Izzy waiting for me in the hallway. The Christmas tree was starting to droop now, reminding us that the festive season would soon be all over, and the new year was around the corner: the time when we were supposed to make resolutions and plans for the year ahead, and I had no clue what mine should be. I had gone along with Heather's costume idea for Hogmanay celebrations at the Glendale Arms. My mum was confused; Izzy, however, burst into a round of applause.

'I'm a character in Harry Potter,' I replied, giving them a twirl. I wore a long cloak, fake glasses, and had made my hair as frizzy as I could. I carried a wand to complete the Hermione look. Heather was going as Harry, of course. 'What do you think, Iz?'

'It's perfect. I want a photo with you. I wish I was coming. I could have been Ginny.'

'You would have made an excellent Ginny.' We posed for Mum in front of the tree as she took a photo on my phone of us. I loved it so much, I made it my wallpaper straight away. I gave Izzy a big hug. 'Now, I'll be back for the fireworks, and your dad is coming too. So, we'll see you before midnight. Will you be okay?'

She rolled her eyes. 'Of course I will, Mum.'

We were hoping most of the people at the pub could be persuaded to come back to the Hall to see the fireworks and had hired a minibus to drive us all over. It felt like the perfect ending to the trail.

'You go and have fun; we'll hold the fort here,' Mum said as we heard a beep from outside.

Heather's dad, Don, had arrived to pick me up, and I climbed into the car with him and Heather and we drove out to the village. The sky was clear and cold, and the stars were out in full force above us. Time was ticking by too quickly. Soon, January would be with us, and my trip home would be coming to an end. I kept pushing it to the back of my mind, but I knew I wouldn't be able to for that much longer.

'It feels like old times: you chauffeuring me and Beth around, Dad.'

'I remember picking you both up, and you pretending you hadn't had anything to drink. I had to force myself not to laugh, to be honest. Not that I condone underage drinking,' he said with a wink to me in the rear-view mirror.

'You'll have all that to come with Izzy,' Heather said to me.

'God, don't. Although, right now she's shocked at the idea of drinking, so let's hope she doesn't take after me as a teenager too much,' I said with a shudder. I thought back to the times I used to stay out with my mum not knowing where I was. I certainly wasn't easy; I knew that now. While I hoped Izzy would stay her sensible self as she grew up, at least I knew all the tricks for sneaking out of the house and might be able to thwart her if she didn't.

'Right, here we are,' Don said as he pulled into the car park. Music and light streamed out from the open door to the pub. 'Have a great time.'

'Are you sure you won't join us for the fireworks?' I asked him as I climbed out.

'Thank you, but I'll be safely tucked up in bed by then. My days of staying up to midnight are behind me now, thankfully.'

I thanked him for the lift, and Heather gave him a kiss before he left. 'I love how close you two are,' I told her, slipping my arm through hers as we walked into the pub.

'With mum gone, we've grown much closer. I like looking after him. I wouldn't want him to be alone. Right – what are we drinking then?'

Heather's words rang in my ears as we weaved our way to the bar. I didn't like the thought of my mum being on her own either.

Glendale Arms was full of people, which was lovely to see. Most people were in costumes, and the atmosphere was lively. Heather got us a bottle of wine and we went through to the back where we spotted Drew with Rory and April. They called us over, and we squeezed into the booth with them.

'Is that really a costume, Drew?' I asked with a laugh seeing that both he and Rory were wearing kilts.

'I didn't have anything else with me. Rory, doesn't have an excuse though,' Drew replied with a grin.

'Yes, I do,' his brother disagreed. 'I wanted to show off my legs. I knew Heather wouldn't be able to resist,' he joked.

Heather arched an eyebrow. 'The big question we need answering though is what you have on under those kilts, boys.'

'Hey, I'm happy to show you,' Rory said, starting to lift his kilt up. Heather shrieked and told him not to scare the whole pub. Drew and I laughed at them. I noticed April had crossed her arms over her chest, looking annoyed.

'What did you come as, April?' I asked, trying to make an effort.

'I didn't have a costume either. But this is my New Year Eve's dress,' she said, uncrossing her arms. She was wearing a little black dress and looked gorgeous. She wrapped her arm through Drew's. Heather poured me a glass of wine and I grabbed it, eager for something to dull the ache I felt seeing them together, but she stopped me.

'We need a toast first. Here's to the new year – let it be happy and healthy for all of us,' Heather said, raising her glass. We all clinked glasses and took a drink.

'I think we need shots,' Rory said, getting up and ignoring our groans.

The pub soon became crowded. Everyone was in a good mood. The music got louder, and with all the drinks that Drew and Rory bought us, Heather and I were soon decidedly tipsy. April, I noticed, wasn't drinking very much and looked quite bored as she played with her phone.

Heather grabbed Rory and dragged him onto the makeshift dance floor that had started up, and they twirled each other around to the cheesy dance song playing.

'Want to dance?' Drew asked April. She agreed and they joined the other two. I watched for a moment. Even though it was a fast song, April had her arms around Drew's neck twirling in a slow dance. I decided that I needed some air and hastily got up and walked out to the garden at the back.

The sky was clear, a crescent moon dangling above, shining its slivery light down on me. I sat at one of the picnic tables, a glass in my hand, breathing in the cool air. I was conscious that it was almost time to make resolutions, to make plans for the year ahead, and I wasn't sure what I wanted mine to be. Change seemed to be dangling like a seductive carrot in front of me, but I wasn't sure whether or not I wanted to take it. Or what it would look like if I did.

'There you are,' Drew said, startling me from my thoughts. He joined me at the table. 'April's family have called her,' he said as if to explain why he was allowed out there with me. 'I can't believe it's almost the new year,' Drew continued. 'This time last year, I had no idea I'd find out I had a daughter,' he said. 'So, God knows what this year will bring.' He smiled at me though.

My head was spinning a little from all the booze. I looked at him and knew our time together was running out, so I had to ask him while I could. 'Drew, can you ever forgive me? For not telling you back then? For running away?' I found myself touching his hand desperately.

Drew met my eyes. 'It's been a shock and a lot to get my head around. But for so long, I was confused. I didn't understand why you cut off all contact. I thought… well, I thought that maybe you had never really felt the same way about me as I felt about you. At least now I know the truth. I know why you left me.'

'Of course I felt the same way,' I told him.

'And you tried to tell me. I still don't understand why I never got your letter, but I get why after I didn't reply you didn't try again.' He sighed. 'I love Izzy. Spending time with her has been really special. I have to focus on the future with her and not what I missed out on. I wasn't sure that I would ever be able to forgive you when you told me but, I think, I already have.'

A sob escaped my throat.

'And now you just need to forgive yourself,' Drew whispered. He held out his arm and I leaned into him. His arms around me felt too good.

I lifted my head and was startled to see how close our faces were. 'I wish I could turn back the clock. To ten years ago,' I admitted. I wanted to tell him that I still felt the same way about him as I had then. Maybe even stronger and deeper because I knew how special the feeling was. 'I wish we were still us,' I said, before I could stop myself.

Drew's eyes searched mine. Then his gaze shifted to my mouth. I found myself parting my lips. And then his lips were on mine. Hesitant. Soft. Just a brush before he pulled back to look at me again. I wanted to grab him. I wanted to kiss him harder, but when I leaned in towards him again, I heard music suddenly get louder and light flood out from the pub, and I froze. Drew turned around as a voice called out. A voice that reminded me we weren't us any more. He was no longer mine and would never be.

Drew stood up abruptly. 'I have to go,' he said turning, and going to April.

I didn't dare turn around to watch them, because I knew that if I did it would break my heart.

Chapter Forty-Four

I drained my glass of wine dry, got up and went back into the pub. I hated that our moment had been stolen but I also felt guilty. April was his girlfriend after all. I had a history with Drew, but it was clear he was in love with her, and even though he obviously still cared for me and seemed to have forgiven me for walking out of his life, I knew that was the end of it. We were drunk and had been talking about our daughter. That was the only reason he had kissed me. To make me feel better. I had been upset. I had to push the kiss out of my mind, and quickly.

I had to try, somehow, to move on from him.

'You okay?' Heather asked, breathlessly, coming back to the table when she spotted me there.

'Yep,' I lied, grabbing more wine and filling up my glass. I checked the time. 'The minibus will be here in a minute, let's round everyone up,' I said, relieved that I could take action and not have to sit there any longer with my thoughts. We got up and told everyone that they were welcome back at Glendale Hall for the fireworks. When we finally got outside, the minibus was waiting and Heather, Rory, Drew, April and I were joined by five others keen to come back with us.

Drew and April sat together, April leaning on his shoulder, and I turned to look out of the window, trying not to let them upset me. I had messed up everything between us ten years ago. I had to accept that we were in the past. All that mattered now was Izzy. I just wished my heart knew that and would stop racing at the memory of his lips on mine. The others talked, laughed and sang along to the radio, but I fixed my eyes on the rolling countryside and tried to ignore the fact that Drew kept looking at me.

I forced on a smile when we pulled into the driveway. I was determined not to start the new year on a downer.

–

'Mum!' Izzy ran from the garden to greet us, and she gave me a big hug. 'Everything is ready,' she said. 'Hi, Dad,' she greeted Drew. The word pierced my heart again. I slung an arm around her and walked back into the garden with her, conscious of Drew and April right behind us.

I paused in shock at the edge of the garden. It was completely full of people, all holding drinks and sparklers, the lights from the trail lighting up their smiling faces. It seemed like the whole village had come out for the night. I smiled despite myself. This was what I had hoped for when we created the trail. It proved there was a community very much alive in Glendale, and it was inspiring to see.

'Wow,' I said when Mum came over.

'Isn't it wonderful? Did you have a nice time?' Mum asked.

I nodded, not trusting myself to answer aloud. 'Gran wasn't up to coming out?'

'No, but I moved her into my room so she can see the fireworks from the window.'

I turned and looked up at the house, spotting a figure looking down on us. I waved but I wasn't sure if she could see me.

'And look who Heather persuaded to come,' Mum said, pointing to a man standing a little bit away from the group, a camera around his neck. 'He's from the local paper – they're going to do an article on the trail and how the community is trying to pull together to stop the redevelopment. As the council won't budge on rents, I thought we needed to get some publicity on the issue and see if that helps.'

'That's a great idea,' I said, hoping it might encourage the council to have a rethink.

'Right, it's almost midnight,' Mum said loudly then to the group.

'It's freezing out here,' April said from beside me. 'Cuddle me, Drew.' She tucked herself into him, but he caught my gaze over the top of her head.

'I'm sorry,' Drew mouthed to me.

I just shook my head and looked down at my boots sinking into the damp grass.

'Mum, it's almost time,' Izzy instructed us, tugging on my cloak. 'Let's go closer.' I followed her to the front of the group. My head was spinning. I wished I hadn't drunk so much. I wished I hadn't kissed him. But, most of all, I wished I hadn't let myself fall in love with him again.

'Here we go,' Mum said, holding up her phone to show us the time. Everyone quietened down. I joined in with the chorus counting the seconds to midnight and sent out a wish that I might get a clue about what the hell I should do in the next year because, right now, I had no idea.

At twelve, a huge cheer went up from the garden and we broke into an off-key rendition of 'Auld Lang Syne.' As we reached the end, the sky exploded into light. John had gone all out with the fireworks. Everyone clapped as a multitude of colours dazzled us in the sky.

'Happy New Year!' I said to Izzy as the final firework exploded, reigning down a waterfall of lights. I hugged her tightly.

'Happy New Year darlings,' my mum said, joining us. And then there was Heather. And I hugged people I didn't even know before I came face-to-face with Drew again. He reached for me, and I let myself fold into his arms for the second time that night. We held on to each other for a moment longer than was needed.

John rejoined us and poured out glasses of Prosecco for everyone. I watched Mum go back into the house, and I drained my drink in one gulp. I knew I'd regret it in the morning, but I wanted to erase any remnants of heartbreak.

'Are you okay?' Heather was beside me. 'Really?'

'Drew and I kissed. Kind of. And then April broke things up,' I told her.

She gasped. 'Blimey. What are you going to do?'

'I have no idea.'

'Heather, I've ordered us a taxi, you better stay at the farm with us,' Rory said, coming over and interrupting us.

'Are you coming on to me, Rory Fraser?' she replied, putting her hands on her hips.

'I wouldn't dare.' Rory grinned, though, and I wondered if he was planning to do just that. I hoped so. Heather deserved some happiness.

'Don't do anything I wouldn't,' I couldn't resist calling after them. Heather turned around and poked her tongue out at me.

'Beth!'

I turned as I heard the desperate call. My mum was in the doorway of the kitchen, waving to me frantically. I ran straight over to her. 'What is it?'

'It's Mum, she's collapsed,' she replied, her face filled with panic.

'I'll help,' Drew said from behind me. I hadn't seen him follow me. John was there too.

'Guys, will you stay with Izzy?' I called to Heather and Rory. I saw Izzy watching us, confused, and they went straight over to her. April was soon there as well, and she quickly wrapped her arms around Izzy. I followed Mum up the stairs, suddenly feeling sober. The festivities felt very far away as we reached my gran and saw her on the floor beside her wheelchair. She wasn't moving.

Drew rushed to her, the doctor in him calmly taking over, telling us to call an ambulance over his shoulder. I pulled out my phone and dialled 999 for the first time in my life.

Chapter Forty-Five

The hospital room was silent. Mum and I sat in chairs on either side of Gran's bed as she slept. Outside, a new day was starting to dawn, not that we could see it. January was beginning on a sober note for us.

We had been up all night. I'd managed to quickly pull off my witch's cloak and replace it with a hoodie before following the ambulance in my car, my mum having jumped in with Gran. Gran had bruised her hips and ribs and was having trouble breathing properly. She looked even weaker than before all of this. I could tell by everyone's faces that they didn't think she'd pull through this fall. She was already far too frail from the cancer. I knew that Mum wanted her at home, but I wasn't sure she'd make it back there.

My phone buzzed in my bag, so I stepped outside to answer it. 'Hi, Drew.' He had helped Gran get into the ambulance, and then stayed on at the Hall to look after Izzy and clear up after the party. Our New Year celebration felt very far away, as did the moment I had with him outside the pub. 'Is Izzy okay?'

'She's fine. I just checked in on her, and she's fast asleep. It took a while to persuade her to go to bed, so I expect she's knackered. I couldn't sleep though. I wanted to check on how Mrs Williams is and how you guys are doing.'

'Gran is conscious now; she didn't break anything but is really bruised and is on oxygen as her ribs are making it hard for her to breathe. She looks so frail. It doesn't look good. And we're okay. Just tired and worried.'

'I'll take Izzy back with me to the farm, once she gets up, and try to take her mind off it all.'

'Thanks, Drew. I'm glad you're there for her.'

'Keep in touch, okay? And try to rest if you can soon.'

'I will,' I promised. I hung up and turned to see my dad walking down the corridor. I had persuaded Mum to let me call him once we had spoken to the doctor, and he had come to the hospital straight away.

'Beth,' he said, coming up to me. 'You both must have had such a shock.'

'It was horrible seeing her on the floor like that. I don't think Mum is taking it too well. I think she thought Gran would stay at home, you know, until the end.'

Dad nodded. 'It was what they both wanted but Margaret is very ill. I'll go in and see them.'

'I'm going to get us some coffees.' I watched Dad go in to the room. Whatever was happening in their marriage, I knew that Mum would appreciate his support. I headed off to the canteen to get us all some much-needed caffeine.

I knew that I had come back to Glendale because Dad had warned me he didn't think Gran would survive another Christmas, but I honestly hadn't expected that she would end up in hospital during my visit. I thought about what Mum said as I carried three paper cups back up to the ward. She had told Gran she forgave her for what she had done in the past. And that forgiveness was often as much about how you wanted to feel as how you wanted the other person to feel. Did I want to hang on to my anger and bitterness over what happened? Time was running out for me to make my peace with her.

Would I regret it forever if I didn't do that?

When I returned, my parents were outside her room. I handed them both their coffees. 'What's happening?'

'She's awake,' Dad said. 'And asking for you.'

'Do you want to go in?' Mum asked me gently.

'Okay.' I took a gulp of the coffee. It tasted like crap. I was nervous but I also knew that I had to do this. They sat down in the chairs in the corridor. My mum looked shattered, and my dad looked grave. I felt like a zombie from the combination of last night's alcohol, the lack of sleep and all the stress, but I knew that I couldn't run from her any more. I took another gulp of coffee and then I walked into the room.

Gran's eyes were open as she lay in the bed, watching me sit down beside her.

'Caroline told me that Drew helped me last night.'

I nodded. 'He was great. He's looking after Izzy right now.'

'I'm glad he's back in your life. This might be my last chance to say it, but I was wrong, Beth. About it all. I know that now. I wish I could have known it sooner and done something about it. I let you go, and I should never have done that. We've all missed you. Having you back at the Hall has been the best Christmas present.' I watched a tear roll down her cheek. 'I thought I'd never get my chance to tell you the truth. Thank you for giving me that chance.'

'Gran, I wish I had known it all sooner, but I am glad that I know it now. I feel like my mum and I are growing closer, and I'm glad that Izzy has had a chance to get to know you all better and see my home. I have missed it more than I realised. Please don't be upset, it's okay. You told me. You did the right thing.' In the end, I added silently but I knew she knew what I meant.

She reached out for my hand, and I wrapped mine around hers. 'Promise me one thing, Beth. That you'll always be honest and tell people how you feel. You may think that it's too late, but it never is. I truly believe that now.'

I thought of Drew straight away. But I couldn't let myself believe that, could I? It was too late for us, wasn't it? Gran was looking at me fiercely, so I found myself nodding. How could I say no to her? 'I promise,' I whispered, hoping that I could live up to it.

'Good.' She raised a small smile. 'It's all in your hands now, Beth. And I know you'll make us all proud.'

I opened my mouth to ask what was in my hands, but Mum and Dad came into the room tentatively to check on us. My gran closed her eyes as if our conversation had tired her out. I took a deep breath. I knew then, as a tear rolled down my own cheek, that I needed to do it: as much for me as for her. For everyone in the room. The time had come to let the past be the past. We had the rest of our lives to live. 'Gran, I forgive you,' I said.

She opened her eyes. 'I know. I don't deserve it; I know that as well. But you're a much better woman than I ever was. And Izzy will be too. You only get one family.' She looked at my parents behind me. 'Make sure you take care of each other.' She drifted back to sleep after that, and they ended up being the last words she said to us.

Because later that day, she passed away.

Chapter Forty-Six

The day had faded by the time I drove to the farm to pick up Izzy. After Gran had died, and we had sorted out what we could at the hospital, I took Mum home and she had gone to bed, exhausted, falling straight to sleep. I had managed a couple of hours napping myself but was keen to see Izzy again. The first day of January was almost over, and I was glad of it. I wanted to put the day behind us. We had known it was coming for a while but, even so, it was still a shock when Gran hadn't responded to us and we realised what had happened. At least we had had the chance to say goodbye, and she had gone in peace. That was something to feel grateful for.

Climbing out of the car, I knocked on the door, and Drew held out his arms to me. I sank into them and couldn't stop myself from remembering Gran's last words to me. *Promise me that you'll always be honest and tell people how you feel.* I pulled away from him before I would be unable to.

'How are you doing?' he said, showing into the hall and closing the door behind us.

'Just tired, really. And still a bit dazed by it all. Worried about my mum, too. Does Izzy know?'

'I thought you'd want to tell her.'

I nodded. 'Thank you for looking after her. And Gran, too, last night.'

'No thanks needed. I'll put the kettle on. Izzy is in the living room. April… she's in town,' he added, and I was instantly relieved. I didn't want her around at that moment. He gave me a reassuring smile, and I felt his eyes on me as I went to find her.

'Hi, love,' I said when I saw her. She was curled up, reading, but jumped up when she saw me and ran over for a hug, gripping my waist tightly. I leaned down into her hair. 'I missed you.'

'How is great-gran?' Izzy asked me, anxiously.

'Let's sit down.' I sat down on the sofa next to her and wrapped an arm around her. 'I'm sorry, Iz, but she passed away at the hospital this morning. She was really peaceful and not in any pain, and we were all with her at the end.'

'She's gone?' Izzy repeated as if she wasn't quite sure whether or not to believe me.

I brushed back her hair. 'Yes, darling. She has. She was very sick, and she couldn't recover from falling. But now, she's not suffering any more.' I felt a sob rise up in my throat. Izzy grabbed hold of me, and I gave her a tight hug. When we pulled back, she was crying. 'Oh, sweetheart, I'm sorry.'

'I never knew anyone who died before. In real life, I mean,' she said, sniffling.

I felt a tear roll down my own cheek. 'I know. And it's so hard realising that we won't get to see or talk to her any more, isn't it? It's okay to be sad, Iz. Come here.' I pulled her into my arms again, wishing I could take her pain away but knowing that she, like all of us, just had to feel it. And it was sad. Despite our ups and downs, she had been my grandmother, and I had loved her. I was glad that we had finally put the past to bed, and I didn't have any regrets to add to the grief.

'Is Granny upset?' Izzy said, looking up at me.

She was always most worried about other people, bless her. 'She is. She lost her mother today, so we need to be there for her, don't we? You can give her a big hug when we get home.'

She nodded. 'I will.'

I wiped her eyes. 'She really loved you, you know that, don't you? She was really proud of you.'

'And you, Mum. She was proud of you.'

I gave Izzy another tight hug as another tear rolled down my cheek. I knew that Izzy was right. At the end, we had made peace with one another.

Drew came in then, and we both wiped our tears away. He brought in coffee for us and a hot chocolate for Izzy. He also had a big slice of ginger cake for us all. He knew us well. 'You both need this,' he said. 'I'm so sorry, you guys.'

I took the coffee from him and nodded. 'Thank you. I'm just glad we got to say goodbye. And that we came home this Christmas.'

He sat down in the armchair. 'I'm glad you did, too.' Our eyes met, and I wondered what he was thinking.

'What happens when you die, do you think? At school, they said some people believe you go to heaven? Do you think that you go there?' Izzy asked us.

'Honestly, I don't know, love. But your great-grandmother went to church and she definitely believed that you go to heaven when you die, so I hope that she has.'

'I wonder what it's like there,' Izzy said, thoughtfully.

'She always said that it was a special and peaceful place where you can live happily with people you have loved in your life.'

Izzy let that sink in for a moment. 'I like that idea. I would want to be with you there.'

Another lump rose up in my throat. 'I'd like that too.'

I realised then we'd be back in Glendale church. I looked across at Drew. 'You won't be here for the funeral,' I spoke my thought aloud. It was selfish but I would have liked him to be there.

'Our flight is in a couple of days,' he confirmed, a frown appearing on his face. 'But I'd like to come back for it. I might be able to change my shifts around. I hate the thought of leaving you. Both,' he added, looking at Izzy.

I hated the thought of it too. I looked at Izzy. 'I don't think we should leave Mum on her own too long.'

'Drew said I can have another sleepover here before they go,' Izzy said.

'If that's okay?' Drew asked me quickly.

'Of course,' I replied. I knew they would both find it hard to say goodbye. I didn't expect there to be so many partings this holiday.

'I wish you didn't live so far away. Boston is stupid,' Izzy declared then.

'I'm starting to think you're right,' Drew said, so quietly as we turned to leave, I wasn't sure if he had meant for us to hear him.

–

I had ordered us pizza for dinner, but Mum had hardly touched it and had gone to bed straight afterwards. We agreed to discuss the funeral arrangements the next day, and then Dad phoned from his hotel to ask if he could come to the house to speak to me about Gran's will. He was the executor and wanted to discuss it with me so I agreed, curious as to why he needed me and not just Mum, but perhaps he didn't want to worry her with it on top of the organising the funeral.

I phoned the head teacher of Izzy's school and asked if it would be okay if we could both have a few more days off so we could stay on for the funeral, and he agreed. I was grateful for having an understanding boss and to be able to put off thinking about going back to London for a little longer. And then Heather arrived.

'Oh, hun,' she said, when I opened the door, giving me a big hug.

'It's good to see you,' I said, letting her in. I led her through to the kitchen and poured us both a glass of wine. 'Izzy has just gone to bed, and Mum is already asleep.'

'How is everybody coping?' she asked as we sat down at the table together.

'My mum isn't doing great, to be honest. She's lost her mother.' I looked at her. 'I'm sorry, you know what that's like.' I squeezed her hand, and she smiled.

'It's fine, honestly. Yeah, I do know. It's so hard. But I'm sure she's grateful that you and Izzy are here. Is there anything I can do to help?'

'Dad is dealing with most of it. We're going to talk about the funeral tomorrow.' I looked out at the garden. 'John dismantled the trail today. It's strange to see the garden without it.'

'It was magical,' Heather said. 'How about you? How are you doing?'

'Honestly, I'm glad she's not suffering any more. You know, I can't pretend to have been her biggest fan through the years, but she was still my grandmother. It's so strange to be here in this house without her. I'm glad, though, that we got to be honest with one another at the end. At the hospital I told her I forgave her.'

'I'm sure that helped her find peace.'

'I hope so.' I took a sip of the wine.

'And Drew?' Heather asked hesitantly. 'Have you spoken about what happened?'

'Not really. He goes back to Boston soon. With April.' I felt despondent and I didn't like it. 'Enough about my woes, please. Tell me something else. I need to stop dwelling on how rubbish everything feels right now. If anyone can cheer me up...' I looked at her, hopefully.

'Oh, God, the pressure!' Her cheeks turned a little pink. 'Actually, I did want to tell you something, but it feels a little silly with everything going on here.'

'I need silly,' I assured her.

'Okay, well, last night. After everything that happened here, Rory and I got a taxi back to the farm with April. It was too late and too far for me to get home, so I stayed there. And... I slept with him.'

My eyes widened. 'Oh my god!'

She put her hands to her face. 'I know right! Drew's older brother. The guy who's taken the piss out of me for years. But, I think I like him. Oh, man.' She buried her head in her arms.

I tried not to laugh. 'This isn't a disaster. This is a good thing. You like him. He likes you. I think that's great.'

'I haven't heard a peep from him since, though.'

'Oh.'

'Yeah, oh. I swear I have the worst luck with men.'

'Maybe he just doesn't think you like him? Maybe you need to tell him how you feel.' I cringed at how hypocritical I was being. Why was it always easier to give someone else advice but not to take the same advice yourself?

'Would you tell him?' she asked pointedly, reading my mind.

'Probably not,' I admitted. 'But that doesn't mean I'm not right.'

She sighed. 'What about you and Drew? Have you told him how you feel?'

It was my turn for my cheeks to turn pink. 'No. He doesn't feel the same way, Heather, I know he doesn't.'

'None of us ever really know what someone else thinks or feels. He might be waiting for you to say something.'

'Or he's happy with his girlfriend.'

Heather rolled her eyes. 'The girlfriend he never mentioned until she turned up. There's no way he doesn't feel something for you; I have seen the way you two are together. Then and now. I don't think you should let him go back without saying something.'

There was only one thing for it – I followed her lead and buried my own head in my arms.

Chapter Forty-Seven

Mum was up and bustling in the kitchen when Izzy and I went down the next morning. 'Morning you two, I'm making us breakfast,' she said, glancing over her shoulder to smile at us. 'Sit down, it's almost ready. Although I must admit I'll be pleased when Sally comes home tomorrow.'

I raised an eyebrow. I hadn't expected her to be up and dressed and bustling around the kitchen but perhaps it was helping to take her mind off things. Izzy and I sat down as we were told. I had phoned Sally to tell her the news of Gran, and she had immediately said she would come straight back, but I had firmly told her to wait until she had originally planned to return. She deserved a break and there would be so much to do when she did get back to the Hall. She had reluctantly agreed.

'Did you sleep okay?' I asked Mum as she brought over two plates of scrambled eggs and toast and a jug of juice.

'Not really. I was up half the night thinking about every-thing. There is so much to do, and my mother wouldn't want us to take our eyes off the ball. We are meeting the council soon, and we have to be prepared. We have to think of a way to save the village. I won't let all our hard work the past couple of weeks be for nothing.'

'But, surely…?'

'Beth,' she said in a warning tone, passing me a coffee and sitting down opposite me with her mug and plate. 'You said it yourself, I need this project. We need to get our Glendale rescue plan back on track.'

'Dad is coming over later to talk to me about Gran, so you could meet up with Heather to come up with a plan for our meeting with the council in a couple of days?' I suggested, seeing how determined she was. If this was her way of coping with her mother's death then what could I do but go along with it?

'I hope we can still work something out with them to stop this development. A compromise at the very least.' She didn't look one hundred per cent convinced that it would be possible though.

I wished I could think of something that would help us. Mum deserved to be able to do that after all that had happened. But I had a sinking feeling that Dad's company would win out, and then the Glendale we knew and loved would cease to exist. I shuffled off after breakfast to shower and get dressed. It was proving hard to buck myself up. Not only was I reeling from losing Gran, and having to deal with planning a funeral, but there was the prospect that Glendale might not be saved after all, and Drew was leaving Scotland. I also soon had to face the prospect of going back to our life in London, and the thought of doing that made me feel a little lonely. I liked having my family, Heather, Sally and John, and of course Drew, around. I had always loved that Izzy and I were a team of two, but it wouldn't be the same. I had had to deal with so much by myself, and I realised that maybe I didn't want to do that any more.

I glanced at the brochure Heather had left last night of the college she had applied to do some art and design courses at. She was planning to study at night and find another day job once the library closed. As I climbed into the shower, I felt a little jealous of Heather. She had everything planned out.

Although the prospect of losing her job had been a huge blow, she was turning it into a silver lining and building a new future for herself. She was going after what she loved. I glanced out of the bathroom window, at the vast lawn below me, and wished that I could do the same thing.

–

Mum left an hour later to meet Heather in the village, and my dad arrived at the Hall soon after that. I left Izzy icing cookies in the kitchen and joined him in his study. I fidgeted in the chair opposite his, the desk between us as the setting felt strangely formal.

'How is Caroline?' he asked as he searched for the papers he was looking for in his drawer.

'She's throwing herself back into the Glendale project. But maybe that's good for her, I don't know.'

'It is probably helping her to take her mind off losing her mother. I wouldn't worry. Your mother is one of the strongest women I know.'

'Well, she's had to be, hasn't she?' I couldn't resist snapping back.

Dad leaned back in his chair and sighed. 'Beth, I wish I could change what has happened, but I can't. I care about Caroline very much. I want to do all I can to help her right now.'

'I know you do. Mum has spoken to the minister and he wants to speak to us about readings and hymns that we'd like at the funeral. I think Mum would like us to go with her, for support. She said we'd see him at the church tomorrow.'

Dad nodded. 'Of course I'll be there. I'll ask Caroline if there's anyone she'd like me to tell about it so she doesn't have to. But first, I wanted to speak to you.'

I nodded, cautiously. 'Okay.'

'I am the executor of Margaret's will, and as such, I shall be sorting out everything regarding that. Her solicitor has arranged to come and discuss it in detail with us, but I wanted to tell you myself what is in her will, and also to give you this.' He pulled out an envelope. 'She wrote you a letter, Beth. For you to read after her death.'

I stared at it as if it was a bomb. 'She wrote to me?'

'She wasn't sure if she would see you before the end, so she wrote this in case. It also explains what is in her will.' Dad leaned forward and looked at me. 'Beth, this is going to take a while to sink in, and you're going to have think hard about what you are going to want to do.'

I felt my pulse speed up. And I wasn't sure why. 'What does it say, Dad?' I asked, wondering if I really wanted to know.

Chapter Forty-Eight

'You and Caroline are the sole beneficiaries of Margaret's will. She created a trust fund a long time ago for each of you, and both contain a significant amount of money. As you know, the family whiskey brand still provides an excellent income as we still receive a percentage of all profits they make, plus the original money that your great-grandfather made when he sold the company has been invested well through the years. Basically, Beth, you're now a very wealthy woman,' Dad said. I stared at him, open-mouthed. 'Additionally, Glendale Hall was signed over to you ten years ago, as part of your trust as well. Which means, you are the owner of Glendale Hall. There are two stipulations included in her will – that Caroline may live in the house for as long as she wants, and that you do not sell it so it will remain in the family to be passed down in the future to Izzy.'

I stared at him in shock. 'Seriously?' He nodded. 'Bloody hell.'

He smiled a little. 'When she wrote her will, she told me that this was to make up for something she had done. She wouldn't tell me what that was at the time, but she wrote it down in this letter to you. Of course, now we know what she meant. This is to apologise for how she treated you when you were pregnant but, more than that, I think she wanted to secure the future of the Hall. She wanted to make sure it would stay in the family, and by passing it down it you, that's what she has done.'

It was so hard to take in. Obviously, I knew how badly Gran had felt about the past, but I had no idea she would go as far as to leave such an inheritance to me. 'I don't know what to say.'

'As I said, you need to let it sink in and have a think about what you want to do. You could, of course, do nothing. Your mother will keep on living here, and you can go back to London with Izzy, and use the money to buy a property there. Or you could choose to stay here at the Hall. The point is now you have options. Margaret has given you freedom to choose what to do next with your life.' He held out the letter. 'Here, why don't you read what she wrote to you, it might help you decide what to do.'

I took it nervously. 'Dad, what do you think I should do?' I asked him. It had been a long time since I had asked my dad a question like that, and he looked surprised but considered it for a moment before answering me.

'I think you should do what will make you happy.'

My eyebrows almost left my face, I raised them so high. My serious, business-minded father was telling me to do what would make me happy. Not the right thing or the sensible thing but what would make me happy. I nodded. 'Does Mum know?'

'Yes, they discussed it. She knew what Margaret wanted. And she told me she thought it was the right decision.'

'Really?'

Dad smiled. 'Really.'

I left his study, still holding the letter, too scared to open it just yet. My mind was racing. I had had no thoughts of what my gran was going to leave anyone, but I would have assumed my mum would inherit everything. Yet, there I was, the new owner of Glendale Hall. I looked around as I walked round the side of the house into the garden. I needed a moment alone before I went to find Izzy. I had no idea what she was going to say when she found out. I slipped my boots and coat on and went outside.

January was beginning grey and dull. The clouds were thick above me as I walked across the lawn, hands in the pockets of my coat, my breath visible in the air. Behind me, Glendale Hall loomed large. It was strange to think that all of it was mine. I suppose I had assumed that one day it would be, but I had thought that would happen at some far-off distant time when my parents were no longer around. To own it, at twenty-six, was unexpected. If anyone had told me just one month before, I would have rebelled against it. I would have gone back to London, and to the safety of my familiar life there with Izzy.

But there was no denying that spending Christmas here had reignited my love for the Hall, especially its grounds. Walking, I felt some of my uncertainty lift as if being out in the garden was healing in itself. I felt relaxed out here. I thought of all I could do as the seasons changed, and I ached to be part of it. To go back to our tiny, if cosy, flat seemed somehow less appealing than it used to. And I knew that my parents needed me. Especially my mum. If she and my dad did split up, she would be alone. I knew she had friends, and Sally and John, but she would have no family around her. And although I knew we'd always be as close as we were now, neither would Izzy and I.

Plus, there was the fact that Izzy hadn't been as happy in London as she had led me to believe. Her problems at school had upset her, and she didn't have any close friends there. She had blossomed in Glendale; I couldn't deny that. She didn't have her head stuck in a book at all hours; she was involved, happy to try new things, to have fun, and was growing close to everyone here. And if her dad did decide to move to Scotland then she would love being as close to him as possible.

It wasn't just the prospect of owning the Hall that was making me question everything. I had also been left a lot of money too. That gave me options for the first time in a long time. When I had run away, I had not only left the house and my family, but the family money too. And I had survived. I'd worked hard for every penny, managed to keep a roof over Izzy and me, and food on the table, but that had been a struggle at times. I had abandoned all ideas of further study, not gone to college or university, and had taken an office job that I really didn't enjoy all that much. Now, Gran had given me a choice. I wouldn't *have* to go back to that.

But if I didn't then what would I do instead?

–

'I finally have some good news,' Mum said when we sat down together that night. 'Someone came into the library to speak to Heather. They came to the trail and were inspired by it and decided to do some research on what we could do to help save the library. There is a national fund that we can apply to, apparently, providing we come up with an idea they like. Heather thought we could set up a homework club for the kids and computer classes for older people. Community projects. Just like the trail – and they will provide funding for it. Which might help persuade the council to keep it open,' she said. 'And look at this!' She slid the local paper across the coffee table towards me. The Glendale trail took up most of the front page, and the headline was big and bold:

Let's save our village!

The report praised the trail and all the work that been put into it. It was scathing about the council planning to redevelop the high street, especially when there were businesses keen to open up shop there. Almost two hundred people, the newspaper estimated, had been to walk our trail, and the whole village was buzzing about it. I looked at the lights in the photo, and my heart swelled. I had never expected such a great turnout or how inspiring it would be for so many. Maybe it had done more than I thought it had. I really hoped so.

'So, Mr Murray got on the phone to me,' Mum said as I was reading it. 'He has finally realised how much the community doesn't want the village to be redeveloped, and the council are finally starting to listen to us. He has brought our meeting forward. He had seemed keen to come to a compromise. He said: "it was clear the people had spoken".'

'That's so great,' I replied, hardly daring to believe it was true.

'I think they've realised that the village isn't going down without a fight but quite what they're going to suggest I don't know,' Mum said. 'Heather and I thought about looking into whether some sort of profit sharing scheme could be set up so that instead of paying high rents, people would pay the council once the shops made money.'

'That could work,' I said. I had had my own thoughts on the subject but wanted to be sure before I said anything to my mum or Heather. I needed to be certain it was the right thing for Izzy, and me, and for everyone else. It was great that the council were coming around, though. I hoped it meant New Horizons would soon be out of the picture.

'What did you say when Gran told you what she was going to put in her will?' I asked Mum then, taking a sip of my wine and curling my legs up on the sofa. The fire in the corner crackled. The evenings were still freezing, but the room was warm and cosy.

'At the time, I was surprised. You two hadn't spent much time together since you went to London as my mother didn't like leaving Scotland, and of course you hadn't been home in years. She was determined though. She thought that the house needed young blood in it again, and by giving it to you, she hoped you'd come back and live here again. Obviously, now I know she also had another motive – to try to make up for how she treated you when she found out you were pregnant.'

'What would you think if I did live here again, one day?' I asked, wanting to gauge her thoughts on it all.

Mum smiled. 'I would love it. Having you and Isabelle here this Christmas has been really special but, Beth, you need to do what is best for you and your daughter. I hope that we can keep on strengthening our relationship, whether you're here or in London, and I know that whatever you decide will be the right thing as you haven't steered yourself or Izzy wrong yet.'

It was still surprising for me hear praise from her. I smiled. 'Thanks, Mum. I keep trying to decide but I don't know. It will be hard to just slot back into our London life. I will miss it here; I do know that. And Gran's money, it means that I could do something different. Dad told me to do what will make me happy but how will I know what will do that?'

'By following what your heart wants. I think you probably already know what will do that,' she said then, surprising me yet again. 'Sometimes you just have to take the leap and do it.' She patted my arm. 'I will support you whatever you decide.'

We sat in silence for a moment, both lost in thought then Mum turned to me again. 'How do you feel about Drew going?'

I shook my head. 'I don't know. We kissed at the Hogmanay party. I don't know what would have happened next, but April was there. I hate the idea of him going back to Boston with her. I hope that he'll take the job in Scotland, for Izzy's sake, but it will be hard to see him building a life here with April.'

'Why don't you tell him that? Tell him how you feel?'

'I feel like I missed my chance, Mum. I left him ten years ago. I can't ask him to choose me again. What if something else happens? What if I end up running again?' That, I realised, was what I was really scared about. In my heart, I did know what I wanted to do next, but it scared the hell out of me. What if I couldn't stick to it? What if I ended up running back to London? I didn't want to hurt anyone again.

Mum looked at me. 'You haven't run from anything that's hard before. You raised your daughter by yourself in the city. That's something to be proud of. You're strong, my darling. You can handle anything. I could never have handled being a single mother but look at what a good mother you've been to Izzy. Don't sell yourself short – whatever you decide to do, you can do it. You've proved that over and over again. You just need to make the choice that you want to make.'

Mum stood up then. 'It's late, I'm going to turn in.' Her eyes fell on the still-sealed envelope on the coffee table. 'Read the letter, don't hide from that. I think it will help you know what to do next. And you're not alone any more, Beth, remember that.' She leaned down to kiss me. 'Good night.'

'Night, Mum,' I mumbled back, my eyes on the envelope and my mind and heart full of what she had just said to me. 'Rip off the plaster,' I said aloud to myself and grabbed the envelope. I ripped it open, before I could chicken out any longer, and read my gran's last words.

The first part explained what she had done in the past as she hadn't known if she would get a chance to ever tell me in person. I skipped those lines. We had talked about it, and let it go, and I didn't want to dwell on it again.

And then she explained why she had given me what she had in her will.

> I am so so sorry. I thought about how I could try to make it up to you and the only thing I could think of was to give you the chance to come back home. To be where you belong. Beth, Glendale Hall is now yours. I want you to be its keeper and pass it down to Isabelle. I don't want you to sell it. That's the only thing I ask of you, and to let your parents stay there as long as they want to, of course. My hope is that you might come back to live here, and that you can be a family again years after I stole that from you all.
>
> I have divided my estate between you and Caroline. I have a lot of money and it's sitting in the bank doing nothing. I know that you can do something with it. I watched you walk away from all of your dreams as a teenager, and I want to give them back to you. Do it for that sixteen-year-old girl, do it for the woman you are now, and I ask that you do it for me too. I never had the courage to go after my dreams. I was content to be a wife and a mother, to stay at the Hall, and live a quiet life. You have never done that. I am envious and proud of the woman you are now. Please take what I want to give you and live the life that you want to live.

I hope that I will get to see whatever it is that you do next from wherever I am going next. Know that I lost myself the day you left, and by giving you this, I hope to find myself again.

All my love,

Your grandmother

Margaret MacKenzie

I clutched her letter to my chest, my eyes blurring from unshed tears. I sat there for most of the night, thinking, trying to let go of the past as I attempted to choose my future.

Chapter Forty-Nine

I pulled up outside the farm to collect Izzy from her sleepover at Drew's. The morning was grey and drizzly, perfectly matching my mood. I had been awake half of the night rereading Gran's letter over and over again.

Climbing out of the car, I walked quickly towards the front door, wishing that the letter hadn't left me so confused. I understood why Gran had left me what she had, and I wanted to do something special with it. It wasn't just about making my dreams come true though. I wanted to do that, yes. But I also wanted to make Izzy's come true too. I knew that Gran had been right: I needed to live the life that we both wanted. First though I needed courage to say aloud the life I wanted, and then I needed courage to do it.

'Hi,' Drew said as he swung the door open. He wore a cosy jumper and jeans, his hair still damp from the shower. 'Izzy and April are out in the field with Rory helping him feed the animals,' he said, stepping back to let me inside.

'Oh, okay,' I said, wishing then that I hadn't left the Hall as early as I had, but I'd wanted to see Izzy and start talking about our future together.

'Coffee?'

'Sure.' I followed him into the kitchen and slipped off my coat, sitting down as Drew made me a coffee and himself a tea. 'Not long until your flight now,' I said, for something to say.

'Tomorrow,' he agreed, bringing our drinks over. 'I can't believe it's that time already. I wish I didn't have to go back. I think April feels the same way.'

'Oh? So, she's coming even more round to idea of moving here?' I took a sip of the coffee, hoping it would revive me a little.

'I think so. But, hey, enough about us – how are you doing?' he asked, touching my hand briefly from across the table.

I flinched a little at his touch. 'I really don't know. My gran – she left me an inheritance, and I'm trying to work out what I'm going to do with it all, to be honest.'

'Wow, really? That's great. Not that it changes the fact she's gone, of course, but I'm glad she left you something.' He gave me a meaningful look.

'I think it was to try to make up for the past,' I said, knowing what he was getting at. 'It could change everything. If I want it to.'

'You don't want it to?'

'I do but it's scary, change, isn't it? It would be a big change for not just me but Izzy too. I want to make sure I do the right thing. I feel like it's a big responsibility, you know? She left me... a lot,' I said. I looked at him. 'And she left me the Hall.'

Drew's eyebrow shot up. 'Wow. That's huge. Beth, I'm happy for you. You deserve it.'

I smiled. 'I never thought I'd leave London, you know? But, Izzy, she really loves it here and now we have this gift from Gran. But it would mean upheaving our whole life and starting all over again.'

Drew nodded. 'I get it. Look at me, I'm still undecided about what to do next, but knowing that you and Izzy might be here… I mean, how perfect would it be for the three of us to be living in Scotland together?'

I smiled but then I remembered. 'And April too,' I said, trying to hide my face in the coffee cup as I took a long gulp.

Drew looked down at his mug. 'April too. Do you ever worry that life is just moving ahead, at full throttle, and you're not sure if you want to stay on for the ride or just take a big leap off and run away?'

'Of course I do,' I replied, trying to ignore the flare of hope in my heart that he was talking about April. 'I've been there, done that and got the T-shirt. That's why I want to make sure I do the best thing this time around, you know? Gran has given me this huge opportunity, and I want to make sure that I make the most of it.'

'You will.' He smiled. 'I just wish I had the same faith in myself.'

I knew I had to say something despite the fact I had told myself to be okay with him and April. 'Drew, if you're not happy then you really should do something about it. You told me that I shouldn't ignore my passion for gardening and just go back to my office job, didn't you? You said I should follow my passion and you were right. That's want I want to do now. Follow my heart. But you should follow your own advice too.' I touched his hand then. 'Do what is going to make you happy.'

He nodded, and he took my hand in his and squeezed it. A current of electricity ran through my hand and up my body. 'Can we talk about what happened? At New Year? Between us?'

Why did it sound so good to hear him use the word 'us'? I took a deep breath. I needed to tell him how I felt. Then he could make his choice. If I didn't then I'd always regret it. 'Drew, that night was—'

The back door burst open then, stopping me in my tracks. Drew and I pulled apart as if a spell had suddenly been broken.

Izzy marched into the kitchen followed by April, who paused when she saw us at the table. Izzy rushed over to me. 'Mum, Rory let me feed the horses today.'

'That's great,' I said, giving her a hug. I glanced at Drew. I knew I couldn't say any more to him then and I didn't know if I ever would be able to. Maybe it was best for us to just go. 'Are you ready to head off?'

'I'll get my things,' she said, dashing off again. I smiled at how carefree she had become lately; it was lovely to see.

April went to Drew and wrapped her arms around his neck. 'She was so sweet with the horses, such a cutie,' she said, smiling down at him before glancing at me. 'She loves it here. Oh, Iz asked if I would send her a postcard from Boston,' she said, letting Drew go and grabbing a notebook and pen. 'Can you write down your address in London, Beth?'

'Well, it might be better to send it here actually,' I said, glancing at Drew before writing the address down.

'Oh, okay,' April said. She leaned over the table, watching me. 'Oh, you don't do stars over your I's any more, then?' she asked, in a slightly mocking tone. 'I guess it was best to grow out of that, wasn't it?'

I stopped writing and looked up at her. 'How do you know I used to write stars over my name?' I asked, frowning at the smug smile on her face.

April straightened up, and her eyes darted to Drew, then back to me. Her cheeks flamed red. 'Oh, I didn't. I mean, I assumed... you know?'

'Not really, no,' I replied. I wondered why she looked so scared suddenly. 'Why would you assume that?'

'You did,' Drew said then, slowly. 'I remember... you always drew stars over your I's; I used to tease you about it,' he said. He looked up at April, questioningly.

'Lots of girls do that,' she said, crossing her arms over her chest, suddenly defensive.

I looked down at the address I had written. 'No, not really. A lot of girls drew hearts at school but that's why I drew stars. I liked to be different.' I had always done stars, but I had stopped after I had Izzy. Precisely a year after actually. When the last letter I wrote never got answered. The letter I wrote to Drew at university. 'Did you see my letter?' I asked April.

'What letter?' she said but her face fell. She knew that I had worked it out.

'The letter I wrote to Drew when Izzy was one. The letter I sent to him at university telling him about our baby. The one he never got,' I replied.

Drew stared at her. 'April, did you see her letter?'

'I don't know... maybe. What difference does it make? It was years ago!'

'What happened to that letter, April?' Drew's voice had a dangerous edge to it.

April noticed and stepped away from the table, her arms falling helplessly to her sides. 'Why is it always about her, Drew? Ever since I met you, she's been there – this cloud over us, one that you can't let go of, even now!' She burst the words out as if she had been keeping them inside for years. It appeared that she had done exactly just that.

'What did you do with the letter, April?' Drew stood up then.

April's face twisted into a pleading expression. 'Drew, baby, I had no idea what was in that letter. How could I? All I knew was that you were heartbroken over this girl from home, and you kept telling me that you couldn't be with me because of her,' she said, choking back a sob at the end. 'When I saw the letter, I saw her name and address on the outside, and I don't

294

know, I thought that you'd be better off if you didn't have to read her excuses.' She started crying properly then. 'I loved you. I'm sorry. I was just trying to help you.'

'What did you do with the letter, April?' Drew said again, his voice louder and harder than I had ever heard it. I held my breath.

April covered her face with her hands, sobbing into them. 'I t… t… threw it away,' she choked out in the end.

Chapter Fifty

'Are you okay, April?'

I turned around to see Izzy in the doorway, her bag in her hand, frowning in confusion at the sight of April in tears, Drew stood by, just staring at her then at me sat dumbfounded at the table. I couldn't believe that she was the one who had stopped Drew getting my letter. I looked at Izzy and couldn't help but see the ten years that he had missed flash before my eyes. I stood up abruptly, my chair squeaking against the tiles. I really didn't want to be in the same room with that woman much longer. 'She's fine, Iz,' I said, firmly, not wanting Izzy to know what was going on.

My voice shook Drew out of his trance. He turned to us. 'You guys should head off.'

'Are you sure?' I asked him, trying to ignore April's sniffling. I searched his face. He looked shocked and betrayed, but he nodded at me. I didn't know where any of us went from here, but whatever happened, the two of them needed to talk. Even though curiosity burned inside me, wanting to know what Drew thought about what April had done, what it meant not only for the two of them but for us as well, I knew that we couldn't stay. 'Right, come on, Iz.' I went to her in the doorway.

'But...'

April looked up then, taking her hand from her face. 'I'm okay, Iz,' she said, trying to wipe her eyes. 'Just upset about going home,' she lied, and I was grateful that she was trying to put a brave face on things for Izzy. I realised then this could well be the last time we saw them before their flight back to Boston.

'I'll see you out,' Drew said, seemingly realising that too. Izzy looked unsure but I steered her out with us into the hallway.

'When will I see you again?' Izzy asked Drew then, her lower lip trembling a little. He wrapped his arms around her, his eyes meeting mine behind her. I really wasn't sure what he was thinking. I was still stunned by April's revelation, so I couldn't imagine how he was feeling.

'I'll be back for your great-grandmother's funeral. I promised you that,' he replied, squeezing her tightly.

I looked away, a lump rising in my throat. Even though he wouldn't be gone that long, he was leaving Glendale and before I had a chance to tell him how I felt. I knew it wasn't the right time after what April had told him. They had to work that out, but I still wanted to throw my arms around him and beg him to stay.

'This Christmas has been the best one ever,' Izzy declared when they let each other go. 'Hasn't it, Mum?'

Their eyes on me, I forced on a smile. 'It has.' I walked towards the door, pausing in front of Drew. 'I'll see you then?'

He leaned down and kissed me gently on my cheek, rubbing my back as he did so. 'Take care, Beth.'

'You too.' I let myself meet his eyes. 'If you need to talk…' He just nodded. 'Right, let's go home then,' I said brightly to Izzy, putting an arm around her. I looked back, once, at Drew, leaning against the doorframe watching us go, and I hoped he would be okay. Izzy waved to him, and he lifted one hand in return.

'Will April come to the funeral too?' Izzy asked me as we walked to our car.

'I don't know,' I replied, honestly. When I opened the car door, I glanced back again but Drew had gone. All I could hope was that when we saw him in a week, I could finally get a chance to tell him that he was still the love of my life; but until then, I had some big life decisions to make, and it looked like he did too.

–

My mum and I stepped out into the frost-covered garden of Glendale Hall early in the morning. January was off to a bitter cold start. I needed to speak to her, and I always felt more comfortable out in the garden, as if the ground beneath my feet gave me greater strength. The sky above us was crisp and clear and we could see our breath in the air. We walked briskly away from the house and across the lawn which crunched under our feet. 'I was thinking about what Gran said in her letter,' I said, breaking our silence. 'That she wanted me to go after my dreams now. I suppose after having Izzy I did have to let go of some of the things I had wanted to do. Gran wants me to do them now.' I turned to look back at the kitchen, where Izzy was having her breakfast. I still found it hard to believe that the house and the garden we were walking in now belonged to me.

Mum nodded. 'I think she wanted to give you back all the opportunities you lost back then.' She hooked her arm through mine. 'Do you want to tell me what you want to do? Have you already decided?'

'I do want to go after my dreams, but most of all, I want Izzy to be happy. It's clear that she was struggling in London, and she loves it up here. Being here has reminded me how much I love gardening and how I do wish I could do something that I'm passionate about. It's also showed me that I love the village and the community spirit here; I really want to help Glendale. So, I have come up with an idea that I want to run past you.' I was nervous about what she would think. I wanted to do something special with my inheritance, but I needed my mum to be on board too. 'You and Heather have hopefully found a way we can save the library – by going for the extra funding and doing more to involve the community. I think Heather has a great chance of persuading the council to rethink their plans, but I thought we could give them further incentive. I'm still worried they are attracted by the offer from New Horizons to buy the high street. We already know that they won't budge on the rents that they were charging. I know we talked about a profit share scheme, but what I thought we could do is put together my money and yours and make our own offer to buy the premises on the high street from the council.' I glanced at my mum who looked surprised but gestured for me to continue. 'As owners of the buildings, we could then offer the premises to the people who told us they wanted to open up a shop, and give them discounted rents to get going, or take a percentage of their profits instead. And you could open up your own shop, like you wanted. The council would not only get money for the properties but as they'd still be shops, they would get business rates too so they'd end up making more than if they let the buildings be turned into flats, plus they would be keeping the community happy.'

My mum thought for a moment. 'It's a generous idea but have you thought about your long-term future. What if we lost the money we invested?'

'I don't think we will. I think Glendale can be successful again, but if it didn't work out, we could just sell the premises down the line to a company like New Horizons. I really don't think it will come to that. Look at how everyone came together when we asked for help. I think it's in everyone's interests for this to be successful.'

'As the shops made more, they could pay us more,' Mum said slowly. 'As you say, it would be like a profit share scheme. I do think the council are coming around to our way of thinking. And I think the village could thrive again but…' she turned to me. 'It's a lot of work, a massive project. I couldn't do it alone, Beth.'

I nodded, relieved that she thought it could work. 'I know. That's the other thing I wanted to talk to you about.' I took a deep breath. I was uncertain how she would take the other part of my plan. Our relationship was already so much better than it had ever been, but it was still early days. 'I'd like to move here for good with Izzy. Izzy loves it so much up here, and I think it will be great for her, for both of us. Being here means I can work with you on this project, but I've also been thinking about how much I've loved working out here again,' I said, gesturing to the garden. 'I've decided that I'd like to go back to college, too.'

'You would?' Mum looked a bit stunned as she tried to take in everything I had told her.

'I want to study gardening like I always wanted to. I couldn't just leave Izzy in the evenings if we were in London to study, but here, I have a free babysitter.' I grinned at her. 'Only if you're really okay with us being here though?' I looked at her timidly, then, crossing my fingers in the pocket of my coat and hoping that, despite the past, we could be a family once again.

Chapter Fifty-One

Mum's face lit up, and she stopped and grabbed hold of my hands. 'Beth, I am delighted!' She pulled me in for a hug, something that still felt strange for us to be doing. 'But are you really sure this is what you want?'

'If you had told me when I came up here before Christmas that I would want to stay, I would have laughed but this just seems to make perfect sense. This feels right for me and Izzy and just seems like the best way to use what Gran has given me. Well, given us. But only if you're on board as well? I want us to do this together.'

'Of course I'm on board! Beth, this is something I could never have dreamed would happen either, but I feel like this is the right decision for all of us.'

'What about Dad?' I asked her then, biting my lip.

'I think I have to accept that he doesn't want to be with me any more but he will be thrilled that you're moving up here. He'll be cross if the council don't accept his company's bid, but I would hope he would be pleased for us as well.'

'I hope so too.' I was sad that my mum felt that their marriage was over, but I hoped that my being there for her, for both of them, would help.

'Your father will be here soon to go to church,' Mum said when we started walking back towards the house.

'After that we need to plan a brilliant pitch to the council for our meeting on Monday. I could ask Heather to come over later, but I don't know if we'll be up to that?'

She glanced at my concerned face. 'It'll be okay. I mean, it'll be hard to say goodbye to my mother, but she was suffering for a long time; it was time for her to go. And she has brought us together, so there are a lot of silver linings to all of this, aren't there?' She smiled at the face in the doorway of the back door as we approached it. 'And now Sally is back, thank God.'

Sally waved at us. She hugged me tightly when we walked in, and she gave my mum a kiss on the cheek. It hadn't felt quite the same at the Hall with Sally in London for New Year. I couldn't wait to tell her my plans. 'I'm so sorry for you both. Now, come into the warm, I'm making breakfast. Izzy was having cornflakes, poor thing,' she said with a brisk shake of her head, rushing back off into the kitchen.

I smiled. Sally liked to feed everybody, and I was not sorry about it. I took off my coat and boots and went to kiss Izzy. 'Will you have room for Sally's bacon sandwich though?' I asked, nodding at her bowl of cereal.

'There's always room for bacon, Mum,' she replied.

'That's my girl.' I looked at Izzy and hoped that she would be as excited by my idea as I felt. I wanted to get through visiting the church with my parents and then I planned to talk to her about it all. I just knew, though, that she would be thrilled: it was written all over her face how happy she was at the Hall.

'Room for one more?' My dad hesitated in the doorway. He was wearing a suit and tie and hovered with unease.

'Sit down, David,' Mum said, formally, joining Izzy at the table. She did give him a small smile though. It was hard to see my parents so estranged. They'd been together for thirty years and you got used to your parents as a unit, not always seeing them as people in their own right with their own hopes and dreams. My mum was doing really well considering everything; I was really proud of her. I knew she was putting all their problems aside so we could say goodbye to my gran but, after that, I knew it would be crunch time for the two of them.

Sally brought over to the table bacon sandwiches, juice and coffee and a basket of freshly baked pastries, and we all tucked in having missed her delicious cooking over the past few days. 'So, did you make any New Year's resolutions?' Sally asked us.

Mum and I shared a look, unsure what we wanted to say about our plans just yet with my dad there with us. Dad looked equally as nervous, and the silence dragged on a little bit too long.

'I am definitely going to eat more of these,' Izzy broke the awkwardness, waving a muffin in the air. Sally burst out laughing, and we all joined in, relieved that the tension had been broken.

'I think I'll make that my resolution as well,' I told her.

'When do you think we'll hear from my dad?' she asked me then, and my smile faded a little. Drew had phoned us from the airport before his flight to say another goodbye to Izzy. I hadn't been able to ask him anything, but he had mentioned that April was there too – so they had flown back together. What happened between them after that, I wish I knew.

'You can phone him tonight, he will have landed by then,' I replied, going back to my breakfast, feeling my mum's gaze on me. I had told her what April had done. I had no idea if Drew would forgive her. I knew myself what a forgiving person he was. I was angry with April and how much she had hurt not only Drew and me but Izzy by keeping them apart even if she hadn't known what my letter said.

303

But I also knew what crazy choices you could make when you loved someone. It didn't excuse what had happened, but I could understand it. And I wanted Drew to be happy, whoever he chose. I hoped though, I wished, that he felt the same way I did, but if he didn't then there was still so much to be grateful for. Coming back to Glendale had already changed so much, I hoped that it would continue to work its magic on us all and everything would work out in the end, one way or another.

–

After breakfast, Izzy stayed with Sally chatting nineteen to the dozen with her, and my parents and I drove to the village church.

It stood at the end of the high street in Glendale, it's tall steeple visible for miles around. Gran used to make us go to Glendale church every Sunday when I was growing up, and as I became a teenager I hated it and sulked so much that in the end my mum told me I didn't have to go any more. In London, Izzy and I had only stepped foot in one once for a wedding of a colleague.

I had grown up believing I'd get married in that church, though, fantasising when I was with Drew that one day I'd walk down the aisle in my white dress to him at the altar. But I'd stopped daydreaming about getting married a long time ago. There hadn't been anyone special enough in my life. And, if I was brutally honest with myself, I hadn't believed that anyone could capture my heart as Drew had. And seeing him again had only confirmed the truth – I had never really got over him to begin with.

The minister welcomed us warmly. Despite the reason we were there, I was taken aback by how young and good-looking he was. Certainly nothing like the minister we had when I was growing up, who had passed away. The Reverend told us to call him Brodie and shook our hands and said how sorry he was that my grandmother had gone. 'Mrs MacKenzie was a real character,' he said with a slight grin. I could well imagine her surprise at him taking over Glendale and was certain she had given him a hard time. But she had continued to go to church until she had become too ill, and I knew he'd visited Gran a couple of weeks before she died, so he must have won her over in the end.

Mum and Dad sat with him in a pew to look over hymns, but I got up and walked over to the altar. I really had no clue about hymns or readings but wanted to be there for moral support. I stopped by the candles that people lit for loved ones. My grandfather had been the only death that I had had to deal with when I was younger. We had never been all that close. Like my dad, he had often been an absent figure from the Hall, working a lot and leaving my gran and mum to run the house and attempt to run me. I thought then about how generations often seemed to do exactly as their parents had. My grandparents had just one daughter, as did my parents and then me, too; although I was a teenager, and out of wedlock, so at least I was doing it my way I supposed.

Picking up a tea light, I struck a match, setting the wick alight with a steady flame, and added it to the row of lit candles. I wasn't sure that I had any kind of faith, but Gran had so it felt like the right thing to do. 'Thank you, Gran,' I whispered into the quiet church. She had guided me home after all and was giving me the chance to change my life. Despite what had happened between us, I was grateful to her for that. I'd had to find my own way in the world away from my often-oppressive family and all the comfortable trappings of Glendale Hall. I was a survivor. I was independent. I was a good mother. All the things that maybe I wouldn't have been if I had stayed with my family ten years before.

But now, I was ready to come back home.

'Would you like to say something?' Dad asked me then after calling out my name. 'Margaret picked out a couple of Bible passages in her will that she wanted to be read. What about this one?' He showed me the passage in the Bible.

It was, of course, about the power of forgiveness.

I allowed myself a small smile. Gran had been consumed with thoughts of forgiveness, and regret, in her final days. She'd asked for my forgiveness, and I had given it to her. I thought of Drew again. He had told me that he forgave me for not telling him that I was pregnant with Izzy all those years ago. He had told me that I needed to forgive myself for it, too. And now it felt like Gran, too, was telling me to do that.

I nodded. 'I'll read this one,' I told them. And I felt myself let go of the past. It didn't matter any more. It had happened. We couldn't change that. And it had made us who we were.

What really mattered was what we were going to do next.

When we got back to the Hall, Dad left us again for his hotel. I looked at Mum watching him drive off through the window. 'Do you want him to come back?' I asked her.

'I appreciated his support today. He'll always be in my life, and I want him to be, but he's chosen her, Beth. And I have to move on from that,' she replied turning away. 'I never thought I'd survive on my own, but I know now I'll be fine. I don't want us to stay together just because he feels he has to stay. I suppose, even at my age I still want to be loved.'

'There's nothing wrong with that,' I told her, fiercely.

'And what about you?' she asked, arching an eyebrow.

'I have a lot on my plate right now, I don't need to add a new relationship to it as well,' I said, lightly.

Mum didn't buy that though. 'You should still tell Drew how you feel. Even if he is working things out with April. Don't regret not saying something. Don't torture yourself with what ifs; Lord knows I have done that a few times.'

'Really? About what?'

'I have to have some secrets from my daughter.' She patted my shoulder as she brushed past me.

'Mum!' Izzy appeared in the hall. 'You're back! Come and see what we made.' She dragged me by the arm, laughing, and I followed her into the kitchen. Mum ducked out into the garden. I wondered what she had meant by her having her own regrets and 'what ifs'. I wondered if there was anything that could be done about them. She deserved to have what she wanted.

'Look,' Izzy said when we were in the kitchen. She proudly gestured to the large pot of delicious-smelling curry on the cooker. 'I helped make it.'

'It smells amazing,' I said, smiling at Sally who gave it a stir. 'You're really enjoying all this cooking, aren't you?'

'It's fun,' Izzy said. 'Sally has taught me loads, so when we go back to London we won't have to eat as many takeaways.'

'Hey, my cooking isn't that bad,' I said, ruffling her hair.

'She's been telling me a few things that have made me very worried for your health down there,' Sally said. She glanced at me. 'How was the church?'

'It was okay. Mum and Dad pretty much sorted it all out, but I said that I'll do a reading. I've never said anything at a funeral before.'

'That's good of you,' Sally said. 'Iz, please pass me some salt, will you?'

I watched Izzy rush to the cupboard and hand it to Sally, and I smiled at how much fun she seemed to be having. 'How was London?' I asked Sally, leaning against the counter.

'Emily threw a great party as always. She misses you guys but she's happy that you're having a great time up here. She said she'll call you. We had afternoon tea in Harrods, which was fun, but London is so packed I was quite happy to see the countryside again. I wish she'd come up here,' Sally said.

'We'll see her soon though, Mum, won't we?' Izzy said, leaning next to me. She frowned a little. 'It's so weird to think about going back there.'

I smiled. 'Well, actually, I wanted to talk to you about that. Go and grab your coat and shoes, I need to show you something outside, okay?' Izzy gave me a curious look but went off upstairs to get her things. 'Did Mum tell you about my inheritance?' I asked Sally when we were alone.

'I knew about it,' Sally replied. Sally knew everything that went on at the Hall, so I wasn't surprised. 'You know what you're going to do with it?'

'I do. If Izzy is okay with it. You wouldn't mind if we became a permanent fixture around here, would you?'

She smiled. 'It only took you ten years, eh?' She gave me a swift, tight hug. 'It's the right thing for you both.'

'Thanks, Sally. As long as you promise not to go anywhere, then we'll be fine.'

'Don't worry, I know how much more I'll be needed with you two causing chaos around here.'

I chuckled, knowing she was probably right.

'Ready!' Izzy reappeared, wrapped up, so I pushed open the back door and led her outside into the garden.

'I only just remembered this last night. I was thinking about when I was your age, living here,' I said as we walked down the lawn towards the trees. 'This garden and the house felt like my castle.'

'I can't imagine you thinking you were a princess,' she replied.

I smiled. 'Not quite, no,' I replied. Izzy knew I was a tomboy growing up, much preferring climbing trees to sitting with my mum in a dress drinking tea, which constantly disappointed her back then. 'But I felt like all of this belonged to me and I wanted to leave my mark on it. Then, one day, I found this tree and realised that I wasn't the first person growing up here to feel that way.'

I steered us towards a towering oak tree. I looked up at it and so did Izzy. It was huge and ancient. Standing there well before any of us, and it hopefully would keep on standing long past us, too. Walking around the thick trunk, I found what I was looking for and pointed to it. 'Look there,' I said. Izzy stepped over to look at the carvings. There were three sets of initials carved into the trunk.

MM

CW
BW

'Was this you?' Izzy asked, tracing her fingers over the final set of initials.

'Yes. That's your great-gran, MM for Margaret MacKenzie, then granny, CW for Caroline Williams, and then me. All three of us grew up here, and we carved our names into the tree. How would you like to do the same?'

Izzy turned to look at me. 'What do you mean? Carve my name or…?' she let her question hang in the air.

'Both. But only if you want to.'

'You want us to stay here?' Her voice had turned a little squeaky, which it always did when she was excited or shocked. I wasn't sure which she was right then. Likely both. Same as me.

'I do. I think it's the right thing for us. I know how much you love it here, and it means we can be here for granny. I can find a new job; I might even go back to studying. Maybe even try gardening, which you know I always wanted to do.'

'What about money?' Izzy asked, instantly anxious. I hoped she would be able to worry less about things soon.

'Your great-gran left us money in her will. We don't have to worry about money any more. And there's more – she also left us Glendale Hall.'

Izzy turned to look back at the house, her eyes wide. 'This is all ours? Really?'

'Really. But we can go back to London if that's what you want. I want us both to be happy. What do you think? Should we stay?'

'Yes, please! I love it here,' she replied, grabbing me and giving me a tight hug. Relief washed over me seeing how excited she was. It was definitely the right decision for all of us.

'In that case...' I took out the wood carving knife I'd borrowed from John from my pocket. I helped Izzy carve her initials below the others on the tree.

'Now I've left my mark here too,' Izzy said, standing back to look at her name under mine.

'That's right,' I replied, feeling a little emotional at seeing her name there and wondering if one day her child would add theirs too. I wrapped an arm around her waist.

'You know what this house has been missing all these years?' Izzy asked then, looking at me.

'What's that?'

'A library.'

I rolled my eyes with a shake of my head. 'Come on, let's see if Sally will let us taste her curry.'

I glanced behind us as we started to walk back to the house, and I saw my mum walking through the trees towards John's cottage.

Chapter Fifty-Three

Heather looked fit to burst when I let her into the Hall. 'You'll never guess what happened?!' she said, grabbing my arm as the door shut behind her, her hair bouncing along with her excitement.

'No, what?' I replied with a smile.

'I've just had lunch with Rory. He told me he thought that I thought what happened between us was a huge mistake. So, I said 'yeah, I'm pretty much sure that it was but I liked it anyway'.'

'You didn't?' I shook my head, wishing I could be as honest as Heather.

She grinned. 'Yep. And he said that I've annoyed him for years and could I please never stop annoying him? I said okay, so we're having dinner this weekend.'

'I actually don't know what to say to that,' I said, leading her into the kitchen. 'But if you're happy then I'm happy.'

'I mean, I never thought that Rory and I would actually happen, but he makes me laugh, and that should never be underestimated, even if he is a little short.' She looked at me seriously for a moment. 'But you don't mind, do you? About us? About the fact he's Drew's brother? Because if you do…'

I held up a hand to silence her. 'Why would I mind? It means Izzy will get to see more of her uncle.'

'And her dad too, maybe, if Drew takes that job here.' Heather gave me a sly look.

'It's a big if; and if he does, April might still come with him.'

'Surely after what she did, he'd be coming over here alone,' Heather said in a low voice as we approached the kitchen where Mum, Sally and Izzy were. 'Can you imagine if you two got back together and me and Rory were a couple.' She looked a little starry-eyed.

'You need to pull yourself together,' I told her, but I couldn't help secretly wishing that as well.

Heather looked a little sulky as she said hello to the others, pouting that I had shut down her happy-ever-after fantasy. But when Mum and I told her our plan, and when she found that Izzy and I were planning to move back to Glendale, she let out a shriek of excitement that shattered all of our eardrums.

–

Izzy and I Skyped with Drew that evening. Izzy was bursting to tell him our news. She hadn't stopped smiling all day, confirming that I had made the right decision in planning to move us to Glendale. Everyone was excited. It was hard to feel glum with everyone talking about our plans, but I was nervous to see and speak to Drew again.

When the call connected, the two of them both started speaking at once. I stared at the laptop, wishing my body didn't react so obviously to him. My pulse sped up straight away, and my cheeks grew warm. His smile and auburn hair in a mess around his face were both welcoming and painful in their familiarity. 'Hey, guys,' he said, the American twang to his voice sounding stronger now that he was back in Boston again. 'How are things over there?'

'We have the best news!' Izzy cried, bouncing in her seat.

'Oh, yeah?'

'We're moving to Glendale!' she cried, a wide smile on her face.

Drew grinned. 'Really?' He looked at me. 'That's amazing.'

'I've been thinking a lot about it after finding out what was in Gran's will. Izzy loves it up here and it means I could go back to school and study gardening, and we get to be with family. We are also going to try and use her money to buy the shops on the high street from the council ourselves.'

'Wow, you are really changing your lives,' Drew said, shaking his head in wonder. 'That's so great. You both look really happy.' I wasn't sure if I imagined a flash of pain in his eyes. 'I'm really pleased.'

'I can't wait,' Izzy declared.

'How are you though?' I asked him, anxiously. I tried to see if there were any traces of April in his living room, but I couldn't see anything beyond a sofa, and picture of a beach hanging up behind him.

'I'm fine, just a bit tired from the flight. I'm back at the hospital in a couple of hours. I found someone to swap shifts with so I can take a couple of days off to come back to the funeral.'

'Are you sure? Drew, it's such a long way for you to come...' Selfishly, I wanted him there, but he was so far away I understood if he couldn't come back.

'It's good timing, actually, as I need to book in a meeting in Inverness at the same time.' He glanced at me and I knew he was talking about his potential new job, and hope retuned to my heart again.

'Oh, that's healthy, doctor,' I replied with a laugh. 'It will be good to see you,' I said, unable to stop myself. 'And is everything okay apart from that?' I asked.

Drew sighed. 'It's getting there,' he replied, ambiguously. 'So, Iz, I finished book two on the flight, so I'm starting book three now,' he said, changing the subject neatly.

'That one is my favourite,' Izzy replied, enthusiastically. I listened to them talk about Harry Potter for a few moments, wishing I knew what was happening with April.

'I'll have to go soon,' Drew said then, regretfully. He looked at me. 'Do you need me to do anything to help, with the funeral, or anything?'

'No. But thank you. It's enough that you're coming to be with us.'

'I've known Mrs MacKenzie all my life, of course I wanted to be there. But, mostly, I want to support you guys. How is your mum doing?'

'It's not going to be an easy day.'

'She has you guys, which will help a lot.'

I nodded. 'Have you heard from your brother, by the way?' I asked then with a smile.

'No, he's hopeless at staying in touch. Why?'

'I think he and Heather have finally got together. They both seem pretty smitten.'

'What's smitten?' Izzy asked me.

'They like each other a lot,' I told her.

'Ew – gross,' she replied.

Drew chuckled. 'Well, it's about time – he's always had a soft spot for her, and I thought something was going on at Hogmanay. I'll text him after this. Right, I better go and get ready for work now. It was good to talk to you both. And I'll see you soon. Okay?'

'I miss you,' Izzy said.

'I miss you, too. I love you, Iz.'

'Love you, too!'

'Have a good day at work,' I said, touched by their goodbye. I ended the call and looked at Izzy beside me. 'You okay, my love?' I pulled her to me and stroked her hair. 'He'll be back with us soon.'

'I hate that he's so far away now,' she admitted, cuddling up to me.

'I know but he won't be away for long.'

'This time,' she replied.

I really hoped that Drew would decide to take the job in Scotland, for Izzy's sake. I just wished that I knew if he'd be moving here alone. I wondered if my mum was right and I should tell him how I felt, but surely if he had chosen to stay with April then there would be no point? It would just make things awkward between us, and we needed to be okay for Izzy's sake. I wished the universe would give me a sign to tell me what to do.

'How long before we can move up here?' Izzy asked, breaking into my thoughts.

'Well, we will have to go back to London for a bit after the funeral, you know that, right? I need to sort out work and a new school for you, and we need to pack up the flat and tell the landlord we're going.' It was strange because it felt as if we already belonged in Glendale, but we had to say goodbye to our old life first. 'But as soon as possible, I promise.'

Izzy smiled. 'Good.'

Chapter Fifty-Four

Mum and I tentatively opened the door to what had been Gran's room. After all, it had been hers for her whole life, so it felt strange to be going in there without her. Like she might burst in at any moment to demand a reason for us being there.

'She requested that she be buried with her pearls,' Mum said as we went in. 'I don't remember a day before she got sick that she didn't have them on.' She walked over to Gran's dressing table.

'I used to think that if Gran took them off, it meant that the world was going to end,' I agreed with a shake of my head. It was fitting that she should have them with her, even though I found it morbid to think about what she'd be wearing when she was buried. I perched on the made bed, all traces that she was in it for so long already removed, watching Mum as she opened up the jewellery box and carefully took the pearl necklace out, letting it slide through her fingers.

'She always said that they would lose their lustre if you didn't wear them regularly.' Mum looked around the room. 'I suppose we need to sort all her things out. Decide if there's anything we want to keep.'

'There's no rush. We can wait until you're ready,' I replied, gently. We lapsed into a short silence.

'I'm sorry,' Mum said then. 'If I was too hard on you when you were growing up.' She came to perch on the bed next to me, draping the necklace across her lap. 'I know that I was strict and you thought that meant that I didn't care, but I was raised to think about how the world saw me and was expected to live up to that. I thought that you should go to university just because it would be something I could tell everyone we knew about, not because I really thought you should have a career. I suppose I just expected you to get married and have a family like I did. I thought that all the times you pushed back against what I wanted was because you wanted to spite me, not because you wanted independence. I suppose I tried to make you just like me, and I think that's what my mother tried to do, too. We didn't give you the chance to bloom. To be your own person. And I know that I can't blame my mother for pushing you away all by herself. If we had been closer in the first place then you would have told me about the baby yourself; you wouldn't have just believed your grandmother when she told you what I thought about it.' Mum shook her head. 'You left because we weren't a supportive family, we weren't… loving. I see the way you are with Isabelle, and I do wish I could have been more like that with you. But it just wasn't in my nature, I suppose. It wasn't how I was brought up, and I couldn't see that I should have tried harder to be the mother you needed, not the mother I thought I was supposed to be.' Mum looked down at the necklace and sighed. 'I suppose I just wanted to tell you that I'm so grateful you're giving me a second chance. That you're coming back here. I know that I can't erase the past but perhaps I can try to make things up to you? If you'll let me?' She turned to me then, hope and unshed tears in her eyes.

A lump rose up in my throat. 'I didn't make things easy either,' I assured her. 'I wasn't very good at telling you how I felt. I thought that I had to fight back when I should have just tried to talk to you. Now I'm a mother, I know how tough it can be, and it was tougher because you had Gran here with her opinions on everything, plus my dad wasn't around to support you. But we have a second chance now so let's embrace it. And this time, let's talk about things before they get to the point where one of us walks out.' I smiled, and she snorted at my poor joke. 'And, you know, it's my house, so my rules,' I added, nudging her with my shoulder. It was the argument that my family had used on me countless times in the past.

Mum shook her head. 'I don't know what we have let ourselves in for,' she said but she smiled back at me.

—

It was a gloriously crisp and sunny morning, so I cried off a trip to the shops with Mum and Izzy and headed into the garden instead. I felt calmer than I had for a long time because I knew what we were going to do. I hadn't realised how restless I had been for so long, running around trying to do everything, desperately trying not to have time to sit on my own and think about my life and how it wasn't shaping up to be what I had wanted it to be. Izzy had been the only bright point in it really.

But I was letting myself breathe again. It wasn't easy, it scared me a little, but I knew that it was what I needed to do. Moving back home would be a gigantic step but it didn't feel like a backwards one: it felt that for the first time in a long time, I was actually moving forwards and not just going around in circles.

I saw John was in the greenhouse so I walked over and let myself into the warmth. 'Do you think I can do it?' I asked him with no preamble. He looked up from the plant he was re-potting, one eyebrow raised, so I explained what I meant. 'Gardening, I mean. Going back to college, studying again, starting all over.'

'Well, of course you can. Gardening is in your blood, like mine. I remember when I first came to work here – you were only six and always running around the grounds, to your mother's despair most of the time.' He shook his head with a smile. 'You were always begging to help me out here. Passion is all you need to succeed, Beth. I think I read that somewhere once.'

'I let go of my passion for a long time.' I kicked at the ground with my boot. 'I pushed it down, I think, just focused on what I needed to do to survive, didn't let myself think about it. But it's like it's suddenly come alive again. Like a plant, I guess, blooming again after a long winter.'

'What's worrying you then?'

I had always appreciated how direct John was. No need to say ten words when two would do. 'That I'm not good enough maybe.'

'If you're not good enough, you just work harder and then you will be. The trail was pretty damn good if you ask me.'

I smiled. 'I suppose change is exciting and terrifying.'

'You did it once before and that turned out pretty good.'

'What about you? Have you always followed your passion?'

He thought about that for a moment. 'When I was able to then yes.'

I hesitated but then I turned towards him. 'John, is there something between you and my mum?'

John looked up sharply. 'Like I said, when I've been able to I've tried to follow my passion. Sometimes, you're just not able to so you get on with that as best you can.' He continued with his weeding, and the two of us fell into silence. I wasn't sure what to say. I hadn't even thought of John as being passionate about anything other than gardening. He had lived at the Hall for twenty years and had never married. Now perhaps I finally knew the reason why. I just wasn't sure what to do with that knowledge. If I should do anything with it. But I knew that it saddened me.

I thought, though, about what he said about passion being all you really needed to succeed. I liked that idea. I knew that I had been passionate about keeping Izzy and raising her in the way I wanted to do, building my own life with her. I was passionate about gardening, and I knew that if I put my mind to it I could make a success of that. I had been passionate about saving the village and we were going to fight until the end to try to do that. And about my family: we'd had our ups and downs, but we were focused on rebuilding, on the future and not the past, and that was already working out better than I could have ever hoped.

And I was passionate about Drew. My heart was full of him. Perhaps had always been even when I had tried to deny it. Maybe always would be.

But what if what happened to John happened to me? If I was never able to tell Drew how I felt, if his heart always belonged to someone else, if I could never tell him that I loved him.

What then?

Chapter Fifty-Five

There was déjà vu in the air as my mum, Heather and I climbed out of the car and walked towards the Glendale council offices, as we had just a couple of weeks before. Sleet was dancing around us and so much had changed in such a short space of time, apart from our determination to do everything we could to keep Glendale village alive.

We were shown into a meeting room. Edward Murray was there again and Tom Walker, the finance officer who had come to the trail, and a woman introduced as Mary Smith. We all shook hands before we all sat down around the round long boardroom table.

'I'm glad you could come in today,' Mr Murray said. 'As you know, we were touched by the impact your Christmas trail has made in the village. The report in the local paper proved that has been the case. We would like to hear your ideas and see if there's anything we can do together to change things.'

Heather handed out a presentation document she had created for the meeting detailing our proposals to them. 'First of all, we'd like you to look at our ideas for the library. We have approached the Public Library Improvement Fund and we believe our bid for money will be successful. We have proposed that we add two initiatives to the library – one to help local children and one to help the elderly. As you can see, the funding would help set up a homework and a computer club and would help fund the library for another two years. During that time, we would be looking to increase the use of the library by the community and continue to look at ways we can fund it for the future. What we'd like from the council is assurance that if the bid is successful, you will keep the library open for those two years,' Heather said, showing them the details in our proposal. 'The fund has been really successful in helping other libraries stay open, and it proves that there is a vital need to keep the library going for our community and for future generations.'

'Who would run these new projects?' Mr Walker asked then, looking up from our plans.

'I would,' Heather said. 'I already have volunteers interested in helping out as well.' He nodded at her response. 'This idea came from someone in the village who came to see the Glendale trail – everyone has been really inspired to offer their help for these projects,' she added.

'And what have you to say about the high street?' Mr Walker asked, leaning back in his chair. I glanced at my mum, unsure if his relaxed pose was a good sign. She nodded at me to explain.

'My mum and I would like to make a competing bid for the premises on the high street. We would like to take over the premises and run them as local businesses. We would offer reduced rents under a profit share scheme. It would mean the high street remains a vital resource for the community, and we might even be able to draw tourists from Inverness and Loch Ness over to Glendale looking for local produce. By keeping the buildings as shops, you'll actually make more with our bid than if you accept the offer from New Horizons, as the shops will obviously pay rates.'

Mr Murray glanced at his colleagues. 'You have the funds to make such a bid, forgive me for my blunt question?'

'We do.' I pointed to the page in the proposal. We had been sneaky. My mum had gone into my dad's study and found the bid from New Horizons. We'd worked out an offer that was as close as we could afford, hoping that the community angle would make up with the slight reduction.

'It's a healthy bid,' Mary Smith commented. 'What if you are unable to make a profit? We wouldn't want to accept your offer and then it ends up being flats in the future anyway.'

'We could draw up an agreement that the buildings must always be used for the community,' Heather suggested. I threw her a smile: that was a great idea.

'We are really passionate about this project,' Mum said then. 'We love the village and you know how much we are willing to do to save it. We brought everyone together by putting on that trail and it showed us just how much of a community spirit there is still alive in Glendale. We are confident that everyone will work with us to make this a success.'

'It's an exciting idea,' Mr Murray said, flicking through our proposal again. 'We must admit that we didn't think there would be any opposition to our proposal to sell to New Horizons. We've tried over the past couple of years to think of ways we can inject life into the village, but it has been an uphill struggle, and with resources stretched to almost breaking point, we really saw no other option. You have, however, provided another option.'

'The report in the paper has galvanised people, it seems,' Mr Walker agreed. 'We've had a lot of emails and phone calls from people worried about our plans and pleading with us to change our mind. We haven't seen such enthusiasm for a long time. We want, of course, to do the best we can for the people we serve in this community. It would be remiss of us to ignore this… what would you call it? People power?' He smiled a little. 'We'll need to go over it all in detail, of course.'

'We are committed to making this work,' I told them. 'This will breathe life into the village again and not only give you money to spend on other things, I think it might even save you some in the long run. The people who might have ended up needing social care might remain more independent if they have a local place to get everything they needed. If they have a community to lean on again. A win-win for all I think.' I could tell, by the look they exchanged, they hadn't thought of that as an outcome.

After asking a few questions about our presentation, Mr Murray said they would come back to us within a week with a decision, and we all stood up and shook hands again. I knew that they knew giving it to us would be the popular decision, that it was what the community both wanted and needed, but I worried that New Horizons might throw more money at them once they heard they might change their minds about redeveloping the village.

'We could talk to Dad,' I said as we walked out into the fresh air an hour later. 'He might be able to persuade New Horizons to not make any counter-offer to the council.'

'I suppose it would be the least he could do,' Mum agreed.

–

The four of us sat down in the dining room that night, Sally bringing us in plates of steaming fish pie and giving me and my mum a reassuring smile, before she left us alone to eat as a family for the first time since Christmas Day. Izzy tucked in to her meal straight away, and I looked at my mum, who nodded, stealing herself with a gulp of wine, for which I couldn't exactly blame her. My dad was back at the head of the table, still in his work suit, having come straight from the office to us, accepting my mum's invitation without knowing why we wanted to see him.

'We wanted to talk to you about our meeting with the council,' Mum said. 'About what Beth and I want to do.' She told him about our plans. He listened in silence having stopped eating.

Dad let her words sink in for a moment before turning to me. 'You want to invest that much in Glendale?'

I nodded. 'I've decided… well, we have,' I said, looking at Izzy, who beamed. 'That we want to move back to Glendale. As well as helping Mum organise all of this, I have decided to go back to college and study horticulture. What I've always wanted to do. Izzy will go to school here, and we'll live here at the Hall.'

He sat back in his chair, trying to take it all in. 'Well, I'm glad that you two are coming home for good, of course I am. But your idea for the high street – have you already spoken to the council about it?'

I nodded. 'We went to see them today.' I told him the offer we had made. 'We're hoping to not only save the shops but the library as well.' I explained Heather's idea for funding. 'We think this will be such a good thing for the community, Dad, surely you can see that?'

'I can see that, yes but, Beth, if the council goes with your idea that means all the work we've put in at New Horizons will have been for nothing.' He frowned. 'You can't expect me to be happy about that?' An edge returned to his voice.

'We hoped you'd see that this is not only a good thing for your family but for Glendale too,' Mum said, losing her cool a little. 'But, then again, when have you thought about either for a long time?'

Dad sighed. 'Caroline, this is business, it's not personal.'

'It's personal to us!' I cried. 'We want to open up a Glendale shop as well. We really believe in this, Dad.'

'What do you want me to say, Beth?'

'I want you to promise us that New Horizons won't make a competing offer to the council, that you'll let them go with our proposal if they want to.'

'I can't do that. I have a board meeting tomorrow. I have to share this information with my company. It's part of my duty as a director.'

'And what about your duty to your family?' Mum cried. She pushed back her chair and stood up. 'Why did I think you would even think about us, David?' She shook her head and left.

'Why is everyone arguing again?' Izzy cried, her knife and fork clattering onto the table.

'Oh, love, it's okay,' I tried to say. 'We're just all very stuck to our own ideas.'

'But why do you need to fight?'

I looked at my dad, wondering the same thing myself.

He stood up. 'I should go.'

I followed him out, telling Izzy I'd be back in a moment. I didn't want her to hear any more arguments. It certainly wasn't what I wanted to move back to Glendale for. 'Dad, please, think about this,' I pleaded with him in the hallway.

'I'm in an impossible situation,' he said, quietly then, his hand on the doorknob, ready to escape. He looked back at me for a moment.

'I suppose you are,' I conceded – he either sided with me and my mum, or his company and, of course, his mistress. It was time for him to choose.

Dad nodded, once, and then walked out of the door.

Chapter Fifty-Six

My mum and I walked to the village together. 'I thought about this one... for us.' She paused at the empty shop right in the middle of the high street, a wide frontage with large glass windows either side of the door. I went to the window and framed my eyes, trying to see what it looked like inside. It went back reasonably far, completely empty at the moment. 'I like it,' I said, trying to picture a wall of plants on one side and maybe a round table in the centre to sell homemade jams and chutneys. I stepped back and looked up at the empty sign and tried to picture one announcing it to be the 'Glendale Hall Shop'. 'It would be great, wouldn't it?'

'And we could sell the family whiskey too,' she said, moving on to look inside the next shop. 'If they'll give us a good deal,' she added, her business hat very much on.

'What do you think Dad will do?' I asked her then.

'Honestly, I think he'll tell the company about our bid. He's pretty much always put business first and he has extra motivation now,' she said, dryly. We carried on walking.

'I can't imagine being with someone for as long as you've been together.' I tried to stop Drew flashing through my mind. I couldn't help it though. He was on my mind more and more as the funeral approached, when I would see him again. We moved passed the final empty shop. One that could very well be filled by Rory soon, selling their farm produce.

'Together for thirty years and still we have trouble telling each other exactly how we feel and what we want. We have been drifting apart for a long time. It's sad to think that it might all be over, but maybe it's just our time. I suppose we haven't worked at our relationship as much as we should have.'

'And he shouldn't have had an affair.'

'No.' She glanced at me. 'But I suppose in a way I can understand him feeling lonely because I have too. I have been lonely for a long time, without even realising it, I don't think.'

'Oh, Mum, I'm sorry.'

'I'm not lonely now.' She touched my arm. 'Having you and Izzy at the Hall has brought it, and me, back to life. I'm so happy we've been working on this project together. Whatever happens, it has given me back my zest for life. Losing your grandmother has made me see that I don't want to sit at the Hall drowning my sorrows and being wrapped up in self-pity. If I'm lonely then I need to do something about it. You know?'

I nodded. 'I do. And I'm so proud of you. It must have been so hard looking after Gran by yourself and knowing that dad was with someone else. I wish I could have been here sooner to help. But I'm here now, and whatever you want to do, I'll support you.' I looked at her. 'Mum, did you ever think about having an affair?'

She glanced at me sharply and then sighed. 'No. And yes. And no.'

'With John?' I dared to ask.

'When John came to work with us, I was happy. Your father worked too much but I had you and my mother and a real social circle then: I wasn't lonely. I felt blessed for what I had. I liked John. He was a great gardener, of course, but as time went on, we became fond of one another, I suppose. I could talk to him. I didn't ever feel that way with your father. Maybe I was too scared to tell him what I really thought or felt because I had so much to lose, but with John, I could just be honest about everything. Does that make sense?'

'You could be yourself.'

She nodded. 'He never judged me. When things started to go wrong, I leaned on him more. When you left, my heart had a hole in it. Your father was absent more and more, and then when your gran got sick, I did get lonely. John was there for me, as he always has been. But, in a way, it didn't help as it once had. Perhaps because I started to want more and knew that I couldn't have it.'

'He loves you,' I said. It wasn't a question and she knew it.

'Yes, but I've never been able to give him my heart fully. He's always known that. I loved your father too much and respected our marriage too much. John was furious when I told him about Cathy. And I can understand why. It was hard to stop him thumping David, to be honest.'

'I bet.'

'I don't know that I've been fair to him. I should have made him leave a long time ago, but I was selfish, I let him stay, even though I knew how he felt. I didn't want him to go.'

I hooked my arm through hers. 'I can understand that.'

We walked towards the Glendale Arms, passing by the church. 'Mum, how did you know that Dad was The One? I mean, what made you want to marry him?' I asked her. It was something that I hadn't thought much about before. They were my parents and when I had come into their world, their relationship was already fixed: they were already committed to one another.

'Your father was the son of some family friends, so I knew him for a long time. We threw a party at the Hall when I was twenty and he came along, with a girlfriend.' She raised an eyebrow. 'I remember looking at him and thinking that he hadn't looked that attractive the last time I had seen him, I was sure. I followed him to the drinks table, and we started talking. He was at Edinburgh University, and I was taking classes at the local college and helping your gran with her charity work. He seemed to have all these big plans. He chatted about what he wanted to do with his life, and he talked about hoping he would get married. I asked him if it would be to the girl he was with and he said: "no, it will be with you". We barely left each other's sides after that.' She chuckled. 'I don't know what it was. It was as if we had finally noticed the other person and realised they had been right there all along just waiting for us.' She opened the door to the pub, me trailing after her, surprised that my parents had been so swept off their feet by one another. I hadn't witnessed anything close to that growing up. It was sad how such a spark had faded.

Mum turned to me then. 'No one knows what's going to happen in life. Whether or not things will work out. But life is about the trying, and the journey. Your father and I have had a lot of ups and downs, but we shared them together, and that's what marriage is all about. You'll know when it's right, when you find that person you want to go through life with. And it might last forever, or it might not, but as long as you start out believing that it will, that's all anyone can ask for.'

I nodded as we made our way to a table close to the crackling fire. 'I always thought I was meant to be with Drew.'

'Maybe you are.'

'I don't know what to do,' I admitted. 'I mean, is it crazy to think there might be something between us? After all this time? We were just teenagers back then.'

'You're not teenagers now, Beth. You know what's real and what isn't. You two have a strong bond, and you have a daughter together. It's complicated, of course it is, and a lot of time has passed, but if the love you had back then is still there then it's not crazy at all. Maybe now is the right time.'

I stared at her. It felt as if I had been fighting my feelings for Drew ever since I walked into this pub and saw him before Christmas. But maybe it wasn't something I should have been trying to fight, but something that I should be grabbing hold of with both hands. Maybe when it was right, you did just know it. Maybe I did know it and that's why I was so scared.

Because if I told Drew how I felt it would mean that I could finally stop running.

Chapter Fifty-Seven

The day of the funeral arrived. It should have been grey and raining to fit our mood, but it dawned crisp and sunny. I glanced out at the garden as the sun shone down on the dew covering the grass, sipping my coffee, waiting for everyone to be ready. I hadn't been able to sleep and had got up and dressed early, suitably sombre all in black. The doorbell rang out in the silence, so I went to answer it, and in the driveway stood the hearse and a sleek black car hired to drive us to the church. White lilies were draped over the coffin. My gran's favourite flowers. They had always stood in a large vase in the hallway when I was growing up.

'It's time to go,' I called up the stairs, my voice echoing in the large hall. I watched as Izzy hurried down in her black dress I had bought her in town, followed by Sally and my mum. I pulled Izzy to me. 'You going to be okay?' I asked her. I didn't relish the fact that it would be the first funeral she had attended, but she had told me she wanted to be there to look after us, which was so like my daughter I had almost burst into tears.

She nodded. 'Are you?'

'I will be,' I promised. There was no point in pretending that this day wasn't going to be difficult. For all of us. I took Izzy's hand, and with my other, I took my mum's. We walked slowly out of the house to the waiting car, pausing at the hearse. It was surreal to think of my gran inside it, so I decided not to. I would picture her sweeping down the staircase at the Hall, instead, in one of her expensive suits, her pearls around her neck, a cloud of Chanel following her, telling me to walk like a lady down the stairs and not to slide down the banister.

I had always ignored her.

The short drive to the village was over in a blink. Outside the church, my dad waited in his dark suit, people were filing past him, the sun shining down on them.

'She would be pleased by the turnout,' Mum said as we climbed out and Reverend Brodie stepped forward to greet us. I knew that the people in the church were all there out of respect for my family and that made me feel proud. We were part of Glendale and that was important. More than I had ever realised before.

We walked into the church, along the aisle to the pew at the front, passing by familiar faces. Heather gave me a small wave. Beside her was her father and in front of them was Rory, and my eyes met Drew's next to them. There was no sign of April. Drew smiled a little at us, and Izzy waved to him. I was grateful to him for coming. More than he probably knew.

I looked at the front where a large photograph was propped up on a stand. It was one of my gran and my mum outside Glendale Hall, my mum holding me as a baby in her arms, the smiles wide on their faces. I felt my breath catch in my throat.

The service was suitably grand for Margaret MacKenzie. The hymns and readings part of her preferred list. My dad read a poem and then it was my turn to talk about forgiveness. I managed to read it without crying but then my mum got up to speak. She didn't waver once as she talked about her own mother, her voice strong in the silent church. 'Family was the most important thing to my mother,' she said, her eyes finding us in the front pew. 'Sometimes to extremes. But she did the things she did because she was fiercely proud of us and wanted us to be the best people that we could be. She wanted us to do everything that she had been unable to do. And for us to always remember to show the people we love how we feel before it's too late. That is her legacy. One that I hope none of us ever forget.'

A tear rolled down my cheek then. I cried for who my gran had been, for who she could have been, all we had but, mostly, for what we could have had.

I felt Izzy take hold of my hand and squeeze it tightly. My mum had been right about Gran's legacy. I wanted to do all I could to be there for the people I loved. I glanced back and met Drew's eyes. He was looking at us, his eyes filled with tears.

My mum took Izzy's other hand, and the three of us sat like that until the Reverend Brodie ended the service, the organ playing as we filed out of the church. Margaret MacKenzie was at peace, her last wish realised – her family all together again.

We drove back to the Hall, where the caterers had laid out a buffet on the long kitchen table and had begun serving drinks in their black outfits, as more and more people came inside, over spilling into the drawing room where we had placed extra chairs.

Drew found me and Izzy in the kitchen. I tried not to notice how handsome he looked in his suit as he gave Izzy a huge hug after she had launched herself into his arms. He turned to me and held out his arms. I stepped into them gratefully, letting him hold me, wishing he would never let go.

'It was a lovely service,' he said when we pulled apart. 'How are you doing?'

'I'm just glad we're here. And that I got to say goodbye to her. We put the past to rest. There's nothing to regret. And what my mum said about us doing everything that my gran wasn't able to do, I really want to do that.'

'You will,' he said. 'Can we talk later?' he asked then.

'Sure,' I replied. I looked across the room at my mum. 'I better go and see if she's okay. You guys stick together.' I watched Drew wrap his arms around Izzy and relief surged through me that he was here. It felt like everything was easier to handle with him here. I had spent so many years handling everything alone that it was such a relief he was here to lean on, for both me and Izzy. The two of them had already developed such a good relationship, and I was so grateful that he had come back to support us. I wondered what he wanted to talk about, but I tried to push it to the back of my mind. I had to focus on getting my mum through the wake. She needed me. And I knew Izzy would be just fine with Drew so I could focus on taking care of her.

Looking around, it felt as if the whole of Glendale was at the Hall. I saw people that I hadn't seen since I was Izzy's age, all wanting to know about my life in London, not knowing that I'd be leaving that behind me soon.

Somehow my gran had made that happen, and I decided that would be what I remembered her for. Not the mistakes she made in the past but how she made up for them. After all, my mum was right about what she said in the church – we had to show the people we loved how we felt. Gran had managed to do that in the end, but I knew she would have been much happier if she had done that sooner.

–

It was late when the last of our houseguests left. The caterers had gone, sweeping away all remnants of the food and drink. My dad left for his hotel. John had retired to his cottage, Sally and my mum went to their rooms, and I took Izzy to bed. She was exhausted and was asleep as soon as I tucked her in. After I shut her door I went along to my mum's room. She was sat up in bed and smiled when I went in.

'She had a good send-off, didn't she?' I said, leaning against the doorframe.

She nodded. 'It was what she had wanted. I still can't believe that she's gone. Every time I walk past her room, I have to stop myself from looking in to check on her. She was ill for so long it feels strange not to be looking after her any more.'

'You looked after her so well,' I said. 'Her last days were as comfortable as they could have been, Mum.'

'She always told me that she wanted to live her last days here. I hated that she had to go to hospital at the end.' A tear rolled down her cheek.

I went over and perched next to her, squeezing her hand. 'She had a fall. It was no one's fault. She got to stay here for as long as was possible. She got to be with her family at the end. You did everything that you could.'

'It just feels so strange to be here without her. She hardly spent any nights away from the Hall. Sometimes I even wondered if she loved this house more than me.' Mum shook her head with a smile.

'She only loved this house so much because you were here,' I replied. My gran had found it difficult to show affection, that was true, and my mum had been the same, but I knew that deep down they had fiercely loved their family and that was why the house meant so much to them.

'And now she's passed it on to you,' Mum said. 'I'm so happy you'll be here now.'

'Me too. And Izzy is so excited. Although she'd like us to build a library for her.'

Mum chuckled. 'Tell her she has to use the one in Glendale to keep it open. I'm so tired.'

'It's been an emotional day.' I stood up and leaned over her to kiss her on the cheek. 'Get some rest.'

'Thank you for your support today, darling. I know it wasn't easy, for any of us, but it's done. We can look forward now.'

'We will,' I promised.

Chapter Fifty-Eight

And then it was just me and Drew. We sat at the kitchen table with a glass of the family whiskey in front of us. I wasn't really a fan of it but it felt like the appropriate drink for us to end this day.

'To Gran,' I said, raising my glass. Drew clinked his against it and we both took a gulp. I winced as it burned down my throat. 'Thank you for coming today,' I said. 'I really appreciate it. I'm glad there was such a good turnout. I wish Gran could have seen that.'

'I think she would have been proud.' Drew took another sip of his drink. 'Funerals really do make you think about time, don't they? How fleeting it can all be. None of us know what will happen.'

'I suppose all we can do is try to make the most of whatever time we do have. I feel a bit like I've been sleepwalking through life, just getting through each day which sometimes is all you can do, but being up here, I've been able to look up and take stock and think about what I want to do.'

'I kind of envy how you know what you want to do,' Drew admitted. 'I feel a bit stuck right now.'

'What happened with April?' I felt brave enough to finally ask him.

'She's gone to stay with her parent's. We're talking but I don't know, Beth. How can I ever trust her again? Yeah, she didn't know what was in your letter, but she guessed it was something important, something that might make me feel differently about her, and she chose to destroy it and not let me read it and make my own choice. She took Izzy away from me.' He sighed. 'She keeps begging me to forgive her, telling me she only did it because she was in love with me and I couldn't let go of the past.' He met my gaze. 'Let go of you.'

'I'm sorry, Drew. What are you going to do?' I didn't want to pin my hopes on them splitting up. I wanted to be okay if Drew chose her. If he was just a friend to me, and Izzy's dad. I was happy he was in my life whatever happened, but I couldn't deny how much I wanted more. But how could I tell him that? I didn't want to burden him with another choice to make. And I was scared, too. What if he had already let me go?

'I'm going to my job interview tomorrow and then I'm going to decide if I want to come back to Scotland. And then I'll tell her what I want. It's good to have this time away, to get some space. It's hard to think when she's there telling me how much she needs me. We've been together a long time, but I never felt ready to take the next step, you know? Marriage. I never felt ready. Maybe that's because she's not the right person. Do you think you just know when it's right?'

I thought about the men that I had met over the past ten years. I had known almost immediately that it wasn't right with them. When I kissed Drew at New Year, my heart had known he was the right one. But obviously he hadn't felt the same. I looked down at the brandy and swished it around in the glass. 'Yeah, I do.'

'That's what I thought. Honestly, I think you have the right idea. Relationships feel more trouble than they're worth right now. I want to do what's right for me, what I want, like you're doing. I don't know if that's selfish.'

His words stung. 'Sometimes you have to be a little bit selfish. To follow your heart. In the long run if you don't, you'll just cause even more hurt. You know?'

Drew nodded. 'I know. When did you get so wise, huh?' He smiled a little.

'I don't think I'm wise at all,' I replied. If I was wise, I would have stopped loving Drew. But I couldn't.

'It would be crazy, wouldn't it, for us both to come back here after all this time? But, I don't know, it feels like something is pulling me back. Is that how you feel?'

I looked up. 'It is.'

Drew held my gaze. I wished I knew what he was thinking. I wished I could tell him what I was thinking. Then he glanced at his watch. 'I should go, it's late. After my interview, can we all do something? You, me and Izzy.'

'I'd like that,' I said. I drained my glass dry.

He smiled. 'Good. And, Beth? Thank you for listening.'

I forced myself to smile back. 'Any time.'

—

I woke up when it was still dark outside and switched on my bedside lamp. I had fallen asleep with the college brochure Heather had given me on my lap. I looked at it now, on the page for the courses in horticulture. There was a night course that I wanted to sign up to, starting in March. I was nervous about going back to school, it had been ten years since I had studied anything, but it helped to know that Heather would be going back as well. There was so much to sort out before all that though. I was beginning to feel anxious about it all. I picked up the notebook I had been writing things down in. We would soon be heading back to London and I had to hand in my notice, talk to my landlord, pack up our flat, say goodbye to everyone we knew there and get Izzy a place at my old school in Glendale.

Before all of that, though, we could have the decision from the council at any time and we would know if our plans to reopen the high street would be getting the go-ahead. And I didn't even want to think about Drew on top of all of that.

Sighing, I climbed out of bed and padded downstairs softly as the house was so quiet. I was in dire need of a strong coffee. When I walked into the kitchen, Sally was there already, pouring herself a cup. 'Do you ever sleep?' I asked her, shaking my head.

'I like getting up early, having a few minutes to myself. Want a cup?' She brought over two steaming mugs of black coffee and we sat down at the table. 'How about you? Why are you up?'

'Too much on my mind, I suppose,' I said, taking a sip of my coffee.

'I thought you were excited about moving back. Are you worried about it now?'

'Not worried exactly. There is just so much to sort out. I just want to get it all done and start our new life up here.' I sighed. 'We're going out with Drew later.'

'You're hoping he's going to be moving back too?'

I shrugged although she was giving me a shrewd look. 'For Izzy, yes.'

'Oh, Beth. I can see the way you look at him. Exactly as you used to do when you were a teenager. You were head over heels for that boy. He's turned into a good man. And you still love him. Why won't you tell him how you feel?'

'I'm scared,' I admitted. 'Scared he doesn't feel the same way. But also worried if he does. What if it didn't work out? Izzy would be devastated. I don't want to make another mistake,' I told her truthfully.

'Mistakes aren't something to worry about, it's what you do after you make them that counts. You should know that better than anyone. If it wasn't scary then it wouldn't be worth doing in the first place, would it now?'

I looked out at the garden, a glimpse of light appearing in the sky, wishing that Sally wasn't right but I knew that she was.

Chapter Fifty-Nine

Drew picked us up and told us he was taking us somewhere for a surprise. We drove for a half an hour before we pulled into the car park, where a large sign for the 'Botanical Gardens' greeted us and made me smile.

'What do you think?' he asked me as he stopped the car.

'I love it here,' I replied. I was taken instantly back to when I was fourteen and I had asked John if he thought I'd be able to make gardening my job. He had driven us to the gardens and talked to me about all the different things I could do in gardening. I was in awe of how they had created such a beautiful garden and all the work that had gone into it. I knew I'd love to work somewhere like that. 'I haven't been here in years.'

'I remembered you telling me that this was one of your favourite places ever,' Drew said as we climbed out of the car. I was amazed that he had remembered that. 'I thought it would be the perfect day out for us. Especially as it's meant to stay dry.'

The January weather did indeed seem to be behaving itself, the sky clear and blue, as we walked into the garden. Izzy was looking less keen about Drew's choice of outing but happy enough because she was with the two of us. I betted I would end up having to buy her something in the gift shop afterwards as compensation though.

'How did your interview go?' I asked him as we entered the outside garden area where a stream ran alongside a beautiful lawn, Izzy skipping on ahead of us.

'It went well. I like the hospital. And the team there. Plus, they do a lot of research, which interests me,' he replied. 'I have a lot to think about.'

'Can we go in there?' Izzy called back, pointing to the glasshouse. The breeze had started to blow up and I could see my breath in the air, so we eagerly went into the tropical warmth, exotic plants towering over us, being dusted with water mist.

'The work it takes to keep these plants thriving up here in Scotland is amazing,' I said, gazing up. 'I can't wait to learn more about it all. Can you imagine what it would be like to work here?' I felt a shiver of excitement.

'You would be brilliant at it,' Drew said. 'Although will you be able to tear yourself away from the garden at the Hall?'

I smiled. 'I suppose it depends if our plan for a shop gets the go-ahead. That will be a lot of work. We want to sell products using the plants and herbs that we grow there. I am trying to persuade John to let me have beehives. Think about what we could make from them.'

'Rory is excited about the idea of having a farm shop, too. I think it will do well. When do you find out what the council have decided?'

'Any day now, hopefully.' I watched as Izzy went on ahead to look at the lily pond. 'What does Rory say about you coming back here?'

'Not much, you know him. He'd never ask me to come back, but I know he could do with some help. There are a lot of incentives for me to come home.' He nodded at Izzy and then he looked at me. 'I honestly don't know what to do. What should I do?'

I stared at him, the palms of my hands turning clammy. Had he given me a chance to tell him how I felt? To tell him to stay. To choose me. To choose us.

'Oh my god, look a lizard!' Izzy cried then. I jumped and stepped back from Drew. My head spun as he went over to look at what she was pointing at. I followed them slowly, annoyed at myself for not being bolder.

Once we got out of the glasshouse, the conversation fell on less important things. Izzy and Drew chatted as we looked around the gardens, and my mind wandered.

I had done everything on my own since I had fled Glendale aged sixteen, and I didn't want to do it any more. I wanted to come home, to be with my family again, and not have to do it all alone. I wanted a chance to make some of my dreams come true. To not have to worry about surviving but to be happy. And that would happen regardless of what happened with Drew, but the question I kept wrestling with was did I want it to happen without him?

After we had seen the rest of the garden, we walked through the gift shop on our way out.

Izzy looked around the shop for something to beg me to buy, and I looked at the gardening books. I felt Drew come over and watch me for a moment.

'I'm sorry,' he said, finally.

'For what?'

'For asking you earlier to tell me what I should do. That wasn't fair. I know that it's up to me. I have to choose, just like you guys have.'

I looked up from the book. 'That's why I forgave my gran in the end. Although she tried, she didn't actually make my choice for me. I decided to run away. And I've done the same thing again now. It would be easy to go back to our life in London, but I know that's not what I want. You need to decide what you want, and to be honest about it, to yourself, your family, to April and to me.' I took a deep breath. 'But, Drew, we would love it if you did come back here,' I said, finally being honest.

He smiled. 'You would?'

'Of course we would.' My heart began to thump in my chest as I smiled back at him. I wanted him so badly to choose us.

'Mum look at this,' Izzy said, coming up to us. She held up a cuddly lizard. 'Like the one we saw!'

'And I've found a book,' I said, knowing she'd be impressed.

'Let me get them for you,' Drew said, taking my book from me before I could stop him. 'I insist. But you have to help me find something for me too,' he said to Izzy, giving me a small smile before he followed her.

Izzy picked up a small pot with a fake cactus growing in it. 'You should get this so you have a piece of Scotland with you in Boston,' she told him.

'That would look very cute on my windowsill,' he said, taking it to look at it.

'Cute?' I said with a grin, hoping to lighten the mood between us. 'Are you a teenage girl?'

'Just because you can't pull 'cute' off,' he replied, marching to the till with our purchases. Izzy waved a mug at me then and I went over to her, leaving Drew to it.

'You need this,' she said, showing it to me.

I laughed at the *Keep Calm and Garden On* slogan on it. 'Hey, I'm always calm.'

'You have been calmer lately,' she conceded, putting the mug back down.

'I have?' Sometimes the way Izzy saw the world fascinated me.

She nodded. 'In London, you were always rushing about, we always had things to do, you always had something to remember, but here you're more chill. I like it.'

I smiled because I knew she was right. 'And I like how you are here too.'

'Me too.'

Chapter Sixty

We drove home, and Drew came in with us. 'Just missed the deluge,' Drew commented as outside the heavens opened, and it started to pour with rain.

'Did you all have a good time?' my mum asked, joining us in the hallway as we took off our coats and shoes.

'It was more Mum's thing,' Izzy said with a shrug. 'But look what Dad got me.' She showed her the lizard she had clutched all the way home.

'Oh. Well, how… nice,' Mum said, eyeing it a little suspiciously. 'Sally has tea and cake in the kitchen if you want some?' Izzy didn't need telling twice and headed that way immediately.

'Have you heard anything from Dad?' I asked her. We knew the meeting at New Horizons was happening that day. She shook her head. I explained to Drew that they were going to discuss our bid to the council. 'We hoped that my dad might persuade them not to counter our bid. But we just don't know.'

'Imagine you being a landlord. I worry you'll be a pushover,' Drew said with a grin.

'My mum and I will be good cop, bad cop so it'll be fine.'

Mum rolled her eyes. 'If people listened to you, they would think I'm a tyrant,' she said, following Izzy into the kitchen. I raised my eyebrows at Drew, and he had to stifle a laugh.

'Let me show you something before we join them,' he said, heading into the living room.

Curiously, I trailed after him. 'What is it?'

'I was waiting for my flight back,' he said, rummaging in the bag from the gift shop. He pulled out a CD. 'And I saw this in HMV. I haven't bought a CD for years, but I wanted a physical copy of this. Let me play it.' He went to the stereo and found the song he was after. 'I haven't listened to it for years.' He pressed play and music filled the silent room. It was our song. The one I had named Izzy after. He turned to smile at me. 'I still can't believe you named her after this.'

'I was in hospital having her, and Emily was with me and trying to distract me from the pain,' I explained, perching on the arm of the sofa. 'She asked me what I was going to name my baby, but I didn't know. She told me to think about names that were special to me, that it would make deciding easier. And a song came on the radio, and I asked her to turn it over as I hated it, and I wished that 'Isabelle' would play. It didn't, of course, but I started thinking about all the times we listened to it that summer, how we had danced to it, and how much I loved it. And how it would always remind me of us... and you.' I felt myself welling up, remembering that day. 'When the midwife put Izzy into my arms, I knew it was the perfect name for her.'

'Your family weren't with you?'

'Just Emily. I didn't let them come for a few weeks. I think I wanted to be sure that I could do without them first.' I wiped the tear that had rolled down my cheek.

Drew stepped forward and reached out, brushing back my hair over my shoulder. 'I wish I had been there with you. It must have been so hard doing it all on your own. You were so brave, Beth.'

The hairs on my arm stood up at his touch. 'I was sixteen and thought I could take on the whole world. I'm not sure I could do it now.'

'Of course you could. You're still being brave. Moving back here, starting over, going back to school and setting up a business. All of that while raising such a wonderful kid as Izzy. You're amazing.'

The song played in the background as we looked at one another. My breath hitched in my throat as I returned his gaze. He was so close. Every fibre of my body wanted to lean into him, to feel his lips on mine again. But I was terrified at the same time.

Then he held out his hand. 'How about we dance to it one more time?'

I liked that he said one more time, and not one last time. I let him pull me up and he started the song again, wrapping his arms around me. I leaned against him as we swayed to the song, closing my eyes. It was as if we had been sucked back to when I was sixteen and he was eighteen, dancing outside his farm, the song playing in his car behind us, feeling like we would be together forever.

'That summer was perfect,' I whispered to him, his hands on my waist burning into my skin. I looked up at him, the stubble on his chin brushing the top of my head.

'It was,' he agreed with a small smile. And we stopped dancing then. Drew leaned down towards me, and I felt myself reach up to meet him.

'Mum! Dad! Where are you?'

We broke apart as Izzy called out to us. Drew stopped the song as she walked in, demanding to know why we hadn't appeared for tea and cake.

'We're coming now,' I told her, feeling my cheeks turn pink as she stood in the doorway, looking at us in confusion. 'Right behind you,' I added, and she finally turned and headed back to the kitchen. I glanced at Drew, but he was bending down looking into the garden shop bag. 'We better go,' I said.

'Uh, yes. I'll just nip to the loo.'

'Okay,' I said. I walked out quickly, hoping my cheeks would return to their normal colour quickly. My pulse was racing. I was sure we would have kissed if Izzy hadn't come in. Did that mean he had feelings for me too? Or was he just caught up in the nostalgic moment we had shared?

I thought back to him calling me amazing and my cheeks turned an even brighter shade of pink.

I went into the kitchen feeling like a teenager again.

–

We were all in the kitchen as Sally, with Izzy helping, cooked the meal when my mum's phone rang. 'The council,' she mouthed to me after she had answered it.

'Oh my god, it's them,' I hissed. We all stopped what we were doing to watch her to talk to them. Drew gave me a reassuring smile. I tried not to blush again.

'Yes… Right, I see,' Mum said as she listened. 'Right. Yes, okay. Thank you, Mr Murray… Yes, we shall see you then.' She hung up and looked at us.

'Well?' I prompted when she didn't say anything.

'They said yes,' she said, slowly. 'They said yes to us. To everything.'

'They said yes?' I stood up. 'They said yes?' She nodded and broke into a smile. I rushed to her and gave her a big hug. 'We really did it!' Izzy joined us for a group hug. 'I can't believe it.'

'That's great news,' Sally said. 'I'll find some champagne.'

'Well done,' Drew said from behind me. He reached for me and I fell into his arms. 'I knew you could do it,' he said, his mouth almost touching my ear. I shivered a little and hoped he hadn't noticed.

'Well, I hardly know what to say,' Mum said, beaming. 'They said they spoke to New Horizons earlier and they've pulled out of the process. They even said, apparently, they were happy that the premises would be staying with the community.'

I gaped at her. 'Seriously? That must be Dad's doing.'

'Maybe what we said got through to him.'

'Oh, I have to ring Heather!' I cried.

'Get her over here for some champagne,' Mum said.

'I'll call Rory too,' Drew said. 'We can make a party of it. I'm flying back tomorrow, and I don't want to miss celebrating this.' As he pulled out his phone, I tried not to let my heart sink at the thought of him going: there was too much to be happy about.

I grabbed my phone to call Heather but then I heard the doorbell ring. 'I wonder who that is?' I popped out into the hall and paused in surprise to see my mum opening the door to my dad.

Chapter Sixty-One

Dad came into the hall. He looked tired. 'I take it you've heard the news?'

'We have,' Mum said, glancing at me as I joined them.

'We had our board meeting. The council had got in touch with us to tell us about your bid. They gave us the option of submitting a counter-offer. We had a rather heated discussion about it and took a vote and agreed that we would back out.' He looked at us. 'I know I haven't been as supportive as I could have been. I was in a difficult situation but still… I also know I haven't been the husband, or father, you both deserve and I'm sorry. I hope this makes up for some of what has happened over the past few weeks.'

Mum nodded. 'Thank you, David. I know that they might have voted another way if you hadn't been there.'

'Well, I'm not exactly popular with some of the board but a lot of us were born and raised in Glendale, or thereabouts, and there are other sites that we can use for the flats.'

I smiled. 'You did good, Dad,' I told him, relieved that he hadn't turned his back on us.

'It was the least I could do,' he replied. He glanced around the hall and sighed. 'I've found a place. Close to the village. To rent. I can't live in that hotel forever.'

'And Cathy?' Mum asked.

'I don't know. She's talking things over with her husband. I don't know what will happen, but I hope…' he trailed off. 'I'm so sorry, Caroline. For everything.'

'I know you are.'

'I'm so pleased you'll be here now,' Dad said to me. 'And Izzy too.'

'Me too,' I replied. 'We're just getting the champagne out. Do you want to join us?'

He smiled. 'Thank you but no, I should go. I am pleased for you though. I'm looking forward to shopping in the Glendale Hall shop.' He reached for me tentatively and I hugged him. I saw Mum duck out but not before I saw tears in her eyes. 'Look after her, won't you?' Dad said to me.

'I will,' I promised, pulling back. 'Are you sure this is what you want?'

'It's time, darling. It's time.'

I nodded. I was sad that it had come to that, but I knew that my parents would both be happier in the long run. 'I'll call you? Izzy and I can come over when you've moved in?'

'I'd like that.'

After I had said goodbye, I went back into the kitchen. Mum was there, looking more composed. Drew was opening up the champagne. Sally and Izzy had been joined by John. Heather and Rory were on their way. The whole family was there apart from Dad. 'Mum…'

'It was time,' she replied, not realising she had said exactly what he had. I hoped they would both be okay, and I was glad that I would be there to make sure of that as best I could.

When Heather and Rory arrived, my mum decided it was time to make a speech. 'Right, everyone,' she called out, clinking her glass for us to quieten down. 'I just wanted to say a few words. First, thank you all for your hard work. Starting with the trail and everything you've done since to help us save the village. We have done it! And I'd like to thank Beth especially for giving me, us… well, to put it crudely, a kick up the butt.' Everyone laughed at my mum saying that. 'We have a lot of work still to do but I know we can make this a success together. So, here's to the future!' She raised her glass and we echoed the toast.

'I can't believe that you pulled this off,' Heather said, giving me a tight squeeze around the waist. 'You, Beth Williams, are a little star.'

'We did it together,' I said, squeezing her back. It was hard to believe that she hadn't been in my life for a long time. I couldn't imagine being without her again.

We all got quite drunk on the champagne, minus Izzy, of course, and Rory and Drew who were driving. I easily persuaded Heather to stay the night so she could have more. And, suddenly, it was late, and Drew was checking his watch.

'Guys, I have a flight tomorrow,' he said. We had moved into the living room in front of the fire by then and there was a chorus of groans at his words. He grinned. 'I know, I'm a party pooper, aren't I!'

'I don't want you to go,' Izzy said, up way past her bedtime and loving it. 'Don't go back to Boston!'

'Ah, Iz.' Drew slung an arm around her. 'It won't be for long, I promise.'

'Hey, how about you come with us to the airport?' Rory suggested. 'I can come and get you on the way? If you can be up early?'

'Of course I can,' Izzy replied, looking insulted. She turned to me. 'Can I, Mum?'

'Definitely,' I said, smiling. I glanced at Drew, wondering if the invitation would be extended to me. He was avoiding my

358

gaze. I looked down at my lap. Perhaps he was remembering the last time he invited me to the airport. I hated that he had stood there waiting for me to say goodbye and I hadn't shown up. No wonder he didn't want to go through that again. I wanted to tell him I'd go anywhere he wanted me to, but I had no idea if that would make him happy.

And then he and Rory got up and everyone was saying their goodbyes. I hovered by the door and I showed them out into the hall. 'So…' My voice trailed off a little as I opened the front door.

Rory glanced at me and then Drew. 'I'll get the car warmed up.' He gave me a quick kiss on the cheek. 'Goodnight, Beth,' and hurried out into the darkness.

My hand rested on the door as Drew stepped into the frame.

'I'll call you guys when I land,' Drew said, looking at his brother outside, and not at me.

'Okay,' I replied, my mouth turning dry. I started to reach for him, but he stepped down into the driveway.

'See you, Beth,' he said, and then he was gone.

I slumped against the doorframe, watching as he opened the car door. He glanced back at me once and I gave him a small wave. I couldn't make out the expression on his face in the darkness and then he climbed into the car and shut the door. It certainly wasn't the goodbye I had been hoping for. I closed the door and leaned against it. I thought about us dancing, how I was so sure he had been about to kiss me, but now he had slipped off into the night with not as much as a second glance.

Had he decided that he had almost made a huge mistake?

Chapter Sixty-Two

I woke up to my bedroom door opening.

'Mum, Uncle Rory will be picking me up in a minute,' Izzy said in the darkness. And then there was a yelp. 'Oh, sorry, Heather!'

I hastily turned on the lamp. Izzy had stepped on Heather in her sleeping bag, waking her up with a jump.

'What's going on?' Heather said, sleepily.

'I just came to say goodbye,' Izzy said, laughing a little. 'Why are you on the floor?'

'Last night, it seemed like a good idea, but my back is killing me,' Heather replied, struggling to sit up. She had refused to sleep in one of the guest bedrooms and had instead curled up on my floor as she had done many times when we were teenagers. 'Wow, we drank way too much last night.'

'We did,' I agreed, struggling to sit up, my head beginning to pound almost instantly. 'Give me a hug,' I said to Izzy. She stepped gingerly around Heather to lean down and hug me. 'Will you be okay?'

'Yeah. Uncle Rory said we can get breakfast afterwards.'

I smiled. 'Okay. Well, we can do something fun when you get back, okay?'

'Okay. See you later.' She practically skipped out of the room again.

I sighed. 'She's really going to miss him.'

Heather looked at me. 'And so are you. You didn't want to go with them?'

'Drew didn't suggest it.' I put my head in my hands and shook it. 'I really thought… God, am I really stupid?!'

'Well, I mean…' She trailed off when I glared at her. 'Sorry. No, of course you're not! You two are meant to be, it's obvious.'

'Not to Drew.'

Heather thought for a moment. 'Maybe he was scared to ask you. I guess it didn't work out last time, did it?'

'That's putting it mildly.' I pulled my hair into a ponytail. 'I honestly thought that last night, he felt the same as I did.'

'Beth, you need to tell him how you feel. Maybe he does. I'm sure he does! But he must be scared. You've only just come back into his life and you have so much history.'

'Plus, he has a girlfriend,' I reminded her.

'Not for much longer. Come on, he doesn't love her and now he's found out what she did… He's going to move back here, and then the three of you can be a family.'

'Could it actually be that simple though?'

'If you let it.' She shrugged.

'I just keep thinking about how I broke his heart. Why would he put himself through that again? What if I tell him how I feel and he doesn't feel the same, or he does but he doesn't trust me? Maybe he thinks I'd just leave him again. And that's what I'm most scared of. What if he's right? What if we did get back together; what if I messed it all up and I ran away again? Izzy would never forgive me. I'd never forgive myself. There's just too much at stake.' There was a strange sense of relief in saying my fears out loud.

Heather absorbed my words then slowly shook her head. 'No one knows going into any relationship whether or not it will work but, Beth, you've loved that man for over ten years, and you guys have been through so much. You've found each other again, that surely has to mean something. You're older and a little bit wiser now.' She smiled. 'You have Izzy, you know how to be there day in and day out for someone. You've decided to come home. You're not running anywhere, Beth.'

Heather was right that I had never really stopped loving Drew. I walked away because I thought I had to, not because I wanted to. I had never given my heart to anyone else. 'Do you really think he might feel the same?'

'The only way to find out is to ask him.' She climbed out of her sleeping bag. 'Right, I'm going to have a shower and then you're going to feed me coffee and bacon, okay?' She headed into the bathroom.

I looked at the book on my bedside table. The one Drew bought me at the botanical garden. I picked it up and put it on my lap. I ran my fingers across the cover. It felt like Drew and I had had so many missed opportunities. What if the universe was trying to tell me that I should just let us go?

Opening up the book, I frowned as a piece of paper slipped out of it. I picked it up and opened it. It was a letter.

'Dear Beth…'

My heart started to speed up almost instantly when I saw it was from Drew. He had written me a letter and left it in the book for me to find. I grabbed it and started to read it eagerly… hungrily.

Dear Beth,

I am writing this in my apartment, looking down at the park, the sun streaming through the window, and wishing I was back in Scotland. Ever since I saw you in the pub that first night, I haven't been able to stop thinking about you. About us.

We've been through so much, haven't we? We loved each other then lost each other. And we've had an amazing daughter together. I hate that I missed out on so much. I hate that we didn't raise her together. And I want to be there for every moment that I can now.

I keep thinking about your letter. I still can't believe that April destroyed it. There have been so many missed opportunities. I'm sat here wondering if I'm crazy to think there might be a second chance for us, but I can't stop thinking about how it felt to kiss you at the Hogmanay party. About how much I wish that you, me and Izzy could be a family. I have no idea how you feel. I've been too scared to ask you. Which is why I'm writing a letter for the first time in years. I'll probably be too scared to even give it to you.

But being with you makes me feel brave. And strong. Like I can do anything. It always has. It still does. And I know that if I don't do this now, say this now, then we will miss another opportunity, and that will be it.

My heart is, and always has been, yours.

If you could ever feel the same way then I need to know. I need you to tell me.

Could you, Beth? Do you?

Drew

I knew then that the reason I hadn't told Drew how I felt was because I wasn't sure I deserved his love. I felt like the choice I had made when I was sixteen meant I should be alone, but Drew was telling me that he did still love me. And not just that

– he also wanted us to be a family, something I had wanted for ten years. God, I had made so many mistakes but, somehow, he had forgiven me for them. I felt like I had been trying to make things right since I came home, but there was one thing left to do. And I really hoped that I would be able to do it, finally.

'Heather!!!!' I leapt up and started hammering on the bathroom door. 'Heather!!!'

'What? Oh my god, what?' She flung the door open, hastily wrapping a towel around her. 'Are you okay?'

'No, I'm not!' I waved his letter at her. 'He does feel the same! Look! He's written me a letter!'

'What?' She stared at it, stupidly.

'It's from Drew,' I said, my words coming out in a rush. 'He loves me, and he wants to know if I feel the same!'

Her eyes widened. 'Oh my god,' she said.

'Exactly! We have to go to the airport! I have to tell him!' I made for the door.

'You're still in your pyjamas!' she cried.

'Crap. Quick, let's get dressed. Can we make it?' I asked her, desperately.

'We have to make it,' she replied, determined. 'What are you standing there for, hurry up!'

I dashed into the bathroom, my heart racing. I had to speak to him before he got on that plane. I had to tell him that I loved him. I wasn't going to let him get on another plane without telling him how I felt.

My heart is, and always has been, yours.

I glanced in the mirror as his words in the letter came back to me. 'Mine too,' I whispered to it.

Chapter Sixty-Three

Heather groaned as she had to slow her car down to join a line of traffic.

I had tried to call Drew as we got into the car, but he hadn't answered, so Heather had called Rory, but he hadn't picked up either.

I was starting to regret not letting Izzy have her own phone as we crawled towards our destination. 'What if we don't make it?'

'Try calling him again.'

I grabbed my phone again. 'Straight through to voicemail again. Maybe his battery has died.'

'If we miss him then you can leave him a message.' She looked across at me, though, with a grimace. Neither of us wanted that to happen. I didn't want another missed opportunity for us. It felt like we wouldn't survive another one. He had poured out his heart in that letter and was waiting for me to do the same. I couldn't bear the thought of him at the airport, looking for me, and thinking that I wasn't coming. Ten years ago, he had waited in the same airport, and I hadn't shown up. This time, I just *had* to be there.

The traffic moved forward a little. My foot tapped against the floor of the car impatiently. 'I can't believe he wrote me a letter,' I said. 'Why didn't he just talk to me last night?' I groaned.

'Because he was too scared just like you were,' she replied. 'I feel like banging your heads together, to be honest.'

'He must have slipped it into the book after we danced. He said he needed the loo.' I remembered then. So, he had felt something in that moment, like me, enough to push him to give me the letter. 'If only he had just said something or kissed me,' I said, shaking my head. But Izzy had come in, I knew that. And neither of us wanted to hurt our little girl. We had been too cautious, too worried about the past, unsure if we really could have a second chance. I just hoped we hadn't left it too late.

'This is so romantic,' Heather said then.

'It'll only be romantic if we make it!' I touched the moon and star necklace around my neck, willing it to give us good luck.

'We will,' she promised, changing lanes to try to get ahead of some of the cars in front of us. 'It's the next exit.'

I tried calling Drew again but there was no response. I stared out of the window, willing us to move faster, as Heather weaved through cars and got into the lane for the airport. 'There it is,' I said as the building started to appear in view. 'What if he switched his phone off because he thought I wasn't going to say anything? That he thinks I read his letter and just ignored it?'

'This will be a nice surprise then,' Heather said. 'Don't worry, as soon as he sees you, he'll know that you feel the same.'

We fell into silence then as Heather navigated the complicated airport signage and finally found the drop-off point. 'You get out here; I'll go and park and catch you up,' she said, slamming on the brakes.

'Thank you!' I called as I jumped out and raced towards the terminal building. I went up to the departures board and scanned the names until I found Edinburgh, where Drew was heading for his connecting flight to Boston. It was due to leave in half an hour. I hadn't missed it at least. My heart in my throat, I looked around for any sign of him.

My phone rang so I answered it instantly. 'Drew?'

'It's me,' Heather said, breathlessly. 'I got through to Rory – finally – they're in the cafe at the top of the escalator,' she said in a rush. 'Hurry!'

I didn't have time to thank her, I just hung up and charged up the escalator, pushing past everyone stood on it with suit-cases. At the top, I looked wildly left and right before I saw the cafe with tables overlooking the terminal. I rushed to it and breathed a sigh of relief when I spotted Izzy sitting with Rory. 'Iz!' I called, causing a few people to turn to look at me. I ran over to them, out of breath. 'Where's Drew?' I gasped out to their surprised faces.

'Right here.'

I spun around, coming face-to-face with Drew. He stood behind me, holding the handle of his small wheelie suitcase, a line of stubble on his chin. My chest sagged with relief. 'I was worried I wasn't going to catch you. I just saw… I just read your letter.'

'And?' He raised an eyebrow.

I didn't answer, I just reached for him, wrapping my arms around his neck. I looked into his eyes and caught his grin before I pressed my lips to his as he kissed me back and picked me up, twirling me around, making me break away from his lips to laugh. 'Sorry I'm ten years too late,' I whispered to him.

'You're right on time,' he replied.

'What's going on?' Izzy demanded from behind me. Drew put me down, and we turned around to face our daughter, and Rory behind her, both looking bemused but smiling.

'Did I miss it?' A voice called out to us then, and Heather popped up at the top of the escalator. She saw Drew's arm still wrapped around me. 'Oh, I missed it, didn't I?'

'What's going on?' Rory asked. 'I'm completely lost.'

'So am I,' Izzy complained.

'I'm in love with your dad,' I said to Izzy. I turned to Drew. 'And I want you to stay. Please.'

'I love you, too,' Drew replied, pulling me towards him to give me a long, slow kiss. Izzy started clapping and the noise grew louder until we broke apart and realised half the cafe were clapping along too. Drew started laughing and I joined in, my cheeks turning red.

'At least I caught that,' Heather said, holding up her phone and videoing us. 'Could you maybe re-enact what happened before I got here?' She saw our faces and put her phone down. 'Okay, I'll take that as a no.'

'Dad, does this mean you'll move back to Scotland with us?' Izzy asked, hopefully.

Drew pulled her to us. 'It does. I've been offered a job at the hospital in Inverness. So, I'll get to see a lot more of both of you, I hope. If that's okay with you?'

'We can go to the Harry Potter studios!' she said with a gasp. I laughed. Trust her to think of that.

Drew grinned. 'Deal.' His face fell a little as he looked at the board. 'I have to go to the gate now. I'm working at the hospital tomorrow so I can't stay.' He saw Izzy's face. 'I'll be back as soon as I can, okay? We all have a lot to sort out, don't we?' he said, meeting my gaze. I nodded. We really did. 'We'll be back together again soon,' he promised. He gave Izzy a big hug and then brushed his lips against mine, making my skin tingle. He turned to Rory and hugged him and Heather goodbye. Picking up his case he headed for the gate. 'See you guys,' he called with a wave, before disappearing from view.

'Rory, I've just realised that I love you and I wanted to tell you,' Heather said then.

Rory turned to look at her and chuckled. 'You're a nut, Heather, and I love you, too.' He pulled her to him, and they kissed.

'Everyone is kissing,' Izzy said. 'I don't get it.'

I pulled her to me, wrapping my arms around her. 'You will one day. So, it's our turn now, we need to go back to London and sort everything out there.'

'But we'll be back soon, too, won't we?' she asked, looking back at me as she leaned against me.

'This is our home now,' I told her.

'Too bloody right it is,' Heather said, pulling away from Rory.

'Heather swore,' Izzy said, her eyes wide.

'She's always been a bad influence,' I told her.

Epilogue

It was the week before Christmas and Glendale Hall was a hive of activity.

'Are you ready, Beth?' Drew called up the stairs to me.

'Coming!' I wrapped my red scarf tightly around my neck and put my beanie hat on. Outside, flurries drifted on the wind and the sun had already set, which meant I could just see the lights twinkling down in the garden signalling that the second annual *Glendale Hall Christmas Trail* was ready for inspection. I hurried down the wide staircase, smiling as I still did when I saw Drew.

It was a couple of months after we said goodbye at the airport before we saw each other again. I had gone to London with Izzy and packed up our life there. Emily had given us a goodbye dinner, and promised to come up to Scotland when she could. Drew had also had to sort everything out over in Boston, and also to finally end things with April. She had collected the rest of her things from their apartment to move back in with her family, and he hadn't heard from her since. Drew now lived at his family's farm and commuted to his new job in Inverness, but spent every moment that he could with us at Glendale Hall.

'I can't wait to see it,' he said, taking my hand in his. We wanted to make sure the trail was as perfect as it could be for when it opened in a couple of days. John and I had spent hours on it, trying to make it twice as magical as it was the previous year. And I couldn't wait to see it all lit up, with Drew by my side.

'Where's Iz?' I asked, looking around as we walked through the kitchen to the French doors. The house seemed oddly quiet all of a sudden. Izzy had blossomed since we moved to Glendale. She loved her new school, especially it's immense library, and made some good friends. She and my mum spent the evenings I studied at college together, and I loved seeing their bond grow. My dad had moved into his place in the village and we saw him once a week, although it was still hard to see him with Cathy, who was preparing to move into his house. My mum had picked herself up and had thrown herself into our village project. I also couldn't help but notice that she and John were spending more and more time together, and I hoped that they would finally let themselves love one another soon. They both deserved to be happy.

So far, the shops on the high street were doing great, particularly the Glendale Hall shop, which we all worked together on. Heather was revolutionising the library, too, and it was lovely to see so many members of the community making use of it. And she was taking classes at the same college as me.

'Oh, I think they're all outside somewhere. Come on, I can't wait to see it.' Drew pulled on my hand, and I laughed at how impatient he was being. We walked out into the chilly garden towards the start of the trail. John had let me become more involved with the garden and I had my own patch again, as I had when I was younger. I also got my way and installed beehives, adding beekeeping to the list of things I was learning, and we hoped to have a range of honey products ready for the shop soon.

We found ourselves at the start of the trail, and a shiver of excitement ran through me. Heather's banner hung across the same two trees at the entrance. She and Rory spent as much time as they could with us at the Hall, and it was wonderful to see her so happy with him. They were joining us later to celebrate the trail being ready. Drew and I started to stroll through the lights. I checked everything as we passed, glancing to see the expression on Drew's face. There were far more lights and we had added glow-in-the-dark stars to the edge of the trail, marking the whole path out with them.

'Well?' I asked as we neared the grotto.

'It's beautiful. Everyone is going to love it,' he said, squeezing my hand. The grotto was decorated as Santa's workshop with a table of crafts that everyone could try their hands at, watched over by a large Father Christmas and elves that we had hired for the occasion.

'Oh, wow,' Drew said as he looked around the room. We also had a fake fireplace hung with stockings and fake crackling flame. 'This is brilliant.'

'Want to make something?' I asked, gesturing to the table.

'Maybe later. I want to see the rest.' We left the grotto and walked into the rose garden where we had staged all the lit-up ornaments this year. There were reindeer, the inflatable snowman and Santa Drew and I had bought the year before and a massive polar bear I found at a garden centre.

'This is my favourite bit,' I told him. We stood by the lights for a few moments. A large snowflake landed on my nose, so I looked up and smiled. 'And then it snows right on cue.' We watched the large flakes start to float down onto us. 'I hope we don't need to cover everything up.' I bit my lip, not wanting the trail to be ruined by a heavy blast of snow.

'I think it's only going to be a light dusting. But I think we need a hot chocolate. Come on.' He pulled me off again.

'What's with you tonight?' I asked with a shake of my head.

We came to the end of the trail where we had draped netting between two trees and hung icicle lights across it so it looked as if they were hanging from the sky. As we approached it, I frowned. There was a banner hanging in front of it. 'What's that?' I asked. Drew let go of my hand and paused as I stepped forward to look at it. When I realised what it said, I stopped too, my mouth hanging open.

In glittering letters high above my head, was the question:

Will you marry me?

I turned to see Drew had got down on one knee. 'Oh my god,' I said.

He smiled. 'Beth Williams, I have loved you since you were sixteen years old. You are the love of my life. I want to spend the rest of it with you by my side. What do you think?' He opened the small box he was holding, and a sparkling diamond glittered in the light from the icicles.

It was the most romantic moment of my life. 'Yes! Of course, yes!' I cried, taking the ring and slipping it on. 'Drew, it's beautiful,' I said when I saw that the diamond was in the shape of a star. 'Can you kiss me now, please?'

Drew chuckled as he got up and took me in his arms. As our lips met, I heard the sound of enthusiastic applause. I let go of him for a moment and smiled as under the banner walked Izzy, my mum, John, Sally, Rory and Heather, and Heather's dad, all clapping and cheering. 'I might have known you'd all be in on this,' I said with a laugh. I pulled Drew back to me and we shared a long, lingering kiss. I heard Rory do a loud wolf whistle.

'It's freezing out here, let's go in for champagne,' my mum said, and reluctantly, I let go of Drew to follow them back to the Hall.

'What do you think, Iz?' I asked as my daughter grabbed my hand. She was grinning.

'I helped choose the ring,' she replied, proudly.

'I love it.' It was a perfect match for the moon and star necklace that always hung around my neck. Drew took hold of Izzy's other hand and the three of us walked into the kitchen together, and I was sure you would have been hard pressed to find a happier trio in the whole of Scotland. As Drew went to open the champagne, Heather gave me a big hug.

'Congratulations,' she said, her baby bump even bigger than it was when I saw her the previous week. It had been a surprise for both her and Rory when she realised she was pregnant, but I knew that they were thrilled. 'We better remember to take that banner down before we open it to the public or everyone will think they're being proposed to.'

'Maybe we should hire it out for that,' I said, widening my eyes.

'Hey,' Drew said, handing me a glass of fizz. 'That was just for you.'

I smiled and kissed him. 'I know but an idea for next year maybe.'

He sighed. 'You'll be offering weddings at the Hall soon.'

'That's actually not a bad idea.'

Drew groaned. 'We better see how ours goes first though.'

'You think we should get married here?'

'I think it would be perfect.'

I looked around us, picturing what the day could look like, and I smiled. 'So do I.'

'Can I be bridesmaid?' Izzy piped up.

'And me!' Heather added, taking an orange juice from the tray with a sigh.

I laughed. 'Who else would I ask?'

My mum cleared her throat then. 'Right, everyone. Time for a toast I think. It's been a year since Beth and Izzy came back to Glendale, and I think we can all agree it hasn't been quiet around here since then.' She smiled. 'And thank goodness for that. I'm delighted that Drew will be joining our family. I know that you two are going to be so happy together, and we can't wait to share in your joy. Here's to Beth and Drew and a lifetime of love.'

I felt myself well up at my mum's unusually romantic speech. I saw her glance at John, and I smiled. I took a sip of my champagne and looked at my family. I couldn't imagine being anywhere other than right where I was, with Drew and Izzy by my side.

We were finally home.

A Letter From Victoria

Dear reader,

First of all, thank you so much for picking up a copy of *Coming Home to Glendale Hall* – I really hope you will enjoy reading it!

I've always been a big fan of Christmas and really wanted to set a book over the festive season. I've included lots of the things I love at Christmas in the book – festive films and music, twinkling fairy lights and, of course, lots of delicious food! As I never really get a white Christmas where I live, I knew this book had to be set in Scotland so that I could include snow too. I love creating fictional places for my books and I hope you find Glendale as special as I wanted it to be. I wish I could take a holiday myself there actually.

I would love to know what you thought of the book once you finish. Please do pop up a review online on Amazon or Goodreads so I can see it, and that helps other readers to discover the book too. And please do come and follow me on social media. I'm addicted to Instagram and you can find me there @vickyjwalters. I'm also on Twitter @Vicky_Walters, and you can like my Facebook page too @VictoriaWaltersAuthor.

Much love,

Victoria x

Acknowledgments

Special thanks to my agent Hannah Ferguson and editor Keshini Naidoo for believing in me, and this book! A big thank you to the teams at Hera Books and Hardman & Swainson for all your hard work and support. Thank you to Cherie Chapman for designing such a beautiful cover, and to my copy editor Janette Currie for all your advice.

Lots of love to all the book bloggers and reviewers who have championed my books – having you guys in my corner means everything! Thanks so much to the Doomsday Writers and The Savvy Author's Snug for all your support and advice. And to the authors who have given me quotes for my books, I'm so grateful. Thanks to my fellow Waterstones booksellers for cheering my books on too. And, of course, everyone who has bought and read my books – your messages and reviews make it all worthwhile.

Thank you to my mum for always being there, and Harry for always trying to distract me. And, thank you to my family for making Christmases so special.